He never lost a battle until he met the one
woman who might succeed in...

CHARMING THE PRINCE

BANTAM BOOKS BY TERESA MEDEIROS

Heather and Velvet
Once an Angel
A Whisper of Roses
Thief of Hearts
Fairest of Them All
Breath of Magic
Shadows and Lace
Touch of Enchantment
Nobody's Darling
Lady of Conquest
Charming the Prince

CHARMING THE PRINCE

Teresa Medeiros

Bantam Books

NEW YORK   TORONTO   LONDON   SYDNEY   AUCKLAND

CHARMING THE PRINCE

PUBLISHING HISTORY
A Bantam Book / April 1999

ISBN 0-553-57502-3

Published simultaneously in the United States and Canada

Bantam Books are published by Bantam Books, a division of Random House,
Inc. Its trademark, consisting of the words "Bantam Books" and the portrayal
of a rooster, is Registered in U.S. Patent and Trademark Office and in other
countries. Marca Registrada. Bantam Books, 1540 Broadway, New York, New
York 10036.

PRINTED IN THE UNITED STATES OF AMERICA

OPM   10   9   8   7   6   5   4   3   2   1

For Irwyn Applebaum, for his unwavering faith in his writers and his continuing dedication to women's fiction.

For Ms. Meriweather, Ms. Silvey, Ms. Truitt, Ms. Warren, Ms. Brown, Ms. Sharon, Mr. Wade Holder, Miss Alma Ferguson, Mr. Fielder, Mr. Johnson, Mr. Jent, Ms. Brenda Watson, Ms. Pat Mickel, Mr. Darvis Snodgrass, Mr. Ted Parrish, Miss Mary Hart Finley, Ms. Amanda White, Mr. Robert Adkins, Ms. Lisa DiPasquale, Ms. Becky Griffin, Mr. David Schuermer, Ms. Patricia Ramsden, Melissa Bregenzer and for all the teachers who strive to give their students a love of learning and reading, especially Mr. Ernie Davis, who once gave me a $\underline{B}$ in trigonometry when I deserved a $\underline{C}$ only because I promised never to take trigonometry again, and who spoke those immortal words—"There's no such thing as a bad book. Some books are just better than others."

For Michael. God has blessed me richly in this life, but never so much as when you fell in love with me.

CHARMING THE PRINCE

Prologue

England, 1347

Lady Willow of Bedlington had been waiting for this moment her entire life. She clutched her papa's hand and shifted from one foot to the other, so excited she feared she might wet herself.

At long last, after six years of wishing and praying, she was finally going to have a mama of her very own.

She stole a furtive look at her papa. He looked as handsome as King Edward himself, standing there so straight and tall in the courtyard of their castle, his undertunic draped with a belted scarlet surcoat. His surcoat might be threadbare and his scabbard tarnished, but Willow had scrambled into his lap and combed his reddish-gold beard for him only seconds before a blast from a herald's trumpet had signaled the approach of his betrothed's chariot.

"Papa?" she whispered out of the corner of her mouth as they waited for the chariot and its retinue of knights to wend its way up the hill.

"Aye, princess?" he replied, inclining his head.

"Will you love the lady Blanche as you loved my mama?"

"I shall never love any woman as I loved your mama."

Stirred by the bittersweet yearning in his expression, Willow squeezed his hand.

He gave her a halfhearted wink. "But 'twill please the king to see me wed to a noble widow such as Blanche. Her lord was killed in the same battle that cost me the use of my sword arm. So she has need of a titled husband and I have need of the generous dowry the king will provide." He swung her hand back and forth. "Think how wonderful 'twill be to enjoy the king's favor once again, Willow! Your little belly won't be growling like a bear anymore. There'll be fresh game on the table every night. We won't have to sell off any more of your mother's treasures. Why, the profit from the timber yield of Blanche's forests alone will overflow our coffers for years to come!"

Willow pretended excitement, but she wasn't the least bit concerned with timber yields or overflowing coffers. She simply hoped the lady Blanche needed a little girl as much as she needed a mama. She wouldn't have been able to endure her papa's prolonged absences from the castle during the recent months had he not been wooing her a new mother.

Her yearning for a mother was the only secret she'd ever kept from him. In truth, most of the time she was perfectly content to be Papa's little girl. Content to mend the rips in his shabby hose with her clumsy stitches. Content to scold him when he went out without his cloak on a snowy winter day and to thaw his icy beard with her kisses when he returned. Content to chortle with delight when he called her "his princess" and rumpled her dark curls. She never even minded that their beans and pottage was more pottage than beans as long as she could fall asleep in the crook of his arm after he'd regaled her with a story from the hand-lettered Bible that had belonged to her mama. 'Twas the only book her papa had refused to sell.

It wasn't until after Willow was settled into the straw tick before the fire with the castle hounds nestled around her that her thoughts would stray to how nice it would be to have a mama to stroke her hair and sing her a lullaby as she drifted off to sleep.

She tugged at her father's hand again. "Will the lady Blanche love me?"

"Of course, pet. How could anyone not love Papa's little princess?"

But this time Papa didn't glance down at her. His grip on her hand tightened until it was almost painful.

Pricked by doubt, Willow smoothed the woolen skirt of her kirtle with her free hand. She had made the kirtle herself from scraps of fabric cut from one of her mother's gowns, working by candlelight until her eyes burned and her cramped fingers cracked and bled. Hoping to impress her new mama with her needle-work skills, she'd even stitched a chain of roses along the square neckline. Although the wind whipping down from the north smelled like snow, Willow chose to shiver rather than hide her handiwork beneath her faded cloak.

She lifted her chin, buoyed by a stubborn rush of pride. Papa was right, of course. How could anyone not love her?

But as the splendid white chariot came rumbling across the drawbridge and into the outer bailey, accompanied by a dozen standard-bearing knights, panic seized her. What if all of her efforts weren't enough? What if *she* wasn't enough?

The covered chariot glided to a halt. Willow gaped, awed by the magnificence of its embroidered damask curtains and cream-and-gilt wheels. Six snowy white steeds stamped their hooves and tossed their heads, flaunting their braided manes. The bells threaded through their leather bridles jingled a crisp fanfare.

Papa leaned down and whispered, "Lady Blanche has a marvelous surprise for you."

The chariot door creaked open. Willow held her breath, dazzled by glimpses of a graceful ankle; a flared sleeve trimmed in sable; icy blond hair gathered into a silver crispinette.

As the lady Blanche emerged fully from her silken cocoon, Willow's heart leapt. Her new mama was even more beautiful than she had imagined.

Her head danced with images of all the things they would do together—sing rounds and recite rondels for her papa on snowy winter nights, spin flax on the spinning wheel that had sat motionless and silent in the solar since her mother's death, gather cowslips and sweet william in the aprons of their gowns when the tender green mist of spring came creeping over the meadows.

As the lady inclined her head and favored Papa with a regal smile, the anticipation of being crushed to her sweet-smelling bosom made Willow feel almost faint.

She took a step forward without realizing it, but

froze when something came tumbling out of the chariot behind her new mama. At first she thought it was a dog—one of the furry, pug-nosed creatures so favored by noble ladies. But as it straightened and shook a mane of white-blond hair out of its eyes to give her a challenging gaze, she realized it was a child.

Willow recoiled. It seemed the lady Blanche would have no need of her. She already had a little girl. Her eyes widened as a second plump little body scrambled out after the first—a boy this time, with rosy cheeks and legs like sausages.

Her confusion mounted as he was followed by another child, then another. She struggled to count them. Three. Four. Five. Every one of them as blond and robust as Lady Blanche, but lacking in any hint of her grace. They scampered around their mother like a litter of white wolf cubs, whining and yelping and tripping over her train.

"I'm firsty, Mama!"

"I'm s'eepy!"

"I gots to piss!"

"Why did we have to come to this horrid old ruin? I want to go home!"

Their pleas and demands were interrupted by a cry that struck dread in Willow's heart.

"Papa Rufus!"

Untangling his fists from his mother's skirt, the largest boy came barreling toward her papa. His cry was a trumpet sounding battle, launching a wild charge across the courtyard.

Willow planted her feet, but the children simply shoved her aside as they surrounded her father, bouncing up and down and clamoring "Papa Wufus! Papa Wufus!"

He was forced to sweep three of them up into his arms or risk being trampled himself. The oldest boy and girl, who appeared to be around the same age as Willow, clung to his neck, while the others attached themselves to his arms and legs.

Their mother swept after them, holding a fur-wrapped bundle in her arms and smiling indulgently. "They've missed you, Rufus. They grew quite fond of you while you were courting me. As did I."

The lady's voice was rich and sweet, like cream that needed stirring. It made Willow's heart contract with yearning. She stood on tiptoe and tried to steal a peek at her stepmother's burden. Perhaps it was the marvelous surprise Papa had mentioned.

Struggling to juggle his own burdens between his strong and weak arms so he wouldn't inadvertently drop one, Papa leaned down to brush Blanche's cheek with a kiss. "I trust you had a pleasant journey, my lady."

"Not nearly so pleasant as the anticipation of what awaited me at its end."

Willow waited for her new mama to notice her, but the woman's hungry gaze remained riveted on her father. It was Papa who finally turned a pained smile her way. "Willow, I told you your stepmother had a surprise for you. You'll never again have to squander your time talking to those imaginary friends of yours. Now you'll have real brothers and sisters to play with."

The children ceased their jabbering, lapsing into a sullen silence broken only by the greedy smacking of a toddler nursing on its thumb.

Five pairs of icy blue eyes surveyed her. None of the lady Blanche's children wore childish kirtles. They were all dressed like miniature adults in cream wool trimmed in cloth-of-gold brocade. The oldest boy even wore a small sword in a scabbard studded with rubies and emeralds. Their silky blond hair hung perfectly straight without a hint of the troublesome curl that had always plagued Willow.

Her stomach sank as she saw herself through those pale, appraising eyes—a gawky child garbed in a dead woman's rags, her neckline hemmed by knots that looked more like nettles than roses.

The oldest girl rested her head on Papa's chest and batted her white-gold eyelashes. "I've never seen hair so black, Mama. Does she roll in the cinders?"

Her brother snorted. "In the stable dung, more likely. 'Tis why her skin is so coarse and brown."

Papa frowned at the boy in his arms. "I say, lad, I'll not have you—"

"Do not mock your stepsister, Stefan," Blanche interjected smoothly. "The poor child cannot help her looks."

"Willow don't sound like a Christian name," the girl said, still eyeing her suspiciously. "Is she a pagan?"

"Willow" had been Papa's pet name for her ever since she'd fallen asleep beneath a willow tree's sweeping boughs as a babe, sending her papa and his villeins on a frantic search that had lasted until the following morning.

Before she could reveal that her Christian name was Wilhelmina, she was silenced by Lady Blanche's low, throaty laugh. "Of course she's not a pagan, Reanna. Her mother was French."

The woman's smile did not waver, but the faint narrowing of her eyes gave it a malevolent cast. Something deep inside of Willow began to curdle.

"The French killed our papa in the war," Stefan said

coldly, his chubby hand caressing the hilt of his miniature sword.

Willow crowded close to her papa's leg and tried to tuck her hand back into his.

"Not now, Willow," he snapped, grimacing in pain as he struggled to pry his earlobe from the mouth of a teething toddler and keep his weak arm from collapsing beneath Stefan's weight. "Can't you see I have but two hands?"

Willow snatched her hand back, flushing with shame. Her father had never before rebuked her in such a tone.

Her stepmother purred, "Don't pout, dear. 'Tis most unbecoming. Here's something to occupy your little hands."

The woman thrust her furry bundle into Willow's arms. Willow didn't even steal a peek at it, watching instead as Blanche linked her arm in Papa's and steered him firmly toward the castle. The stray children toddled after them while Reanna leaned over Papa's shoulder and poked her tongue out at Willow. Papa cast her one brief, helpless glance before they all disappeared into the shadows of the great hall.

Willow might have stood there all day, dazed and bereft, if she hadn't become aware of a most curious warmth spreading down the front of her kirtle. Her burden began to squirm. Her eyes widened in horror as a wisp of white-blond hair stuck atop a fuzzy pink scalp slowly emerged from a gap in the fur. The gremlin's puckered face flushed crimson as it threw back its head and let loose with an earsplitting wail.

Only then did Willow realize she was holding yet another of her stepmother's whelps. Only then did she hear the snide chuckles of Blanche's knights as they elbowed one another and pointed at her. Only then did she realize exactly what was soaking her precious kirtle and dripping into her shoes.

Resisting the urge to add her howls to the baby's, Willow lifted her chin and leveled a stern gaze at the smirking men. "What are the lot of you gawking at? Have you never seen a lady pissed upon before?"

As the knights snapped to attention, choking back their mirth, Willow swept the sodden hem of her skirt around and went marching toward the castle, trying not to stagger beneath the weight of her squalling burden.

Sons are a heritage from the Lord
  children a reward from him.
Like arrows in the hands of a warrior
  are sons born in one's youth.
Blessed is the man
  whose quiver is full of them.

Psalm 127
The Holy Bible

One

England, 1360

Sir Bannor the Bold raced through the shadowy stone corridors of the castle, his brow pouring sweat and his heart hammering in his chest like a war drum. He dashed around a corner, then ducked into the alcove of a recessed window, fighting to still the hoarse rasp of his breathing long enough to listen for his pursuers.

For a blessed moment, there was silence. Then came the relentless patter of their feet, the savage cries portending his doom.

His trembling hand went instinctively to the hilt of his broadsword before he remembered the weapon would be useless against them. He was defenseless.

If any of the men who had fought by his side against the French for the past fourteen years had seen the shudder of dread that wracked his massive body in that moment, they would have surely doubted their own senses. They had seen him scale a castle wall with his bare hands, dodging the steaming gouts of boiling oil that rained down like hellfire from the heavens above. They had seen him leap off his warhorse and race through a deadly hail of arrows to heave a fallen man over his shoulder and carry him to safety. They'd seen him rip the blade of a French sword from his own thigh with nary a flinch of pain, then use it to dispose of the man who had stabbed him. Much to King Edward's delight, his enemies had been known to toss down their arms and surrender at the merest whisper of his name on the battlefield.

But never before had he faced an adversary so formidable, so utterly lacking in mercy and Christian compassion.

As they stampeded past his hiding place, he shrank against the wall, his lips moving soundlessly in a prayer for deliverance to the God who had always fought so valiantly by his side.

But in the month since the treaty with the French had been signed, even God seemed to have abandoned him. The triumphant howl that assaulted his ears might have come from Lucifer himself.

They had spotted him! Too panicked to consider the consequences, he bolted, darting back the way he had come. The devils were almost on him now, so close on his heels he could feel their hot breath scorching the back of his doublet.

He scrambled up the winding stairs, hoping to reach the sanctuary of the north tower before they brought him down and began to tear him apart like a pack of snarling mongrels. The wooden door loomed before him. He lunged for its iron latch and shoved, praying his sweaty grip would hold. Something groped at his ankle. For one bone-chilling instant, he feared he was lost. Then the door swung open.

He lurched across the threshold, shaking off the grip of the thing that had seized him, and slammed the door behind him. Only when the crossbar had thudded securely into its iron brackets did he dare to collapse against the door and suck in a great, shuddering breath. The enraged howls and demands for his surrender escalated, then subsided into ominous silence.

"Please, Lord," he muttered, not yet willing to give up on his old ally. "Not *that*. Anything but *that*."

He had once endured four months in a Calais dungeon, chained to a dank stone wall with only lice and rats for company. When his captors had fed him rancid gruel, he'd choked down every bite and asked for second helpings. After they had stretched him on the rack, he'd confounded them by enjoying a most satisfying nap. When they had branded his flesh with a glowing iron, he'd bit back his howls of pain and laughed in their faces. But not even his most diabolical enemy had managed to devise a torture so cruel, so likely to break a man's will and make him beg for mercy as . . .

"Papa?"

Bannor groaned in mortal agony.

It came again—the dulcet lisp of an angel. "Papa? Won't you come out and pway wif us?"

Bannor swore beneath his breath. 'Twas just like that shrewd imp Desmond to send his six-year-old sister to bargain for a truce. None of his children were as fair or as sweet as wee Mary Margaret.

Or was it Margaret Mary? Bannor struggled to remember what his daughter looked like, but could summon nothing beyond a vague impression of misty blue eyes and golden ringlets. According to Father Humphries, the castle priest, she had the look of her mother about her. Bannor was shamed to realize that he'd been absent from the castle for so much of his marriage to his second wife that he couldn't remember precisely what *she* had looked like either.

"Go away, honeypot," he whispered to the door. "Papa doesn't want to play anymore." He despised the pleading note in his voice, but was helpless to banish it.

"We only want you to be our pony. I pwomise we won't tie you up again."

"Or pour pepper in your helm," piped up another hopeful voice.

"Or set your whiskers afire," trilled another.

As Bannor stroked the singed remnants of his beard, the chorus of entreaties reached a crescendo with Mary Margaret's "Pwease, Papa!"

Bannor steeled himself against the plaintive refrain. "Begone with you," he thundered. "Papa has matters of import he must attend to."

"Of more import than us, no doubt. Piss on the bugger, I say."

Bannor's lips tightened as he recognized the sullen snarl of his eldest son and heir. Thirteen-year-old Desmond had a mouth like a privy. Bannor itched to grab the lad by the scruff of his grimy neck and rebuke him for his insolence. But that would mean opening the door.

Desmond's voice brightened. "I know! Let's use the bellows to pump Cook's flaming pudding full of lamp oil!"

The crestfallen groans shifted to whoops of delight as he and his loyal minions went scampering down the stairs like a brood of Satan's imps.

As their footsteps faded, Bannor slumped against the door, undone by the indignity of it all. He, Lord Bannor the Bold, master of Elsinore, pride of the English and terror of the French, was a prisoner in his own castle, held captive by an army of bratlings.

His bratlings.

He shook his head, but only succeeded in releasing a cloud of pepper from his hair. When his fit of sneezing had subsided, he drew himself up to his full height and rested his hand on the hilt of his sword, the set of his jaw grim enough to chill a foe's blood to ice. 'Twas not in his nature to surrender without a fight. Determined to find a way to prove to his rebellious offspring that they had chosen the wrong man with whom to do battle, he marched to the window, wrenched open the wooden shutter, and roared for his steward.

When a panting Sir Hollis arrived at the top of the stairs in response to his lord's thunderous summons, he was surprised to find the tower door closed and bolted.

Troubled by the silence within, he pressed his mouth to the door. "My lord?"

"Are you alone?" came a savage whisper.

He peered over one shoulder, then the other. "Quite."

The door creaked open. A muscular arm shot through the crack, jerked him inside, then slammed and bolted the door behind him.

Hollis barely had time to catch his breath before it was knocked out of him again by the fearful sight of his lord. Bannor stood with legs braced and chest heaving, his powerful hands clenched into fists. His dark hair hung around his face in a wild tangle, framing eyes that were red-rimmed and feral. But most startling of all was the condition of his fine black beard. Or what was left of it. Hollis leaned nearer to his jaw and sniffed. 'Twas not his imagination. His master positively reeked of smoke.

"Good God, man! Have you been attacked?" Hollis looked around wildly. "Is there an assassin lurking within the walls of the castle?"

"Aye," Bannor replied grimly. "Ten of them to be exact. All armed with naught but their wits and their whining."

"Ten?" Hollis frowned, then nodded slowly as comprehension dawned. "Oh, you mean the children."

"Children?" Bannor snorted. " 'Tis too gentle a name for those demon spawn. Had I not counted his toes myself when he was a babe, I would insist that you check Desmond for a forked tail and cloven hooves."

The steward wisely suppressed a smile. "I suppose they are a bit . . . rambunctious. Perhaps 'tis only the natural exuberance of youth."

"Exuberance? Malevolence, more likely." Bannor flung himself into a chair and swept his arm across the table, scattering several scrolls and sending up a cloud of dust. "Curse this wretched peace anyway! Would that the war with France had lasted a hundred years!"

Hollis sighed wistfully, wishing the same. If Edward hadn't signed the treaty at Brétigny, he and Bannor would be sitting in a tent on a distant battlefield, toasting their latest victory. After years of being comrades, the end of the war had thrust them into the awkward roles of lord and vassal. He feared he was as ill-suited to being steward of a vast holding such as Elsinore as his lord was to playing doting papa to a passel of brats.

Hollis blew the dust out of a goblet and poured Bannor some ale from the earthenware flagon resting on the table, hoping to soothe his temper. In case he failed, he poured some for himself as well. "You've been off on one campaign or another since you were little more than a lad yourself, my lord. Perhaps the children are simply in want of some discipline."

"You don't understand." Bannor leaned across the table and lowered his voice to a hoarse whisper, as if to confess a terrible sin. "They're not afraid of me."

Hollis had to sink down on the hearth and swallow a generous mouthful of ale to digest that startling revelation. He'd fought at Bannor's side for over thirteen years and had yet to encounter any man who didn't wince with dread when Bannor rose to his full height or raised his voice above a murmur. Why, only this morning, he'd sent a page scurrying from the great hall in tears simply by baring his teeth at the lad and wishing him a pleasant morn.

"Well, you can't spend the rest of your life locked in this tower," Hollis said thoughtfully. "Perhaps you need to make them afraid of you."

"And how would you suggest I do that? Throw them in the dungeon? Threaten to lop off their little heads?" Bannor rose and paced to the window, sloshing ale over the rim of his goblet with each furious stride. Intrigued by the gleeful shriek that wafted in on the wind, Hollis joined him.

Chaos reigned in the courtyard below. Angelic little Mary Margaret was busily pumping lamp oil into the deflated skin of a blood pudding while two of her sisters played at dismembering their dolls. Desmond and three of his brothers had captured one of the younger pages and were holding him upside down by his ankles over an open well.

"Desmond!" Bannor shouted, leaning out the window. "Free that lad this instant!"

Before he could recant his unfortunate choice of words, a splash and a hollow wail drifted to their ears.

As a squire went trotting over to drag the howling boy out of the well, Desmond gave the tower window a fawning bow and shouted, " 'Tis ever a pleasure to do your bidding, sir."

Bannor growled beneath his breath. " 'Tis the Elsinore curse, you know. My own father, heartless wretch that he was, sired seventeen legitimate children and thirty-six bastards, two on his deathbed. You'd think the family motto wasn't 'To conquer or die,' but 'Be fruitful, and multiply.' "

Hollis did not have to be reminded that his master had been one of those bastards. Had he not endeared himself to the king with his unflinching loyalty and skill in battle at the tender age of seventeen, Bannor might still be a penniless man-at-arms instead of lord of one of his father's richest holdings. A holding he had wrested from his eldest legitimate brother with the king's hearty blessing. His brother and all the rest of his half-siblings had fled to one of their father's castles in the south upon hearing that Bannor the Bold, one of Edward's most dangerous and trusted young knights, had amassed an army and was preparing to march upon Elsinore.

Bannor looked despairingly at Hollis. "God must be punishing me for my lust. 'Tis my only failing, you know. I've never been given to strong drink, uncontrollable rages, or taking the Lord's name in vain."

"You cannot bear all the blame for your children's existence, my lord. Both of your wives adored you.

Even when you sought to grant them a respite from your attentions, they would creep into your bed in the dead of night and insist upon fulfilling their marital duties." He gave Bannor a look that was both sympathetic and slightly envious. " 'Tis that wretched face of yours the ladies cannot resist."

Bannor shook his head and sighed. "If only I'd been born homely like you . . ."

Hollis, who considered himself more than passably handsome with his bristling mustache and thick head of brown hair, shot his friend an offended glare before he caught the mischievous twinkle in Bannor's eye.

He parried with a smirk of his own. "Given your fine looks, my lord, this might be just the beginning of your brood. After all, you're only two-and-thirty. Why, I've heard of men siring babes as late as their seventy-fifth year!"

Bannor shuddered. "God forbid. I should geld myself first."

A knock sounded on the door. Panic flickered across Bannor's face. "Find out who it is before you open it. Desmond is more cunning than the Black Prince," he said, referring to King Edward's son, who had been wily enough to take the French king hostage at Poitiers. "It could be a trap."

Hollis obeyed. " 'Tis Fiona, my lord."

At Bannor's nod, he opened the door to reveal the wizened Irish nurse standing at the top of the stairs holding a squirming bundle.

Bannor drained the rest of the ale before dropping his head into his hand and muttering, "Dear God in heaven, not another one."

"I'm afraid so, m'lord," Fiona said, bustling into the

tower. " 'Tis the second one in a fortnight. I found her in a basket outside the gatehouse."

"Did this one come with a note?"

"No, m'lord. Just a blanket and a rash."

Although Bannor remained firmly at arm's length, Hollis could not resist peeling back the threadbare blanket to steal a curious peek. The babe's face was even more wizened than Fiona's.

Hollis frowned, perplexed. "Why, this child can't be more than a few weeks old. Wouldn't you have been in Gascony with Edward when—"

Bannor cut him off as if he hadn't even spoken. "Send to the village for a wet nurse, Fiona. And tell the priest to christen her and give her a name. The poor creature at least deserves a name." He pointed a warning finger at the beaming nurse. "But not Margaret. Or Mary. We already have three Margarets, one Mary, and one Mary Margaret. 'Tis enough to muddle a man's thinking."

"Aye, m'lord," Fiona replied, bobbing a clumsy curtsy.

As she turned to go, the babe began to wiggle and fret. The nurse lifted the child to her shoulder, crooning softly in Gaelic. The babe subsided as if falling beneath the spell of some sweet enchantment, blowing joyful bubbles of spittle and cooing like a dove.

Bannor watched them go, a most curious expression on his face. "Perhaps 'tis not a man's firm hand my children require," he said musingly, "but a woman's gentle one."

"Fiona's a woman," Hollis pointed out.

"Aye, but she's getting on in years." A wistful shadow passed over Bannor's face. "And there's still no touch so tender as a mother's."

As he turned to fix Hollis with a piercing stare, all traces of softness vanished from Bannor's face. His rugged features took on the ruthless cast they always bore when he was plotting a campaign . . . or an ambush. Hollis took an instinctive step backward, fearing he just might be its target.

His fears were proved justified when Bannor began to stalk him, a predatory smile curving his lips. "Why, Hollis, I do believe you might be just the man to find my children a mother."

"Me?" Hollis backed into the table, rattling the ale flagon. "B-b-but, my lord, would it not be wiser for you to choose your own bride?"

Bannor waved away his objections. "I have no wisdom where women are concerned, only folly. If it were left to me, I'd choose another buxom, sweet-smelling beauty like Mary or Margaret. Before I could clear her perfume from my head, I'd have a new litter of brats to terrorize me."

He marched to the other side of the table and began to sift through the scattered scrolls until he found a scrap of blank parchment. He dipped the tip of a feathered quill into a flask of ink and began to scribble furiously. "The king is rumored to be at Windsor, overseeing the castle's renovation. If he grants my petition, you shall have full authority to choose a bride for me, arrange a betrothal with her family, and make my sacred vows to her before a priest."

Hollis's panic mounted. "You want me to marry your wife?"

Bannor stopped scribbling long enough to shoot him an exasperated look. "Of course not. I simply want you to stand in my stead while the banns are read and the priest blesses the union." He sealed the missive with a dab of melted wax, then rose to slap the scroll into Hollis's hand. "When you return to Elsinore with my bride, the deed will already be done. I will be wed to this woman in the eyes of both God and the king." He clapped his friend on the shoulder. Hollis tried not to stagger. "I'm trusting my future to your hands, my friend. What I need is some maternal, bovine creature who will prove to be no temptation to my appetites."

Hollis tucked the scroll into his belt, sighing in defeat. He knew better than anyone that there was no dissuading Bannor once a course of action had been decided upon. "Since you're known throughout the kingdom as one of Edward's favorites, finding you a bride shouldn't prove too great a challenge."

Bannor arched one dark brow. "It might be more of a challenge than you think. I did kill my first two wives."

"Through no real fault of your own, my lord."

Bannor returned to the window and stood gazing down into the courtyard, his hands locked at the small of his back. A child's giggle floated to their ears—innocent and wistfully sweet.

Bannor's expression softened, betraying the desperation beneath his gruffness. "Find her for me, Hollis. Find the woman who will love my children as if they were her very own."

As Hollis gazed upon the troubled countenance of the most devoted friend he had ever known, his heart surged with loyalty. "I shall find her, my lord." He dropped to one knee and rested his hand on the hilt of his sword. "I swear it upon my very life."

Two

Bannor was going to kill him.

Hollis trudged through the moss-shrouded forest, leading his exhausted mount and glumly contemplating what gruesome form his death would take. A simple skewering with his lord's sword would surely be too merciful. He deserved nothing less than a slow dip into a vat of boiling oil, a leisurely devouring by dungeon rats, a midnight rendezvous with a hooded axman. Perhaps he could request that Bannor pike his severed head on the barbican as a warning to other young knights foolish enough to undertake such an impossible quest.

"Sir?" ventured one of the men-at-arms who was plodding along behind him. "We've passed that same oak four times."

"I fear we may be lost," said the other.

"Lost," Hollis mumbled, still caught up in his own bleak reverie. "Aye. All is lost."

The very act of putting one foot in front of the other seemed to be draining him of the last of his strength. He and his men had been combing the English countryside for over two months. He'd visited every noble household from Windsor to Wales with daughters of marriageable age in residence, but had yet to find his lord a suitable bride.

Despite Bannor's dour prediction, he'd found no lack of fathers eager to thrust their daughters upon his master. But if the eldest was too sweet and pretty, the youngest was too sour and plain. One would confess she cared nothing for children while another would rub her belly and promise to give his lord many fine sons to bless his household. He'd been briefly heartened by the discovery of an earl's daughter with an ample girth and a mustache thicker than his own until she'd grabbed his knee beneath the trestle table, batted her lashless eyes, and croaked 'twas a pity a virile young man like himself was not seeking a wife. A terrifying vision of Bannor being crushed between her massive thighs had sent him fleeing from her father's castle in the dead of night.

A defeated sigh escaped his lungs. The carpet of leaves crackling beneath their feet would soon be smothered by the first snowfall of winter. He had no choice but to return to Elsinore and confess to Bannor that he had failed. Perhaps he wouldn't be too frightfully unattractive carrying his head about in the crook of his arm.

He stumbled to a halt and peered through the shimmering gloom, realizing with consternation what his men had tried to tell him. They were lost and most likely had been for quite some time. The ancient trees towered over them in eerie splendor, their autumn crowns of gold and scarlet diffusing the fitful sunlight.

Just ahead of them he spied a break in the foliage. He might have dismissed it as a trick of the shadows had the faint echo of a high-pitched giggle not lured him forward.

His men hung back, exchanging a dubious glance. "I'd draw yer blade if I was you, sir," one of them warned. "It might be a wood sprite."

"Or a fairy," suggested the other man, tracing a cross on his breast.

"Aye," added the first. "Them fairy wenches like to carry mortal men off to their underground lairs and steal their seed."

Hollis snorted. "They'd probably toss us back and send for our lord. Bannor could populate an entire fairy kingdom."

Dropping to one knee, he parted the glistening bracken only to find himself overlooking a meadow draped in a patchwork of sunlight and cloudshadow. Its wee inhabitants raced and tumbled through the tall brown grass in gleeful abandon, both fair of hair and fleet of foot. At first glance, Hollis thought they might have actually stumbled upon a fairy kingdom—until one of the creatures tripped over a root and went sprawling, his outraged wail proving that he was indeed mortal.

Before Hollis could consider rescuing the lad, a shepherdess separated herself from the gamboling flock of children and rushed to the side of her fallen lamb. As she gathered the bawling child into her lap, Hollis's curiosity sharpened. He squinted into the sunlight, but could make out nothing of her features. Although she moved with the grace and swiftness of youth, her garb gave no clue to her age. Her hair had been gathered into a russet wool cap and she wore a drab kirtle and apron of the sort any serf or castle maidservant might wear.

It wasn't her appearance that intrigued him so much as the protective curve of her shoulders as she hugged the child to her breast. They were too far away to hear her voice, but he could well imagine the gentle words she must be crooning to soothe the lad's sniffles.

Hollis sank back on his heels. Perhaps he'd been going about his quest in entirely the wrong way. After all, Bannor had never insisted his bride had to be of noble birth. Why not present him with a young Fiona—some shy, sturdy peasant girl who would welcome the care of his unruly brood and make few demands on her new lord and master?

A grin slowly spread over his face. The men-at-arms crept closer, gazing down at his dazed visage in alarm. One of them passed a hand in front of his face; Hollis didn't even blink.

"What is it, sir? Have ye seen a vision?"

"Aye, I have at that. The answer to all my prayers." As the men exchanged a perplexed glance, Hollis's grin softened into a blissful smile. "A Madonna."

He was tempted to drive his mount straight down the hillside into the meadow, but he feared startling both the girl and her young charges. 'Twould be a simple enough task to seek out the nearest village or castle. Surely someone there could tell him who she was and where she lived.

He parted the bracken again, unable to resist stealing one last look at his find before he took his leave. As he watched, the lad wiggled out of her lap and went shimmying up the gnarled trunk of an apple tree. She scrambled to her feet and stood beneath the tree with arms outstretched, as if to catch him should his hands slip or his little feet falter. The broad expanse of her hips did indeed give her a distinctly bovine look.

Hollis sighed with anticipation as he rose and groped for the reins of his horse, already hearing in his head the sweet, coaxing music of her voice.

"If you don't come down from that tree this instant, you wretched little troll, I'll climb up and toss you down."

"Will not."

"Will, too."

"Will not." A half-rotted apple came sailing through the branches, striking Willow's temple with a solid *bonk*. The other children erupted in scornful laughter.

Gritting her teeth, Willow tucked her foot into the crook of the trunk, fully prepared to make good on her threat.

Yowling like a treed cat, ten-year-old Harold came sliding down the trunk. He had almost reached the ground when his foot became tangled in Willow's skirt and he went sprawling on his stomach for the second time in that day.

His high-pitched wail set Willow's teeth on edge. While she was trying to decide whether she should pick him up and dust him off again or throttle him, he rolled to a sitting position.

"She t-t-twipped me!" He gulped for air, his plump cheeks turning redder than the apples she'd gathered in the pockets of her apron. "Willow twipped me! I'm going to tell my papa!"

Eight-year-old Gerta stomped to his defense, her flaxen braids bristling with indignation. "I saw her trip you. She's an ugly, hateful girl and I shall tell Papa, too."

"And Mama!" chirped the nine-year-old twins in near unison. "We shall tell Mama. Mayhaps she'll send her to bed without supper again."

Undaunted by the familiar chant, Willow simply leaned against the tree, folded her arms over her chest, and narrowed her eyes. As a wicked smile spread over her face, the children grew very still. Even Harold stopped his sniveling.

"I hope they send me to bed without supper," she said softly. "For if they do, I shall soon grow fiercely hungry. Then I shall creep out of my bed in the black of night and go in search of something to eat." She deliberately lowered her gaze to the white little belly protruding from beneath the hem of Harold's tunic, then ran her tongue along the edge of her gleaming teeth. "Something plump and tender and succulent . . ."

As her voice deepened to a growl, Harold surged to his feet, bellowing in terror. His brother and sisters followed, squealing at the top of their lungs as they scattered across the meadow, fleeing toward the sanctuary of the castle.

Willow collapsed against the tree, weakened by laughter. When her mirth finally subsided, she slid to a sitting position and took an apple from her apron, savoring the rare bliss of solitude. There seemed to be little point in continuing to coax and cajole, reason and threaten, when her every effort to make her brothers and sisters behave was thwarted by her stepmother's indulgence.

She sank her teeth through the apple's crisp skin, remembering how eagerly she had anticipated Harold's birth. After three years of serving as nursemaid to her pampered step-siblings, she was finally going to have a brother or sister of her own blood. But Blanche had used the occasion of his birth to pour more of her poison into Papa's ear. As Willow had approached the bed to steal a peek at her new brother, Blanche had gently reminded her papa that it was Blanche, and not Willow's mother, who had fulfilled the sacred duty of giving him a son.

Willow snapped another bite from the apple. Harold had been a sweet-natured babe, as had been the three babes born after him, but his natural affection for her was soon tainted by the disdain his older step-siblings showed her. The chasm between them was simply too great for his chubby little arms to bridge.

They were sturdy. She was slender. They were blond. She was dark. They had blue eyes. Hers were the tempestuous gray of a storm at sea. They had icy Saxon blood flowing through their veins, while hers surged with the warm, passionate blood of the French. They were loved. She was . . .

Willow tossed away the half-eaten apple, abruptly losing her taste for it. She had not been her papa's little princess for a very long time. From the moment Blanche had arrived at Bedlington, she had deposed Willow with all the ruthless ambition of a conquering queen determined to set her own heirs on the throne.

In the beginning, Willow had been too bewildered to accept her defeat. She would try to crawl into her father's lap only to find it already occupied by a clinging Reanna or a smirking Stefan. Hungry for a story, she would wiggle her way into the circle of children crowded around her papa's knee. Just as Papa would reach out an arm to draw her nearer, Blanche's hand would descend on her shoulder like a pale spider.

"You're growing too old for such nonsense, dear," Blanche would whisper, the honeyed venom of her voice paralyzing Willow more effectively than her biting grip, "Why don't you run along upstairs and see if Beatrix needs her napkins changed?"

Willow would creep from the great hall, stealing a yearning glance at her papa over her shoulder. More than once, she would have sworn she glimpsed a reflection of her own trapped panic in his eyes. His mouth would open, but before he could call her back, Blanche's children would swarm over him, clamoring for his undivided attention. Eventually, his unspoken words had swelled into a silence so deafening it could never again be fully broken.

Sometimes Willow wished she couldn't even remember when Papa had loved her. Perhaps then she wouldn't waste her time dreaming that someone might love her that way again. The yearning ran deep, deeper even than her craving for a single hour of freedom to call her own.

Seduced by that bittersweet dream, she leaned her head against the tree. As her eyes drifted shut, it was not her papa's face she saw, but the face of another man.

Her prince, she had christened him when she'd still been young and foolish enough to believe in such fancies.

His hair was as dark and lustrous as samite, his jaw

strong and his brow kind. It mattered not what color his eyes were so long as they brimmed with love for her and her alone. He would not love her for a brief, sweet season, but forever.

Willow could not have said how long she lingered in that meadow, hearing his whisper in the rustling of the grasses, feeling his touch in the caress of the breeze. She didn't even realize she'd puckered her lips for an imaginary kiss until the first drop of rain spattered against them, vanquishing both her prince and her dreams.

She scrambled to her feet, her alarm rising with the wind. She might be getting too old to be sent to bed without supper, but she had no doubt Blanche could devise some more subtle punishment for her rebellion. She tucked a stray tendril of hair into her cap. The last time she'd dared to defy her stepmother, Blanche had threatened to shear her of her unruly curls.

Tying up her apron so as not to spill the apples from the pockets, Willow went dashing across the meadow toward the castle she had once called home.

Willow burst into the musty gloom of the kitchen only seconds before the fitful shower swelled into a genuine downpour. She ducked around the stream of rain pouring through a crack in the ceiling, shivering as she discovered the fire had been allowed to go out again. If the cold hearth and deserted spit were any indication, she might not be the only one going to bed without supper. Perhaps 'twould be wise to hoard the apples in her apron.

Blanche's spending was bleeding her papa dry. The overflowing coffers he'd dreamed of when he'd wed the wealthy widow had long ago dried to a meager trickle. As long as she was draped in jewels and fur and her little darlings garbed in samite and wool, Blanche cared not that the castle's defenses were rotting or that her father's villeins and men-at-arms had deserted him for fairer and more prosperous masters.

The king's wrath would have descended on them long ago had Blanche not wed her two eldest daughters, Reanna and Edwina, to wealthy barons. Driven to distraction by the incessant whining of their wives, the barons had agreed to pay the castle taxes Blanche's own threats and bullying had failed to raise.

Willow and her papa might have been poor before he'd married Blanche, but at least they'd had each other. Now they had nothing between them but regrets and strained silences.

Willow started up the winding stairs, hoping to creep around the balcony that overlooked the great hall and reach the bedchamber she shared with her sisters before her stepmother could waylay her. She fully expected to hear Harold lisping out a detailed recitation of her sins. She did not expect to hear the stern ringing of masculine voices.

Willow crept toward the balcony railing and peered through the smoke of the rushlights. Oddly enough, there wasn't a child in sight in the great hall below. Three strangers stood before the raised dais where Blanche insisted that Papa receive all visitors to the castle. Papa hunched in a canopied chair, his red-gold hair faded to a lackluster gray, his once proud shoulders stooped beneath the burden of his wife's debts and demands. Blanche reclined next to him on a gilded bench, presiding over the dusty squalor of the hall like some mythical Saxon queen.

The man who was speaking wore the golden spurs of a knight. "If a dowry cannot be arranged at this time, I'm sure my master would be willing to provide a generous bride-price."

" 'Tis barbaric! I'll not hear of it!" Papa shouted, pounding on the arm of his chair.

"Just how generous?" Blanche asked, resting a pale hand on Papa's sleeve.

The stranger shifted his scrutiny to Willow's stepmother, his thick mustache twitching with amusement. "Generous enough. My lord has already secured the blessing of the king. He is *very* eager to make this match."

"Ah, but she is *very* dear to us," Blanche said before Papa could speak.

Willow clung to the railing. They could only be discussing the betrothal of Blanche's youngest child from her first marriage. But Beatrix wasn't yet fourteen! Blanche must be desperate indeed if she was considering bartering her off to the highest bidder. By rights, Willow knew she should be glad to see the girl go. After pissing in Willow's shoes all those years ago, the brat had gone on to inflict a host of indignities upon her. Willow pressed a hand to her belly. Perhaps the pang she felt there was simply a twinge of envy for Beatrix's good fortune. Surely she wouldn't actually miss the spoiled little minx.

Shaking off Blanche's grip, Papa glowered suspiciously at the knight. "Just why does your lord want her so badly?"

Willow was straining forward to hear the man's answer when something wet slithered across the back of her neck.

"Eeeewww!" she groaned, recognizing it as an eager male tongue.

Spinning around, she backed her assailant into the shadows. "I'd suggest you keep that viper in your mouth before I yank it out by the roots."

Her stepbrother chuckled and cocked a smug eyebrow. "Ah, but why should I keep it in *my* mouth when yours is so much sweeter?"

Stefan's gleaming fall of thick, blond hair and bulging bands of muscle might make the castle maidservants swoon, but to Willow, he was the same smug little boy who had mocked her mercilessly since their very first meeting. Only now he wore a much larger sword.

"Even the sweetest of berries can poison you," she retorted, hands on hips.

His pale blue eyes narrowed. "I do believe this particular berry has grown a bit saucy." He nodded toward the balcony. "Before your opinion of yourself ripens any further, you might wish to remember that this mysterious lord is offering to buy you for his bed as if you were naught but a village whore."

Willow was too stunned to take offense at his insult.

"Me?" She touched a tentative hand to her chest, betrayed by a treacherous surge of wonder. "This lord wants *me* for his bride?"

Stefan's smirk darkened into a scowl. "You needn't look so calf-eyed. Mama will never let you go."

Willow's wonder faded as she recognized the bitter truth in his words. "Of course, she won't. If she did, she might have to find another nursemaid for her brats."

Unable to bear hearing her papa send the earnest young knight away, Willow turned toward the bedchamber.

Stefan stepped in front of her, blocking her path. "Mama wouldn't give you to another man because she knows I want you for myself."

Willow recoiled. Her stepbrother had never before dared to be so brazen. She forced herself to meet his taunting gaze with equal boldness. "Well, you can't have me. Blood may not bind us, but you're still my brother. The king would never allow us to wed."

Stefan caught her shoulders in a painful grip, his voice deepening to a husky growl. "Who said anything about wedding you?"

As he licked his plump lower lip, as if in anticipation of savoring some juicy morsel of meat, Willow almost regretted teasing Harold. She forced herself to wait until the glistening tip of his tongue was only an inch away from her parted lips before whispering, "I warned you to keep that viper away from me."

Jerking herself out of his grip, she drove a knee into his padded codpiece. He doubled over, grunting an oath.

Before he could recover, Willow darted left, then right, driven by a primitive urge to flee. Her bedchamber no longer felt like a refuge, but a trap. Without conscious thought, she plunged down the stairs that wound into the great hall, stumbling to a halt in the shadows beneath the balcony.

" 'Tis a tremendous sum, Rufus," Blanche was saying, a dreamy sheen softening the avaricious glitter of her eyes. "Enough to pay the taxes for the next two years."

"I won't hear of it, woman! I'll not sell my own daughter!"

Longing only to escape a future as ugly as her stepbrother's sneer, Willow stepped out of the shadows, her voice ringing like a bell. "And why not, Papa? 'Twouldn't be the first time."

Hollis's jaw dropped as his meek Madonna came marching into the great hall, her shoulders squared for battle. He squinted at her through the gloom, the smoke from the poorly trimmed rushlights making his eyes water. The girl's homely cap had slid down over one eye, casting a shadow over her features.

He still couldn't quite believe his good fortune. His mysterious angel hadn't turned out to be some common village wench, but the spinster daughter of an impoverished baron. She'd probably long ago resigned herself to living out the remainder of her life as a weighty burden to her family. She would no doubt be pliable and eager to please a mighty lord such as Bannor. Especially since Bannor would laud the very plainness that made her repugnant to other men.

Hollis stole a glance at the ceiling, where cobwebs drifted in place of the colorful banners that must have once adorned the rafters. She should also be most humbly grateful to be rescued from this place. Upon their approach, he and his men had been appalled by the disagreeable stench of the weed-choked moat. Rain seeped steadily through cracks in the ceiling, running in dank rivulets down the crumbling stone walls. The stale rushes beneath their feet were littered with oft-gnawed bones and the droppings of hounds, both dried and fresh.

As the girl marched toward the dais, Hollis gallantly made way for her, prompting his men to do the same.

He expected the girl's arrival to intensify her father's blustering, but the old man began to toy with the folds of his moth-eaten surcoat, taking great care to avoid her eyes. "What are you doing here, child?"

"I'm not a child any longer, Papa. If I were, you wouldn't be discussing my betrothal with these strangers."

He wagged a finger at her. "The matter is none of your concern."

"On the contrary. 'Tis very much my concern. I had no say in the matter when you sold me into servitude for the price of the king's approval and Blanche's dowry. Perhaps I should be allowed to choose my next master."

Turning her back on her sputtering father, she took a few steps toward Hollis, then hesitated. Although the gloom made it impossible to determine her expression, Hollis could not help but be touched by the dignity of her stance. Her fists were clenched at her sides, her chin tilted to a proud angle.

"Do you speak the truth, sir? Does your lord want me for his bride? Does he truly want me?"

Remembering the longing he'd glimpsed on Bannor's face when he had charged him with finding a mother for his children, Hollis nodded and said softly, "Aye, my lady. He wants you more than you can imagine."

She tilted her chin even higher. "Then he shall have me."

Hollis broke into a grin, oblivious to her father's groan, her stepmother's triumphant laugh, the garbled exclamation of rage that came from the balcony above them.

The girl reached around to loosen the ties of her apron. As she cast away the rumpled garment, a crimson shower of apples went bouncing across the floor.

One came to rest against the toe of Hollis's boot, but he never felt it.

His grin had frozen on his face as she'd peeled away the bulky apron. His wide-eyed gaze slowly traveled up her slender, high-breasted form, following the graceful path of her hands as she reached up to drag off the russet cap. She shook her head, freeing a shimmering cloud of raven curls, before baring her own pearly white teeth in an answering smile.

Hollis's grin faded.

He groaned aloud.

Bannor was going to kill him.

Three

"Leg o' mutton, my lady?"

Willow tore her gaze away from the chariot window to eye the enormous hunk of meat gripped in Sir Hollis's fist.

"No, thank you," she murmured.

The knight's hopeful expression fell, and she was tempted to reconsider. But her hands were none too steady, her stomach was all aflutter, and she didn't want to risk staining her beautiful new kirtle with even a drop of grease.

While Sir Hollis delved back into the seemingly bottomless hamper of food he'd purchased at the last village they'd passed through, Willow smoothed her skirt, marveling at the absence of little muddy handprints on its plush green velvet folds. She knew she was no beauty, as Reanna and Beatrix were, but arrayed in such finery, she could almost pretend she was. 'Twas the happiest she had felt since that long ago day when Blanche had arrived at Bedlington to wed her papa.

Willow smiled, bemused by the irony. Today she was the one rocking along in a splendid chariot drawn by six handsome steeds. She was the one guarded by a retinue of knights bearing rippling pennons adorned with their lord's standard—a magnificent red stag rearing up against a field of gold. She was the one racing toward the arms of the man who had made her his bride. Her heart thudded in time with the horses' hooves as she leaned out the window to embrace the crisp autumn afternoon.

As they had traveled north, the towering trees of Bedlington Forest had given way to the rolling hills and sharp crags of Northumberland. A hint of snow laced a distant peak.

"Fig sweetmeat?" Sir Hollis leaned forward to wave the delicacy beneath her nose, as if hoping to tempt her with its rich nutmeg scent.

She shook her head, tempering her refusal with a polite smile.

He returned to pawing through the hamper, muttering something that sounded curiously like, "Mount my head in the great hall, won't he?"

Willow's world tilted as the chariot began to climb a steep and winding hill. She settled back into her seat and drew the hood of her fur-trimmed cloak up over her hair, shivering with a mixture of exhilaration and apprehension.

All she knew of the mysterious lord who was now her husband was that he was a generous man. As soon as his steward had sent word by one of his men-at-arms that she had agreed to become his bride, he had dispatched not only the chariot and knights, but a wagon bearing two massive chests filled to overflowing with exquisite gowns woven of velvet, sendal, and damask; half a dozen pairs of shoes stitched from the softest beaten doehide; and several vials of precious perfumes and rare spices.

The sight of all that bounty spilling across the great hall had made Blanche sick with regret, Stefan sick with jealousy, and Beatrix sick with envy. Blanche had bemoaned the fact that she hadn't demanded a higher bride-price, while Stefan sulked and Beatrix fled up the stairs, wailing that Willow had stolen the man who should have been *her* husband.

Willow stroked the supple mink tippets trailing from the sleeves of her kirtle, smiling wryly. If not for her husband's extravagance, she would have arrived at his castle with her scant belongings tied up in a rag bundle on the end of a stick. Perhaps he thought her the sort of woman who could be wooed by the caress of silk against her skin or the tantalizing aroma of myrrh. She hoped he would be pleased to discover that her affections could be bought far more cheaply, costing him nothing more than his devotion.

"Sugar comfit?"

"No!" Willow said sharply, growing ever more perplexed by the knight's persistence. "I'm not the least bit hungry."

Her curt refusal made his thick mustache droop with despair. For the first time, Willow caught the brief downward swipe of his lashes and followed it with a questioning glance of her own. The kirtle hung loose on her, almost as if it had been fashioned for a much larger woman. She'd always felt lacking next to her robust siblings. Stefan had oft mocked her for being as skinny as a willow wand and twice as knobby. Perhaps Lord

Bannor preferred strapping wenches with ample hips, and breasts as buxom as young Beatrix's were already promising to become.

The poor child cannot help her looks. Blanche's pitying murmur was so clear that Willow wouldn't have been surprised to find her stepmother perched on top of the chariot like some malevolent harpy.

Still glaring, she snatched the sweet from the knight's hand and wolfed it down in a single bite. He looked so mollified that she also accepted the fig sweetmeat he timidly proffered. But when he fished the mutton leg out of the hamper and waved it at her, she abruptly lost what little appetite she had.

Her doubts made her feel like a child tugging at her father's hand once again.

Will the lady Blanche love me?

Of course, pet. How could anyone not love Papa's little princess?

She'd been naive enough to believe such a lie once. If she'd deluded herself again, she would have a lifetime to repent her reckless decision.

"Tell me more of this Lord Bannor," she demanded. "You've told me all about his bravery in battle and his devotion to king and country, but I still don't know what manner of man would beseech another to choose his bride."

Sir Hollis gave the mutton leg a thoughtful nibble. "A prudent one."

A chill shot down her spine. Perhaps it was not she who was lacking, but her husband.

"Is he . . ." she leaned forward on the bench, hardly daring to speak her suspicions aloud, ". . . ill-favored?"

Sir Hollis nearly choked on his mouthful of mutton. "I wouldn't exactly say that."

Willow found his reaction less than comforting. "Was he disfigured in the war? Did he lose a limb? An eye?" She suppressed a shudder. "A nose?"

The knight's mustache twitched as if he was fighting back a sneeze. "I can assure you, my lady, that Lord Bannor returned from France with all of his significant parts intact."

Willow frowned, wondering just which parts a man might consider significant. "What of his temperament, then? Is he a kind man? A fair man? Or is he given to brooding and violent fits of temper?"

Sir Hollis blinked at her. "My lord would be the first to assure you that he is not a man given to strong drink, uncontrollable rages, or blasphemy."

Willow settled back on the bench, folding her hands in her lap. "I suppose a woman can ask no more than that of her husband."

Yet once she had wanted more. Much more. A fleeting vision of her prince drifted before her eyes, evoking a bittersweet pang of yearning. She would never again hear the rich echo of his laughter. Never again taste the honeyed sweetness of his imaginary kiss. The time had come for her to exchange her girlish dreams for a man wrought of flesh and blood, sinew and bone. She closed her eyes, bidding her prince farewell with a wistful sigh.

She was determined to make this Lord Bannor a good wife. It mattered not if he was old and infirm, harelip, or disfigured in service to king and country. If he was willing to pledge his devotion to her and only her, she could certainly do no less for him.

Fortified by her resolve, Willow opened her eyes. Or at least she thought she did. But the vision framed by the chariot window persuaded her that she must have drifted into a dream.

A castle seemed to float upon the cliff that over-looked the sparkling waters of the River Tyne. It bore no resemblance to her papa's crumbling keep. Graceful round towers jutted toward the clouds, crowned by conical roofs of gray slate. A crenellated wall enfolded the massive palace in a sweeping curtain of sandstone.

Willow blinked. She must surely be dreaming, for who but a prince could live in such a majestic abode?

She didn't realize she had spoken the question aloud until Sir Hollis replied, "Why, you, of course."

She shifted her wide-eyed gaze to the knight.

His tense smile sent a shiver of foreboding down her spine. "For that majestic abode is Elsinore, and you, my dear, are its new lady."

"The chariot approaches! The chariot approaches!"

As the lookout's cry echoed from the watchtower, followed by a braying blast from a hunting horn, Bannor yawned and stretched his long legs, refusing to budge from his chair. Twice in the past week, Desmond had lured him from the tower with a similar ruse. He'd emerged the first time only to go skidding across the buttered planking and down the stairs. If the wall hadn't broken the force of his headlong tumble, he might have snapped his neck. He'd taken more care the second time the horn had sounded, tiptoeing gingerly down the stairs and peeping around corners until the greased pig Mary Margaret had lured into the great hall with a handful of acorns went sprinting between his legs, knocking him flat.

He'd endured many sieges while defending his king's holdings in Guienne and Poitou, but never one so prolonged or so relentless. Since Hollis had departed to seek a mother for his children, Bannor had conducted most of his business from the tower, daring to leave its sanctuary only in the dark of night while the children slept.

One morning near dawn, he'd slipped into the warren of interconnecting chambers they shared to find the lot of them nestled like a litter of pups in an enormous four-poster bed. Mary Margaret slept with her golden hair spread across Desmond's breast, her thumb tucked between her little pink lips. A faint snore drifted out of Desmond's open mouth. Studying his son's freckled cheeks and snub nose, Bannor shook his head, marveling that so angelic a visage could be capable of such devilment.

The sense of helplessness that plagued him was utterly foreign to his nature. He knew all there was to know about being a warrior, but nothing at all about being a father. How was it that he could command a legion of twelve hundred of the king's most powerful and dangerous men, yet couldn't coax one scrawny boy into granting his simplest request?

He was reaching to smooth a tousled lock of the lad's chestnut hair when Mary Margaret's misty blue eyes fluttered open.

"Papa?" she whispered. "Are you a ghost?"

"No, honeypot," he murmured. "Just a dream."

She had closed her eyes and drifted back to sleep with a contented sigh, leaving Bannor to slip out of the chamber without a sound.

The lookout's cry did not come again. Bannor settled deeper into his chair and rested his chin on his chest, hoping to steal a nap. Sleep had become an elusive prize since he'd taken to roaming the night, haunting his own castle like a beleaguered ghost.

When a banging sounded on the door, he jumped to his feet, instinctively grabbing his broadsword.

"M'lord, m'lord!" Fiona cried, her brogue muffled by the thick oak of the door. "Yer standard's been spotted on the south road less than a league away! 'Tis yer lady!"

His lady. Bemused by the notion, Bannor slowly lowered the sword. He hadn't had a lady to call his own since Margaret had died over six years ago.

He could hear the old nurse clucking with impatience as he heaved aside the stout bench he'd been using to block the door and lifted the crossbar. Fiona stood on the landing, wringing her apron in her gnarled hands. " 'Tis yer lady, m'lord! She comes at last!"

Bannor snatched his burgundy doublet from the back of the chair and shrugged it on over his shirt. As his large fingers fumbled with the ivory buttons of the closely tailored tunic that flared over his hips, he wished that he was donning mail hauberk, plate armor, and helm to ride into battle instead of marching out without armor or arms to greet his new bride. He looked longingly at his broadsword, knowing how vulnerable to attack he would feel without its familiar weight at his hip.

"Have the children been gathered to welcome their mother as I ordered?"

"Aye, m'lord. Every last one o' them. Even the babes." Fiona beamed up at him, quivering with joy at the prospect of having a new lady for the castle. She'd adored her first two mistresses and grieved as deeply as Bannor when they'd died so young and so tragically.

He draped a chain of braided silver around his hips, then smoothed his disheveled hair. "I suppose I should inspect them before she arrives. A warrior never sends his men into battle without giving them a few words of instruction and encouragement."

"Aye, and eager for yer counsel I'm sure they'll be, m'lord," Fiona promised.

A less wary man might have been inclined to believe her, Bannor thought as he strode the length of the inner bailey, surveying the children gathered in the walled courtyard. They were actually standing in something that looked remarkably like a row. Fiona brought up the tail of their ranks, juggling the two most recent additions to his household. From the largest to the smallest, the children gazed straight ahead with nary a fidget or a smirk among them. The innocence of their expressions made Bannor distinctly uneasy.

Although Desmond looked no less angelic than his siblings, the crow with the splinted wing perched on his shoulder glared at Bannor, and the furry tail protruding from the neck of the boy's tunic twitched in annoyance.

Wisely deciding its origins were best left unexplored, Bannor clasped his hands at the small of his back and leaned down to sniff the dirt-ringed neck of the slender, fair-haired boy at his side. "And when was the last time you had a bath, young Hammish?"

The boy counted backward on his fingers. "Less than a fortnight ago. But I'm not Hammish, sir." He drove an elbow into the ribs of the solid little fellow standing next to him, eliciting a muffled *oomph*. "He is."

"Hmmmm . . ." Bannor masked his chagrin by turning a thoughtful scowl on Hammish. The lad had stout legs and thick, straight cinnamon-hued hair that made him look as if he was wearing an earthenware bowl on his head. "So you would be Hammish?"

"Aye, my lord."

"There's no need to address me as your lord. You may call me 'Papa.'"

"Aye, my lord."

Bannor sighed. His head was beginning to ache. He couldn't very well introduce the children to their doting new mother if he couldn't remember their names. He scrambled to come up with a convincing lie. "Before we march into battle, 'tis common practice for all the men fighting beneath my standard to shout out their names. Would you care to try that?"

The children leaned forward and craned their necks to the right, looking to the boy who headed their ranks. He lifted his shoulders in a sullen shrug, then dutifully barked, "Desmond!"

The others followed in turn.

"Ennis!"

"Mary!"

"Hammish!"

"Edward!"

"Kell!"

"Mary Margaret!"

"Meg!"

"Margery!"

"Colm!"

The two babes added a goo and a gurgle. Fiona gave Bannor a grin as toothless as the babes'. "We just call these wee angels Peg and Mags."

Bannor pinched the bridge of his nose. The ache in his head had deepened to a throb, yet he was no closer

to being able to pick one of his own children out of a
mob of strangers. Hell and damnation, they *were* a mob
of strangers.

He plastered on a smile. " 'Twas a fine effort. Suppose we try it once more?"

"Lackwit," muttered Desmond.

Bannor gave him a narrow look. "What was that,
lad?"

The boy gave him a cherubic smile. "I said, 'As you
wish.'"

Before Bannor could confront his insolence, a
mighty blast from the lookout's horn sent a tremor of
excitement through the courtyard. The jangling of
chains was followed by a grinding creak as the gatehouse portcullis inched its way upward. The musical
jingle of spurs and rhythmic thud of hoofbeats her-
alded the chariot's final approach.

Bannor fell into line between Hammish and Mary,
choosing to make his stand with his troops. As the retinue of knights split away and the chariot rolled to a
halt, he tugged at his doublet and reached to smooth a
beard that was no longer there. He was not yet accustomed to his clean-shaven jaw, but given his beard's
alarming tendency to burst into flames whenever his
offspring were near, he decided he soon would be.

He was not a man given to fidgeting. Noting his un-
easiness, Fiona came over and thrust the youngest babe
into his arms. Bannor would have been no more appalled had she handed him a severed head. He tried
holding the cooing creature at arm's length, but when it
started to squirm, he tucked it under his arm as if it
were one of the dried pig bladders his squires spent
hours tossing and kicking about the courtyard.

Exasperated, Fiona rescued the blanket-wrapped

bundle and situated it neatly in the crook of his arm. "Don't fret, m'lord," she crooned, standing on tiptoe to tweak his cheek. "I've yet to meet a lass who could resist a strappin' fellow with a babe in his arms."

Bannor opened his mouth to protest that the last thing he needed was a bride who found him irresistible, but 'twas too late.

An eager young squire had already rushed over to throw open the door of the chariot, revealing one slender doeskin-clad foot.

Four

As the chariot door swung open, Willow hesitated, glancing uncertainly at Sir Hollis.

The knight hung back. "Perhaps I shouldn't have eaten that entire mutton leg, my dear. You'd best go first. I'll be right behind you."

Willow took a deep breath and gingerly slipped one leg out of the chariot. It would hardly do to come spilling out at her husband's feet like a sack of barley. Thankful for the deep recesses of her hood, she kept her eyes fixed demurely on the cobblestones as she climbed down from the chariot, vowing to herself that she would not flinch when she first looked upon his face, no matter how deformed or unsightly it was.

Only when she stood upon her own two feet did she dare to look up. And up. And up.

Into the face of her prince.

Willow gasped, convinced for the second time in that

day that she had drifted into a dream. A dream sweeter and more enchanting than any that had come before it.

But even she could never have dreamed the man who stood before her. She would never have thought to draw the shallow brackets around his mouth or to shade his chin with the merest hint of beard shadow. It had taken the kiss of the sun to bake faint furrows into his brow and darken his skin to a rich, deep gold. His hair was not lustrous samite, but raw silk, cropped to just above his shoulders and shot through with rare threads of silver. Both wit and humor glinted in the midnight blue depths of his eyes, and an elusive dimple in his right jaw only served to emphasize the sulky-sweet cant of his mouth.

He was not slender as she'd fancied him to be, but broad and muscular. The determined jut of his jaw warned her that he was no boy, content to steal chaste kisses, but a man who would not rest until he possessed all she had to give.

Her man.

Flustered by her thoughts, she lowered her gaze. Only then did she realize he was holding something in his arms—perhaps another gift for her. Some costly treasure, no doubt, to be accompanied by a tender pledge of his affection.

Willow lowered her hood, then tipped back her head and smiled at him.

As Bannor gazed down upon the cloaked beauty who was now his wife, only one thought pierced his fog of desire.

He was going to kill Hollis.

If his hands hadn't been otherwise occupied, he

might have lunged past the woman and jerked the coward out of the chariot by his throat. As it was, he could only gaze down at her in paralyzed horror.

A simple fillet circled her brow, the delicate band of gold making a valiant, yet futile, effort to tame the cloud of dark curls that framed her face. She had a small mouth. Her upper lip was slightly plumper than her lower, the perfect shape for a man to gently seize between his teeth in the breath before he kissed her. Her dark-lashed eyes were large and gray, but 'twasn't so much the look of them that stirred him, but the look *in* them. He'd had women gaze adoringly up at him, so sated with pleasure they could barely whisper his name, but he'd never had one look at him as if he was the answer to her every prayer. 'Twas both compelling and unsettling.

Bannor opened his mouth to welcome her to Elsinore.

"Are you my mama?"

Bannor clamped his mouth shut. Little Mary Margaret had broken ranks and was blinking up at the new arrival.

"Are you my mama?" the little girl repeated, her golden ringlets bobbing as she tugged at the sleeve of the woman's cloak.

Willow's gaze slowly shifted to the child. She blinked rapidly, as if she couldn't quite comprehend what she was seeing. Before she could form a reply, Desmond said scornfully, "Of course she's not your mama. Your mama's dead."

Mary Margaret's blue eyes welled with tears.

Five-year-old Meg patted her on the shoulder, her own plump bottom lip beginning to quiver. "Don't cry, Mary Margaret. At least you had a mama. Me and Margery and Colm, we never had no mama a'tall."

"That's 'cause you're all bastards," Edward informed her cheerfully. "So is Peg and Mags."

Kell glowered, his small hands clenched into fists. "Don't call our sister a bastard, you clod!"

"There's no shame in being a bastard," Hammish said earnestly, tugging at Bannor's free hand. "You're a bastard, aren't you, my lord?"

"Aye, son, that I am," Bannor murmured, watching his bride's expression shift from wonder to confusion to horror. As she slowly took in the row of squabbling children, she began to shake her head as if waking from a dream.

Or tumbling into a nightmare.

Despite Meg's attempts to console her, Mary Margaret's sniffles soon escalated into sobs. Four-year-old twins Margery and Colm burst into sympathetic tears, striking up a mournful chorus better suited to a Greek tragedy than the farce that Bannor's once well-ordered life was fast becoming.

Kell broke ranks to give Edward a shove. "Now, see what you've done, you oaf! You made them all cry."

"I didn't make them cry," Edward protested, shoving him back. "Mary Margaret made them cry."

As lanky twelve-year-old Ennis dove between the two boys, the blows began to fall, punctuated by grunts and oaths. Desmond's crow took to the air, flapping its splinted wing and cawing madly. Something small and furry scuttled down the leg of his breeches and up Meg's kirtle, making her squeal. Hammish took one or two stray blows hard enough to make him stagger, but remained staring dutifully ahead, the only remaining link in their shattered chain. The boy's stoicism reminded Bannor eerily of himself. The baby in Fiona's arms soon took up the battle cry, squalling at the top of its lungs and shaking its little fists in the air.

Only the babe Bannor was holding remained blissfully oblivious to the shouts and howls that threatened to deafen them all.

"I will have silence!" Bannor roared.

For the first time since his return from the war, the children obeyed him, lapsing into a hush so complete he could hear the flutter of the crow's wings as it settled back on Desmond's shoulder, and the shallow whisper of his bride's breath.

He sensed that his bride was only a step away from bolting. Fiona's words came back to him—*I've yet to meet a lass who could resist a strappin' fellow with a babe in his arms.*

In an effort to erase her stricken expression, he thrust his burden into her arms. "My children and I would like to welcome you to Elsinore, my lady."

She eased back the blanket, then stood gazing down at the feathery perfection of the babe's head.

Her eyes were as cool as the ash from yesterday's fire. "No, thank you," she finally said, handing it back to him. "I've already eaten."

Sweeping the fur-trimmed train of her cloak behind her, she turned and climbed right back into the chariot, slamming the door in his face.

Bannor stared, dumbfounded, at the stag carved into the chariot door. It wasn't until the children began snickering that he realized the warmth slowly spreading through his groin had nothing to do with the spark of lust his bride had kindled in his loins, and everything to do with the toothless babe grinning up at him from its nest of blankets.

Five

Willow sat stiffly on the chariot bench, her hands clenched in her lap, her eyes staring straight ahead. She had not stirred for a long time, not even when the door had flown open and a muscular arm dusted with dark hair had grabbed a handful of Sir Hollis's tunic and yanked the cowering knight out of the chariot. She had half expected to be removed with a similar lack of ceremony, but it seemed her new husband was content to leave her alone.

Alone. 'Twas her destiny to be ever surrounded by others, yet ever alone. Her heart beat low and hollow in her ears, a mocking reminder of how freely and carelessly she would have offered it to a stranger. A stranger, it seemed, who had no more need of it than her stepmother had.

Although the voices outside the chariot had subsided

to hushed whispers, then silence, long ago, their queru-
lous echoes still rang in her head.

Are you my mama?

Of course, she's not your mama. Your mama's dead.

At least you had a mama. We never had no mama a'tall.

That's 'cause you're all bastards.

Willow shook her head to silence them. While ex-
tolling his master's virtues, Sir Hollis had neglected to
mention that several of Lord Bannor's conquests must
have been of an amorous nature.

How many children had the man sired, for heaven's
sake? Ten? Twelve? Twenty? She hadn't awakened from
her horrified daze until the moment he had handed her
the youngest babe, beaming as if he expected her to
clasp the bratling to her breast and swoon with maternal delight. He would never know it was not the babe's
soft coo that had made her knees go weak, but the
rugged charm of his smile. A smile that made promises
and broke them in the same treacherous breath.

You're a bastard, aren't you, my lord?

Aye, son, that I am.

His rueful confession should have warned her. He
was no noble prince offering her his heart, but a wicked
ogre commanding an ill-tempered army of dwarves.
Willow touched a hand to her sooty curls, remembering his horrified expression when she had pushed back
the hood of her cloak. At this very moment, he might be
nursing a disappointment as bitterly keen as her own.

"M'lady?"

Willow started in dread, but the beseeching voice
was neither a man's nor a child's, but a woman's lilting
brogue.

"I've made ready yer chamber, if ye'd care to come
inside."

Willow lifted the curtain and looked outside. A hunched figure was silhouetted against the shadows of night. She couldn't very well remain in the chariot forever, she thought despairingly. Nor could she demand to return to a home where she was no longer welcome. Her papa would never allow her to defy Blanche's wishes, and her stepmother would never return Lord Bannor's gold.

If she fled back to Bedlington, Blanche would no doubt have her trussed up, tossed over the back of a horse, and delivered right back into her husband's arms. Even now, the prospect of being bound to such a man sent a strange shiver down her spine.

"Come now, lass," crooned the woman. "Ye've nothin' to fear from our lord."

Willow swung open the door, abandoning her haven, though she knew in her heart that the woman was wrong.

As the stooped crone led Willow through the broad, flagstone passages of the castle, she cast a toothless grin over her shoulder. "There's no need to apologize fer yer shyness, lass. After I wed m'darlin' Liam, God rest his randy soul, it took him two days and three flagons o' ale to coax me out from under the bed. By then I was too drunk to do anythin' but lay there with m'skirts over m'head." She gave Willow an impish wink. "Not that Liam seemed to mind."

Shaking away a dark image of Lord Bannor ravishing her insensible body, Willow followed the crone up a winding staircase lit by fat beeswax candles perched on stone corbels.

"Ye can't blame a man for bein' eager to sample his

bride's wares. But there's no need to fret, lass. He's gentle as a lamb, our Bannor is, despite what they say 'bout his bein' able to rip a man's head off with one hand."

Willow swallowed hard, imagining Lord Bannor ravishing her insensible, *headless* body.

"Aye, and if any man knows how to pleasure a lady, 'tis our lord."

" 'Twould appear he's had ample practice," Willow said dryly.

Fiona paused on the landing, drawing her nearer with one bony claw, as if to share a girlish confidence. " 'Tis whispered he's so potent he can make his babe quicken within a woman's belly simply by lookin' deep into her eyes."

Willow shuddered. "Then I shall endeavor to avert my gaze whenever he is near."

The woman cackled, her dried apple of a face puckering into a leer. "Such a vow would be easier to keep were the lad not so comely to look upon."

Willow could find no retort for the truth. Her steps grew more leaden as they climbed a second set of winding stairs. It seemed her prison was to be a tower. She had expected a spartan cell, or perhaps a straw pallet laid at the foot of one of his bratling's cradles, identical to the one she'd slept on at Bedlington. As the door at the top of the stairs swung open at Fiona's urging, her breath caught in a startled gasp.

The moment Blanche had arrived at Bedlington, she had laid claim to every treasure Papa had not yet sold. She'd stripped the remaining tapestries from the walls of the great hall and hung them over her bed. She'd sipped her mead from the silver chalices once used to offer the holy sacraments in the chapel. She'd slept in the pearl-encrusted girdle that had belonged to Willow's mother. Over the years, Willow had forgotten how seductive such luxury could be.

The plastered walls of this bower had been hung with palls of purple silk. Fragrant sprigs of sweet fennel and pennyroyal had been strewn across a timber floor hewn from the finest Norwegian fir. A fire crackled merrily within the belly of an arched fireplace capped by a stone hood.

Her bed was no straw pallet, but a grand four-poster, curtained with hangings of embroidered linen. Most wondrous of all was the lancet window set deep in the thick stone wall. Unlike the arrow loop on the landing, it was not veiled with crude oak shutters, but glazed with glass—a treasure so rare and precious Willow had never dreamed she would see it in her lifetime.

The chamber looked as if it had been prepared for a pampered princess. Or a cherished bride.

As Willow caught a glimpse of her own stunned reflection in the window glass, she resisted the urge to spin round and round like a giddy child.

"I do hope the chamber pleases ye, m'lady," Fiona said, beaming up at her. " 'Twas Lady Margaret's chamber, and Lady Mary's before her." The old woman crossed herself. "God rest their gentle souls."

Willow's giddy delight faded. "Lady Margaret and Lady Mary?"

"Aye—m'lord's first two wives. As sweet-tempered and dear as angels, they were." She shook her head and made a sad little *tsk*ing noise with her tongue. "The poor lad has always blamed hisself fer their untimely deaths."

"As well he should," Willow muttered beneath her breath. They'd no doubt died spewing out his babes in that very bed.

The old woman's words cast a pall over the cozy chamber. The precocious Beatrix and her married sisters had sometimes whispered of men who measured the vigor of their manhood by the number of children they could sire. Men who looked upon their wives as little more than fertile fields to be plowed thoroughly and repeatedly until their seed took root. Perhaps this Lord Bannor was just such a man. Perhaps he hadn't sought her out to be a chattel to his children, but a slave to his insatiable lusts.

Her thoughts must have been apparent for Fiona wrapped an arm around her and gave her a quick, hard squeeze. "If ye're tempted to cower under the bed as I did, lass, just remember that Lord Bannor won't need a flagon o' ale to coax ye into his arms. 'Tis said he has charms no maiden can resist."

"That's just what I'm afraid of," Willow whispered.

But the woman was already gone, leaving her all alone to await her lord's pleasure.

"Give me one good reason why I shouldn't throttle you?" Bannor demanded for the dozenth time as he paced the north tower, glancing off the rounded walls like a cornered stag.

"I'm your only worthy chess opponent," Hollis suggested hopefully.

Bannor leveled an icy glare at him. "I defeated you the last eleven times we played."

"Ah, but it took you more than five moves."

"Only because I felt sorry for you. A weakness I'm in no danger of succumbing to at the moment."

"More's the pity," Hollis said glumly, slumping deeper into his chair as if hoping such a pathetic posture would make him a smaller target for Bannor's wrath.

"I send you out to find me a maternal, bovine dowd to mother my children, and you bring me a . . . a . . ." Bannor sputtered to a halt, at a loss to describe the exquisite creature who had emerged from the fur-lined depths of the hood. His voice both roughened and softened as her piquant features and cloud of sable hair danced before his eyes. "A goddess!"

"Not a goddess—a Madonna," Hollis protested. "You should have seen her with her brothers and sisters. She was the very soul of tenderness and devotion. The moment I laid eyes on her, I knew she would welcome your own children with open arms."

"Aye, that she did." Bannor slapped at his chest through the thin linen of his shirt. "That's why I'm marching around the tower in naught but my shirt and hose while the maidservants scrub piss out of my finest doublet."

Hollis heaved a defeated sigh. "When I first saw her, she was wearing a cap. And apples."

Bannor swung around to blink at his steward, wondering if the man had well and truly lost his senses.

"By the time I got a clear look at her, 'twas too late. The bargain had been struck. She had defied her own father to plight her troth to you."

"So you chose to defy me by accepting her pledge."

It was a statement, not a question, and Hollis wisely held his silence. Until he muttered beneath his breath, "You would have done the same."

Bannor gave him a narrow look.

Hollis dared to meet that look. "If you had seen the heartless manner in which her family treated her while we were waiting for the banns to be read, you would have done the same. Her father ignored her. Her stepmother disdained her. Her brothers and sisters ordered her about as if she was no better than a slave. And her stepbrother . . ." Hollis shook his head, his mouth thinning to a grim line. "I cared naught for the look in his eyes whenever they lingered upon her."

The thought of such a delicate treasure being ill used made Bannor want to slam his fist into the wall. Made him long to march upon this Rufus of Bedlington and burn his keep to the ground. Made him yearn to pound that lecherous stepbrother of hers until he begged for mercy.

"Did they beat her?"

"I think not. 'Twas her spirit that was bruised by their lack of kindness, not her flesh. Bruised, but not broken."

Bannor had caught a glimpse of that spirit when she'd thrust wee Mags back into his arms and slammed the chariot door in his face. During the war, he'd grown so accustomed to everyone scurrying to obey his commands that he'd been startled by an urge to applaud her defiance.

He should have followed his warrior's instincts and worn armor to their first meeting—a helm to shield him from her beauty and a breastplate to protect his heart.

He raked a hand through his hair. "I trusted you to find me a wife who would not tempt me to get her with child, and you bring me a woman who makes me think of nothing else. Just how long do you think 'twill be before her body begins to ripen with my seed? A fortnight? A sennight? A night?"

Hollis brightened. "Perhaps you should consider a vow of celibacy. I've no doubt God would find it a most impressive sacrifice, much more pleasing in His eyes than if you had wed some stout fishwife with a mustache."

Bannor planted both palms on the table, looming over his steward. "If you'd care to keep your tongue, perhaps you should consider a vow of silence."

Hollis snapped his mouth shut.

Bannor straightened, shaking his head. "I fear there's only one way to undo this wretched mischief you've done." He went to the door. But he did not open it until after he'd looked furtively out the window and determined that the children should be safely abed.

"Where are you going?" Hollis demanded.

"To inform my bride that a terrible mistake has been made. To tell her that we must petition Edward for an annulment before the union can be consummated."

Hollis rose to his feet, drawing himself up to his full five feet nine inches. "I cannot bear the thought of her returning to live in such squalor and neglect. If you don't want her, then I'll keep her for my own wife."

Bannor tried to imagine Hollis stroking his bride's creamy skin, Hollis sifting his fingers through her raven curls, Hollis tickling that delectable upper lip of hers with his mustache. He could not have said what his expression was in that moment, but his steward took a fearful step backward.

"I appreciate your noble offer, Hollis, but I could never ask you to make such a terrible sacrifice." The sarcasm drained from his voice, leaving it somber with regret. "If Lady Willow does not wish to return to her father's household after the annulment is granted, then I shall escort her to the sisters at Wayborne Abbey. 'Tis the only fit refuge for such a woman."

It pained Bannor to imagine a woman as desirable as Willow devoting herself to a life of pious virtue, but 'twas preferable to the thought of another man enjoying her.

As he turned to go, Hollis said softly, "Was it not you who claimed that when I returned to Elsinore with this woman, she would be your wife in the eyes of God?"

Bannor hesitated, his friend's rebuke piercing his armor of resolve like the tiny blade of a misericorde. "Then I can only pray that He will forgive me for what I am about to do."

Willow never would have thought that she would miss Harold's whining or Beatrix's imperious commands, but as she gazed around the bedchamber, the unfamiliar hush unnerved her. Once she had longed for silence and solitude—for a few precious moments to think and dream. Now that she was alone at last, she was afraid to do either.

A curious peek behind the bed curtains did nothing to ease her fears. The sable pelts had been folded back and the linen sheet sprinkled with velvety rose petals, confirming her dark suspicion that Lord Bannor intended to waste no time in getting his brat on her.

After shrugging out of her cloak, she lifted the linen napkin on the table. A mincemeat pie sat on a silver plate, still warm to the touch. Nibbling its flaky crust, she wandered into a curtained alcove to discover not a chamber pot, but the decadent luxury of an actual privy. The queenly throne was outfitted with a wooden seat and surrounded with fresh handfuls of straw. She barely resisted the childish urge to yell "Halloo" down its murky shaft.

An ornate cupboard had been set against the wall opposite the bed. Willow swallowed the last of the pie and approached it. The rearing stag carved into its door seemed to leer at her, his mighty antlers a threat to any maiden who dared to trespass upon the secrets he guarded.

" 'Tis a wonder Lord Bannor didn't choose a rutting stag for his coat of arms," she muttered darkly.

As the cupboard creaked open, she braced herself, half expecting to find the crumbling bones of Lord Bannor's most recent wife. But its silk-lined interior yielded only a silver comb and a chemise woven of a sendal so fine she could see her splayed fingers through two layers of the stuff.

Its very existence invited fondling. But as Willow held the garment up to her chest, testing its length against her own, 'twas not her hands she saw caressing the gossamer silk, but a man's hands—their backs dusted with crisp, dark hairs.

Cursing her vivid imagination, she dropped the chemise and scuttled backward. Her heel caught on an uneven board, sending her tumbling through the bed curtains. The feather mattress swallowed her up in one hungry gulp. The bedframe's leather springs creaked madly as she struggled to escape before Lord Bannor discovered that she'd stumbled right into his perfumed trap.

Bannor's determined strides did not slow until he reached the foot of the winding stone staircase that led up to the south tower. The dismay he'd felt at confronting his children was only a twinge compared to the panic roiling inside him now. He'd challenged the grim specter of death without flinching too many times to count, but the prospect of facing one willowy slip of a girl iced his palms with sweat and made his heart thud with dread.

He was afraid not so much of her as of himself. Every time he'd taken a brief respite from the war and climbed these very steps to visit the bed of one of his wives, a babe had been born nine months later. As much as it galled him to admit it, he was no different from his father in that respect. No lord of Elsinore had ever been able to touch a woman without getting her with child. And Bannor feared that once he started touching this woman, he wouldn't be able to stop.

He marched up the stairs, resolved to explain to this Lady Willow that his steward had made a terrible, if well-intentioned, mistake. He had just reached the landing when the door crashed open and his bride came flying from the chamber.

Bannor made an instinctive grab for her, hoping to keep them both from tumbling headlong down the stairs. As he caught her, she jerked up her head and he found himself gazing deep into her dark-lashed eyes.

He expected her to be startled. He did not expect her to let out a scream that curdled his blood in its veins and sent him staggering backward with an unmanly yelp of his own.

Six

Willow backed away from the towering stranger who was now her husband, the echo of her scream still ringing in the narrow stairwell.

Even as she averted her eyes and clapped a protective hand over her stomach, she knew she was being absurd. She had ten siblings. She wasn't so foolish as to believe a man could make his babe quicken within a woman's womb simply by gazing into her eyes. Yet how to explain that dart of lightning she'd felt deep in her belly at the precise moment their eyes had met?

She stole a sidelong glance at Bannor. He wore only an ivory linen shirt—belted to flare over his lean hips—black hose, and leather calf boots. With his shirt unlaced at the throat to reveal a dark *V* of chest hair and his hands resting on his hips, 'twas almost possible to believe him capable of such wicked sorcery. Willow had always thought blue eyes were cold and soulless, but this man's eyes crackled with passion, especially with the raven wings of his brows arched over them like forbidding storm clouds.

"Sweet Christ in heaven, woman!" he thundered. "Are you trying to break my neck or yours?"

Willow shifted her hand from her belly to her heaving chest, still avoiding his eyes. "Forgive me, my lord. You startled me."

He raked a hand through his hair. "Not nearly as much as you startled me. Just where were you headed in such haste? Is the tower afire?" His eyes narrowed. "Has that naughty son of mine tossed another stinkpot into the privy shaft?"

Embarrassed to admit she'd been panicked by nothing more than a feather mattress and a nest of rose petals, Willow shook her head. " 'Tis a habit of mine to take the night air. I was simply going for a . . . a stroll along the battlements."

His left eyebrow shot up. "Without your cloak?"

"How foolish of me," Willow replied, seizing the opportunity to escape. "I'll go fetch it this very moment."

She darted for the chamber, but Bannor followed, his challenging gaze warning her that he had no intention of having a door slammed in his face for the second time in that day.

As Willow yielded to allow him grudging entry, they were both forced to step over one of the sable pelts that littered the floor. Half the bed curtains had been torn clear from their moorings, revealing rumpled sheets and scattered pillows.

Bannor sauntered over to the bed and plucked a downy white goose feather from what appeared to be a fatal gash in the mattress. He held it up for her perusal.

"Had I a more jealous nature, I might be tempted to check beneath the bed and see if one of my bolder squires was lurking there."

"I took a nap," Willow lied. "I'm a restless sleeper."

"So I gathered." He squatted to retrieve a fallen rose petal, shaking his head. "Fiona's been at it again, hasn't she? When she's not playing mother hen to whatever chick needs her the most, the woman's a shameless champion of romance."

"A trait you do not share?"

The crumpled bloom fell from his fingers as he straightened. "I'm a warrior, my lady, not a sentimental old Irishwoman."

The boldness of his gaze coaxed another flutter from Willow's belly. 'Twas as if a pack of tiny butterflies was beating their wings against an irresistible breeze.

Flustered, Willow fumbled beneath the scattered bed-clothes. "I was sure I left my cloak right here."

Bannor frowned. He couldn't help noticing that Willow was avoiding his eyes. She'd shown no such shyness earlier. Perhaps she regretted her defiance and feared his reprisal.

The next time she stole a fearful glance at him, he leaned against one of the bedposts and offered her the boyish smile that had been known to ease the fears of even the most timid maiden.

It had the opposite effect on Willow. She paled as if he had struck her, then scowled down at the floor. Per-plexed, Bannor captured her chin in his hand and tilted her face toward him. Had her eyes not fluttered shut, he might have been able to resist the temptation to stroke his thumb across that petal-soft rosebud of a lower lip.

"Why do you tremble so, my lady?" he murmured.

"Have I so fierce a countenance as to make you cower at my glance?"

Her eyes flew open. Bannor was gratified to find not fear, but defiance, glittering in their depths. "Perhaps I'm simply in danger of falling beneath the spell of your legend. After your maidservant had finished describing your rather gruesome habit of ripping off men's heads with one hand, she warned me that you could get me with child simply by gazing into my eyes."

He cocked one eyebrow. "And you believed her?"

Willow stiffened. "I should say not. Contrary to the manner in which I'm presently behaving, I'm not a simpleton."

"Good. Because I can assure you that I'd have to use both hands to rip off a man's head." When her pursed lips failed to soften into a smile, he added, "As for getting you with child, I could never hope to accomplish such a feat with a mere look. I'd have to follow my glance with a wink or . . ." his gaze drifted of its own volition to her mouth, ". . . perhaps even a kiss."

"Do you mock me, sir?"

"Never," he said softly.

When Bannor realized his thumb was once again straining toward her lips, as if hoping to coax forth the smile his jests had not, he released her. He paced across the tower, trampling the fallen rose petals beneath his boots.

How best to spare her pride? he wondered. How best to inform her that she was not destined to be his bride, but Christ's?

He swung around to face her. "I'm afraid Fiona spoke in haste, my lady. For I cannot get you with child at all."

Willow's lips curved in a brief, but dazzling smile.

"Have you suffered some grievous wound? Sir Hollis assured me that you returned from the war with all your parts intact. All your *significant* parts anyway." Her sympathetic frown didn't quite hide the shy downward dart of her gaze. Bannor felt himself harden as if she'd caressed him with more than just her eyes. "Of course, perhaps Sir Hollis doesn't consider—"

Bannor held up his hand, hoping to silence her before she gave him yet another reason to murder his steward. "I can assure you, my lady, that my significant parts are not only intact, but in full vigor." Fuller than he would have liked at the moment, he thought grimly, thankful for the generous cut of his shirt.

An unmistakable grimace of disappointment flickered across Willow's face.

Bannor stepped closer to peer into her face. "You are a most perplexing creature. I've never had a woman recoil with horror at the prospect of bearing my child."

"Obviously," she murmured, a rueful smile flirting with her lips.

"Should I be offended or merely curious? Don't most women believe as the Church does, that the creation of offspring is God's divine purpose for marriage?"

"If that is so, my lord, then you must be a very devout man indeed."

Bannor was taken aback. He had not expected to find his bride's wit as irresistible as her beauty.

"I suppose children can oft be considered a blessing," she added, "but there are women who choose to wed for other reasons. Security. Rank. Riches." She ducked her head and slanted him an engaging glance. "Love."

Bannor gave a scornful snort. "I know naught of love, my lady. Only of war."

"You must have once loved the lady Mary and the lady Margaret."

His brow furrowed. "I bore a great and most tender affection for both my wives. I chose them for all the virtues a man most admires in a woman and strove to be the most devoted husband I knew how to be. But love?" He shook his head. "Love is an affliction to be suffered only by fools and lads."

"You were a lad once."

"And a fool as well."

Willow turned away from his cynical smile. As she stretched her hands toward the flames on the hearth, their crackling cheer failed to warm her.

"We've spoken of the reasons a woman might choose to wed. But what about a man?" She turned back to face him. "What about you, my lord?"

It was Bannor's turn to avoid her eyes. He paced to the window, then back again, stroking the hint of beard that shadowed his jaw. " 'Twasn't precisely a wife I was seeking."

Willow folded her arms over her chest. " 'Tis the usual outcome, when a man plights his troth to a woman and has his steward stand before the priest and make his vows for him."

"I'm well aware of that. But I had a more pressing need of a mother. Not for some child yet to be born, as Fiona might have led you to believe, but for the children I already have. Someone to care for them."

Willow managed to keep all but the faintest trace of bitterness from her voice. "Then I suppose you chose the right woman. I all but raised my ten siblings."

"So my steward assured me. But I must confess that when I sent Sir Hollis to seek out a bride for me, I expected him to bring back someone less . . . well, more . . ."

Bannor never had any trouble barking commands at his men, but his eloquence deserted him in the face of Willow's unblinking gaze. "Someone who wasn't quite so . . . so . . ."

"Me?" she offered.

"Exactly!" he shouted, a smile breaking over his face.

"So you are suggesting that we do not suit."

Although Willow's expression did not betray so much as a flicker of reproach, Bannor's relief quickly faded to consternation. Hoping to soothe the sting of his clumsy words, he gathered her hands into his own.

And froze before he could speak.

Had he not been gazing into Willow's exquisite face, he would have sworn he was holding the hands of a peasant. Roughened and chapped, they sported nearly as many calluses as his own. He must have betrayed himself with a downward flicker of his eyes, the ghost of a pitying wince, for she tugged her hands away from his, but continued to meet his gaze with a pride as unflinching as any he had faced on the battlefield.

Bannor knew then that he could not bear to strike that pride a mortal blow. He could not send her back to her family against her will or imprison her behind convent walls. He briefly entertained the notion of allowing Hollis to keep her as his wife, but his mind rejected the image of Willow in his steward's arms before it could fully form.

Bannor hadn't earned his reputation as a master strategist on the battlefield and the chessboard for naught. Perhaps there was a way to make her believe she was still mistress of her own fate. If he could somehow goad her into spurning *him*, she could depart from Elsinore with both her pride and her innocence intact.

It took him little more than a brief mental calculation, masked by an innocent blink, to plan his campaign. If he wanted to drive his opponent's queen from the board, he would simply have to send in his army of pawns to stage an attack.

A single fortnight in the company of his children should be enough to bring Willow marching up the stairs to his tower, demanding to be released from their vows. He would then play the part of wounded husband, flattering her with his passionate protests before reluctantly agreeing to petition Edward for an annulment.

Bannor recaptured Willow's hands in a grip too tender to resist. "On the contrary, my lady. I'm simply suggesting that I give you some time to become better acquainted with my children."

"With the children?" she echoed wanly.

"And with me, of course," he hastily added. Even as Bannor uttered the lie, regret coursed through him. He could never hope to know her in the one sense he most longed to—the biblical one. Desperate to escape before he betrayed himself with a whispered endearment or careless caress, he brought one of her callused palms to his lips and pressed a gallant kiss upon it. "Forgive me for tarrying so long, my lady. 'Tis late and you must be exhausted from your journey. I shall leave you to your dreams."

He was already drawing the door shut behind him when Willow's reply came, so soft he might have imagined it. " 'Tis far too late for that, my lord."

Seven

Willow fully expected to be awakened before dawn by the fretful squalls of a hungry babe. To crawl out of bed and stumble blindly to the castle kitchen where she would dole out lukewarm gobbets of porridge to Lord Bannor's whining brats. To spend her day enduring their howls and dodging their kicks when they were denied even the smallest indulgence.

She also expected her slumber to be as devoid of dreams as her heart, but her sleep was invaded by a dark stranger, more phantom than prince, who brushed her lips with his own, then vanished into the mist.

Willow rolled to her back, groaning as she sank deeper into a rose-scented cloud. Golden warmth flickered across her face, warning her that the cloud must be drifting too close to the sun. She pried open her eyes. Sunbeams slanted through the glazed window of the tower, reproaching her with their midmorning brilliance.

She saw that an earthenware basin had been left upon the table for her. Tendrils of steam drifted up from the ewer beside it, curling around a stack of linen towels.

She bounded to her knees in the middle of the enormous bed, swiping a rose petal from the tip of her nose. Perhaps 'twas not a baby's hungry cry that had awakened her, but Lord Bannor's bellow of rage as he discovered his bride was naught but a shameless sloth intent upon starving his precious children.

At that moment, the chamber door flew open to reveal two squires carrying a large chest between them. She snatched the sheet up to her chin, her eyes widening in alarm as the oldest boy let his end crash to the floor.

"Watch my toes, won't you?" his companion whined between gasps for breath. "I've only got ten o' them."

The gangly lad gave his sweaty forelock an obsequious tug. "A thousand pardons for disturbing your rest, m'lady, but the wagon just arrived from Bedlington and Lord Bannor thought you might have need of your garments. Make haste, Rob," the lad barked, jerking his head toward the door. "We've one more to fetch."

Rob groaned and rubbed the small of his back. "Maybe we should use a pony to haul it up the stairs."

When they were gone, Willow clambered down from the bed and padded toward the chest. She couldn't fathom why it would be so heavy. Her stepmother had had ample time to plunder its most costly treasures. Willow had expected it to arrive at Elsinore barren of all but a few stray threads and a puff of dust. She was reaching for the leather latch when her ears caught a faint rustle from within.

She froze, cocking her head to listen, but heard nothing more threatening than the whisper of her own breathing. Shaking away her fancies, she once again reached for the latch.

And heard a scrabbling too violent to be produced by even her overactive imagination. Willow stumbled backward, seeking to put as much distance between herself and the chest as possible. She shuddered. What if one of the enormous rats that haunted the moat at Bedlington had found its way into the chest?

She cast about for a weapon, finally settling on the charred remnants of a log she fished out of the cold grate.

She sidled back to the trunk. She reached down and gingerly unbuckled the latch.

The scrabbling subsided. Willow was already drawing in a breath for a sigh of relief when the trunk lid sprang open with a resounding crash. She shrieked, but stood her ground and lifted the makeshift weapon high over her head.

A tousled mane of white-blond hair popped into view, making Willow recoil with a different kind of horror.

"Beatrix!" Willow slowly lowered the log, regretting that she hadn't brought it down on her stepsister's head when she'd had the chance.

Beatrix sneezed twice and spat out a mouthful of flaxen hair before hooking one shapely leg over the side of the chest. "Where on earth did Lord Bannor find those pathetic weaklings? You'd have thought they were carrying in a boar for the roasting!"

"Or a bore," Willow retorted, eyeing her stepsister's lush hips with more than a trace of envy. She tossed the log back on the grate and planted both hands on her own narrow hips. "Just how did you come to end up in that chest? Did you back into it while admiring your reflection in a goblet of water?"

Beatrix giggled as she staggered to her feet. "Don't be a silly mouse. 'Twas Stefan who tucked me in."

"Stefan?" An ugly seed of suspicion was beginning to flourish in Willow's mind.

"Aye. And I can tell you that the rascal should have carved me a much larger air hole."

"Or a much smaller one," Willow muttered as Beatrix craned her pale, swanlike neck to peer around the chamber.

Acting purely on reflex, Willow groped for the hand mirror on the table behind her and handed it to her stepsister. She knew only too well how vain Beatrix was about her rump-length tresses. She'd been the one ordered to comb them five hundred strokes before bedtime each night.

While Beatrix raked her fingers through a snarl and preened for the benefit of her adoring reflection, Willow tapped her foot impatiently. "Don't you think your mother is going to be just a wee bit upset when she discovers you've gone missing?"

Beatrix lowered the mirror, admiring the ample cleavage exposed by her square-cut bodice. "Once Stefan explains our scheme, I'm sure she'll be too busy marveling at our brilliance to miss me."

Knowing her stepsister enjoyed nothing so much as an audience, Willow gently suggested, "Why don't you explain your scheme to me so I can marvel at your brilliance, too?"

" 'Tis quite simple, really. I've come to present myself to this wealthy lord of yours. The moment he lays eyes on me, he'll realize he married the wrong sister. Then you can return to Stefan and I can take my rightful place in Lord Bannor's bed." Forsaking her reflection, Beatrix studied Willow with a wisdom beyond her years. "Unless you already have."

Wearing only the flimsy chemise she had discovered in the cupboard, Willow felt exposed beneath her stepsister's scrutiny. Then Beatrix went to the bed and tossed back the pelts to reveal the snowy linen sheets.

"How curious," Beatrix observed. "Although last night was to be your first in your husband's arms, not even a drop of maiden's blood has been spilled here."

Her stepsister sauntered back over to her. Willow refused to flinch as Beatrix brushed a coral fingernail over her cheek. "And what's this? Tearstains? Poor Willow. Could it be that you spent your wedding night crying yourself to sleep?"

Willow slapped Beatrix's hand away. "What makes you think any man would want a child in his bed?"

"Better a child than a dried-up old hag. Had Mama realized how wealthy your fine lord was, she would have never wasted him on the likes of you."

The words wouldn't have stung had they not rung with truth. Willow gazed at Beatrix for a long moment before saying softly, "You forget yourself, little sister. Your mother is not mistress here."

She found one of her kirtles in the trunk, dragged it over her chemise, and jerked the side-laces tight. Then she turned and headed for the door.

"Where do you think you're going?" Beatrix asked.

"To request an audience with *my* husband. To inform him that you've run away from home and to insist that he return you to Bedlington without delay. You can decide whether you would prefer to travel by chest or by horse." Willow wrenched open the door.

"Willow, wait!"

Although the quaver in her stepsister's voice should have warned her, Willow still wanted to groan when she turned around and saw the tears swimming in her stepsister's enormous blue eyes. Willow wasn't any more immune to the beseeching tremble of that ripe lower lip than she'd been when Beatrix had been a cherub-faced toddler.

Beatrix lowered the lid of the chest and plopped down on top of it, her bravado seeping out of her on a dispirited sigh. "I only agreed to this mad scheme of Stefan's because they intend to make me take your place. Mama has always favored your father's brood over us and with you gone, I'm the only one left to tend to them." The girl's imploring gaze could have melted a block of granite. "Please don't send me back there, Willow. If I squander my youth caring for Mama's brats, what man will ever want me?"

Willow knew all too well what Beatrix was talking about. She couldn't send Beatrix back to the same fate that she had so narrowly escaped. And in truth, Willow was not so eager to be surrounded by strangers. At least Beatrix would be a familiar face, if not always a friendly one.

"Very well. You may stay. But only," Willow added sternly, "if you promise to behave yourself and go along with everything I say."

Beatrix rushed across the chamber and threw her arms around Willow, beaming through her tears. "Oh, Willow, you're too good! Of course I'll do whatever you say. I'm sorry I said such wicked things. I was just jealous, you know. Because you managed to snare some rich old baron with naught better to do with his gold than lavish it on you. With any luck, he'll be dead soon and all of this will be ours!"

At the sound of approaching footsteps, Willow struggled to squirm free of her stepsister's overzealous embrace. "We're left with only one dilemma. How ever shall I explain you to Lord Bannor?"

While Willow was urging her toward the chest, driven by some half-baked notion of stuffing her back inside and slamming the lid, Beatrix chattered merrily on. " 'Twas petty of me to envy you. Why, I told Stefan that any man willing to wed a woman he'd never seen must surely be as homely as a troll. 'Tis undoubtedly a blessing that he didn't come to your bed last night." She shuddered. "Can you imagine him blowing his sour breath in your face? The few teeth he has are probably all pointy and yellow, and I'm sure he must be far too old and shriveled to—"

Before she could finish detailing the gruesome short-comings of Willow's husband, he ducked through the door, balancing the second chest on his brawny shoulder as if it weighed no more than a goose feather.

Eight

"Forgive me for trespassing upon your privacy, my lady," Bannor said in his rich baritone, "but I was passing through the bailey when I came across two lads arguing over who should have the privilege of bringing this to you."

Willow would have had no trouble extracting herself from Beatrix's clutches at that moment. Her stepsister's limbs had gone as limp as her jaw. Her gaze slowly traveled from the toes of the leather boots that hugged his muscular calves to the sparkling indigo of his eyes to the rumpled silk of his dark hair.

"How very g-gallant of you, my lord," Willow stammered, waiting with dread for the moment when Bannor's gaze would alight on Beatrix. When his own jaw would drop and he would realize, just as Beatrix had predicted, that he had wed the wrong sister.

But to Willow's shock, he passed the girl as if she

were invisible. As he lowered the chest to the floor, a splendid pageant of muscles rippled beneath the jade green brocade of his doublet.

"Who the devil is she?" The query came not from Bannor as Willow had expected, but from Fiona, who had appeared in the doorway wearing two dozing babies in a sling on her hunched back.

"She's my . . . my . . ." Seized by a wicked burst of inspiration, Willow blurted out, "My maidservant!"

Beatrix's mouth fell open even farther, but Willow gave her a hard squeeze to remind her of their bargain.

"Her name is Bea," Willow added spitefully, knowing how much her stepsister despised the nickname.

As Fiona shuffled over and began to unpack one of the chests, she said suspiciously, " 'Tis most odd. I never saw the lass last night."

"She was traveling in . . ." Willow cleared her throat "*with* the baggage. She's a genuine treasure—quite devoted to her duties. Aren't you, my dear?"

Beatrix responded to Willow's stranglehold with a dazed nod.

Bannor spared her an indifferent glance. "What ails the child? Is she mute?"

Remembering all the times her stepsister's ceaseless twittering had made Willow long to smother her with a pillow, Willow laughed. "I should say not."

Nor was she accustomed to being ignored. The merest flutter of Beatrix's flaxen eyelashes had always sent any male within winking distance into a lovesick swoon. Before Willow had time to regret loosening her grip, her stepsister sauntered over to Bannor and sank into a curtsy so deep it left her gawking hungrily at a codpiece that appeared to be in no need of padding.

Her voice deepened to a throaty purr. " 'Twill be a

privilege to serve you, my lord. You have only to tell me how I might best pleasure . . . um, please you."

Bannor cleared his throat and averted his eyes from her overflowing cleavage before shooting Willow an amused glance. "Your *devotion* is commendable, my child, but you can best please me by serving your mistress."

Willow caught her by the elbow and gave her a shove toward the other chest. "You heard Lord Bannor, didn't you? Be a good girl and fetch my slippers."

Beatrix stumbled to a halt, glaring at Willow. "Shall I fetch them in my hands or my mouth, Your Highness?"

"Whichever one most needs to be kept occupied," Willow retorted.

Beatrix bent over the trunk, deliberately twitching her saucy rump in Bannor's direction.

If he found anything curious about the exchange, he chose to hide it behind an impassive smile. "Given the uncommon warmth of the day, my lady, the children have chosen to breakfast in a meadow just beyond the castle walls. I'm sure they would be delighted by your company."

"Will you be joining us?" Willow asked, regretting the wistful words as soon as they were out.

An expression that might have been regret flickered over his face. "I'm afraid not. I have some castle accounts to review with my steward." Without further ado, he made a curt bow and took his leave.

Beatrix straightened, holding Willow's slippers to her chest and gazing dreamily at the empty doorway. "No wonder you cried yourself to sleep last night. No woman should have to sleep alone with such a man beneath her roof."

Shaking her head, Fiona muttered something in a brogue so thick Willow could only make out, "brazen strumpet" and "ought to be taught a lesson."

Willow tugged her slippers from the girl's hand. "You're absolutely right, Fiona. Bea's a spirited child and when left to herself, she does tend to get into mischief. After she finishes helping you unpack, why don't you see to it that she . . ." Willow tapped her pursed lips consideringly, eyeing the fingernails Beatrix had ordered her to buff to a coral sheen only a few days ago ". . . scrubs out the privy."

As Willow tripped lightly down the stairs, she was accompanied by the pleasing melody of her stepsister's outraged shriek.

Bannor watched from the window of the north tower as Willow went strolling across the bailey, her head held high and a hint of a smile playing around her lips. Her name suited her, he thought despairingly, admiring the gentle sway of her slender hips. She looked so delicate he could almost believe the slightest breeze would snap her in two.

As she passed beneath the gatehouse arch and started down the drawbridge, he had to grit his teeth to keep from shouting out a word of warning. Sending her out to confront his children without armor or weapon was a bit like tossing a kitten to a pack of snarling dogs.

Better a pack of snarling dogs than a ravenous wolf, he reminded himself in an attempt to soothe his conscience.

He already regretted breaching her bedchamber that morn, but he had feared she might grow suspicious if he didn't make an occasional appearance outside the tower. Not even the presence of her impertinent little maidservant and a glowering Fiona had stopped him from wanting to tumble her into that rumpled, rose-strewn bed, though.

Biting back a groan, Bannor slammed the shutter, imprisoning himself in the murky gloom. His tower was becoming as much of a cell as that dungeon in Calais. He had no choice but to forfeit his freedom until Willow demanded hers. He no longer dared to spend the endless hours between midnight and dawn prowling the shadowy maze of the castle. Not with Willow nestled in that lavish four-poster, her cloud of curls spilling across the pillows, her skin ripe with the sweet musk of night-blooming jasmine. 'Twas too great a temptation for even a monk to bear.

And contrary to the way he was living at the moment, he was certainly no monk. His first seven children had been conceived and born in that very bed. He had sired Desmond on his wedding night at the tender age of nineteen. 'Twas the only night he and Mary were to share before Bannor was summoned to rejoin Edward's forces in France. He'd returned ten months later to find his beaming young bride standing in the courtyard, holding a freckled elf of a babe in her arms. Both proud and bewildered, Bannor had barely had time to count his son's fingers and toes before Mary had handed the tiny fellow to Fiona, taken him by the hand, and led him up the stairs to that same bed. He had ridden out the very next morning, leaving Desmond in his cradle and Ennis safely tucked in Mary's womb.

Bannor sank into a chair, flinging one of his long legs over its arm. Once he might have welcomed the end of the war. Welcomed the chance to be a real husband to a woman like Willow. But all of that had changed five years ago when the sins of the father had finally been visited upon the son.

Bannor straightened, that bittersweet memory strengthening his resolve. As long as Willow stayed at Elsinore, he was determined to stay away from her.

As Willow strode across the meadow, her face tilted skyward to drink in the sun's warmth and a genial breeze teasing her hair, she felt the stirrings of an emotion she hadn't felt in a very long time—hope.

It had naught to do with Bannor's amused indifference toward her beautiful stepsister, she told herself sternly. 'Twas simply the blessing of a fickle autumn day that had chosen to flirt with the pleasures of summer rather than surrender to the icy embrace of winter. Her strides grew longer as she kicked her way through the rustling grasses, and before she knew it, she had lifted her skirts high and broken into a run. She'd never been allowed to run at Bedlington unless she was chasing a child or rushing to do her stepmother's bidding. The pure, sweet freedom of the motion made her heart sing with delight.

Until she went tearing over a hill and ten scowling little faces swiveled around to glare at her, reminding her that her freedom was only an illusion.

Willow stumbled to a halt. Bannor's children were scattered across a shallow dip in the land—some sitting with their chubby legs crossed, others lying on their stomachs with their chins propped on the heels of their hands. A woven basket perched in their midst, spilling tarts, walnuts, dates, and apples across the carpet of fallen leaves. The children didn't seem to be suffering for her neglect. They appeared to be plump and well fed, and she doubted the dirt embedded in the creases of their rosy skin could have been removed in a single scrubbing, no matter how vigorous.

"What have we here?" she exclaimed, struggling to inject a note of false cheer into her voice. "It looks suspiciously like a band of pixies to me."

Her teasing failed to brighten their dour expressions or break their stony silence. They continued to eye her as if she were a small green worm that had wiggled its way out of one of the apples. The hardest face belonged to the freckled boy who reclined in the crook of a gnarled old oak. A crow with one splinted wing perched on his shoulder, and a huge yellow tomcat with a torn ear and one malevolent gold eye was draped across his lap.

"You, sir, must be their king," Willow ventured, bobbing an exaggerated curtsy. "One must always curtsy in the presence of royalty, you know."

The boy and the cat eyed her with identical contempt, the cat's tail twitching lazily. The crow cocked his sleek head, his beady gaze making Willow feel as if she were a particularly enticing scrap of carrion.

She lowered her voice to a whisper just loud enough for the other children to hear. "If I fail to show you proper respect, you might decide to have me carted off to the dungeon, or shout 'Off with her head!'"

A wicked sparkle lit the boy's green eyes, revealing that he would have liked nothing more. But his lips remained locked in a mutinous line.

Sighing, Willow turned to the blue-eyed, golden-haired moppet sitting cross-legged on the ground beneath the tree. "If that handsome lad is the king of this band of pixies, then you must be the fairy princess. But where are your wings?" She peered over the little girl's shoulder, frowning in mock dismay. "Did you leave them under your bed?"

The child cupped a hand over her mouth, but not before a merry giggle could escape.

"Mary Margaret!" spat the boy in the tree.

Shamed by her brother's rebuke, Mary Margaret ducked her head and muttered, "Sorry, Desmond."

" 'Twould appear the king is a tyrant," Willow murmured as Desmond dislodged both cat and crow and slid off the branch, landing lightly on the balls of his feet.

She could tell he regretted the maneuver almost immediately, for he was forced to tip back his head an inch to look her in the eye. But his chagrin didn't stop him from drawing nearer, his swagger an unconscious imitation of his father's.

"His Highness is displeased." Willow folded her arms over her chest, mirroring his posture. "Perhaps he'll be gracious enough to tell me what I've done to offend him?"

"You married our father," the boy said flatly, squaring his narrow shoulders. "We haven't had a mama for a very long time and we don't need one now. I take care of my brothers and sisters. We don't need no *mother*"—he spat the word as if it were a profanity—"mucking about in our doings."

"Aye!"

" 'Tis the truth!"

"Don't need no mama!"

The other children chimed in, coming to their feet to support their brother. A solid little boy of about nine, with dull reddish hair and bashful brown eyes, was the last to rise.

Willow refused to be daunted by their show of unity. "Your father believes you do."

Desmond snorted. "How the hell is he to know what we need? He can't even remember our names. He'd rather be somewhere in France lopping off heads and licking the king's boots than spend so much as an afternoon in our company."

Willow was less disturbed by the boy's insolence than by the nearly imperceptible quiver of his chin. "You shouldn't speak of your father so," she said gently. "If he didn't care for you, he never would have married me." The confession stung, but she made it anyway, hoping it would soothe the boy's wounded pride.

A nasty smile curved Desmond's lips. "We heard he bought you, just like his men-at-arms plunk down their coins for a roll in the feathers with old Netta down in the village."

His boldness earned snickers from all of his siblings, except for the lad with the bashful eyes.

Willow could feel her own smile begin to fray at the edges, but she struggled to curb her temper. "My papa couldn't afford a dowry, so your father paid a bride-price for me. 'Tis an honorable custom, if a somewhat ancient one."

Desmond shrugged lazily. "Why would he be willing to pay for something he can get for free any time he wants it?" He jerked his head toward three of the smallest children. "Meg and the twins there are proof that there's not a woman in the village who wouldn't welcome my father into her bed."

'Twas no great boon to Willow's pride to discover that Bannor apparently found every woman he encountered irresistible. Every woman but the one he had wed. As her smile faded, the children huddled closer together, as if fearing she might fly at them in a rage.

Instead, she leaned forward until her nose nearly touched the freckled tip of Desmond's and said softly, "Perhaps you're right. Perhaps you don't need a mother as much as you need to be taught some manners."

Whirling around, she gathered her skirts and began to march back up the hill.

She'd nearly reached its crest when Desmond's voice rang out, freezing her in her tracks. "Whatever he paid for you, 'twas more than you're worth."

Willow might have challenged the taunt if, somewhere deep in her heart, she didn't believe he just might be right. There was nothing left for her to do but keep walking, head held high, until she could no longer hear the mocking echo of Desmond's laughter.

When Willow trudged into her bedchamber late that evening, she found Beatrix buried up to her pert nose in a tub of myrrh-scented water.

Her stepsister's mouth was already moving when it emerged. "Oh, Willow, thank heavens it's you! For a moment I thought you were that vicious little leprechaun come back to torture me. Can you believe she made me draw my own bath? She would have begrudged me the water itself if I hadn't lied and told her the bath was for you."

"You poor dear. It grieves me that you should suffer so," Willow said dryly, remembering all the times Beatrix had ordered her to lug bucket after bucket of freshly boiled water up the long, winding stairs at Bedlington.

She crossed to the cupboard, perfectly willing to forgo her bath until morning. She longed only to crawl into bed, draw the pelts up over her head, and pretend she had never crawled out of it that morning.

"Just look at my fingernails," Beatrix demanded, extending the claws in question over the rim of the cloth-lined tub. "They've been shredded like so much cabbage. Of course, that's partly your fault for insisting that evil troll make me scrub out the privy. She all but cackled with glee every time she heard one of them snap." Beatrix's lips pursed in a reproachful pout. "You needn't have been so petty, you know. If I was going to play the role of your maidservant, I thought it only fitting that I swear my fealty to your lord."

"The way you threw yourself at his feet, I would have sworn 'twas the role of his paramour you were seeking," Willow retorted, drawing a clean chemise from the cupboard.

Beatrix breathed a besotted sigh. "I'd be content to spend only a few glorious moments in the company of a man like that."

Willow jerked her kirtle over her head. " 'Twould be more than I've enjoyed. Lord Bannor spent the day locked in his chambers with Sir Hollis, while I strolled alone in the garden, prayed alone in the chapel, and supped alone in the great hall."

Even more disconcerting had been the peculiar sensation that she'd never truly been alone. Although she hadn't caught so much as a fleeting glimpse of Bannor's children since their disastrous meeting in the meadow, she had whirled around more than once during that interminable day, convinced she saw a flicker of movement out of the corner of her eye or heard the ghostly echo of a giggle. 'Twas like being hunted through an enchanted castle by a band of invisible sprites.

While Willow drew the fresh chemise over her head, Beatrix stood without a hint of shyness, streaming water from her skin like some pagan goddess rising from the sea. Unable to bear the sight of all that rosy perfection, Willow jerked a linen towel out of the cupboard and tossed it over her stepsister's head.

Beatrix used it to blot her waterfall of flaxen hair. "I can assure you that supping alone in the great hall is better than having to choke down a cold bowl of broth and a stale oatcake while standing up in the kitchens. Although I must confess 'tis the best place to glean all the latest gossip." Wrapping the towel around her and stepping out of the tub, she slanted Willow a coy look. "Is what they say about Lord Bannor true? Has he really sired a dozen babes?"

Willow frowned, tallying children on her hands until she ran out of fingers and had to begin again. "I suppose so."

"Want to hear something truly delicious?" Beatrix asked. "Some of Lord Bannor's children are baseborn. It seems that shortly after Lady Margaret died, babies began to arrive at the castle gate in baskets. They're believed to be the result of Lord Bannor's dalliances with several of the village maids. He's taken in five of them so far."

Willow kept her expression bland. "Lord Bannor doesn't seem to make any distinction between his children, no matter which side of the blanket they happened to be born on. 'Tis a most admirable quality. Most men don't even bother to claim their bastards, much less welcome them into their homes."

"Perhaps he doesn't feel 'twould be fair to deny them, when he's naught but a bastard himself?" Beatrix clapped a hand over her mouth. "He did tell you, didn't he?"

"Of course he told me," Willow snapped, unable to bear her stepsister's pity. "I simply thought he was referring to his temperament, not the circumstances of his birth." She padded toward the bed.

Beatrix went around to the opposite side of the bed, preparing to shed the towel before she climbed into it. "They're already laying wagers, you know, on how soon you'll be breeding." Her stepsister stole a sly glance at Willow's stomach. "Since their lord paid a visit to your chambers last night, some of them are whispering that you already are."

Willow might have indulged herself with a bitter laugh if she hadn't been distracted by the small, dark shapes clearly visible beneath the sheet.

"Fiona," she murmured, shaking her head. "Perhaps the sentimental old fool will soon learn 'twill take more than a handful of rose petals to lure her lord into *my* bed."

Weary of hiding her hurt, Willow yanked back the sheet. She was still trying to figure out why the rose petals had suddenly began to chirp when the first cricket took flight, striking Beatrix square in the nose.

High above the castle in the refuge of the north tower, Sir Hollis was desperately seeking a maneuver that might save his queen from the ruthless clutches of Bannor's knight when a bloodcurdling scream shattered the cozy silence.

"Good God!" Hollis shouted, bounding to his feet. "It sounds like someone's being murdered!"

As the screams—shrill, feminine, and punctuated by hysterical shrieks and a peculiar stamping sound—

swelled in intensity, he fully expected his companion to snatch up his sword and race for the door.

But Bannor acknowledged the interruption with nothing more than a wary flicker of his eyelids. " 'Tis your move."

Hollis slowly sank into his chair, groping for his rook with a trembling hand. He slid the piece into the square next to it, realizing even before Bannor murmured "Checkmate" that he'd surrendered his queen to the rapacious white knight and left his king helpless before the onslaught of one of Bannor's craftier pawns.

Although Bannor seized his prize without hesitation, caressing the delicately carved queen between his thumb and forefinger, he found it impossible to take his usual satisfaction in his victory.

Because, unlike Hollis, he knew the game hadn't ended.

It had only just begun.

Nine

Bannor was free.

Free to joust and spar with his knights in autumn sunshine so bright it stung his eyes. Free to train his garrison of soldiers beneath the cottony clouds floating across the crisp blue sky. Free to gallop across the stubble of his shorn fields on his mighty white destrier and praise his grinning villeins for reaping such a plentiful harvest. Free to sup each night at the head of the high table in the great hall, surrounded by the angelic faces of his children.

He'd never been so miserable.

He might have been able to savor his freedom had Willow not been required to pay the price for it. Now that his children had discovered a more gratifying target for their mischief, they hastened to obey his every command, murmuring, "Aye, Papa," "Nay, Papa," and

"As you wish, Papa" with all the humble piety of saints, all the while packing Willow's cupboard, bed, and bath with enough bugs, rodents, and reptiles to rival any plague Moses had cast on the Egyptians.

Bannor forced himself to turn a blind eye to their devilish doings, promising himself that every humiliation Willow endured at their hands would only serve to spare her pride when she was finally goaded into spurning him.

When they dumped enough pepper in her stew to make her sneeze a dozen times in rapid succession, he commented upon its savory tang and handed her a kerchief to wipe her streaming eyes. When they loosed Mary Margaret's favorite pig in her bedchamber, he behaved as if deaf to its shrill squeals, even going so far as to step absently over the beast as Willow and her scowling little maidservant herded it through the great hall. When they tossed a stinkpot down her chimney, he ignored the pungent odor of sulfur that clung to her mane of silky curls for days.

After that first night, there were no more screams. Unable to bear the strained silence, Bannor would find himself standing in the shadows of the courtyard, waiting for the moment when Willow would throw open the shutters, her delicate nostrils pinched between thumb and forefinger, and calmly toss out the rancid eggs Desmond had stuffed in the toes of her shoes. Once or twice, he would have almost sworn he felt her accusing eyes searching the darkness, as if she sensed his presence.

Bannor's desperation grew as the fortnight approached its close without Willow making so much as a whisper of complaint. The winter snows would soon be upon them. If he was forced to spend the long, dark winter nights in her company, he knew a babe would come as surely as the spring.

He was breaking his fast one cold, sunny morning, ringed by the bland faces of his impeccably behaved children, when Fiona marched into the great hall and slammed his trencher down on the table. "I'm afraid there isn't any honey this morn, m'lord. Ye'll have to eat yer bread dry." She glowered at him from beneath her scraggly brows. "I hope ye don't choke on it."

As Fiona stomped back into the kitchen, Bannor exchanged a wry glance with Hollis. He'd been forced to confide in his steward, but all the other denizens of the castle remained baffled by his thoughtless behavior toward his bride. Even his knights and men-at-arms, who would have never dared question his authority on the battlefield, had taken to muttering among themselves and casting him disapproving glances. If Willow didn't spurn him soon, he might very well have a full-scale rebellion on his hands.

Bannor had just taken a hearty bite of bread when Willow appeared on the broad stone steps that cascaded down into the great hall. For one moment, he believed he truly might choke. His labored swallow was audible in the stunned silence, as the eye of every knight, squire, and page who had chosen to break their fast in the great hall turned toward the stairs.

It seemed the mystery of the missing honey had been solved.

Golden gobbets of it dripped from Willow's hair and clung to her throat and shoulders, draping her alabaster skin in a glistening amber veil. Bannor fought an absurd temptation to race up the stairs and lick her.

As she descended, her slippers adhering to the floor with each painstaking step, Fiona emerged from the kitchen. The old woman threw up her hands to cup her horrified face. The earthenware platter she'd been carrying shattered on the floor. "Jesus, Mary, and Joseph, lass! Ye look like a banshee!"

Desmond exchanged a sidelong glance with Kell and Edward, his triumphant smirk leaving no doubt as to who had propped the missing pot of honey over Willow's doorway. Bannor had to grip the edge of the table to keep from dunking his son's head in his bowl of porridge.

The stunned silence swelled as Willow picked her way to the foot of the table and simply stood there.

Acutely aware that everyone in the hall, from the burliest knight to the smallest page, was holding his breath in anticipation of his reaction, Bannor simply popped another chunk of bread into his mouth. "Good morning, Willow. I trust you had a pleasant night's sleep."

She did not reply. She simply gazed at him down the length of the table, the bitter reproach in her stormy gray eyes informing him that he had finally won. He had finally succeeded in making his bride despise him. Oddly enough, as she turned her back on him and trudged back up the stairs, her head held painfully high, Bannor felt no flush of triumph, only an overwhelming sense of defeat.

Willow paced the length of her bedchamber as she sawed through another sticky curl, waving it like a battle flag when it finally came off in her hand. Honey would have washed out of her hair easily enough, but her tormentors had been diabolical enough to lace the viscous syrup with tree sap. "Lord Bannor the Bold indeed! Why, I've never met such a dastardly, craven, cowardly, lily-livered . . ."

"Pusillanimous," Beatrix provided cheerfully.

"Pusillanimous, fainthearted . . ."

As Willow lapsed once again into sputtering, Beatrix wrested the dagger from her hand and gently propelled her toward a stool. "Why don't you let me finish this? If you persist as you have been, Lord Bannor the Bold will be wed to Lady Willow the Bald."

Willow threw herself down on the stool, clenching the sticky folds of her skirt in her fists. "You won't have to worry about that. I wouldn't stay married to the wretch if he was the last man on earth and the survival of mankind depended on my bearing one of his horrid little brats."

"I can understand that," Beatrix said, divesting her of another honey-and-sap-laden curl. "I just don't understand why you let it go on so long. I would have insisted that he throw the nasty little trolls in the dungeon the first time they emptied a bucket of soot down my bedchamber chimney."

"And give the little monsters the satisfaction of knowing I went running to their father to tattle on them? I think not! Besides, I've endured much worse at the hands of Stefan and Reanna. Remember the time they nailed my shoes to the floor? *While* I was wearing them?" Willow sighed woefully as another gooey strand of hair plopped into the growing pool on her bedchamber floor. "I suppose I thought that perhaps in time, Bannor would come charging to my rescue to slay the naughty dragons, like a knight or a . . . a . . ."

Beatrix leaned over her shoulder, an impish smile playing around her lips. "A prince?"

Willow swiveled around to gape at her stepsister.

"I used to hear you talking to your imaginary lover when you thought I was asleep," Beatrix confessed. "Once I even saw you kissing your hand and pretending it was him."

"Why, you meddlesome little minx!"

As Willow lunged forward, Beatrix danced backward, holding the dagger out of her reach. Only then did Willow realize that she felt curiously light-headed.

She touched a tentative hand to her shorn locks. " 'Tis a most curious sensation. My hair has done naught but vex me since the day I was born. I never realized how very *attached* I was to it."

Proudly surveying her handiwork, Beatrix thrust a mirror into Willow's hand. Willow slowly raised the mirror to her face, only to behold a stranger gazing back at her. A stranger with hair that bristled around her head like a cornered warthog's, and enormous eyes like those of the trained ferrets that used to somersault their way across the great hall at Bedlington in more prosperous times.

Beatrix twined one of her own long, flaxen locks around her finger as she crowded close to steal a glimpse of herself over Willow's shoulder. " 'Tis really quite fetching. You'd make a very pretty boy."

Willow's eyes widened until they were livid circles in her pinched face. When she slammed down the mirror and surged to her feet, Beatrix hopped backward.

"Where are you going?"

"To slay my own bloody dragon." Willow marched toward the door, her face pale, but resolute.

Beatrix trotted along behind her, hefting her skirts high to avoid the puddles of honey still scattered across the floor. "If you don't want Lord Bannor anymore, might I have him?"

Willow spun around in the doorway, a scathing smile curving her lips. "With my compliments!"

The echo of Willow's angry footfalls had yet to fade when Beatrix darted for the cupboard. She tugged a creamy sheet of vellum, a quill, and a bottle of ink from one of the cubbyholes carved into the door.

Dear Stefan, she scribbled. *You'll be delighted to know that Willow has given her blessing to my union with Lord Bannor. 'Twill be only a matter of time before I summon you to Elsinore.*

Beatrix signed her name with a flourish. Now all she had to do was coax one of the bumbling squires who was so enamored of her to deliver the letter to Bedlington. As she held the sealing wax over a candle flame to soften it, she fought to ignore a twinge of guilt. She wasn't exactly betraying her stepsister. She was simply striving to remain in the good graces of her brother.

As Beatrix tipped her hand, the scarlet wax spilled over the parchment, sealing its secrets inside.

The flat of the sword slammed into Bannor's head, sending him crashing to the ground. He struggled to a sitting position and dragged off his helm only to find a disbelieving Hollis standing over him. Shaking his head to stave off the ringing in his ears, he reluctantly took the gauntleted hand Hollis extended to him and allowed his steward to pull him to his feet.

The dozens of knights and men-at-arms who had gathered in the list to train were all gaping at him with the same astonishment as Hollis. They'd never before seen anyone best their master in a contest of skill or strength, and weren't sure whether they were expected to cheer Hollis's victory or fall upon him with swords drawn.

"Excellent effort," Bannor rasped, giving his steward a hearty clap on the back. "Most commendable."

The men exchanged several dubious glances before sending up a half hearted *huzzah*.

"Th-thank you, my lord," Hollis stammered, looking as if he'd rather be back inside the castle calculating taxes.

While the next two combatants circled each other, swords at the ready, Bannor leaned against the fence surrounding the sand-sprinkled field.

Hollis joined him. "I do hope you'll forgive me," he said sheepishly beneath the ringing of the swords and hoarse shouts of encouragement. " 'Twas not my intention to dishonor you."

"I'm quite capable of dishonoring myself. I proved that this morning." Bannor dragged his forearm across his sweaty brow. " 'Twould have been no more than I deserved had you cut my head off. Then you could have drenched it in honey and had Fiona present it to my bride on a trencher. 'Twould have been a sweet revenge for her to savor."

Hollis used a kerchief to dab at his own brow. "I'm quite relieved to learn your loathing is for yourself and not for me."

Remembering the look Willow had given him before she had exited the great hall, Bannor murmured, "My loathing is only a shadow of hers."

"Ah, but the lady does not know that your neglect was prompted by the purest of motives."

"Nor will she ever know. She will leave Elsinore believing me the most heartless of wretches—too cold and unfeeling to defend the honor of my lady against a band of rebellious children."

A fortnight ago, Willow's contempt might not have troubled Bannor. But as his gaze traveled down the length of the list to the grassy field where those very children were staging their own mock tournament, his expression was bleak.

Ennis and Kell were galloping toward each other with Mary Margaret and Margery perched on their respective shoulders. The girls clutched makeshift lances in their chubby little paws. Since no one had been able to get Hammish off the ground or coax him into moving any faster than a waddle, he'd appointed himself herald, and announced each unseating with an off-key blast from an ivory hunting horn. As the lad endured an accidental kick in the head without even staggering, Bannor shook his head, marveling at his fortitude. When they tired of that game, Desmond donned one of Bannor's own cast-off helms and began to best each child in turn, no great feat of strength or skill considering he towered head and shoulders over even the tallest of them.

Bannor might have been tempted to challenge the arrogant brat himself had an excited murmur not swept through the list. He knew even before he turned that this was the moment he'd been waiting for. The moment when he could at last claim victory for his own.

But as Willow came striding toward him, he felt only dread.

He had already decided that he would accept whatever rebuke she chose to give him, but as he caught sight of her butchered hair, he knew he wouldn't utter a whimper of protest if she wrested his sword from his hand and plunged it through his heart.

With her stained skirts and shorn head, she should have looked ridiculous. Instead, she looked as regal and magnificent as a hostage queen, stripped of her crown, but not her majesty. As she neared, Bannor realized that what he'd mistaken for cool gray ash in her eyes had always been banked embers, now fanned to glowing flame by her wrath.

His men instinctively cleared a path between them as Bannor stepped away from the fence and stood with hands on hips, bracing himself for the blow she'd come to deliver.

She marched right past him without sparing him so much as a contemptuous glance.

Speechless, Bannor swung around to watch as she descended upon the group of children. Their eyes widened in alarm and they scattered before her.

All but Desmond, who had just used a thick branch to sweep Edward's legs out from under him. As Edward scurried to safety, Desmond's triumphant bray of laughter drowned out the ominous silence that rippled in Willow's wake.

"Who'll be next?" he shouted, Bannor's oversized helm hanging crooked over one ear. "Who'll be the next churl to challenge Sir Desmond the Invincible?"

"I believe I'd like to have a go at it," Willow said mildly, plucking the branch from his hand. Before he could squint through the eye slits at his new challenger, she delivered a ringing blow that sent him staggering to his knees.

Having so recently been the recipient of just such a

blow, Bannor might have winced in sympathy had he not been struggling to choke back an astonished shout of laughter.

"Hey!" Desmond cried, his voice a hollow wail. "You can't hit me when I'm not looking. That's not fair!"

The boy dragged off the helm. His petulant scowl faded when he saw the avenging angel standing over him, the glistening spikes of what was left of her hair haloed by the sun. Something in Willow's eyes must have warned him, because after one wild look around to confirm that his siblings had deserted him, he began to scuttle backward through the grass on his heels and elbows.

"Fair?" Willow echoed, scorn ringing in her voice as she stalked him. *"Fair?* What would a bully like you know about *fair?* I've seen your kind before. You delight in preying on those who are weaker than you, but when it comes to fighting fair, you're naught but a sniveling little coward!"

As Willow grabbed the sputtering boy by the ear and hauled him to his feet, Bannor wondered how he could have ever thought her delicate.

"Mary Margaret! Ennis! Kell! Help me!" Desmond wailed as Willow began to drag him toward the castle.

His brothers and sisters remained huddled behind a hawthorn tree. Even his pet crow, newly relieved of its splint, took to the sky, cawing in distress, as Desmond's voice rose to an enraged howl. His face flushed so red his freckles all but disappeared. Willow marched on, giving him no choice but to follow or abandon his ear to her unrelenting grip.

As they approached Bannor, the boy's howls melted to a whimper calculated to rend even the most hardened heart. "Papa, oh, Papa, do save me! I'll be good. I swear I will!"

Willow halted directly in front of Bannor, her taut jaw and forthright gaze daring him to deny her. She could not know that in that moment he would have denied her nothing.

"Might I have a word with your son, my lord?"

Desmond clutched at the front of the quilted gambeson Bannor wore to protect his armor. "Please don't let her take me, Father! She's a madwoman!"

Bannor leaned down and said in his son's ear: "In future contests, Sir Desmond the Invincible, I'd advise you to choose your opponents with more care." To Willow, he extended a hand toward the castle. "Be my guest."

Willow proceeded to haul a disbelieving Desmond toward the bailey. The younger pages, who had most often been the victims of Desmond's bullying, were the first to break the stunned silence. They scampered gleefully along behind him, sending up an elated cheer. The men-at-arms followed, adding their own shouts of approval to the growing din.

Hollis clapped a hand on Bannor's shoulder. "What in the devil is she doing?"

"Something I wish I could have done long ago," Bannor murmured.

Shrugging off Hollis's grip, he joined the procession, as eager as the others to learn what fate Willow had chosen for his son. As they entered the courtyard, servants streamed out of the surrounding buildings to see what all the commotion was about. The beekeeper who had been stung on the nose when Desmond had capsized his hives began to clap, as did the candlemaker, who had been dipped in his own vat of tallow when Desmond had snuck up behind him and shouted "Boo!" The maidservants who had been forced to rewash all the sheets after Desmond had hurled fat globs of mud at their freshly washed laundry hooted with delight.

A thunderous surge of applause rocked the bailey as Willow marched the bellowing boy up the stairs to the wooden platform that housed the gallows.

Bannor began to shove his way through the crowd, afraid she might actually be planning to hang the lad. But she dragged him past the gallows, past the stocks, and past the flogging post, finally halting in front of the finger pillory that was most commonly used to punish harmless drunkards, petty thieves, and unruly peasant children.

Steering Desmond to his knees, Willow folded his fingers into the hollows carved into the wooden crossbar. She lowered a second piece of wood over his knuckles and fastened the latch with an unmistakable flourish.

Bannor smiled. She had chosen well. Although Desmond's imprisonment was painless, no matter how hard he squirmed or how loud he howled, he could not free his fingers from the tiny tunnels.

As Willow straightened, her gaze met his over the heads of the cheering mob. Bannor touched a hand to his brow to acknowledge her triumph. She spread her skirts in a mocking curtsy, as graceful in victory as she'd been in defeat. Tearing his gaze away from hers, Bannor turned blindly toward the north tower, determined to retreat before she captured far more than just one of his pawns.

Ten

Willow sank her teeth into the apple she'd confiscated from the page who had been about to hurl it at Desmond's head. The lad and his companions had rapidly dispersed after Willow had disarmed them, still grumbling and kicking at the dirt because they were to be deprived of the pleasure of throwing bruised apples and rotten cabbages at her surly prisoner.

As the sun had began to set behind the west tower, deepening the chill in the air, the rest of the crowd had drifted away as well, growing bored with the spectacle of Desmond glaring at Willow and Willow cheerfully ignoring him. Soon the two of them were left all alone in the courtyard, their pointed silence broken only by the distant strains of music and merriment wafting out from the great hall.

Desmond's crow perched on the sinister arm of the

gallows, looking more inclined to tuck his head into his breast and take a nap than to pluck Willow's eyes out.

Willow sat with her back against the flogging post, her skirt draped between her splayed knees. From the corner of her eye, she saw Desmond's hungry gaze trace a trickle of apple juice down her chin.

"Care for a bite?" she asked, holding the apple beneath his chin.

He bared his teeth, warning her that he'd rather rip her throat out.

She shrugged. "I would imagine your brothers and sisters are enjoying some nice fat pomegranates and rose-sugared raisins right about now. If you'd like to join them, all you have to do is apologize."

"I'd rather rot!"

Willow tossed away the apple core, hiding her gratified smile. 'Twas the first sound he'd made since his outraged howls had faded to sullen silence. "That could be arranged. Although I suspect your father would protest when the vultures started plucking the flesh from your bones."

"Ha! He'd be glad to be rid of me."

"Why would you say such a thing?" she asked softly.

Desmond was no longer glaring at her, but staring straight ahead, his freckled jaw set so tight it hurt to look at it. "Because 'tis the truth. He cares naught for me, or for any of my brothers and sisters. He cares only for war and the king." Now that the floodgates had been opened, Desmond couldn't seem to stop his torrent of words. "During the war, we had to be content with him coming home every few months—bringing a sack of presents, rumpling our hair, telling us what fine children we were and how proud our mothers would have been had they lived. When he came home to stay, I thought 'twould be different. We all did. But he shut himself up in that tower and wouldn't pay us any heed, no matter what we did." He fixed her with a baleful glare. "Then *you* came."

Willow wanted to recoil, but she was forced to watch helplessly as that rigid jaw began to quiver. "You with your big gray eyes and your soft black hair. We saw the way he looked at you that day in the courtyard! We knew he'd never come to love us if he had you to love!"

A single tear spilled down the boy's cheek. He pressed his face to the crossbar, but could do nothing to hide the sobs that wracked his narrow shoulders.

Willow drew in a shaky breath of her own. So their mischief was not wicked or malicious as Stefan's and Reanna's had been, but was only a desperate bid for their father's attention. And they weren't seeking his attention so much as they were seeking proof of his love. She knew only too well how futile a quest that could be.

Willow tore at the pillory's iron latch, shredding one of her fingernails. When she lifted the crossbar, she half expected Desmond to bolt, but he crumbled into a sitting position on the platform, burying his face in the crook of one arm.

Willow longed to comfort him as she had so often longed to comfort Harold or Gerta. She resisted the temptation by drawing her knees to her chest and wrapping her arms around them. She sat quietly while he cried, her gaze fixed on the frosty opal of a moon that had just begun to peep shyly over the castle ramparts.

She waited until he swiped at his nose with the back

of his hand before choosing the apple with the least bruises from her pile of missiles and holding it out to him.

He scowled suspiciously at her.

"I may be a wicked stepmother, but 'tis not poisoned, if that's what you fear."

"I s'pose I couldn't blame you if it was," he confessed sheepishly, snatching the apple from her hand and biting a juicy chunk out of it. "Not after that horrid thing we did to your hair."

" 'Twill grow back in time. I hope." Willow hugged her knees even tighter, also hoping that the sooner she made her own confession, the less painful it would be. "You needn't consider me a rival for your father's affections, Desmond. Although he is noble enough to honor his vows, Lord Bannor has made it quite clear that he was very disappointed in Sir Hollis's choice of a bride." She blinked up at the moon. "He will never love me."

"Oh, we know that now," Desmond said cheerfully, nibbling his way around the gutted apple core. " 'Twas him who gave us the idea of driving you away."

Willow whipped her head around to stare at him. "Oh, he did, did he?"

"Aye. We were just going to play a couple of pranks on you in the beginning. Then Kell climbed up on the roof to drop a stinkpot down the chimney of the tower, and overheard Father tell Sir Hollis that the best way to get you gone was to let you spend as much time as possible in our company."

Willow felt as if she had been the one struck over the head with a branch. She knew Bannor regretted marrying her, but she hadn't suspected that he was so eager to be rid of her that he would use his own children to drive her out of his life.

"You needn't look so insulted," Desmond said, tossing the apple core over his shoulder. " 'Twasn't very flattering to us, either."

She frowned. "No, I don't suppose it was."

"But it made sense of what Edward heard the night you came to Elsinore. Edward's a bit of a dunderhead when it comes to spying, so we thought it was just gibberish at the time."

"And just what did Edward hear the night I came to Elsinore?" she asked, although she was almost certain she didn't want to know.

"Well, he was peeping through the squint in the north tower wall—"

"The squint?"

"Aye, 'tis a tiny hole in the mortar that connects to the secret passageway in the wall." Desmond shrugged as if living in a castle honeycombed with secret passages and peppered with peepholes was the most ordinary thing in the world to him. "Most of the chambers in the castle have got them. Fiona told us our grandfather had them built so he could spy on his female guests while they disrobed, then smuggle them into his chambers after his wife was abed."

Well! Willow thought. That would certainly explain the niggling sensation that she was always being watched, and the spectral giggles that haunted her whenever she was alone. "What a miserable old lech your grandfather must have been! I suppose I should warn Bea to start wearing a chemise to bed."

"Oh, must you?" Desmond blurted out, his dismay unmistakable. He had enough manners to blush beneath Willow's frigid stare. "Anyway," he hastily continued, ducking his head, "Edward was peeping through the squint when he heard Sir Hollis say that swearing a vow of celibacy would be much nicer than bedding you or some fat old fishwife with a mustache. Father couldn't bear the thought of giving up women for good, so Sir Hollis offered to keep you for himself. Father told him it would be unfair to ask him to make such a terrible sacrifice."

Willow gasped. Was there to be no end to the insults she must endure from the wretch's faithless tongue?

"Then Father mentioned a convent. He and Sir Hollis both agreed 'twas the only fit place for a woman such as you."

Willow would have gasped again if her breath had not frozen in her chest. A convent! Bannor found her so abhorrent that he would lock her way in a convent? He would doom her to a life of piety and celibacy. She would never know the kiss of her prince or that of any other man. She would never know his kiss.

Desmond peered into her pale, still face, a hint of panic flaring in his gamin green eyes. "You're not going to cry, are you? I hate it when the girls cry. I'd rather you whacked me on the head again."

"No," Willow said calmly, rising to her feet. "I'm not going to whack you on the head. And I'm not going to cry."

She had no intention of wasting another tear on his traitorous father. Just as she had no intention of wasting another moment struggling to earn the love of a man who was so stingy with his affection he wouldn't even spend it on his own children. She'd already squandered too many tears and too many moments striving for a love that could not be won or earned, yet was never freely given.

Rage poured through her, washing her heart clean of the blood from its fresh wounds and searing the old wounds into scars that would serve her well in the battle to come.

Unnerved by her icy calm, Desmond stammered, "D-don't not cry for my sake. Blubber all you want if 'twill make you feel better. I'll just stick my fingers in my ears."

Before he could, Willow said, "I was just remembering something my father once told me."

"And what would that be?" Desmond asked.

She tugged the boy to his feet. He hung helpless in her grasp, plainly captivated against his will by the storm of mischief brewing in her eyes. She gave his freckled hand a squeeze before bending down to whisper, "All it takes to make allies of foes is a common enemy."

Eleven

When Bannor emerged from his tower the following morning, an uncommon spring lightened his step. He felt almost as he had the morning after a resounding victory over the French. 'Twas a most perplexing sensation. Had he won yesterday's contest, his petition for an annulment would be on its way to Edward, and Willow would be on her way to Wayborne Abbey.

He threw back his shoulders as he bounded down the stairs, whistling the first few majestic bars of "Might Triumphant O'er Evil." As he entered the great hall, he expected to find a demure Willow holding court over a penitent Desmond and a table full of meek and obedient children, cowed by the example she had made of their mischievous brother. But the high table was empty, its oaken surface barren of all but a scattered handful of crumbs.

Bannor's whistle died on a hollow note. What if Willow was gone after all? What if she had run away to punish him for his indifference? He swept an anxious gaze across the hall, oblivious to the curious glances cast him by the knights and squires being served by the bustling pages.

Fiona emerged from the kitchens, one of the babies draped over her shoulder. Bannor squinted at it, but still couldn't tell if it was wee Peg or wee Mags.

"And where is Lady Willow this morn?" he inquired, hoping to give the impression that her answer was of little import to him.

Fiona shrugged, dislodging a cheerful burp from the babe. "Off with the wee ones somewhere, I s'pose, m'lord. They gobbled up their porridge, then darted off as fast as their legs would carry 'em."

"And did Willow gobble up her porridge as well?"

"Aye, I believe she finished first. 'Twas her who was urgin' 'em to make haste."

Bannor frowned. An honorable man would be pleased that his new wife and his children were getting along so well, but Fiona's words made him uneasy. He shook off the sensation, telling himself he was being absurd. He ought to be looking forward to a day of spirited combat and mayhem in the lists. Now that Willow had put an end to Desmond's reign of terror once and for all, he was free to devote himself to training his men with his old relish.

He helped himself to a chunk of brown bread from a squire's trencher and started for the door, nearly stumbling over the enormous heap of goods piled in the middle of the floor.

"Fiona! What's the meaning of all this?"

Fiona came bustling over, beaming a toothless smile. " 'Tis a tribute to yer lady, m'lord. Gifts to thank the lass for takin' young Desmond in hand." She pointed to each item in turn. "The beekeeper sent a dozen jars of honey. The candlemaker sent a bushel of wax candles. The butcher sent a salted ham. The mat weaver sent a—"

Bannor held up a hand to silence her. "Very well, Fiona. I think I understand."

He frowned down at the bounty. None of his people had ever sent him gifts, except for those due him as their lord and master on ceremonial feast days. He wasn't sure how he felt about them paying homage to *his* bride. Especially not when he should be the one showering her with extravagant gifts—a silk wimple to crown her newly shorn curls, a delicate silver chain to drape around her alabaster throat, a glowing teardrop of a ruby to nestle between her plump, succulent . . .

"Gak."

"Hmmm?" Bannor murmured, still lost in his reverie.

"Gak!" the baby in Fiona's arms repeated, reaching out to bop him in the nose with one tiny, pink fist.

Bannor flinched. The baby chortled. Eyeing the child ruefully, Bannor shook his head. If he didn't stop dwelling upon them, 'twould be only a matter of time before those plump, succulent breasts of Willow's were put to use nursing a creature identical to this one. Then another. And another . . . He shuddered.

"I'm sorry, m'lord," Fiona said, struggling to re-arrange her burden. "The wee imp has a way o' slippin' out o' m'grasp."

"No harm done," Bannor replied, tweaking the baby's nose. "I suspect she was only trying to warn me of a danger I'd do well to remember."

• • •

By the time Bannor reached the lists, the spring had returned to his step. The mere prospect of battle, genuine or mock, was enough to make his blood quicken. His nostrils flared, drinking in the musky perfume of leather and horse sweat. Only on the battlefield were the lines of engagement clearly drawn. Only on the battlefield was he allowed to employ both his wit and his might to defeat his enemy. He never had to worry that one of his men might burst into tears if he raised his voice to a roar, or that a clumsy blow might crush his opponent's feelings instead of his head.

The sand-sprinkled field was already teeming with men engaged in casual swordplay and halfhearted wrestling matches. The clash of steel faded as he made his way through their ranks, answering their murmured "My lord's" and deferential bows with a nod and a smile of his own. He still missed the easy camaraderie of war, where need and desperation had made brothers of them all—lord, vassal, and lowliest servant.

A gangly squire came scampering out of the stables that bordered the list as he approached. "What's it to be, m'lord? Shall I fetch your sword or your lance?"

Bannor gave the field a measuring look. "What do you say, men?" he called out. "Shall we joust?"

A rousing cheer greeted his words. Not one of them could resist the challenge of controlling over a thousand pounds of straining horseflesh between their thighs. Nor the opportunity to unseat the most recent rival produced by their constant taunting and petty squabbling.

A few of them even dared to shoot their lord a

speculative glance. They were no doubt remembering how Hollis had so soundly trounced him yesterday. Bannor bit back a smile. They would not find him so easy to best on this day.

The squire sprinted back from the stables, fighting to juggle lance, shield, and helm.

"Slow down, lad, before you impale yourself." Bannor put out a hand to arrest his headlong flight. "Or me."

He inclined his head, inviting the boy to slip the helm over it. As he did so, Bannor found himself enveloped in a choking cloud of white. He fumbled blindly for the helm, jerking it off and shaking his head. Flour flew everywhere.

The squire stumbled backward, aghast with horror. "Oh, my lord!" It was impossible to determine whether he was beseeching his heavenly or his earthly master. " 'Twas not my doing, I swear it."

Bannor swiped the coarse stuff from his eyes and mouth, knowing he ought to be thankful it wasn't pepper. Or honey. Someone in the crowd snickered.

"Silence," he shouted, snatching the lance from the lad's hand and banging it on the ground. The weapon slowly folded in on itself until its top half hung by a thin sliver of wood.

"Maybe that's why that bride o' his ain't breedin' yet," one of the men murmured. "His lance has gone limp."

A helpless wave of laughter rippled through their ranks.

Bannor tossed down the shattered lance, sweeping a murderous glare over them. They snapped to attention, swallowing their grins. His nape prickled and he swung around, scanning the tree-dotted meadow just beyond the list. He could not shake the sensation that he was being watched by unseen eyes. Was that a woman's laughter he heard or simply the mocking echo of the wind?

"Shall I f-f-fetch you a fresh helm and a new lance, my lord?" the squire stammered.

Realizing that the unfortunate lad was only a snivel away from wetting his braies, Bannor resisted his first impulse to roar a reply. "Just fetch my horse, son," he said through gritted teeth. " 'Tis all I need."

He no longer had any interest in jousting. He simply wanted to escape his men-at-arms' pitying looks and sly asides.

Bannor stood at rigid attention, his hands locked at the small of his back, while he awaited the squire's return. His men exchanged nervous looks, but only one of them dared to clear his throat. The awkward silence stretched until it was broken by the tinkling of bells, so delicate and ethereal that Bannor once again scanned the meadow, half expecting to see a band of fairy folk frolicking among the toadstools.

The tinkling swelled as the squire emerged from the stables, leading the white stallion who had carried Bannor into more battles than he could remember.

La Mort Galloping, the French had christened him. Standing over seventeen hands high, the pale horse had cut a swath of terror through the ranks of his enemies, rippling like molten moonlight through the blackest night.

But that was before someone had woven pink ribbons through his silky tail and mane and draped a harness of silver bells over his neck. They jingled merrily with each plodding step he took until at last the stallion stood before Bannor. As he hung his mighty head in shame, a crown of chrysanthemums slid down over his brow, leaving him to eye Bannor with one soulful brown eye.

Bannor rubbed the beast's velvety nose, knowing exactly how he must feel.

"I only left him alone in his stall for a moment, my lord, I swear it," the squire said, beginning to babble in earnest. "I can't imagine who would have done such a dreadful thing."

"Nor can I." Undeterred by the violent jingling of the harness, Bannor jerked the reins out of the lad's quaking hands and swung himself astride the horse. "But I intend to find out."

He kicked the horse into a canter. He'd traveled only a few paces when the saddle slid sideways, dumping him on his ass hard enough to jar his teeth. A cloud of flour flew up from his hair.

He sat there for a long time. Long enough for the horse to trot around the list once, then return to nudge him in the shoulder. Bannor fingered the leather cinches dangling from the stallion's back. They hadn't been cut. They'd been deliberately frayed to the point where they would be sure to give way as soon as they were forced to bear the weight of a rider—especially a rider of his weight and stature.

As Bannor climbed to his feet, every man on that field took an involuntary step backward. A piteous whimper escaped the squire's throat.

Bannor paced before them, his hands once again locked at the small of his back. "Today," he called out, his masterful baritone silencing every whisper, "I will teach you the hardest lesson that any warrior, no matter how bold or courageous, must learn before he rides into battle."

The men exchanged expectant glances and craned their necks.

"How to make a graceful retreat." Bannor sketched them a brief bow, then started for the castle, dusting grass and sand off his backside as he went.

Bannor paced the north tower, feeling nearly as frantic as he had on the night Hollis had returned to Elsinore with his bride. Then he had longed only to be rid of her. Now he longed only to find her. He paused at the window, drawn there against his will by the hellish glow drifting up from the courtyard below.

A crackling bonfire spat stinging clouds of brimstone into the night sky. A band of imps cavorted around it, their sinister shadows an unsettling contrast to the merry giggles wafting to his ears. Although Samhain had come and gone over a fortnight ago, Bannor would have sworn his offspring had declared a pagan celebration of their own—a decadent feast where they might pay homage to the god of unruly children.

A savage pounding sounded on the door, mirroring his own desperation. "Make haste, my lord! 'Tis Hollis!"

Bannor was forced to heave aside three chairs, a table, and a bench before he could lift the crossbar and bid his steward to enter.

Sir Hollis staggered into the tower, weaving his way through the makeshift barricade. Soot blackened his handsome face, and the right side of his mustache was smoldering.

"Where the hell is she? Why isn't she with you?" Bannor demanded, handing him a goblet of water.

Hollis snatched the cup from his hand and drained it

dry. "She is nowhere to be found," he rasped. "I have searched everywhere. Even among" —a violent shudder wracked him —"*them.*"

Bannor poured him a second goblet of water, taking care this time to point to his mustache before he handed it over.

"Oh!" Hollis exclaimed, dousing the side of his face.

"Could she have run away?" Bannor's heart surged with a panic that had naught to do with his offspring's tyranny. "Is that why the children are celebrating?"

Hollis shook his head. "She's been spotted throughout the castle all the day long. But every time I send a servant to fetch her, she vanishes again. 'Tis most vexing."

Bannor returned to the window. He gazed down at the carnage with growing despair. "You saw how she handled Desmond. I must seek her counsel. I'm convinced she's the only one who can help me put an end to this wretched mischief."

At that precise moment, an arrow came sailing through the window of the tower. It thudded to a halt in the wooden shutter, the feathers adorning its haft tickling Bannor's nose.

"We're under attack!" Hollis shouted, dropping to all fours and scrambling toward the door. "Shall I alert the guard?"

"Not . . . quite . . . yet," Bannor replied, wrenching away the scrap of parchment impaled by the quivering shaft.

While he studied the missive, Hollis climbed sheepishly to his feet. "Shouldn't you come away from the window, my lord?" When Bannor ignored his timid query, he stood on tiptoe and craned his neck, but still couldn't see over Bannor's shoulder. "What is it?"

"A list of demands."

"Demands? Oh, dear God, your enemies have seized Lady Willow, haven't they? They must be holding her hostage. Whatever do they want? Gold? Jewels? Weapons? The castle itself?"

Bannor handed the parchment to him, his face strangely devoid of expression. While Hollis held it up to the torchlight, Bannor turned back to the window, his narrowed gaze searching the night.

"These demands are so much gibberish." Hollis frowned as he scanned the crumpled paper. "Honeyed pomegranates and fig pudding for breakfast, lunch, and dinner. Baths no more than once a month. Bedtime no earlier than midnight. Why, they're the ravings of a lunatic. Or . . ." He lifted his head, comprehension slowly dawning. ". . . a child."

Bannor paid him no heed. He seemed to have found what he was looking for. An enigmatic half-smile curved his lips.

"If this is just another of the children's pranks, albeit a dangerous one, then I don't understand this last demand," Hollis said. "The one that calls for your unconditional surrender."

"Ah, but you soon will," Bannor said, drawing him toward the window.

Hollis squinted down into the courtyard, struggling to see through the smoke and shadows. At first he believed, as Bannor must have, that the slender figure silhouetted against the writhing flames was Desmond. Only when the flames shot higher could he make out the gentle swells filling out her breeches and tunic and the inky cap of curls that clung to her head. Lady Willow gazed boldly up at the window, making no attempt to hide the bow in her hand or the challenging jut of her jaw.

Hollis shook his head, torn between shock and amusement. "You'd best devise a new battle plan, my lord. For it appears your lady has decided to join the game."

Bannor flexed his powerful hands on the windowsill. "This is no game, my friend." He swung around, his eyes gleaming with a raw excitement Hollis hadn't seen since King Edward signed the treaty with the French. "*This* I understand. *This* is war."

Twelve

On day two of the siege, Bannor paced the length of the bailey, surveying the orderly ranks of his garrison. The men-at-arms Sir Hollis had assembled for the briefing gazed straight ahead, the stern set of their jaws assuring him that they understood the serious nature of his commands. Bannor's pawns had betrayed him to the black queen, leaving him no choice but to send his knights into battle.

"Make no mistake, men," he said, sweeping a grave look across them. "This castle is under attack by an enemy far more cunning and ruthless than any we've faced before. You cannot afford to underestimate them. They are utterly without honor or mercy."

The men who had been sent to scale the south tower the day before only to have their ladders shoved away from the wall by a golden-haired imp wielding a forked stick nodded knowingly. They were still nursing their aching backsides and bruised pride.

"I would never ask you to commit yourself to such a dangerous campaign if I didn't feel that this reign of terror must be brought to a swift and conclusive end."

The gatehouse guards who had had the castle mangonel stolen from beneath their very noses only to have it used to catapult them with fresh cow dung shuddered their agreement. Since then, their comrades had spent most of their time either sidling away from them or breathing through their mouths.

"We must learn to think like them. To exploit their every weakness. We must be willing to seek out their soft underbellies and . . ." Bannor trailed off, imagining just how soft Willow's underbelly would be beneath his hand. When he continued, a hoarse note had deepened his voice. "We must be willing to use every weapon at our disposal to probe their deepest, darkest, most secret . . ." He lapsed into silence again, picturing just where his hand might wander after he'd stroked the velvety softness of Willow's underbelly.

Hollis cleared his throat, snapping him back to attention.

The man who had been constable of Bannor's garrison for over eleven years stepped forward. "Am I to understand, my lord, that the chief objective of our campaign is to subdue the pawns?"

"I should say not, Sir Darrin," Bannor replied. "Your chief objective is to capture their queen."

The men exchanged uncertain glances.

Sir Darrin's grizzled brow furrowed with puzzlement. "And should we succeed?"

Their eyes followed Bannor's as he tipped back his head and gazed up at the south tower. The red-and-

gold standard that had rippled boldly over the walls of
Elsinore since Bannor had wrested the castle from his
half-brother over thirteen years ago now hung upside
down. Instead of rearing into the air, the red stag
pawed at the ground, his mighty heart skewered by the
airy branch of a willow.

Bannor's lips curved in a smile so ruthlessly tender
it had been known to make even his most worthy and
courageous foe beg for the chance to surrender. "Bring
her to me."

Willow withdrew into the shadows of the tower, shivering despite the sunbeams slanting through the window. She almost wished it had a wooden shutter to
slam. The glazed glass seemed far too fragile to shield
her from the primal heat of Bannor's gaze.

Although she could not hear the orders he was giving to the soldiers gathered in the bailey, she could
easily deduce their nature. Bannor's determination had
been written in his stance as surely as his motto was
emblazoned on the cupboard beneath the rearing stag—
To conquer or die. She lifted her chin. If he could not conquer her with his indifference, he certainly wasn't going
to conquer her with his enmity.

She swung around, hands on hips, to survey her
own ranks. Unlike Bannor's men, they did not stand in
orderly rows, gazing straight ahead with their shoulders thrown back. Instead, they scampered about the
chamber, each engrossed in the task Willow had set before them. Their concentration was frequently broken
by a fit of giggles or a shoving match when they dis-
agreed over how to proceed. It was not yet noontime,
and Willow had already had to break up two fistfights

and dry a flood of petulant tears. The latter had belonged to Beatrix, who resented being asked to turn her dainty hands to the task of whittling table legs into arrows.

Willow shot a wry glance heavenward. Those genteel ladies, Mary and Margaret, would no doubt rise wailing from their crypts if they could see what Willow and the children had done to their elegant bedchamber.

Kell and Edward had torn the palls of purple silk from the walls and were using them to fashion bold sashes they could all wear over their tunics. The fine floor of Norwegian fir now sported numerous scars, gouged when Ennis and Hammish had dragged all the nonessential furniture from the chamber and shoved it down the stairs, creating an impromptu barricade. Mary and Mary Margaret had stripped the hangings from the bed and were slicing them into bandages. Although no one had suffered anything more life-threatening than a splinter or a skinned knee while scampering out of the reach of Bannor's men, Willow believed in being prepared.

The youngest children were tearing feathers from the mattress in great handfuls, hoping to use them in some diabolical plot of Desmond's involving a vat of pitch and a garrison of sleeping soldiers. The children required no bed. They preferred to sleep wrapped in blankets on the floor just like the soldiers they were pretending to be.

Last night, Willow had joined them there. There was something oddly comforting about being surrounded by their snug little bodies. As she had lain in the dark, listening to their various snores, snorts, and snuffles, she had realized that she was having something she hadn't been allowed to have in a very long time—fun.

Kell and Edward suddenly broke into a noisy tug-of-war match over one of the sashes. Willow was moving to separate them when Desmond came tumbling out of the cupboard.

She had been shocked to discover that her very own cupboard was a door to one of the secret passages Desmond had described that fateful evening on the gallows. The passages and peepholes scattered throughout the castle made it possible for them to come and go without being detected. Bannor might be a master of strategy, but he'd yet to figure out how Willow and the children were privy to his battle plans practically before he made them.

Willow's mouth curved in a tight little smile. Perhaps if he had spent more time at home with his children and less time indulging his appetites for war and women, he might be familiar with the passages his children had been traversing since they were toddlers.

Desmond's face had lost its pinched, sullen look. The crow on his shoulder let out a triumphant caw as he swept them an exaggerated bow. "Captain of the guard reporting for duty."

Ten-year-old Mary stopped shredding the bed hangings long enough to shoot him a resentful look. "I don't see why you always get to be captain of the guard."

"Because I'm the oldest."

"No, you're not. I am." Beatrix scrambled to her feet, her nose still red from her fit of tears. She was the exact same age as Desmond, but she towered over him like an Amazon princess.

He tried to sneer up his nose at her, but couldn't seem to coax his gaze into traveling any higher than her heaving breasts. A flush crept into his freckled cheeks. "You can't be captain of the guard. You're naught but a maidservant. And a girl."

Willow cleared her throat pointedly.

Desmond jerked his gaze away from Beatrix's chest and flushed deeper. "Beg pardon, Willow. But you're not a girl. You're our commander." His bony chest swelled. "And I've come to bring you tidings of great import."

Beatrix rolled her eyes while the children crowded around, eager to hear his news.

"Proceed," Willow commanded, waving a regal hand.

Desmond threw a nervous glance over his shoulder, as if he feared one of his father's spies might come bounding out of the cupboard. "I was hiding in the passageway behind the hearth in the kitchen just waiting for a chance to snatch a hare from the spit when I heard one of the maidservants say that Fath—" his face hardened, "—the *enemy* had just given the order that all the food stores were to be removed to the spice cellar, where they're to be kept under lock and key." Desmond paused for dramatic effect. "He plans to starve us out."

The children gasped as one, but it was Hammish's piteous whimper that cut straight to Willow's heart. The shy lad could bear any physical blow without wincing, but the prospect of having his food cut off made his plump cheeks go pale with dread.

Willow wrapped an arm around the boy's shoulders, stirred by a rush of fierce protectiveness. Gerta or Harold would have squirmed out of her embrace, but Hammish only snuggled nearer. What manner of monster would starve his own children? she thought bitterly. It seemed her husband was a prince after all. A prince of darkness.

"Don't you fret, sweeting," she assured Hammish, ruffling his cinnamon-colored hair. "We'll find something for you to eat. I swear it."

The boy's hopeful gaze strayed to the crow on Desmond's shoulder.

Desmond stroked the bird's sleek feathers and glared back at his brother. "We might just have to eat you. At least there'd be plenty to go around."

Before Willow could chastise him, Edward piped up. "We won't have to eat none of us. I'll just wait 'til the pigeons come to roost on the battlements for the night. As soon as they fall asleep, I'll sneak up behind 'em and bash 'em over the head with a club." Edward mimed the entire hunt. Kell staggered beneath the blow of the invisible club, then collapsed onto his back, his fingers curled into rigid talons.

Beatrix groaned. "I'm not eating a filthy pigeon. My constitution is far too delicate."

"You didn't look so delicate yesterday when you were wolfing down that lark pasty I brought you," Desmond reminded her, earning a scornful look.

Willow struggled to hide her own grimace of distaste. " 'Tis a fine idea, Ed. We can roast the pigeons right here on the hearth. Margery and Colm can turn the spit."

The four-year-old twins beamed, delighted to be included in the adventure.

The devilish mischief melted from Desmond's face, leaving it curiously sober. "There's more you should know, Willow."

The children ceased their fidgeting and fell into a grave hush. A claw of foreboding tickled Willow's nape. "Go on."

"My father told his men that if they should succeed in routing us, there's only one thing he wants."

"And that would be?"

"You."

The single word shivered Willow to the core. The children exchanged wide-eyed glances, their eyes glassy with dread.

"We've heard tales about what Papa does with the prisoners he captures," Mary whispered.

"Aye, we have," Ennis said somberly. "Some say he cuts off their heads, strings them on a rope, and hangs them from his saddle."

"Others say he pitches them into a deep, dark hole and covers them over with dirt," added Kell. "While they're still alive."

"I heard he boils 'em in a big pot," Edward offered cheerfully, "then sucks the marrow from their bones." He lifted an invisible bone to his lips and made smacking noises.

Mary Margaret rushed over and buried her face in the leg of Willow's breeches. "Oh, Willow," she wailed, "what if Papa eats you all up?"

Willow stroked Mary Margaret's ringlets, as much to hide the trembling of her own hand as to comfort the child. She never wanted the little girl to learn that there were far more diabolical punishments a man could visit upon a woman.

"If he takes you hostage," Beatrix declared, striking a noble pose that didn't quite hide the hungry dart of her tongue over her ripe, pink lips, "I shall offer myself in your place."

Desmond snorted. "He'll be paying us to take you back."

Before Beatrix could box the boy's ears, Willow said, " 'Tis a grand gesture, Bea, but that won't be necessary. Lord Bannor would have to capture me first. And I have no intention of letting him do that." She managed a bold smile. " 'Twill be only a matter of time before your wicked papa is forced to surrender."

"Once he does," Desmond asked eagerly, "what will *you* do with *him*?"

It wasn't until Willow's gaze had traveled the expectant circle of their bloodthirsty little faces that she realized she hadn't the faintest idea.

On day four of the siege, Willow and Desmond huddled in the secret passageway tucked into the wall of the north tower. For both of them to see through the narrow peephole bored in the stone, they had to crouch with their faces pressed cheek to cheek.

Despite the cozy grace of the chamber Bannor had prepared for her, it appeared that he had been living in spartan squalor since returning to Elsinore. The walls of his tower were bare stone, with no trace of the richly hued tapestries scattered throughout the rest of the castle. Crude shutters veiled the windows, their wooden teeth chattering beneath each bullying gust of the wind. The table and chairs were littered with crumpled sheaves of parchment and a veritable arsenal of weapons—the rusty head of an ancient battle-ax, a massive crossbow it should have taken two men to handle, maces, shields, and at least half a dozen broadswords, their deadly blades polished to a gleaming sheen.

Bannor didn't even allow himself the luxury of a bed, but instead chose to sleep on a straw-stuffed mattress beneath one of the windows. He ought to at least drag it in front of the fire, Willow thought irritably, now that the nights had turned so bitter cold. Of course, half the time he didn't even bother to light a fire, but slept huddled beneath a thin blanket. 'Twas almost as if he equated comforts with weakness and sought to deny himself even the most primitive of them.

"Here he comes," Desmond hissed, jabbing an elbow into her side as the tower door swung open.

Willow rubbed her ribs. "Let's pray Sir Hollis is with him so we can learn what they've got planned for the morrow."

Willow could not help wondering how she would feel if Bannor drew a woman into that candlelit tower behind him. One of the women from the village, perhaps, who had already welcomed him into her bed and borne his child. But the door drifted shut to reveal he was alone.

As he secured the crossbar, then wandered toward the window, his gait seemed to lack its usual swagger. He gave the parchments scattered across the table a rueful glance, then reached around to rub the back of his neck, almost as if he wished there was someone there to do it for him. He unlatched the shutter and stood gazing up at the stars, his silent sigh hanging in the frosty night air. Willow wondered if he was pining for one of his lost wives, or perhaps for the woman who had taught an innocent boy that love was naught but an affliction to be scorned rather than suffered.

As he closed the shutter and began to tug wearily at the buttons of his doublet, Desmond sank back on his heels, snorting in disgust. "We might as well retreat. There's naught to see here."

Willow wasn't so sure about that. As Bannor shrugged out of his doublet, the supple roll of his muscles sent a strange languor melting through her limbs, robbing her of both the strength and the will to rise.

"You go along," she murmured, her eye still plastered to the peephole. "It might be prudent for me to observe him a bit longer. To seek out his weaknesses."

But as Bannor drew his linen shirt over his head and tossed it carelessly aside, then propped one foot on a bench to peel down his hose, she had to admit that he didn't seem to have any. Even in the dim candlelight, 'twas evident that his powerful chest was perfectly complemented by powerful thighs and powerful calves, all lightly dusted with dark hair.

Desmond shrugged. "Suit yourself. But *don't* get captured."

As the boy scrambled away on all fours, Willow was too chagrined to confess that she had already been captured. Captured by the mellow bronze glow of Bannor's skin in the flickering candleshine, by the crisp coils of dark hair that thatched his chest, by the sweet melancholy of his expression.

She was so beguiled by that hint of vulnerability amidst all that power that it took her a moment to realize he had stripped down to naught but a scrap of linen no wider than one of the bandages Mary Margaret had torn from the bed hangings. Willow's eye widened in alarm as he gave it an absent tug. At the precise moment it fell away, he turned his back on her and padded naked to the mattress, stretching with the effortless grace of some magnificent male animal who isn't aware it is being observed.

It wasn't until he'd rolled to his side, presenting her with his broad back, and dragged the blanket over his hips that Willow was able to pry her eye away from the peephole. She collapsed against the wall. Her mouth had gone dry and her breath was coming in short pants, as if she'd been the prey this night instead of the predator.

As Willow waited for her breath to steady and her limbs to regain their strength, she was shaken to the core to realize that she hadn't discovered Bannor's weakness, but her own.

Thirteen

On day five of the siege, Bannor lurked in the shadows of the buttery, his anger mounting as he listened to the shameless rustling of the rat who had descended the stairs to the spice cellar only minutes before he'd arrived.

He could no longer deny it. He had a traitor in his midst. His suspicions had been confirmed earlier that evening when a contrite Sir Darrin had reported to the tower.

" 'Tis just as you suspected, my lord," the grizzled old knight had blurted out. "At last count, we were missing two wheels of cheese, six rashers of bacon, five loaves of barley bread, a barrel of salted stockfish, and one smoked ham."

"I knew it!" Bannor exclaimed, slamming a triumphant fist into his palm. "The pampered little bratlings should have raised the white flag the first night they were deprived of their fig pudding. There's no way they could have held us off for three days if they weren't getting food from somewhere." He fixed the knight with a forbidding glower. "Or someone."

Sir Darrin took an involuntary step backward. "The spice cellar has been locked the entire time, my lord, just as you ordered. No one could have come or gone except for them that has the keys. Shall I post a guard?"

Bannor stroked his jaw, pondering the man's words. "I don't believe that will be necessary. I'd prefer to tend to the matter myself."

As the knight wheeled around to make a hasty exit, Bannor squinted at the back of his head. "Whatever is that thing in your hair?"

" 'Tis a goose feather, my lord," he admitted. He tugged, but the downy wisp was held fast to his graying locks by a gooey wad of pitch. "The gatehouse suffered an attack last night while my watch was sleeping."

The proud old knight's sheepish confession had only made Bannor more determined to catch the thief who was betraying them all. The rustling coming from the spice cellar suddenly ceased. The muted thud of a door being drawn shut was followed by the stealthy click of a key turning in a lock. Bannor pressed himself to the wall, resting his hand on his sword hilt.

His quarry began to mount the stairs, humming an off-key Irish ditty Bannor knew only too well. His mouth fell open in disbelief, then thinned into a sardonic smile.

He waited until the interloper had crept past before folding his arms over his chest and stepping out of the shadows. "Hungry, Fiona?"

The old woman let out a startled shriek and spun around, dropping her entire armload of pilfered goods.

Bannor nudged a shattered egg with his toe. "Thank God that wasn't one of the babies you were carrying." He surveyed the carnage, clucking in sympathy over the tragic remains of several meat pies, a slab of salted beef, and a sack of apples. "How thoughtless of me. It appears I've gone and ruined your supper."

The old woman's mouth puckered into a pout that would have done Mary Margaret proud. "Me mum always said I was cursed with a most fierce appetite."

Bannor arched one eyebrow. "Fierce indeed. Although I would have thought even the most voracious appetite would have been satisfied by two wheels of cheese, six rashers of bacon, five loaves of barley bread, a barrel of salted stockfish"—his voice rose to a roar—"and one smoked ham!"

Fiona thrust out her wizened arms in surrender. "Go on," she wailed. "Call yer soldiers. Have me clapped in irons and dragged off to the dungeon. I promise to go quietly. Bein' eaten by the rats is no more than I deserve for smugglin' supplies to the enemy." She dabbed at her nose with the hem of her apron. "I'm an old woman. I wasn't goin' to live much longer anyway."

Bannor rolled his eyes, exasperated by her theatrics. "Don't be ridiculous. I've no intention of casting you into the dungeon for feeding my children. In truth, I can't even blame you for taking their side in all this. After all, you're the one who practically raised them while I was off fighting the king's war all those years."

"The children?" Fiona repeated, her long-suffering demeanor shifting to a fierce glower. "Why, I taught those children to fend fer themselves from the day they was born. Wee Edward alone could keep 'em fed fer months on naught but pigeons." The old woman drew herself up to her full height, which put the topknot of her bun squarely at the middle of Bannor's chest, and stabbed a finger at his chest. "I'm not doin' this fer the children. I'm doin' it fer *her*."

"Her?" Bannor echoed weakly, already dreading Fiona's response.

"Aye, *her*—yer lady! 'Tis that poor lass I'm sidin' with, and I can tell ye right now that I'm not the only one. After seein' the heartless way ye treated her, most of the women in the castle feel the same way."

"I suppose that explains why my doublets have been returning from the laundry with all their buttons snipped off."

Fiona cocked her head to the side, her beady little eyes making her look remarkably like Desmond's crow. "Do ye remember the night we met?"

"I'd be hard pressed to forget." Bannor rubbed his temple with the flat of his palm. "You hit me over the head with an iron kettle."

The night he'd seized Elsinore, he and his men had managed to battle their way through the halfhearted defenses of his brother's men-at-arms with nary a scratch. But upon emerging into the castle kitchens, Bannor had been laid low by a howling banshee. He'd dropped his sword and sat down abruptly on the floor, clutching his ringing ears.

Fiona shook her head. "Those of us that had been at Elsinore long enough to remember what yer da had done were sure ye'd come to raze the castle and slaughter us all. When I clobbered ye with that pot, I was shiverin' in me boots. I knew 'twas only a matter of time before ye recovered yer wits and lopped me head off."

"As I remember it, old woman, you were every bit as saucy and unrepentant as you are right now. You stamped your foot and accused me of putting a dent in a perfectly good pot." That was when Bannor had thrown back his head and roared with laughter. He smiled at the memory. "I'll never forget how you dropped to your knees, cradled my head to your bosom, and crooned, " 'Poor lad! I've gone and made ye daft, haven't I?'"

"And when ye claimed the castle fer yer own," Fiona asked, "wasn't I the one who spoke up on yer behalf? 'He's a bastard by birth,' I told 'em all, 'but not a bastard by nature like that wretched brother o' his.'"

Bannor's half-brother had been a notorious tyrant, just as his father had been, and in truth, most of the castle denizens had been relieved to be rid of him. "They would have never accepted me as their lord with such ease had you not appointed yourself my champion."

Fiona's head bobbed in a self-righteous nod. "I always praised ye to the heavens fer yer kindness and gentleness toward yer sweet lady wives. And in all the years I've known ye, ye've never given me cause to regret me loyalty or to be ashamed o' ye." She wagged a grizzled finger in his face. "Until now!"

Bannor barely resisted the urge to duck his head like a chastened page. He'd rather be stripped of his spurs by the king than endure one of Fiona's lectures. His chagrin mounted when he realized Fiona's staunch bottom lip was beginning to quiver.

"And ashamed o' ye I am! Ye let those children make mock o' that poor lass when all she wanted was to be a fit bride to ye. When I think o' the look on that dear child's face when she came marchin' into that hall all smothered in honey and ye just smirked down yer arrogant nose at her . . . Why, it put me in mind of somethin' yer da would do, aye it did!"

Fiona's face crumpled. Just as Bannor reached for

her, she threw her apron over her head, burst into noisy sobs, and fled down the darkened passageway.

When the last echo of her sobs had faded, Bannor slumped against the wall, deeply shaken. He had sought to escape his father's legacy, not preserve it, yet the old man seemed to haunt him at every turn.

It was Bannor's most bitter regret that his father hadn't lived long enough to feel the point of his son's sword at his throat as Bannor demanded the surrender of all he held dear. He had eluded that fate by dying in the arms of a buxom maidservant, coming and going in the same moment as it were. She'd later been overheard to remark that the randy old goat had been no stiffer in death than in life. His legend had only been enhanced when she had borne what would be the last of his many bastards.

Those bastards had been scattered from one end of England to the other. Bannor could never quite meet the eyes of even the lowliest of village peasants or castle servants without wondering if they were a brother or sister he would never know.

He raked a hand through his hair. Perhaps Fiona wouldn't think so ill of him if she knew how hard he was fighting to atone for his father's sins and just how much that battle was costing him.

Bannor had always prided himself on his honor on the battlefield, but if he ever hoped to put an end to this conflict with Willow, he could not afford to fight fair. His eyes narrowed as he gazed down the shadowy passage that had swallowed Fiona and her sobs. It seemed that Willow had found a devoted ally in his camp. Perhaps 'twas not too late for him to find one in hers.

· · ·

On day six of the siege, Beatrix lifted the iron grate set in the ceiling of the privy, poked her head out, and looked both ways. After making sure that the ramparts were free of Bannor's guards, she hiked up her skirts and clambered to freedom, drinking in hungry gulps of the frosty air whipping across the battlements.

She couldn't bear to spend another minute in the company of those surly brats. If she did, she might just yank sweet little Mary Margaret bald or stuff one of her stockings down Edward's throat to stifle his incessant chattering.

She marched faster along the battlements, working herself into a fine huff. Desmond was the most intolerable of the lot, always bossing her about as if he was already lord of the castle instead of just a scrawny boy no older than she was. His voice had developed a strange tendency to crack whenever she was near, causing him to croak like a toad just when he was struggling to be at his most haughty.

Why, only yesterday he'd ordered her to fetch one too many things and she'd been forced to sit on him until he'd bellowed for Willow, forgetting for a satisfying moment that such a scuffle was beneath her dignity.

And Willow! Who could make sense of her stepsister? Beatrix sighed, her steps slowing to a dreamy meander. If Lord Bannor wanted to conquer her, she would surrender herself into his arms and his bed without so much as a squeak of protest.

"Bea?"

The husky whisper drifted to her ears, sending a shiver that had naught to do with the cold fluttering over her skin. She hugged her cloak tighter around her just as the object of her wicked fantasies came sauntering out from behind one of the stone chimneys. With a woman's instincts far beyond her years, Beatrix recognized immediately that this wasn't Lord Bannor the warrior she was facing, but Lord Bannor the man. The man who had fathered a dozen children on only God knew how many women. The man who could wield his charm as ruthlessly as he wielded his sword.

She took a cautious step backward, making ready to flee.

Bannor's beguiling smile and outstretched hand cut off her retreat more effectively than an entire garrison of soldiers. His dark blue eyes twinkled with good humor. "There's no need to be frightened, child. Contrary to what your mistress may have told you, I'm not your enemy."

Beatrix blinked up at him adoringly, longing to blurt out the truth. To tell him that she wasn't Willow's maid, but her sister. The sister he should have pledged both his heart and his troth to from the very beginning. But some damnable loyalty to Willow stopped her. However, that same loyalty didn't prevent her from moistening her lips with the tip of her tongue or pushing back her hood so her silvery tresses could ripple in the wind. After all, she thought, squelching a twinge of guilt, Willow had all but said she was welcome to him.

"How could I be frightened of you, my lord, when you've shown me naught but kindness?" she purred, deliberately loosening her shawl so it would fall away from her bosom. Bannor's amused gaze flicked briefly downward to acknowledge her efforts. "Have you a message for my mistress?"

"Oh, I have several messages for your mistress." That sulky-sweet mouth of his tightened, sending a faint thrill through Beatrix. "But I'm patient enough to wait until I can deliver them with my own lips."

"Then why did you *waylay* me?" she asked breath-lessly, savoring the feel of the word in her mouth.

"Because I would like to propose a truce." He leaned closer and winked at her. "Just between the two of us."

"The two of us?" Beatrix echoed, dazed by the possi-bilities. "You and me?"

When he nodded, she shot a furtive glance behind her. 'Twould be just like Kell or Edward to come pop-ping out of the privy grate and catch her conversing with the enemy. Sensing her reticence, Bannor backed toward the chimney and crooked a finger at her, invit-ing her to follow him.

Beatrix hesitated, torn between her allegiance to the woman who had all but raised her, and the irresistible dimple that had just appeared in Lord Bannor's jaw.

Fourteen

On the seventh and final day of the siege, Willow was scrambling around on hands and knees in a shadowy tunnel on the second level of the castle, trying to gather up the arrows her stepsister had just dropped for the third time.

"What on earth is the matter with you tonight, Beatrix? You're as nervous as a rabbit!"

Beatrix looked fearfully over her shoulder, her half-hearted fumbling scattering more arrows than she retrieved.

Willow thrust the last arrow into the quiver, then shoved the quiver back into her stepsister's hands. "If I didn't know better, I'd swear *we* were the ones about to be ambushed."

The quiver slipped from Beatrix's hands; the arrows spilled over Willow's feet. Willow took a deep breath before shooting her stepsister a look of pure exasperation.

"Sorry," Beatrix whispered, looking uncharacteristically contrite.

As Willow groped once again for the stray arrows, her hands weren't much steadier than Beatrix's. When the quiver was full, she slung it over her own shoulder, where it joined Desmond's small bow, and led the way down the tunnel. They'd gone on many such missions in the past sennight, but none so important as this one. Tonight they weren't going to bombard the garrison with pitch and feathers or drop a stinkpot down the chimney of the great hall. Tonight they were going to strike at the very heart of Bannor's defenses.

'Twas the only heart the man possessed, Willow thought grimly as Beatrix took the lead.

Oddly enough, the inspiration for the attack had come from Beatrix. She had been the one to point out that although Bannor's tower was even more impenetrable than theirs, since it contained no secret entrances, the path he must take to reach that tower was not. If they situated themselves somewhere along his nightly route, it might be possible to trap him. Once they had Bannor at their mercy, his men would have no choice but to lay down their own arms and surrender.

The prospect of having Bannor at her mercy made Willow's skin prickle with a most unsettling mixture of dread and delight.

Beatrix had began to feel her way along the wall. "Here," she pronounced, dipping her fingertips into a shallow groove. "This must be the one."

"Are you certain?" Willow whispered.

Her stepsister proved she was by sliding aside the panel of wainscoting and poking her head into the torchlit passageway. Willow followed suit. They looked first one way, then the other. The narrow corridor appeared to be ideally suited for their purposes. Willow had only to seek shelter in one of its recessed windows, while Beatrix tucked herself behind the oak door at the far end of the corridor. When Bannor ambled through the door, Willow would leap out in front of him, brandishing a nocked arrow, and order him to stand and surrender.

Willow would have loved to have Desmond and Ennis handy to cast a giant net over his head in that moment, but she couldn't risk one of them getting hurt in the fray that was sure to follow. She had no illusions that Bannor would surrender without a fight. Which was precisely why Beatrix was going to tiptoe up behind him while he was distracted and bash him over the head with the sack of sand she had tied in her skirt.

Before they could take up their positions, Beatrix grabbed her hand and squeezed it just like she used to do when she was a very small girl. "Do take care, Willow. Swear you will."

Touched by her concern, Willow squeezed back and gave her a reassuring smile. " 'Tis Lord Bannor who should take care on this night."

While Beatrix huddled behind the door, Willow curled up on the broad stone windowsill. She slotted an arrow, praying she could manage not to shoot herself in the foot before Bannor appeared. Mist obscured the moon beyond the iron grate in the unshuttered window, veiling her in shadows. Soon there was nothing left to do but wait, while tension stretched her nerves as taut as the bowstring.

Footsteps approached. Heavy yet fleet footsteps that could belong to only one man. Willow held her breath, but was still terrified he would hear her heart throbbing in her ears. She forced herself to wait until he was past the door, past Beatrix, past any chance of escaping their trap, before she rolled to her feet, coming face to face with the enemy for the first time since she had learned of his treachery.

"Stand and yield," she called out, her voice far steadier than her hands. "For I cannot allow you to pass."

Bannor's crooked grin was somehow more intimidating than a snarl. 'Twould have been far easier to despise him if he'd been cursed with horns and a tail instead of twinkling blue eyes and a dimple in his jaw. "What would you have me yield, my lady? My sword or my heart?"

Willow gasped out a laugh, not sure whether to disdain or admire such unbridled arrogance. "Your heart, although no doubt prized by many a mewling female, is of little value to me. 'Tis your sword I demand."

"Then 'tis my sword you shall have." He slid the weapon from its scabbard and tossed it to the floor between them, before nodding toward the bow. "You wouldn't shoot an unarmed man, would you?"

"Not unless he gave me good cause." The ease of his surrender unnerved Willow, but honor compelled her to shift the aim of the arrow from his chest to the floor.

"I must confess to being a bit curious," Bannor said. "Now that you have me, just what do you intend to do with me? Will you ransom me to my men? Cast me into my own dungeon?" He arched one of those diabolical eyebrows, the wicked sparkle in his eyes deepening. "Or perhaps keep me for your own pleasure?"

Willow raised the bow again. The motion did not seem to deter him. He began to saunter toward her. Willow's first instinct was to retreat, but the sight of Beatrix creeping out from behind the door emboldened her.

She tossed her head, a motion she was beginning to

enjoy now that she'd become accustomed to her sprightly curls. " 'Twill be a pleasure indeed to accept your surrender."

"Ah, but sometimes surrender can be as sweet for the vanquished as for the victor."

He kept coming, his smile so tender that Willow took an involuntary step backward. If Beatrix didn't act soon, she would be forced to either shoot him or yield.

He was nearly upon her when her stepsister drew back the sack of sand. Willow bit back an absurd urge to shout out a warning. She flinched as the sack struck Bannor's head with a dull thud. He went down like a stone.

Beatrix faced Willow over his crumpled form, white with horror. "Oh, dear Lord, I think I've killed him!"

"Don't be ridiculous," Willow snapped, laying aside the bow and dropping to her knees beside him. "According to what Fiona told me, he's nearly impervious to pain. I'm sure he's just stunned." She tangled her fists in his doublet and rolled him to his back, grunting with the effort it took.

Bannor's open-mouthed vulnerability only emphasized the dark sweep of his lashes against his cheeks. A wistful pang seized Willow's heart.

How often had she dreamed of her prince in just such sweet repose? How many times had she imagined smoothing a tumbled lock of hair from his brow before leaning over and gently pressing her mouth to . . .

She was already leaning forward, her lips parting instinctively, when Beatrix blurted out, "Is he dead?"

Willow started. "No," she gritted out. "He's not dead. He's just . . . sleeping."

Beatrix began to back toward the secret panel. "I'll go fetch Desmond. He'll know just what to do."

Willow sank back on her heels, eyeing her stepsister askance. "Just this morning you said Desmond was a lackwit who couldn't find the cheeks of his rump with both hands."

Beatrix shrugged, her eyes darting between Bannor and the panel. "Perhaps he's learned something since then."

"Wait!" Willow cried as Beatrix slid aside the panel and ducked into the wall. "Don't go! Don't leave me—" the panel slammed shut; her voice died to a whisper, "—alone."

The sigh of Bannor's breath against her cheek reminded her that she wasn't alone at all. She sank back on her heels. She had dreamed of having him at her mercy, but now that she did, she wasn't sure she could bear to hurt him. Lying on his back like that with his lips parted and one arm outflung, he looked so utterly . . . noble.

Her breath quickened as she stole a guilty glance over her shoulder. What could be the harm in pretending, just for a moment, that he was the man she had dreamed he would be?

Her hand trembled as she smoothed the raw silk of his hair from his brow. Drawing in a ragged breath, she leaned forward and touched her lips to his, thinking only to steal a sweet, brief taste of what might have been.

A warm, rough hand clamped down on the back of her neck. With one breath she was kissing him; with the next he was kissing her. But this was not the chaste sip of pleasure she had anticipated. Bannor's mouth opened beneath hers in hungry demand, forcing her to yield before each hot, silken thrust of his tongue. He did not waste his breath entreating her to surrender.

He simply battered down her defenses, as if to claim the spoils that had belonged to him all along.

He kissed her until all the fight melted from her rigid limbs and clenched fists, until she could do nothing but sprawl across his chest, an eager and willing captive of everything she had sought to escape.

When Bannor finally took mercy on her, she barely had the strength to lift her head. His chest heaved beneath her throbbing breasts, warning her that his breathing was no steadier than her own.

She glared at him, as outraged by her own shocking behavior as she was by his. A triumphant smile curved the lips that had just kissed her so thoroughly, as he stroked her tumbled curls away from her face and murmured, "Checkmate."

Fifteen

Bannor hauled Willow up the stairs, his grip on her wrist as implacable as an iron manacle. He cleared two steps with each of his long strides, forcing her to trot in a most undignified manner or be dragged along behind him. She was tempted to plant her feet and refuse to budge, but knew he would most likely just throw her over his broad shoulder like a sack of meal.

She was still simmering over the realization that she had been the one trapped. She had been the one betrayed. Beatrix had been white-faced not with fear, but with shame. She should have known better than to trust the little minx. Especially with a man like Bannor.

The door to the north tower loomed before them. Bannor marched her across the threshold, then left her standing in the center of the room while he slammed down the crossbar and heaved a heavy oak bench in front of the door as if it weighed no more than a footstool. After a moment's thought, he shoved the table after it.

His message was clear. She was beyond rescue. Beyond redemption. Beyond hope.

He swung around to face her, his brooding silence more terrifying than a bellow of rage. He was her lord. She was his wife. If he chose to beat her for her defiance, he could do so with the blessing of both the king and the church. Nor was there anyone to stop him from locking her away for the rest of her life, from burying her alive deep beneath the stones of his dungeon. If he considered that too much of a bother, he could arrange an unfortunate mishap. She might tumble out a window. Or fall down a well. But none of those tragic fates compared to the one she feared above all others.

He might kiss her again.

An unbearably sweet shiver of dread and desire rippled down her spine. 'Twas the one punishment she had no defenses against. If he took her in his arms again, she feared she would willingly betray not only her comrades, but her own heart. A heart she had sworn to protect in that moment she had first learned he didn't possess one of his own.

Of course, if he kept glowering at her like that, she would begin to babble anyway. She would tell him the location of all the secret passageways and hidden peepholes. She would admit that it had been her idea to braid Mary Margaret's pink ribbons into his warhorse's tail. She would confess to spying on him as he disrobed, and spill out the sordid details of the fevered dreams that had swept her sleep every night since then as punishment for her indiscretion. Willow bit her bottom lip, praying she could hold her silence beneath his condemning glare.

The accusation he finally hurled at her was not the one she had expected. "Why did you kiss me?"

Out of all her recent offenses, it was almost as if her kiss had wounded him the most. Since it was the one question Willow dared not answer, she had no choice but to toss it back in his face. "Why did *you* kiss *me*?"

"Because, contrary to your conduct, you're a bit old for spanking." His speculative gaze raked her from head to foot. "At least I thought you were . . ."

"If your kiss is naught but a punishment, I shudder to imagine what you do to women who truly offend you."

He took a step toward her, the light in his eyes sharpening to a dangerous glitter. "Would you care to find out?"

Willow took a step back. "Was it your kiss that tricked Bea into betraying me?"

He shrugged. "Not every woman considers my kiss a torture to be endured."

"If you touched her, I'll kill you." Willow blurted out the words before she realized she meant them.

A mocking smile played around Bannor's lips. "Jealousy becomes you, my lady. It kindles a blush in your cheek and a fire in your eyes."

She was so caught off guard by the unexpected flattery that it took her a moment to realize he hadn't denied her accusation. "I'm not jealous. I'm appalled! You ought to be ashamed of yourself!"

His smile vanished. "If I had seduced your maidservant, I would be. But I can assure you that my carnal tastes don't run to precocious children." He drew closer

and began to circle her. "You dare to chide me for sins
I've yet to commit, but what about your own transgres-
sions, my lady? Since you came to Elsinore, you've in-
cited my children to open rebellion. You've hardened
their hearts against me."

"I didn't harden their hearts!" she cried. "You did!
The same way you hardened mine—with your inatten-
tion and your indifference." Willow turned away from
his probing gaze, realizing that she had revealed more
than she meant to.

His voice softened as he captured her chin in his
hand and tilted her face toward him. "Those are sins I
cannot deny. But I am coming to regret them."

Unable to bear the mockery of his caress, she jerked
away from his touch, but continued to meet his gaze
boldly. "Just as you regret marrying me?"

"And why shouldn't I?" he replied hoarsely, his
empty hand curling into a fist. "I haven't known so
much as a moment's peace since I first laid eyes on
you."

Willow stiffened. At least he had spared her a stammered denial or an outright lie. "Then I suppose all that
remains is to determine my fate." She ducked out of his
reach and began to pace the tower. "Since you find me
no more appealing than some fat fishwife with a mustache, perhaps 'tis not too late for you to swear that
vow of celibacy you considered." She shot him a look of
mock sympathy. "But 'twould be a shame for you to
have to give up all your other doxies." She marched to
the hearth, then back again. "You could allow Sir Hollis
to take me off your hands, but we wouldn't want the
poor fellow to have to make such a *terrible sacrifice*, now
would we?" She spun around, snapping her fingers. "I
know! Why don't you just have me locked away in a

convent where I can die a dried-up old virgin. After all, 'tis the only fit place for a miserable creature such as me."

Bannor's mouth had fallen open halfway through her recitation. Willow reached up and firmly nudged it shut. "There's no need to deny any of it. Your own son heard the entire exchange."

He swung away from her, bracing his hands on the mantel over the stone hearth. At least he had the decency to hang his head in shame, Willow thought bitterly.

"Why did you have to use your children to drive me away? If you wanted to be rid of me, why couldn't you just tell me? I wouldn't have held you to your vows. I would have set you free."

Bannor turned to face her. Why, the wretch wasn't cringing in shame! He was laughing! Mirth had crinkled his eyes and deepened that wicked dimple in his jaw.

Furious, Willow marched to the door. The clumsy barricade Bannor had erected loomed before her. She shoved at the table with all of her might, but it refused to budge. Only then did she realize that Bannor had come around and was holding the other end of it steady with one hand.

All traces of merriment had disappeared from his face, leaving it as grave as Willow had ever seen it. "When I told Hollis I couldn't allow him to make the *terrible sacrifice* of keeping you for himself, I was mocking him, not you."

Willow strode to the window and peered down, measuring the distance to the cobblestones below.

Bannor's voice followed her, more relentless than his touch, more compelling than his kiss. "I didn't swear a vow of celibacy because I knew I could never resist a temptation as sweet as you."

Rejecting the window as a possible escape route, Willow began to tap her way along the wall, hoping to find a stone she could dislodge to reach the secret passage.

"And I almost locked you away in a convent, because I couldn't bear the thought of any man but me putting his hands on you."

Willow froze, forgetting to breathe. Forgetting *how* to breathe. She slowly turned, feeling as if she'd wandered into one of her dreams.

But Bannor was still there, leaning against the table with his arms folded over his chest like a shield. He wore a look on his face Willow hadn't seen since her papa had last ruffled her hair and called her "his princess"—part yearning and part pain over some loss he could anticipate, but was powerless to prevent.

Willow took one step toward him, then another. Then she threw back her head and began to laugh.

Bannor was both baffled and enchanted by Willow's laughter. It wasn't sweet and tinkling as he'd expected, but deep and rusty, like the sound an iron portcullis might make if it hadn't been raised for a very long time.

"I knew you'd want revenge on me," she said, her throaty chuckle making him ache with desire, "but this is truly a jest more cruel and petty than any Desmond could have devised."

Bannor shook his head in bewilderment. "The jest must be on me, dear lady, for I am well and truly ignorant of it."

"Do you think me an utter lackwit? We may not have lived in splendor at Bedlington as you do here at Elsinore, but we did have mirrors." She gave the soft, dark curls that framed her face a cruel yank. "My hair is the color of soot. My skin is as swarthy and coarse as a troll's. My arms and legs are as knobby as the limbs of a willow. And my breasts!" She cupped the offending objects in her open palms. "Just look at them!"

Bannor cleared his throat with a great deal of difficulty. 'Twas impossible *not* to look, with the small, plump globes hefted so alluringly in her hands.

She let them fall, then gazed despairingly down at her chest. "They're naught to speak of. Barely half the size of Bea's." Her face brightened with a curious mixture of anguish and pride. "Now Bea is beautiful. She has big blue eyes, long flaxen hair, and skin like fresh-poured cream. If you were to tell me you couldn't resist a temptation as sweet as Bea, I would believe you."

"She's only a child!" Bannor protested. "And I really don't mean to be unkind, but isn't she just a little bit . . . plump?"

Willow gaped at him for a long moment before saying softly, "I do believe that's the nicest thing anyone has ever said to me."

"Yet," Bannor said, moving resolutely toward her. She stood her ground, her expression wary, but intrigued.

There might have been a thousand mirrors at Bedlington, but Bannor suspected Willow had never truly seen herself. She had seen only her warped reflection in the spiteful eyes of those who sought to belittle her. Anger surged through him. Perhaps he should rethink his decision not to burn her father's keep to the ground.

Willow would have been alarmed by Bannor's fierce expression if she hadn't been mesmerized by the tender glow in his eyes. She stood as still as a marble statue, waiting to be brought to life by his touch.

It did not disappoint. His hand brushed against her hair. As he twined one curl around his finger, then stroked her scalp with his broad, blunt fingertips, she had to turn her face away to keep from sighing with delight.

"Your hair," he whispered, the spicy-sweet warmth of his breath caressing her ear, "is a cloud of the softest sable. Any man would long to bury his face in it. Your skin . . ." he murmured, sliding his hand around to cup her cheek, "is as gold and sweet as nectar warmed by the sun. Your limbs . . ." he stroked his hands down her arms until they were palm to palm, then laced his fingers through hers, holding her hostage to the gentle press of his body against hers, "are delicate, yet strong enough to bind me to your heart."

Willow was beginning to rue her frankness. He wouldn't, she thought breathlessly. He couldn't . . .

But he did.

Bannor claimed her breasts as boldly as he had claimed the rest of her, first kneading them through the coarse linen of her tunic, then supporting their weight with his palms while his thumbs stroked her rigid nipples. Willow gasped, no more prepared for the raw throb of pleasure than she was for the thick, sweet surge of liquid desire between her thighs.

"And your breasts . . ." Bannor's hoarse rasp deepened to a wordless groan that was more eloquent than any tribute ever composed by a poet or minstrel. He inclined his head to press a reverent kiss upon each gentle swell.

Willow twined her fingers in his hair, coaxing his head back up. "I've always thought my mouth was rather . . . plain," she confessed, daring to give him a provocative look.

"Well, you were wrong," he said gravely, touching his fingertips to her lips. " 'Tis a thing of uncommon beauty."

Her eyes fluttered shut as he lowered his head to graze her lips with his own. This time, he took his pleasure in tender sips, molding his mouth to hers, then gently nibbling her upper lip until she was the one hungering for the fulsome sweetness of his tongue in her mouth. He did not leave her wanting for long. She moaned her delight as he seized the prize of her mouth with rough, lavish strokes that charmed her own shy tongue into joining the fray. She cupped the nape of his neck in her small hand, coaxing him closer, urging him deeper.

Bannor accepted her invitation with a growl of satisfaction, bearing her back against the wall. There was no need for his body to ripen against hers. It already had. For Willow, not even the foreign shock of that discovery could compare to the sheer wonder of realizing that this magnificent man—this warrior prince—truly wanted her.

He wrapped his arms around her, lifting her until the undeniable proof of everything he'd said nudged at the juncture between her legs. Her thighs parted instinctively, welcoming him as eagerly and artlessly as her mouth had welcomed his tongue. The coarse wool of her breeches created an exquisite friction as he cupped her bottom in his hands, lifted her hips high, and ground himself against her.

Fearful that he was in danger of spilling his seed in his braies like some callow squire, Bannor began to tug Willow's breeches down her slim hips. They wouldn't be slim for long once her body began to swell with his child. The image should have panicked him. Instead, he felt a savage rush of pride.

Biting off an oath, he broke away from her, leaving her to collapse against the wall in a bewildered heap. He staggered to the window, flexing his hands on the stone sill. The night's wintry breath failed to cool his fevered brow.

If he turned around in that moment, he knew he wouldn't be able to resist Willow's moist, parted lips or the luminous invitation in her misty gray eyes. Perhaps 'twas not too late to make her believe his attentions had been naught but a twisted game of revenge. But even as he considered the ploy, he knew she would not believe him. If his body didn't betray him, his eyes would. Fiona had always said he was a wretched liar.

He gazed up at a distant star, stripped of every defense except the truth. "I wasn't trying to drive you from Elsinore because I did not want you, my lady, but because I feared I would never stop wanting you."

"And that would be bad?" Willow squeaked, still reeling from the wonder of being wanted at all.

" 'Twould be terrible," he replied, his profile bleaker than the winter sky. "Because every time I touched you, your body would quicken with my child."

Willow's breath caught as she realized for the first time just how sorely she had misjudged him. She crossed to the window, drawn toward him by a tide of tenderness, and rested her hand on his forearm. "You mustn't allow your grief and guilt to rob you of all future happiness," she said softly. "After all, any man would be reluctant to bed his bride after his first two wives had lost their lives bearing his children."

Bannor turned to stare at her. "Who told you such a thing?"

"No one had to tell me," Willow murmured, growing bold enough to lift her hand to his cheek. "Fiona said that you'd always blamed yourself for their untimely deaths."

"As well I should. If Mary hadn't been waiting in front of the castle to greet me after the Battle of Guisnes, she wouldn't have been standing on the bank of the moat when the drawbridge chain snapped. And if I'd been home with my family instead of off wresting Poitiers from the French, I would have never allowed my sweet-tempered, absentminded Margaret to gather wildflowers in the meadow while the squires were practicing their archery."

Willow's hand went limp, falling away from his jaw. "Do you mean to tell me that neither one of your wives died in childbirth?"

"I should say not. They were both as hale and hearty as broodmares. They would have each been happy to bear a dozen of my children." He shuddered as if someone had walked over his own grave.

As he began to pace the tower, much as she had done earlier, Willow sank down on the windowsill, gazing at nothing in particular.

"Potency has always been the bane of our family," he explained, raking a hand through his hair. "My own father sired fifty-three children before he died. His father before him sired sixty-nine. So you see, Willow, 'tis not that I don't want you. I just don't want any more bloody children!" When she replied to his outburst with a dazed blink, he knelt beside her, cupped her hands in his own, and peered up into her face, his expression as earnest as young Hammish's. "I cannot give you the one treasure every woman yearns for—a child of her very own."

Willow laughed. "Is that what you think I want from you—a child? Some sniveling creature to cling to my apron? Some cunning imp who whines and sulks and throws tantrums until it gets whatever it wants? Why, I can't abide the wretched little monsters!"

Bannor looked genuinely puzzled. "You seem to get along well enough with my wretched little monsters."

Willow scowled, surprised to realize that was true.

"Well, I can abide *your* children," she amended, "but not the rest of them. They're selfish."

He nodded. "And greedy."

"They fidget."

"And wriggle," he concurred with a grimace.

"And gobble up all the choicest morsels," she pointed out.

"They're sticky."

"And rude," she snapped, her voice rising.

"And crude."

"And petty!" she yelled.

"And spiteful!" he roared.

They both stopped shouting at the same time, nose to nose, mouth to mouth, their breath mingling. They eyed each other warily, realizing that for the first time they were in perfect accord and that their accord just might be more dangerous than their enmity.

"Thank God Fiona was wrong," Willow murmured, unable to tear her gaze away from his. "At least you cannot get me with child simply by gazing into my eyes."

" 'Twould take a wink," he agreed, nodding soberly.

"Or perhaps even a kiss," she whispered, her lips parting of their own volition.

Willow moaned softly as he drew her into his arms. Resisting the ripe temptation of her mouth, Bannor feathered his lips over her brow, her eyelids, the bridge of her nose. The sensation was so delicious she had to fight a shameful urge to beg him to kiss her in all the places she'd never been kissed. He nibbled at the corner of her mouth, coaxing a sigh of pure delight from her lungs.

Her sigh was all the invitation he needed. He bent her back over his arm, taking her mouth with a kiss so deep and sweet it made her knees crumple with desire.

Willow knew from Bannor's agonized groan that he never intended to lower her to the straw mattress, never intended to come down on top of her, never intended to nestle the bulk of his weight between the cradle of her thighs.

So when he did just that, she could not bear to reproach him. She could only cling to his shoulders and arch against him, baring her throat to the moist, searing caress of his lips.

Was it any wonder she mistook the rhythmic pounding she heard for the passion-thickened throb of her pulse? Or the trickle of sandstone for the sound of the wall around her heart crumbling to dust beneath Bannor's tender siege?

But there was no mistaking the deafening crash that followed, or Mary Margaret's shrill cry. "Oh, Desmond, he's biting her! Make him stop before he gobbles her all gone!"

Sixteen

Bannor rolled off of Willow, his warrior's instincts returning to life an instant too late to save either of them. For a dazed moment, all Willow could see was feet—a forest of grubby little feet crowned by chubby little toes. Her bewildered gaze fixed on the pair of feet directly in front of the mattress. They were larger and dirtier than the rest, but not so dirty she couldn't make out the freckles peeping through the grime.

She traced those angular feet up to a familiar bow gripped in a pair of freckled, white-knuckled hands, up even farther to a pair of narrowed green eyes, then back down to the arrow pointed at Bannor's heart.

Acting on pure instinct, Willow flung herself across Bannor's chest, arms outstretched, and shouted, "Hold your fire!"

It wasn't until she saw the disgusted shock on Desmond's face that she realized she had betrayed not only the children, but herself as well. It took the boy a heartbeat longer than she would have liked to lower the bow.

"I should've shot the wretch in the back while he was wallowing all over you," he snarled.

"At least I'd have died a happy man," Bannor murmured into her hair.

Desmond's comrades were similarly armed. Ennis wielded a sickle, Mary a pair of sheep shears, Edward a club, Kell a blacksmith's awl, and Mary Margaret a pitchfork. Hammish was clutching something that looked amazingly like a ham bone, while Meg and the twins balanced a miniature battering ram between them. Given the amount of dust drifting through the air, it must have been the same battering ram they'd used to smash their way through the stone wall.

"How did you find me?" Willow asked.

After returning the arrow to its quiver and shrugging the bow back on his shoulder, Desmond reached behind him and dragged forth a flushed and rumpled Beatrix. Willow might have been tempted to believe her stepsister had suffered an attack of conscience if the girl's hands hadn't been bound in front of her and her contrite grunt hadn't been muffled by the kerchief stuffed between her lips. She wiggled her fingers at Willow in a sheepish wave.

"When Bea returned from the mission without you, I sensed something was amiss." Desmond cast the girl a smug glance. "It didn't take much to wring a confession from the little traitor. All I had to do was make Hammish sit on her while I tickled her feet."

Hammish hung his head while Beatrix tossed hers, the haughty glare she shot Desmond promising retribution.

Ennis lowered his sickle. "You can imagine our alarm when we learned Father had taken you."

"Don't I wish," Bannor whispered, his devilish chuckle making Willow's earlobe tingle.

Willow dug her elbow into his stomach, but she might as well have been elbowing a rock.

Edward brandished his club in the air, as if to vanquish an invisible enemy. " 'Twas me who founded you for 'em. I was peepin' through the squint when I heard Papa say your hair was soft as dog fur, your skin was all sticky like somethin' that'd been left out in the sun all day, and Bea here was fat as a pig."

The gag failed to muffle Beatrix's outraged gasp.

Willow blushed, more concerned about what Edward might have *seen* through the squint than what he might have heard.

"He makes a rather eloquent spy, doesn't he, my little fishwife?" Bannor muttered.

Mary Margaret planted the tines of her pitchfork in the floor, scowling ferociously. "If Papa wasn't biting you, then what was he doing?"

Extricating herself from the haven of Bannor's lap, Willow rose to her feet with as much dignity as possible. She was as aware of her rumpled tunic, tousled hair, and glistening, kiss-swollen lips as she was of Desmond's suspicious gaze. "Your papa and I were . . . um, we were . . ."

Bannor sprang to his feet. "Negotiating a truce."

"A truce?" Desmond spat.

The rest of the children groaned in disappointment.

Willow smiled sweetly. "I cannot blame your father for seeking to spare his pride, but what we were really negotiating was his surrender."

"My surrender?" Bannor glowered down at her.

Desmond still looked skeptical. "If he's surrendering, then what is there to negotiate?"

"Terms, of course." She dared to give Bannor's chest an amicable pat. "After all, compromise is the very nature of surrender, is it not, my lord?"

"I wouldn't know, my lady," he said through clenched teeth. "I've never surrendered before."

"So I gathered," she murmured. "Which is why we shall strive to make this as painless as possible." She beamed at the children. "You'll be delighted to know that your father has agreed to all of your demands."

"Like hell I have—" Bannor's protest died to a grunt as Willow's heel came down hard on his toes.

"But in exchange," she continued before the children could unleash their triumphant cheers, "he has one demand of his own." Both Bannor and the children seemed to be holding their breath, awaiting her next words. "He wants to spend more time in your company."

"He does?" Desmond asked, barking out a dubious laugh.

"I do?" Bannor echoed, panic rising in his voice.

Willow ignored them both. " 'Twould be a great boon to him if you would allow him to share all of your meals and to tuck you into bed each night."

"At midnight," Kell confirmed, testing the sincerity of his father's pledge.

"Aye, at midnight," Willow agreed.

Beatrix rolled her eyes as the children huddled together, engaging in a muttered and hissed parley that concluded with a shoving match between Kell and Edward. When they separated, it was Mary Margaret who approached Bannor.

"We wants one more thing," she proclaimed, the pitchfork clutched like a royal scepter in her chubby little fist.

Bannor shot Willow a wary look before squatting down to his daughter's eye level. "And just what would that be?"

"We wants you to pway wif us."

Bannor rolled his eyes heavenward, then chuckled ruefully. "Very well, princess. I shall be honored to do your bidding."

That familiar endearment on Bannor's lips made Willow's heart contract with a longing she'd hoped never to feel again. As he reached over to rumple his daughter's ringlets, she had to turn away.

Desmond was watching her, his gaze as sharp and predatory as his crow's. The sullen quirk had returned to his lips. "So tell me, Father," he said, folding his wiry arms over his chest, "just what has Willow gained for her efforts? After all, she was the one who *persuaded* you to surrender."

Bannor straightened. He gazed at Willow for a long moment before saying softly, "Willow has won her freedom, if she so desires it."

Mary Margaret dropped the pitchfork and threw her arms around Willow's leg. "You're not going to leave us, are you? You promised to teach me how to braid ribbons in a horse's tail and shoot a bow. Oh, Willow, say you won't go!"

For a painful moment, Willow couldn't say anything at all. Then she scooped the child into her arms. "The only place I'm going right now is to bed. Which is where you all belong, since 'tis well after midnight."

Ignoring Mary Margaret's groan of protest, she thrust the child into her father's arms. Bannor held the scowling moppet at arm's length for a moment before heaving her over his shoulder. Mary Margaret's groan turned into giggles. "Just what am I to do with the little imp?" he asked, glowering at Willow.

"Tuck her in." Willow smiled sweetly and pointed toward the newly made door in his wall. "If you follow that passageway down to the next level, you'll find it leads right to her chamber."

Desmond waited until his father and Mary Margaret had squeezed through the jagged hole before drawing a wicked-looking dagger from his stocking. "You might be a traitor, Bea," he said, slicing through the girl's bonds, "but at least you're not sleeping with the enemy." He ducked into the passageway, giving Willow a bitter look over his shoulder.

Willow sighed, fearing that she had lost a cherished ally, perhaps for good.

As if sensing her melancholy, Hammish tucked his plump hand into hers. "Don't pay Desmond any heed, my lady. I think you were ever so brave to beard Papa in his den. I'm sure it must have been quite terrible for you to end up in his clutches."

"Simply horrid," she murmured wistfully, remembering the gentle press of Bannor's hands against her flesh, the delectable taste of his kiss, and the helpless hunger on his face when he had confessed to wanting her.

Seventeen

As Willow struggled down the castle drawbridge the next morning, frigid gusts of wind whipped the folds of her cloak around her ankles. The day had dawned cold and bright, but the dazzling sunlight promised little more than the memory of warmth. As she passed beneath the arch of the gatehouse, she drew up her hood and averted her face from the curious stares of the guards. 'Twould never do for the lady of the castle to be caught running such a shocking errand.

Turning toward the village, she shifted the woven basket on her arm from one side to the other. The laden hamper might slow her steps, but she hadn't wanted to march empty-handed into a stranger's camp. Especially not when she was the one who had come to do the begging. She'd packed the basket with several of the gifts the generous castle-dwellers had bestowed upon her—jars of honey, slabs of salted meat, scented wax tapers that would surely seem the height of luxury to anyone accustomed to the overripe stench of tallow.

She wandered through the maze of narrow dirt streets, realizing too late that she hadn't the faintest idea where she was going. When a pack of exuberant boys sprinted past, nearly knocking the basket from her arm, she seized the smallest lad by the arm.

Ignoring his frantic squirming, she leaned down and whispered something in his ear. He flushed and pointed toward a row of identical wattle-and-daub huts crowned by hay-thatched roofs before scampering off to join his friends.

Willow was trying to decide which one to approach first when the door to the end cottage flew open and a man came spilling into the street. His face was flushed and the drawstrings of his hose untied. Willow shrank into the shadows, feeling a wicked thrill to learn that someone could be indulging in such debauchery while most of the castle residents were still in the chapel dutifully reciting their morning prayers.

The man reeled in a drunken circle. "Lord, woman, you've got me so addled, I don't know whether I'm comin' or goin'."

"You're no better at one than the other," came a woman's tart voice from inside the cottage. "So you might as well be going."

The door slammed in his face.

"Saucy bitch," he muttered. The poor confused fellow spent several interminable moments fumbling with his dangling drawstrings before finally lurching down the street, still cursing beneath his breath.

Willow waited until he had disappeared around a corner before creeping toward the door. In response to her timid knock, the woman within shouted, "Unless you'd care to buy a dose of pox with your shilling, you'll give me a moment to wash up."

"Well," Willow murmured, thankful there was no one around to witness her blush. "I do believe I'm at the right cottage."

She had time to shift the basket between her aching arms three times before the door finally creaked open. A tall, rawboned woman appeared in the doorway. Willow's courage wilted beneath her suspicious gaze. At an utter loss for words, she held out the kerchief-draped basket.

The wariness on the woman's face immediately sharpened to contempt. "I know your kind. I've seen it on my doorstep before. You bundle up in your warm cloak, creep out of your cozy cottage, and draw your hood up over your face so only God will know you took pity on the village whore. Well, you and your fine Christian charity can go straight to the devil," she snarled, "for I'll have none of it!"

She would have slammed the door in Willow's face had Willow not wedged the basket between door and frame. "Please don't send me away! I haven't come to offer you pity or charity. 'Tis I who am in need. *I* who require something from you."

The woman showed no sign of relenting. Desperate to sway her, Willow shoved back her hood.

The woman froze, then reached over almost absently to finger one of Willow's butchered curls. An enigmatic smile touched her lips as she stood aside and jerked her head toward the shadowy interior of the cottage. "Let it never be said that old Netta would turn away her lord's lady."

•　•　•

The fire sputtering upon the ash-encrusted hearth revealed that "old Netta" was probably no more than a dozen years older than Willow. With her slender waist and mane of honey-brown hair, she had probably been what most men would call a handsome woman before time and disappointment had etched a permanent sneer on her lips and carved gaunt hollows beneath her soaring cheekbones.

Although a basin and cloth perched on a stool in front of the hearth, there was no mistaking the musky aroma that still hung in the air. Willow kept her gaze averted from the rumpled bed, trying not to imagine how many men must have taken their pleasure there. That task became more difficult when Netta plopped down on the foot of it and leaned back on her elbows.

Painfully aware of the woman's measuring gaze, Willow moved the basin to the hearth, sat down stiffly on the stool, and rested the basket at her feet.

"So how do all the fine folk at the castle fare?" Netta asked lightly. "Your lord? His brood?"

'Twas not the question Willow had expected. "My lord and his brood are quite well, thank you. And they're precisely why I've come to see you today." She toyed with the sleeve of her kirtle, finding it impossible to keep from fidgeting. "It has been brought to my attention that you are a woman of some . . . um . . . experience."

Netta arched a plucked eyebrow, urging her to continue.

"Which is why I was hoping you could teach me . . ." Willow faltered.

"To satisfy your man?" Netta ventured. "There's no need to stammer and blush, you know. You're certainly not the first bride to seek my counsel. Nor will you be the last."

"Oh, I don't think my man is going to be very difficult to satisfy," Willow confided, blushing even more furiously than she had on the doorstep. "What I am seeking is some way to satisfy him without ending up with his babe in my belly."

Netta surveyed her for a bemused moment, then threw back her head and cackled with laughter. "I'm a whore, not a witch, child. I've no potions or spells to prevent a man's seed from taking root in his woman's womb. Especially not *your* man's."

" 'Tis not a potion or spell I seek," Willow said desperately, "just some sensible advice. Surely you must practice such tricks. If you didn't, this cottage would be overrun with children, would it not?"

Netta's smile faded. She gazed at the hearth, cocking her head as if she could hear the ghostly laughter of all the children who would never play there. "Aye, I suppose it would," she said softly.

"I can pay you." Willow fumbled for the satin purse she'd tucked into her sleeve.

Netta rose from the bed, her face hardening once again to a resentful mask. "You can keep your coins, my lady. I won't do it. 'Tis far too dangerous a game you play. I've known men who had their wives burned at the stake for less. I'll not help you deceive your husband."

"But I have no intention of deceiving my husband. On the contrary, I believe Lord Bannor will be delighted to learn that I'm partaking of your instruction. Why, I plan to tell him this very night!"

Netta rested her hands on her hips and blinked at Willow. "What they're whispering about you in the village is true, isn't it? You really did declare war on our lord and take his children hostage. You're quite mad, aren't you?"

"Would you help me if it was a lover I sought to thwart?" Willow asked, her growing desperation making her bold.

Netta snorted. "I'd never believe you. Why would any woman be unfaithful to such a man as Lord Bannor?"

Willow opened her mouth, unable to keep from asking the one question she'd promised herself she would not ask. "Has Lord Bannor ever . . . ? Have the two of you . . . ?"

Netta did not reply for a long moment. When she finally did, her husky laughter was edged with regret. "I might risk my bones in the arms of a drunken soldier, but I'm not fool enough to risk my heart for any man. Bones will heal, but hearts. . . ?"

Willow lowered her eyes, reluctant to reveal that she might be just such a fool.

Netta held out her hand. "Have you a shilling on you?"

Willow looked up, startled. "I thought you told me to keep my coins."

"I did," Netta replied, an impish grin transforming her careworn face. "And I'm about to show you where."

"Four hundred and ninety-five. Four hundred and ninety-seven. Four hundred and ninety—"

"Oh, Beatrix," Willow crooned, interrupting her stepsister's long-suffering recitation, "I do believe you missed a stroke. Perhaps you should begin again. At four hundred."

As Beatrix glared at her stepsister's reflection in the hand mirror Willow was holding, Willow stole a look at the glazed window of her chamber. The moon seemed to be creeping across the sky with agonizing slowness.

Beatrix gritted her pearly white teeth and began to drag the silver-handled brush through Willow's hair once again, giving one of the sleek curls a spiteful tug.

"Ow!" Willow cried, springing up from the stool. " 'Tis not as if you have any right to sulk. Combing my hair five hundred strokes is no more punishment than you deserve for betraying me to Bannor last night."

"When I agreed to deliver you into his hands, Lord Bannor swore to me that he wouldn't hurt you." Beatrix's petulant gaze raked her up and down. "And you certainly don't seem to be any the worse for enduring his heartless tortures."

For once, Willow was tempted to agree with her stepsister. She held up the mirror, hardly recognizing the lustrous dark curls, sparkling eyes, and flushed cheeks of the woman gazing back at her. 'Twas almost as if she was seeing herself through the tender glow in Bannor's eyes.

While Willow was distracted, Beatrix snatched the mirror from her hand. The girl had always had little patience for anyone's vanity but her own. As she turned the mirror this way and that, surveying her face, her breasts, and her plush hips from every conceivable angle, her usual smirk of satisfaction was marred by a shadow of doubt. "Did Lord Bannor truly say I was fat?"

"Of course not," Willow assured her. Since Bannor had actually said Beatrix was plump, she hoped God wouldn't count it as a lie. "You know better than to pay any mind to Edward's gibbering. Lord Bannor said you were . . . fair. Exceedingly fair." As the gloating smirk returned to Beatrix's face, she could not resist adding, "But far too immature for his tastes."

Ignoring her stepsister's infuriated gasp, Willow plopped back down on the stool. "I believe you stopped at four hundred." She smiled sweetly. "Or was it three hundred and fifty?"

While Beatrix resumed her reluctant ministrations, Willow tried not to squirm. She should have been aching with exhaustion from all that she'd accomplished that afternoon, but anticipation tingled through her veins like the most potent of meads, making even the pretense of sleep impossible. Beatrix had reached a sullen four hundred and twenty-two when the chapel bells began to toll, their crisp cadences ringing sweetly through the night.

Willow sprang to her feet, leaving Beatrix's hand hanging in mid-stroke, and raced out the door.

"Where on earth is she going in such haste?" Beatrix murmured just as the chapel bells tolled their twelfth stroke.

Bannor plodded up the winding steps, more exhausted than he'd ever been after a day of battling the French. His head pounded, his knees throbbed, and no matter how hard he tried, he couldn't shrug away the nagging ache between his shoulder blades.

The pain in his knees was certainly no mystery. He'd spent the last two hours scampering about the flagstones of the great hall on hands and knees while Meg, Margery, and Colm took turns straddling his back, tugging at his hair, digging their sharp little heels into his ribs, and shouting, "Faster, Papa, faster!" If the chapel bells hadn't tolled midnight when they had, he'd have been tempted to rear up, toss one of his hapless little riders into the air, and gallop to freedom.

It hadn't taken him long to realize he was going to regret promising to do Mary Margaret's bidding. The child was no princess crowned by golden ringlets, but a blue-eyed tyrant who made Attila the Hun look like the most benevolent of masters. After only a day of fetching this and destroying that, he could understand why most of her dolls were missing both their heads and their limbs.

Kell's and Edward's constant squabbling was still ringing in his ears. Ennis and Mary had spent most of the day with their dour little noses poked into the air, trying to prove that at twelve and ten, they were far too old and sophisticated to be "played with." Only the good-natured Hammish had applauded all of Bannor's desperate efforts to entertain them. He'd especially enjoyed making mock war with the soldiers Bannor had fashioned using green apples for their bodies and twigs for their arms and legs. Until he'd been compelled to eat the entire French army. Bannor shuddered. He'd spent nearly an hour holding the lad's head over a privy shaft while he groaned and retched out his misery.

At least he'd been spared the acerbic lash of Desmond's tongue. The boy had scorned all of their attempts to coax him into joining their frantic merry-making. Bannor had glanced up more than once to find him perched on the ramparts with his crow on his shoulder, brooding over them like a sullen gargoyle.

Willow had remained even more elusive. Bannor had caught only a single glimpse of her during that in-terminable day. Before he could seek her out, the twins had tugged at his hands and Mary Margaret had bellowed out another command at the top of her little lungs.

He yawned as he reached the landing at the top of the stairs, longing only to stumble to his mattress and collapse. Even though the chill was just the sort to claw itself deep into a man's aching bones, he refused to waste time or effort building a fire. The cold rarely troubled him. He'd spent too many nights sleeping on the frozen ground in some dense thicket of French forest, only to wake up more often than not shrouded in a blanket of snow.

He dragged open the tower door, that feeble effort sapping the last of his strength.

The tangy aroma of wood smoke drifted to his nose, startling him nearly as much as the cozy snap and crackle of the fire on the grate. An invisible cloak of warmth enveloped him. The relentless fist of the wind knocked in vain, for the rattling of the shutters had been muffled by the burgundy palls of velvet draped over each window to thwart the icy drafts.

A rug woven of wolf skins had been spread before the hearth. The plank floor had been strewn with winter savory and fresh mint. The oak table held only a chess set, its carved soldiers arranged with rigid military precision, and a pile of scrolls bound in tidy ribbons. The hole his children had punched in the west wall was now veiled by a gold-and-scarlet-hued tapestry depicting a knight inclining his head to receive the tender blessing of his lady before riding off to war.

Bannor rubbed his bleary eyes, wondering if perhaps in his exhaustion he'd taken the wrong set of stairs. But no. 'Twas definitely his own treasured collection of weapons that had been mounted with loving care on the curve of the wall beside the door. He reached up to absently run his fingers over the blade of the broadsword that had been given to him by the king, upon emerging triumphant from his imprisonment in Calais.

A faint creak drew his gaze to the oak-and-leather bed frame that had replaced his narrow straw tick. A nest of quilts draped its plump feather mattress, and emerging from that nest was a woman garbed in a gown of rich green velvet trimmed in mink. A woman whose short-cropped curls and shy smile gave her heart-shaped face a gamine charm he could never hope to resist.

When she started toward him, Bannor did not hesitate. He snatched the massive broadsword from the wall, leveled it at her heart, and growled, "Don't take another step, my lady, or I shall run you through."

Eighteen

Willow gazed at Bannor in disbelief, not sure whether she should laugh, or snatch one of his shields down from the wall to protect herself. The wild glint in his eye made him look even more dangerous than the grim determination etched on his features.

She took a tentative step forward. Bannor took a step backward, as if even the two and a half feet of icy steel that lay between his hand and her heart was an inadequate defense.

"Have you declared an end to our truce, my lord?" she asked softly, taking another step toward him.

"No, you have," he ground out from between his clenched teeth. "By plotting this diabolical ambush."

She took another step, daring to rest her fingertips lightly on the tip of his blade. "On the contrary. I've come here to lay down my arms. Why don't you do the same?"

Bannor glowered at her from beneath the sooty sweep of his lashes as she traced the shimmering length of steel down to his clenched fist. If it hadn't been for the heated whisper of his breath in her hair, she would have sworn he'd been forged from the same immutable metal. But his rigid fingers unfolded at her touch, allowing her to disarm him with surprising ease.

Before she could drop the heavy weapon, Bannor caught it in one hand and returned it to its pegs on the wall. "I should have known a sword wouldn't be enough to deter you. Perhaps I should send to the chapel for a crucifix and a rope of garlic."

His expression was so grim that Willow could not help laughing. "That won't be necessary. I can assure you that I'm quite harmless."

"Isn't that what the serpent said just before he coaxed Eve into eating that nice shiny apple?"

Bannor strode to the cupboard and flung open the door. He spent several minutes pawing through its contents and swearing beneath his breath, giving Willow ample time to retrieve the flagon of ale he was searching for from the hearthstones where it had been warming. When he slammed the cupboard door and wheeled around, she was already holding out a goblet brimming with the amber brew, an inviting smile curving her lips.

Their fingers brushed as he reluctantly accepted her offering and took a long, thirsty swig. "I thought I granted you your freedom. Why are you still here?"

"You granted me my freedom only if I so desired it. Perhaps I don't."

He paced to the far side of the tower, positioning the table as a barricade between them. "Just what do you desire, my lady? To invade my every refuge? To leave me no haven where I can escape your smile, your scent?" His voice softened as he fingered the velvet ribbon binding one of the scrolls. "Your touch?"

A tingling warmth crept through Willow. "Perhaps when you hear what I have to say, you won't be so eager to escape. I believe I know what ails you, my lord. And I believe I may have found the cure." He eyed her warily as she approached the table. Mustering all of her courage, she blurted out, "Did you know that there are ways a woman can prevent a man from getting her with child?"

"Such as forcing him to spend a day in the company of his children?"

Willow gave him an exasperated look.

Bannor sank into a chair and propped his boots on the table, heaving a defeated sigh. "Of course I know of such tricks. I'm not some callow lad. But I also know 'twould be a sin for you and me to practice them."

Willow frowned. "Why would such a thing displease God?"

"Because He created the marriage bed for procreation, not pleasure."

Given her husband's history, she could not quite let that pass without challenge. "And if a man should choose to seek his pleasure outside of the marriage bed? Isn't that a sin as well?"

Bannor's expression was as bland and innocent as an angel's. "Fornication is a venial sin, preventing conception a mortal one."

Willow blinked at him. "I'm beginning to understand why you have a dozen children."

He drained the rest of the ale and averted his eyes, the gesture curiously furtive in such a forthright man.

Willow paced back and forth in front of the table,

deep in thought. "If we don't actually consummate our union, we can hardly be accused of defiling the marriage bed."

"Go on . . ." Bannor murmured, bringing the empty goblet to his lips.

"Therefore, we shall remain sinless in the eyes of God," she finished brightly, planting her palms on the table.

Bannor cleared his throat. He seemed to be having great difficulty choosing his words. "I trust 'twas not Father Humphries's counsel you sought to come to this conclusion."

"Not precisely." It was Willow's turn to avert her eyes. "If you must know, I paid a visit to the village whore."

Bannor jerked his feet off the table and sat up straight. "You spoke with Netta?" For just an instant, Willow would have sworn he looked more guilty than she did.

"Aye, I did. And very forthcoming she was." Willow leaned across the table, lowering her voice to a whisper. "Did you know, for instance, that a man can give pleasure to a woman without ever taking his own?" When Bannor's expression didn't even flicker, she sighed ruefully. "No, I don't suppose you did."

An endearing flush began to creep up his throat. " 'Tis not fitting that a husband and wife speak so frankly of such matters. I've certainly never done so before."

"Not even with Mary or Margaret?"

The notion seemed to horrify him. "Most certainly not with Mary or Margaret. Such things should only be dealt with in the most hushed of whispers." When Willow continued to look dubious, he added firmly, "In the dark. Beneath the blankets." He waved his hand in a vague motion. "A touch, a smile, a satisfied sigh should be utterance enough between any man and woman."

Willow shrugged, sighed, and turned away as if to take her leave. "Very well, my lord. 'Twas my intention to please you, not displease you."

Before she could quite reach the door, Bannor barked, "Just what else did this woman teach you?"

Willow slowly turned, struggling to hide a smile. "Netta claimed she didn't wish to overwhelm me on my first visit, so she chose to share only one of her tricks with me." Willow fumbled in her skirt pocket, drawing forth a shiny coin. She held it up for Bannor's perusal.

"A shilling?" he said, arching one dark brow. "And what do you plan to do with that? Make it disappear into your ear?"

Willow giggled. "Don't be ridiculous. Netta told me *precisely* where I could put this coin to prevent you from getting me with child. And it most certainly wasn't my ear."

Both of Bannor's eyebrows shot up as Willow sat down primly on the edge of the bed and began to lift her skirt. As her trim ankles came into view, followed by the shapely curves of her calves, the goblet rolled out of his fingers and hit the floor. She had to wiggle a bit to hike her skirt high enough to expose her knees. By then, Bannor's breathing had deepened to an audible rasp.

She slanted him a shy look. He was still staring, seemingly entranced by the deft motion of her fingers as she parted her legs and firmly tucked the coin . . .

. . . between her knees.

"There," she said, squeezing her knees together.

"Netta swore to me that no man has ever gotten a woman with child while she was holding a shilling between her knees."

All of Bannor's breath seemed to leave him in a mighty sigh. His eyes glittered with dry amusement. "This Netta must be a very wise woman indeed."

"Oh, she is! She told me you could do anything you wanted to me, as long as you took care not to dislodge the shilling."

"Anything?" If Bannor had been a wolf, his ears would have pricked up. He rose and came around the table. He sauntered around the bed in a predatory half-circle, making the hairs on Willow's nape tingle. "Anything at all?"

"Within reason," she amended, eyeing him nervously.

Her trepidation mounted as he disappeared from her line of vision. The bed creaked beneath his weight as he climbed to his knees behind her, sinking deep into the feather mattress.

His husky whisper warmed her ear. "Then I suppose there would be no harm at all in my doing this."

He ran his hand beneath the curls at her nape, lifting them to expose her tingling flesh to the moist brush of his lips. Willow could not help but moan as all the tension melted from her body, leaving her as boneless as one of Mary Margaret's rag dolls.

The shilling clattered to the floor.

"Sorry," she muttered, scrambling to retrieve it. She stole a glance over her shoulder at Bannor as she wiggled back into place. "I have a feeling this is going to be much more difficult than it sounded."

"I certainly hope so," he murmured, nuzzling the sensitive shell of her ear.

Willow struggled to keep both her eyes and her

knees clenched tightly shut as his lips tenderly traced the feather-soft hairs at her temple, the sleek plane of her cheekbone, the vulnerable curve of her jaw—finally coming to nestle against the pulse throbbing beneath the silky skin of her throat.

Willow's appetite was whetted by the delicious sensation of his mouth against her flesh. She turned her head, blindly seeking a taste of him. But he would kiss only the very corner of her mouth, lightly flicking it with the tongue she longed to draw deep inside of her. The gentle press of his hands on her shoulders held her captive to that delectable torment, until they began to glide downward, his broad thumbs lingering against the fluted arch of her collarbone, then hooking in the bodice of her kirtle.

Willow's eyes flew open. "What are you doing?" she demanded, both frightened and stirred by the inexorable descent of those hands.

"Only what you gave me leave to, my sweet lady," he whispered. "Anything. Anything at all."

He leaned over her shoulder, pressing his cheek to hers. Raw excitement flickered through her, its pulsing flame fed by the beguiling prickle of his beard stubble, the intoxicating spice of the ale on his breath, the ragged pounding of his heart against her back. Both of their hearts seemed to skip a beat as Bannor peeled down her bodice in one smooth motion, leaving her naked to the waist.

Nothing could have prepared Willow for the icy flush that heated her skin as her breasts were exposed to the firelight and to his gaze for the very first time.

For a timeless eternity, it seemed as if he would be content only to look, to drink his fill of her with his smoldering eyes.

Then he curled his palms around her, filling them as if with the most bountiful of treasures. As his knuckles grazed their pebbled tips, his groan of pleasure mingled with her gasp of delight.

Willow wanted to close her eyes, but she could not drag her gaze away from the sight of Bannor's callused fingers tugging gently, but firmly, at her distended nipples. A greedy mewling welled up from deep within her throat. She clenched her legs together even tighter, not to hold fast the shilling, but in a vain attempt to assuage the sweet sting between them.

It was the same dart of lightning she had felt in her belly the first time their eyes had met, a white-hot flame that licked lower and hotter with each deft squeeze of Bannor's fingertips, threatening to engulf everything in its path.

When Willow could no longer bear its fevered kiss, she pressed her small hands to the backs of his, molding both of their hands to her breasts. She never dreamed that he would take her unspoken plea as an invitation to slide his hand out from beneath hers and slip it beneath her skirt. And not even when his hand drifted gently up her thigh did she guess he would be so bold as to seek to soothe that sting himself.

Which only rendered the shock of his big, blunt forefinger raking through her silky nether curls that much greater. A shudder of pure reaction seized her as he slid his finger into the throbbing cleft between her legs, burrowing as deep as he dared.

"The shilling, Willow," he reminded her, his voice resonating with the same urgency that was mounting deep within her. "Remember the shilling."

It was an exquisite torture to squeeze her legs together when her every instinct was begging her to let them fall apart, entreating her to let him dabble his fingers in the warm honey melting from the feminine heart of her.

The shilling might prevent him from reaching that overflowing cup, but it could not stop him from finding the glowing ember nestled in her damp curls. He stroked it to raw flame using nothing more than the supple twist of his finger. Willow bucked and writhed, but there was no escape from the sweet madness pulsing through her womb.

She clung to his powerful forearms as pleasure began to spill through her, culminating in a surge of rapture so deep and hard she never even heard her own wail, or the musical tinkle of the shilling striking the floor. Bannor's hand slid down, cupping her so hard she had no choice but to ride another wave of pleasure to its soul-shattering crest.

She was still being rocked by lingering tremors of delight when he drew her hard against him, burying his lips in her hair.

"Oh, my!" she gasped, her breath coming in convulsive little pants. "I never . . . I never ever . . . I never even dreamed . . ." Clutching her bodice to her heaving breasts, she twisted around to give him a fierce scowl. "You miserable knave! You did too know it was possible to give a woman pleasure without taking your own!"

Bannor smoothed a sweat-dampened tendril of hair from her cheek, a crooked smile quirking his lips. "Indulging you, my lady, was one of the greatest pleasures I've ever known."

Willow's heart melted at his gallant declaration. She pressed her mouth to his, kissing him with passionate fervor.

When he finally managed to disengage himself, the strangled note in his voice was unmistakable. "You mustn't forget the shilling, Willow. There's one more thing you must do to ensure its success."

She blinked at him, still drunk on the potent sweetness of his kiss. "And what would that be?"

"Leave," he said firmly.

"Leave?"

"Aye, leave. Now. This very moment."

Before she could gather her scattered wits or her shilling, Bannor had drawn her off the bed and to her feet. He tucked her back into her gown, his hands as matter-of-fact as if he were dressing one of his children, then hauled her to the door. He gave her a hot, hard kiss that left her weaving, then shoved her onto the landing and closed the door in her face.

Before she could stagger toward the stairs, it flew open again. "Oh, Willow?"

"Hmmm?" she murmured, bestowing a dreamy smile upon him.

Bannor leaned against the door frame, his tousled hair and heavy-lidded gaze making him look every bit as deliciously wicked as the satyr she had once believed him to be. "Come back tomorrow night. I've a few tricks of my own to show you."

Nineteen

Hugging her cloak tight around her, Willow darted across the bailey, hoping she could make it to the drawbridge before the dozing guard awoke from his slumber. Even in her haste, she could not resist stealing a look at Bannor's tower. A smile touched her lips as she imagined him sprawled across the feather mattress, his hair rumpled, and his skin smelling of sleep. She hoped the embers of the fire she had kindled would still be glowing when he awoke, a smoldering reminder of what had passed between them only a few short hours ago.

"M'lady! M'lady!"

Willow clapped a hand to her pounding heart as Fiona came lurching out of the dawn mist. "Good heavens, Fiona, I thought you were a haint."

The old woman certainly looked the part. Despite the morning chill, she wore naught but a ragged shawl draped over her white gown. Her tidy bun had unraveled, leaving her hair to hang in lank wisps around her face. Willow had never seen the little woman look quite so frazzled.

"Forgive me, m'lady. I saw ye from the nursery window and knew I'd have to make haste if I was to catch ye. Mags has taken the colic and sweet Peg here has hardly got a wink o' sleep all night. Every time the poor creature starts to drift off, Mags wakes up screamin' and there they both go, howlin' their wee heads off." Fiona thrust the basket dangling from her wizened arm at Willow. "I was hopin' ye wouldn't mind lookin' after the poor mite fer a spell?"

Willow took an involuntary step backward. "Oh, Fiona, I really don't think—"

"I'd ask one o' the maidservants to do it, but they just haven't got yer tender touch with the wee ones." The old woman's bottom lip quivered so piteously Willow feared she might burst into tears herself.

Willow sighed. "Very well. Give her over." She hooked the basket over her arm. "It's certainly not as if I've never had a baby foisted off on me before."

"May God bless ye, m'lady!" As a second baby's strident shriek pierced the morning hush, Fiona's toothless smile tightened to a wince. Muttering beneath her breath, she hastened back toward the castle, leaving Willow alone with her new charge.

Willow started to tighten the hood Fiona had fashioned, but some foreign impulse prompted her to peel back its folds and steal a look at the child's face. She expected the baby to be sleeping, not gazing up at her with a wide-eyed curiosity no less keen than her own.

"Well, hello there," she murmured, nonplussed by the babe's unwavering stare.

Peg's rosy cheeks had already began to ripen. She

was becoming less puckered and more puckish, looking less like a wizened old man and more like a jolly elf. The head that had been bald only a fortnight ago was now covered with fuzzy blond down. Willow could not resist brushing her fingertips across it.

A bubble of laughter escaped the baby's lips, so merry and engaging that Willow was startled to find herself laughing.

"Aren't you a good-natured thing," she said, gently tweaking the creature's pug nose.

The baby wiggled her fist free of her blankets and grabbed Willow's finger. As Willow gazed down into that happy little moon of a face, she was caught off guard by a bittersweet rush of tenderness. This wasn't just any baby. This was Bannor's baby. A baby he had created with some nameless and faceless woman—a woman who had known the full measure of his desire, not just a tantalizing taste of it.

Willow tucked the baby's flailing arm back into the blanket and drew up the hood to shield her from the wind. Once Willow might have pitied the child's mother, but as she trudged toward the drawbridge, the basket clutched to her chest, she feared she was coming to envy her.

When Netta yanked open her door to find Willow and wee Peg waiting on her doorstep, she paled as if she'd seen a ghost.

She stared at the basket for a long moment before jerking her gaze back to Willow. "If I didn't want your jars of honey or your fancy candles, I don't know why you'd think I'd want *that*."

Willow braced herself, waiting for Netta to slam the

door in her face, but instead the woman wheeled around and marched back into the cottage, leaving it agape.

'Twasn't quite an invitation, but Willow decided to pretend it was. She slipped her head into the cottage to find Netta standing in the middle of the room with her back to the door. She was hugging herself, as if simply appearing in the doorway had chilled her to the bone. Her hair was unbound and her feet bare, but her bed was empty.

"I hope you don't mind me bringing the baby along," Willow said cheerfully, lugging the basket through the door. "Fiona asked me to mind it while she tended to one of Bannor's other babes."

"Put her on the hearth," Netta commanded without turning around. "So she won't catch a chill."

Willow gently rested the basket on the warm stones before shrugging off her cloak and settling down on the stool. "How did you guess she was a girl?"

Netta shrugged her wiry shoulders. "A girl? A lad? It makes no difference, does it? They're all destined for the same life of toil and heartache."

Willow chuckled. "Oh, Bannor would never stand for that. His children might sorely vex his patience, but I'd wager he would lay down his life to ensure their happiness."

Netta turned around, her lips twisted in a bitter smile. "Then the child should count herself well blessed to have such a fine father."

"Aye," Willow said softly, thinking of her own papa. "Indeed she should."

"Why is she making those noises?" Netta demanded, her expression curiously fierce. "Is she hurting? Or hungry?"

"Just bored, most likely." Willow stretched out her leg and rocked the basket with her foot, a skill she'd perfected while learning to juggle Blanche's brood. The baby's fretful whimpers soon subsided into blissful chortles. She kicked away the blanket and began to play with her toes.

Netta's tension also seemed to ease. She sank down on the foot of the bed, eyeing Willow with a mixture of wariness and curiosity. "To be honest, I never expected to find you on my doorstep again."

"And why not? Your shilling trick was a most splendid success."

Netta's hazel eyes widened. "It was? Why, I thought Bannor would laugh you out of his chamber!"

Willow stiffened before saying softly, "And why would you think that?"

Netta bit her bottom lip as if realizing too late that she'd revealed too much. Her shrug seemed to lack its usual indifference. " 'Twas naught but a harmless bit of mischief, my lady. An innocent jest."

"And I suppose 'twas my innocence that was the jest. Or was it my ignorance? Did you spread word of my visit throughout the village so that Bannor's villeins would know that their lord's bride was as foolish as she was mad?"

Willow could hardly bear to think that Bannor might have been laughing at her as well. That their tender encounter might have been nothing more to him than a virgin's folly. She rose from the stool, jerking up her cloak and wrapping it around her.

She fought to keep her voice cool and her hands steady as she drew a velvet purse from her sleeve and tossed it on the bed. "I hope that will be enough to

compensate you for any coins you might have lost
while you were tarrying with the village idiot."

As she started for the door, Netta sprang up from
the bed, dogging her steps. "So what's to be my punishment for mocking the grand lady of Elsinore? Will you
have me tarred and feathered? Driven out of the village? Stoned?" Although Netta hurled the words at her
with brash bravado, Willow sensed the undercurrent
of fear.

She hesitated, her hand on the door latch. She had
been powerless for so long that it had never even occurred to her that she now had the authority to indulge
in something as petty and rewarding as revenge. She
remembered all the times Stefan and Reanna had so
cruelly mocked her, all the times Blanche had punished
her for some imagined offense, all the times her papa
had turned his face away rather than meet her pleading gaze.

She cut Netta a cool, clear glance. "Twould hardly be
fair to punish you for my folly, now would it?"

Willow slipped out of the cottage without bothering
to draw up her hood. 'Twas still early and there were
only a handful of villagers scattered along her path. She
answered their curious glances with a defiant stare.
She was halfway up the hill that led to the castle when
she realized with an icy start of horror that she'd forgotten Peg.

She spun around and sprinted through the winding
streets, her cloak flapping behind her. As she turned
down Netta's lane, a baby's shrill cry rent the air. Willow thought it might very well be the worst sound
she'd ever heard, until it ceased as abruptly as it had
began.

The cottage door was still standing open. Willow

stumbled through it without bothering to knock. Her fright swelled to panic when she saw the empty basket on the hearth.

Had the thundering of her heart not completely ceased for a beat, she might have never heard the husky, off-key humming. She whirled around to find Netta perched on the end of the bed, gazing down at the blanket-wrapped bundle in her arms. A bundle that squirmed, cooed, then let out a resounding burp more suitable to a burly ale master.

Netta lifted her head, offering Willow a smile as winsome as Peg's own. "I do believe she likes me. She quieted right down as soon as I started to sing."

Willow staggered over and plopped down on the stool, wiping her brow with her sleeve. "I'm delighted to know the two of you are getting along so well. Perhaps we can all sing a round together as soon as I catch my breath."

Netta dragged her gaze away from the baby's face, her smile fading. She rose and thrust the baby at Willow. "Forgive me, my lady. I forgot myself. I should never have touched her with these hands."

Willow studied the woman's stricken face for a moment before waving her away. "And why not? They're clean and sturdy, aren't they? Just make sure you keep one of them under her head and one of them under her rump, or she'll flop about like a beached pike."

Netta hesitated for a moment, then drew the baby back to her chest. When she lifted her eyes this time, the wariness within them was tempered by reluctant admiration. "I've met many ladies in my life, but none who deserved the title. If you still want me to, I'll teach you whatever you wish to know about pleasing your precious Lord Bannor."

Willow's lips curved in a thoughtful smile. "Every-thing. I wish to know everything."

By noontime the morning mist had drifted down the river, leaving the inhabitants of Elsinore with the prom-ise of a crisp, sunny afternoon. They came spilling out of the castle, eager to savor every moment of freedom they could steal before the coming snows imprisoned them behind the high stone walls until spring.

The bailey resounded with the shrill giggles and pelting footsteps of running children while the list rang with the clash and thunder of mock skirmishes. Even the washerwomen had dragged their tubs out of the dank laundry and into the sun, their massive forearms jiggling as they swapped jests and gossip.

Willow, Beatrix, and Mary Margaret trudged out to the meadow bordering the list, dragging a straw-stuffed dummy behind them. Willow knew that giving in to Mary Margaret's persistent pleas to teach her to shoot a bow might not be the wisest decision she'd ever made, but at least it would help her pass the inter-minable hours until midnight. A sweet shiver of antici-pation rippled through her. Thanks to Netta's generous tutelage, tonight she would storm her husband's tower armed with far more than just a smile and a shilling.

"You're blushing."

Willow jumped as her stepsister's accusation shat-tered her reverie. "No, I'm not. I'm simply flushed from the heat."

Beatrix's skeptical snort made a cloud of fog in the chilly air. "From the heat of your daydreams perhaps." She leaned over to whisper, "Or perhaps from the heat of dreams that have already come true, judging how late it was when you crawled into bed last night."

Willow glared at her. There were certain disadvantages to sleeping with a meddlesome stepsister. Especially one who knew her so well.

While Beatrix lashed the dummy to a nearby tree, Willow ushered Mary Margaret to a small rise in the land. The child's bow was even smaller than Desmond's; its feathered arrows weren't much larger than darts. As Willow knelt behind her, she prayed the only consequence of teaching her how to use it would be a row of headless and disemboweled dolls riddled with arrow holes.

"My mama got shooted by an arrow and went to heaven," Mary Margaret announced as Willow slotted one of the shafts and sought to arrange her small fingers on the bowstring.

"My mama went to heaven, too," Willow informed her.

"Did she get shooted by an arrow?"

"No, she got very sick when I was born." Willow pressed her cheek to Mary Margaret's, steadying the child's hand with her own. "Perhaps both of our mamas are smiling down upon us right now."

"Or cringing in horror," Beatrix muttered, eyeing the deadly tip of the arrow.

Confident that the child had a firm grasp on the weapon, Willow withdrew a few steps and nodded toward the dummy. "See that red heart painted on his chest? I want you to aim straight for it. Can you do that?"

Mary Margaret nodded. Her eyes narrowed to a fierce squint as she drew the bowstring taut. Willow held her breath, waiting for the telltale *ping*.

"But what if I shoots him in the head?" Mary Margaret suddenly blurted out, swinging the bow around.

Beatrix ducked while Willow reached over and gently plucked the bow from the child's grasp. "Rule number one, pixie. You must never take your eyes off your target."

"Why, look," Beatrix murmured, plucking a stray leaf from her hair as she gazed toward the list. "There's Lord Bannor."

"Where?" Willow whirled around, forgetting that she still held the bow.

At first she thought her stepsister was teasing her again, but there was no mistaking the noble bearing of the man strolling along the fence with Sir Hollis. He stood head and shoulders over his companion and most of the other men in the list. As he inclined his head toward Sir Hollis, the sun glinted off his hair, gilding it to a raven sheen. Kell and Edward dogged his every step, their own bright and dark heads bobbing in uncanny imitation of the two men. When Bannor paused to inspect a knight's armor, Edward crashed into the back of his legs, earning an exasperated look.

Willow might have believed Bannor was too preoccupied to notice her, had it not been for the brief sideways flicker of his glance and the dazzling flash of his smile.

She heard the *ping* she had been waiting for. The arrow left the bow, sailing across the meadow and toward the fence in a neat arc.

She was still standing frozen in shock when Mary Margaret tugged at her sleeve. "Oh, Willow, you shooted my papa! Is he going to heaven, too?"

Twenty

The last thing Willow expected Bannor to do was draw the arrow from his shoulder, give it a puzzled glance, then toss it over his shoulder, all without missing a step. Surely, she thought, 'twould be only a matter of seconds before he crumpled face first into a pool of his own blood.

Jerking herself out of her horrified daze, she lifted her skirts and went running across the meadow. She cleared a sagging rail of the fence in a graceless bound and went staggering right into his arms.

Her words came spilling out in a jumbled torrent. "Oh, Bannor, can you ever forgive me? I forgot I was holding the bow and then I saw you and you smiled at me and I had just rebuked Mary Margaret for taking her eye off the target and oh, I never meant to shoot you, I swear I didn't!"

He cupped her elbows, holding her steady. "Was

that *your* arrow? I thought one of the pages had mis-fired again."

She tugged at his arm. "Make haste, my lord! You must lie down before you collapse!"

"But I feel fine," he protested, shooting Hollis a be-mused look.

"Of course you don't! The pain and blood loss are simply impairing your judgment."

Willow threw her arms around his neck, attempting to drag him to the ground. Their scuffle was beginning to attract the curious stares of Bannor's men.

"All right! All right!" he shouted, sinking to his knees in the sand-sprinkled grass. "There's no need to throttle me. I'll go quietly."

As a crowd gathered around them, Willow drew his head into her lap and began to stroke his hair tenderly. "There, now. Doesn't that feel better?"

"I do believe it does," he murmured, snuggling his head deeper into her bosom.

Hollis rolled his eyes. "I can assure you, my lady, that there is no need for alarm. Lord Bannor has en-dured far worse insults at the hands of the—"

Bannor cleared his throat, cutting him off. "Perhaps Lady Willow is right." He allowed his eyes to drift shut. "I am beginning to feel a bit light-headed."

Bannor was beginning to feel other things as well, most of them centered in the region of his loins. He never dreamed he'd allow his men-at-arms to see him stretched out full-length on the ground with his head in a woman's lap. But Willow's wordless murmur was like the haunting notes of a siren's song, both sweet and seductive. He was no stranger to the gifts of women. He had partaken eagerly of their many pleasures. But he had always denied himself their comfort, equating its solace with a weakness he could not afford.

Desmond's flat voice penetrated the silken web Willow had woven around him. "What happened to him?"

"Willow shooted him. He's going to heaven."

Bannor opened one eye to find his daughter standing over him, her mane of golden curls haloed by the sun. "Would you miss me, sweeting, if I died?"

Mary Margaret thought about it for a minute, then shrugged. "Don't s'pose so. It can't be much farther away than France."

"He can go straight to hell for all I care."

Willow gasped and both of Bannor's eyes flew open to meet Desmond's defiant stare. Kell and Edward cupped their hands over their mouths to smother their shocked giggles. The men gathered around them shuffled their feet and exchanged uneasy glances as they awaited their lord's explosion of wrath.

Bannor sighed wearily. "I hate to disappoint you, lad, but the only place I'm going right now is to bed."

"Can you walk, my lord?" Willow inquired, shooting Desmond a savage look. "Or shall I have your men fetch a litter?"

"I believe I can walk." Bannor blinked up at her, using his thick, dark lashes to their full advantage. "With your help."

She braced her slender shoulder beneath his, helping him to his feet.

As they went staggering toward the castle, Sir Darrin dragged off his helm and scratched his grizzled head. "That's most odd. Lord Bannor never needed any help the time he crawled out of that moat in Poitiers with a dozen arrows poking out of his back."

"Or the time he escaped from that dungeon in Calais after they'd starved and tortured him half to death," one of his companions added.

Sir Darrin shook his head. "I do hope he's not going soft on us."

Hollis poked his nose between the two men. "As long as Lady Willow is around, you needn't fret yourselves about that."

Willow kept her arms wrapped tightly around Bannor's waist as she led him through the broad passages of the castle, bellowing orders that sent the flustered maidservants and pages scurrying to fetch bandages, hot water, and a cornucopia of healing herbs.

As they made their way up the winding stairs, she glanced over to find Bannor eyeing her askance. "What is it, my lord?"

"I can't believe I ever thought you had a small mouth."

Willow might have chided him for the jibe if he hadn't suddenly grabbed his shoulder and let out a heartrending groan. Only after she had him settled in his bed did she dare leave him long enough to retrieve the supplies she'd requested from the servants hovering outside the door.

Bannor reclined on a nest of pillows while Willow arranged the bandages, a basin of steaming water, and a bowl of fresh herbs on a bench beside the bed. "Desmond didn't mean what he said, you know," she said without looking at him.

Bannor snorted. "Of course he did. The lad loathes me."

Willow crumbled a pinch of marjoram into the water, shaking her head. "If he loathed you, he'd be indifferent to you, not furious with you."

Bannor cocked his head to study her. "How is it that you know so much about that wayward son of mine?"

She devoted all of her attention to folding the bandages into narrow strips, then dipping half of them into the water. "Because there was a time in my life when I would have done anything to make my father take notice of me. Even told him to go straight to hell." She gave Bannor a wry glance. "Or insisted upon wedding a man I'd never laid eyes on."

A shadow flickered across Bannor's face. "An act of mutiny you've no doubt had great cause to regret."

Instead of replying, Willow said lightly, "Let's take a look at that wound, shall we?"

Bannor winced as she gently pried his hand from his shoulder. Her brow furrowed in puzzlement as she smoothed her fingers over the flawless linen of his shirt. She glanced at the opposite shoulder, where a narrow slash marred the fabric.

Bannor immediately shifted his grip to that side. "It must have been phantom pain. 'Tis a most vexing sensation."

"Most vexing indeed," Willow murmured, surveying him through narrowed eyes. His sun-bronzed skin didn't betray even a trace of pallor.

She peeled the shirt from his shoulder with less care than she had been taking, but all of her sympathy and remorse came flooding back when she saw the puckered wound that marked his smooth flesh.

"Oh, Bannor, I should have never been so careless." She wrung out one of the bandages and gently dabbed away a thin trickle of blood. "Can you ever forgive me?"

He heaved a ponderous sigh. "Fortunately for you, I've never been one to hold a grudge."

She tried to tug his shirt farther down his shoulder, but the rich linen resisted her pull. "I believe I'd be able to better dress your wound if we took this off." Without waiting for his reply, she began to wrestle the garment over his head.

"That might not be the best idea," Bannor said, his voice muffled by the material.

But it was too late. The garment had already unfurled in Willow's hands, leaving her to gaze in naked amazement upon his exposed chest. It was God who had wrought a masterpiece from the powerful slabs of muscle and crisp coils of dark hair. And it was man who had done all in his power to destroy it.

When she had spied upon him in the tower, the flickering candlelight had shielded her from the most shocking of his secrets. Robbed of speech, Willow reached out her trembling hand and stroked her fingertips across the jagged scar that ran from the top of his breastbone to the bottom of his rib cage.

"I earned that one in my first tournament," Bannor said softly, keeping his gaze on her face. " 'Twas a blessing that the lance just grazed me."

Still mute, she traced the thin rope of scar that bisected his left nipple and curved around his heart, then looked at him questioningly.

"A dagger. King Philip of France hired an assassin who crept into my tent while I was sleeping, stabbed me, and left me for dead." A dangerous smile quirked his lips. "The man was most surprised when I paid a visit to his tent the following day and returned his dagger."

She touched the pocked circle to the right of his

breastbone, then the identical scars on each side of his heart.

"Arrow. Another arrow. Yet another arrow," he confessed, rolling his eyes.

He drew in a ragged breath as her hand skated lower, grazing the shiny, rippled flesh that covered half the plane of his abdomen, then disappeared into his hose.

"Boiling pitch." He shrugged. " 'Twas my own fault really. I didn't roll over the top of the wall fast enough."

He stiffened, but didn't protest when she urged him forward. As his back came into view, Willow finally found her voice, choking out a gasp.

His back was pocked with arrow scars even more numerous and vivid than the ones on his chest. It wasn't those souvenirs of battles both won and lost that made her eyes sting, but the pale wheals that crisscrossed the satiny expanse of flesh from his broad shoulders to his lower back.

He tensed as she traced one of them from beginning to end. "A mere twenty lashes. My French jailers were most displeased when I strangled one of the guards with the whip he was using to beat me."

Overcome by emotion, Willow wrapped her arms around his waist and pressed her cheek to his ravaged back, wishing there was some way she could heal him with the balm of her tears.

Bannor's breath left his lungs in a raw shudder. He was a man born with an almost inhuman tolerance for pain, yet Willow's tears sent a jolt of pure agony through him.

He struggled to hide it behind a rueful laugh. "I cannot blame you for hiding your face. I know this battered body of mine is a frightful sight to behold. Now you know why I always chose to bed my wives in the dark. Beneath the blankets."

Willow's lips flowered against his back, leaving him suspended somewhere between pain and pleasure. "You wear your scars as badges of honor, my lord. They are beautiful to behold."

Bannor held himself rigid as she kissed each one in turn. "I never dreamed you'd be so cruel as to torture a confession out of me," he said unevenly. "Very well. I confess. The wound you gave me is naught more than a scratch. I simply used it as an excuse to escape the clutches of my children and lure you to my bed before midnight. I was never even light-headed. Although I'm beginning to feel that way now," he muttered. His eyes drifted shut as Willow began to nibble her way around the muscular column of his throat.

Willow was remembering the first time she'd seen him—how she had longed to explore each of his imperfections just to prove he was real. Her prince seemed only a pallid ghost of a man, as she nuzzled her lips against the tantalizing shadow of a beard that always darkened Bannor's jaw and breathed in the fragrant spice of his skin. His eyes were closed, his thick lashes fanned against his cheeks. He groaned deep in his throat as she touched her lips to his.

Her prince's teeth had been without flaw, which only made the chip in one of Bannor's front teeth more beguiling. She traced its jagged edge with her tongue, driving him to the verge of madness. Before he could seize that elusive prize for his own, she had drifted lower.

Her prince's chest had been as smooth and hairless as a boy's. Willow raked her fingernails through the whorls of dark hair that swirled over Bannor's chest, savoring their crisp texture, before pressing her mouth to the broad ribbon of scar that ran from his breastbone to his rib cage.

She rained moist kisses down its length, longing to give pleasure where before there had been only pain. If Bannor's ragged breathing was any indication, he was suffering a bit of both. Her fingers sought the grave insult carved by the assassin's dagger. It made her tremble to think that someone had tried to still forever the mighty heart beating beneath her hand. As she swirled her tongue around the rigid nub that had been bisected by that treacherous blade, Bannor tangled his hands in her hair, breathing an oath that sounded more like a prayer.

Her puckered lips caressed the puckered flesh around each arrow scar before gliding down, down, down, until they reached the burn scar on his abdomen.

Bannor would have sworn he hadn't had any sensation in the area of that scar for over a decade, but just watching Willow's ripe mouth glide over his ruined flesh was enough to make him dizzy with longing.

When her luscious lips traced the scar all the way to the top of his hose, his muscles contracted with crazy anticipation. He seized her by the shoulders, drawing her up to his eye level. "Now might be a good time to warn you, my lady," he growled, "that I don't have a shilling on me."

A bold and silky smile curved her lips. "You won't be needing one, my lord, unless you wish to hold it between *your* knees."

Bannor's wariness melted to shock when she inclined her head to tug at the drawstring of his hose with her teeth. The slight sag in the fabric was all she needed to reach a belly that had rarely even been exposed to the

kiss of the sun. As her questing mouth eased the hose
even lower, Bannor would have sworn he was on fire
again, the flickering flame of Willow's tongue a taste
of both heaven and hell. He nearly came off the bed
when she gently cupped her hand around him through
the hose.

" 'Tis a most imposing codpiece, my lord," she whispered, her breath tickling his belly.

"I'm not wearing a codpiece," he gritted out between his clenched teeth.

"Oh!" she exclaimed, managing to sound both sultry
and innocent at the same time.

Bannor collapsed against the pillows, throwing an
arm over his eyes.

Willow decided to take his hoarse groan as one of
surrender. She held her breath as she eased down his
hose. In her innocence, she had never even dared to
imagine her prince as possessing such a mysterious
wonder.

Her breath escaped in a reverent sigh. The imperfections that had come before only made the perfection of
him seem that much more overwhelming. She cupped
him in both hands this time, shyly measuring both the
length and breadth of him. His fulsome splendor only
made the hungry ache within her deepen.

Bannor's hips bucked as Willow's lips tenderly enfolded him. 'Twas a boon neither Mary nor Margaret
had thought to grant him, and one he would have been
too proud to propose. He could not resist watching as
Willow took him, not in darkness, nor beneath the blankets, but in the dazzling sunlight that spilled through
the west window, limning her hair in silver.

He fisted his hands in those dark, silky curls, unable

to decide if his bride was a she-devil or an angel. In truth, he did not care. He only knew that he was blessed to be held in her tender thrall for as long as she would have him. And have him she did. He threw back his head and roared with ecstasy as she delivered a sweeter death than any assassin, an arrow to the very heart of him.

He was still suffering fierce aftershocks when he dragged Willow into his lap and tangled his tongue with hers in a long, hot kiss.

They both started guiltily when an impatient knock sounded on the door, followed by Mary Margaret's imperious tones. "Willow, has Papa gone to heaven yet?"

Bannor buried a chuckle in Willow's hair. "Indeed he has," he whispered, "and you, angel, are the one who sent him there."

The chapel bells were just beginning to chime twelve times when Willow slipped into Bannor's tower that night, a wooden platter tucked in the crook of her arm. She deposited her burden on the table, arranging cheese, bread, and flagon of mulled wine in a welcoming tableau.

She took one of the torches dipped in pitch from its iron bracket and used it to light the nest of kindling she had arranged on the hearth earlier that evening. A cozy crackling soon filled the tower, along with the crisp fragrance of burning pine. She doused the torch in the bucket of water kept in the corner for just that purpose, preferring the gentle flickering of the firelight.

Willow surveyed her efforts with satisfaction. But as she wandered to the bed, she knew the warmth, food, and wine were only a shadow of the pleasures to come. Her breath quickened with anticipation as she remembered the promise of sweet revenge Bannor had whispered in her ear, before reluctantly extracting himself from her embrace and going to reassure Mary Margaret that her papa wasn't going to heaven just yet.

The quilts were rumpled and the mattress still bore the imprint of Bannor's body. Unable to resist the temptation, Willow kicked off her shoes and clambered up on the bed. She curled her body into the larger hollow left by Bannor's, feeling as snug as a baby animal in its burrow.

When Willow awoke, the chapel bells were tolling again. Once. Twice. Three times.

She sat up and rubbed her eyes, both puzzled and disoriented. The cheese and bread sat untouched on the table; the fire burned low on the hearth, casting little more than shadows.

"Bannor?" she whispered. Her timid query was greeted by silence.

Without bothering to don her shoes, Willow slipped from the tower and padded down the stairs.

She poked her head in the first door she came to. Although the children had several beds between them, they nearly always ended up in the massive four-poster shared by Desmond, Ennis, Kell, and Edward. But tonight Desmond slumbered there alone, looking impossibly lost in the middle of that enormous bed. With his mouth hanging open and his lashes resting against his freckled cheeks, he looked closer to five than thirteen. Willow gently drew the blanket over him, wondering if he remembered ever having a mother to do so.

Growing more perplexed by the moment, she crept

down the broad stone stairs that cascaded into the heart of the castle. Since it was not uncommon for drunken stragglers and weary travelers seeking shelter from the cold to linger after an evening of merriment, she was not surprised to find a heap of bodies huddled around the hearth.

She was surprised to discover that the heap of bodies belonged to the lord of the castle and his offspring.

Willow bit back a smile. It appeared the children had lost their valiant battle to stay awake until midnight. And so had their father.

Bannor lay in their midst like a fallen giant cast into an enchanted slumber by a sparkling pinch of fairy dust. Meg, Margery, and Colm had their little heads pillowed on his muscular thighs. Ennis and Mary sprawled on the two benches flanking him while Hammish, Edward, and Kell curled up at his sides. Edward was mumbling in his sleep and Hammish's mouth was pressed to Kell's ear. Willow could only pray the lad didn't dream he was partaking of some tender delicacy.

Bannor held Mary Margaret snuggled in the crook of one arm. Although she had claimed not to care if he went off to heaven or France, her little hand clenched the front of his doublet as if she had no intention of ever letting him go. When she whimpered in her sleep, Bannor's arm tightened around her, forming a brawny shield that no night terror, no matter how bold, would dare to challenge.

When the chapel bells had tolled midnight only three short hours ago, Willow would have sworn she had everything she had ever desired. But as she gazed at the dark and gold heads of father and daughter through a blur of tears, she discovered that she was really no better than a greedy child herself, always craving more than she had.

'Twas no longer enough that Bannor should want her. She wanted him to love her, too.

Just as she loved him.

The realization made her heart ache with a bitter-sweet yearning more keen than any she had ever felt for her prince. Until that moment, she had never understood how Bannor could consider love an affliction. But as she slipped silently from the hall, she was already beginning to shiver with a fever from which there was no cure.

Twenty-one

When Willow awoke the next morning, she had good
reason to shiver. The temperature had plunged during
the night, leaving sparkling diamonds of frost on the
glazed window of her chamber. A sullen sky brooded
over the castle, mirroring her mood.

Although she knew that Beatrix had rarely risen before noon at Bedlington, she still felt compelled to try to
shake the girl out of her stupor. Beatrix simply mumbled a protest, snuggled deeper into the feather mattress, and drew the pelts over her head. Willow sighed,
wishing she could do the same.

Instead, she donned a fur-lined gown cut from crimson wool and hastened downstairs to seek the warmth
and cheer of the great hall. A fat yew log burned on
the massive stone hearth. Bannor, Sir Hollis, and the
children were gathered around the high table while
various knights, squires, and men-at-arms broke their

fasts at the long trestle tables scattered throughout the hall.

Bannor interrupted his conversation with Sir Hollis as she approached. "Good morning, my lady," he murmured, his eyes narrowing as he studied her face. "I trust you had a satisfying night's sleep?"

" 'Twas most fulfilling, my lord," she replied, wondering if he'd been disappointed to find his bed cold and empty when he'd finally retired to his tower.

The chair beside him was empty, but she deliberately joined Hammish on one of the benches. Let Bannor think she was sulking because he'd failed to keep their midnight tryst. 'Twas better than having him suspect the truth.

Garbed in brown hose and a crisp doublet of emerald green camlet, Bannor looked none the worse for having spent most of the night sleeping on the stones before the hearth. His jaw was freshly shaven, and his eyes possessed their usual sparkle. His children, however, didn't seem to have fared as well. Mary poked at a sticky pomegranate with one finger, while Ennis sluggishly stirred his fig pudding. Kell and Edward slumped over the table, their eyes drooping and their chins propped on opposite hands. A dozing Mary Margaret was in imminent danger of falling face first into her bowl. Even Hammish seemed to be making only a perfunctory effort to lick his plate clean.

Desmond was the only one eating with grim ferocity, as if he intended to choke down every honeyed pomegranate and spoonful of fig pudding in the castle, even if it killed him.

The children's attention sharpened when a squire emerged from the kitchens, staggering beneath the weight of a pewter platter laden with a succulent array of meats. Mary Margaret snapped out of her doze, her pert nose twitching like a rabbit's.

As the squire lowered the platter to the table, Bannor rubbed his hands in gleeful anticipation. Willow shot him a suspicious glance. She'd never seem him partake of anything before noon more hearty than brown bread washed down with ale.

As he stabbed a thick slab of bacon with his knife, popped it into his mouth, and began chewing with deliberate relish, the children followed his every move, their mouths hanging open. "Would you care for some bacon," —their faces brightened, then fell again as Bannor gallantly added—"my lady?"

"No, thank you, my lord," Willow replied, hiding a reluctant smile. "I'll just have what the children are having."

"You can have mine," Ennis said, shoving his bowl and spoon at her. "If I never see another bowl of fig pudding, 'twill be too soon for me."

Willow twirled the spoon in the bowl with even less enthusiasm than he had. It seemed her unfortunate affliction had also robbed her of her appetite.

"I'd like some of that pheasant," Sir Hollis said cheerfully, knife already in hand.

Bannor stretched halfway down the table to hand the platter to him. The children licked their lips as it passed only inches beneath their noses, then watched through glazed eyes as the knight helped himself to a slice of roast pheasant dripping with a piquant plum sauce. Desmond shoveled another heaping mouthful of fig pudding into his mouth, swallowing with an audible gulp.

While Bannor and Hollis savored their feast, pausing only long enough in their vigorous chewing and swallowing to swap effusive praise for the cook and all of his minions, Edward began to claw at his chest. "Might I have a bath today? I'm starting to itch."

Scowling, Kell inched away from him. "You're starting to smell, too."

Bannor tucked a hearty bite of pork savory in his mouth. "I'm sorry, son, but according to the terms of our treaty, you're not due for a bath for at least another fortnight."

Kell pinched his nose shut and made a gagging noise.

Edward elbowed him in the ribs. "Don't know what you're going on about. You don't exactly smell like the queen yourself." He sniggered. "Or maybe you do."

Plainly hoping to avoid a round of fisticuffs, Bannor dabbed at his mouth with a linen napkin and rose to his feet. Before his offspring's hopes could rise with him, he gestured for the squire hovering behind the buttery screen to remove the platter from the table.

When it was gone, his cheerful gaze traveled the circle of glum little faces that ringed him. "So what are we to play today? Is it to be hoops and tops? Or perhaps a few rousing games of hot cockles and hoodman blind?"

Desmond glared into his bowl, while the rest of them simply blinked at him, their eyes drooping at half-mast. Mary Margaret hid a yawn behind her hand.

Bannor shrugged and sighed, managing to look nearly as crestfallen as Hammish. "Well, if no one wishes to play with me this morning, I suppose I'll just wander out to the list and see if perhaps I'm needed there." Shooting Willow a wink that made her heart do a somersault in her chest, he turned away from the table.

"Perhaps you should go to Windsor. The king might need his arse wiped."

Although Desmond's head was inclined, his voice still carried throughout the hall. All talking and chewing seemed to cease at the same moment. Some of Bannor's men gaped openly at the high table while others took a sudden and profound interest in the red-and-gold banners strung from the rafters.

Bannor slowly pivoted on his heel, his hands curling into fists. "What was that, son?"

Willow held her breath, waiting for Desmond to mutter some falsehood or denial, but he shocked them all by surging to his feet. She realized then that the crimson creeping into his rigid jaw was not a stain of embarrassment, but anger.

He faced his father squarely, his own hands clenched into fists. "Please don't let me detain you, Father. You'd best hasten to the lists and whip out your mighty sword because you never know when the French might declare war on us again. And you know what? I pray they do! Then you'll have to rush to the king's side, won't you? Only this time, I hope you never return. Unless it's draped belly-down over your horse's back!"

Bannor loomed over his son, his face so still and fraught with menace it might have already been a granite effigy carved on a tomb. Willow clutched Hammish's trembling hand beneath the table, waiting for Bannor to backhand his eldest son. In truth, she could not say the boy didn't deserve it.

When Bannor finally spoke, his voice was so dangerously silky they all had to strain to hear it. "If the king requires me to fight at his side, lad, I will most certainly heed his command. But I've no intention of dying beneath a French blade. Not even to please you."

Leaving the echo of his words hanging behind him, Bannor turned and strode from the hall, shouldering his way through a cluster of gawking squires.

"Bannor!" The quavering cry pursued him across the meadow, more relentless than the icy flecks of snow stinging his face.

Bannor doubled the pace of his long strides, crunching the frozen grasses beneath his boots. He had spent most of his life making war, but now all he desired was a moment of peace. The sluggish ripple of the river drifted to his ears, promising just that.

"My lord!" This time the cry was more urgent. And more breathless.

"Leave me be, Willow," he called over his shoulder without slowing. "I've no wound for you to tend today."

"Not even the one inflicted by your son?"

Bannor halted at the rim of the riverbank, swearing beneath his breath.

He refused to turn around, even when he heard a desperate panting behind him. Willow came stumbling into his line of vision, her hair dusted with snow and her skirt stained with mud, as if she'd fallen more than once in her stubborn pursuit of him. She would have probably gone rolling right into the river if he hadn't reached out a hand and snagged her.

As soon as he had her steadied, he took his hands off of her and started down the bank. "You may accompany me if you insist, but I'll thank you to speak no more of my son."

She scrambled after him. "How can I speak of anything else? Didn't you see his face? He was deliberately trying to provoke you."

"Just as you are?"

She continued as if he hadn't spoken. "The poor lad was all but begging you to snatch him up by the scruff of his neck and give him the shaking he deserved. When you turned your back and walked away, I thought he was going to burst into tears right there in front of God and everybody. And if he had, I don't think he would have ever forgiven you."

Bannor kept walking.

"I don't understand why you let the boy run wild when he ought to be training in the list with you and your men." Willow's voice rose. "And I don't understand how Lord Bannor the Bold, Pride of the English and Terror of the French, can be afraid of one scrawny thirteen-year-old lad!"

Bannor whirled around on the edge of the river, his eyes blazing, and roared, "I'm not afraid of him! I'm afraid of me!"

Willow stumbled to a halt.

Bannor raked a hand through his hair. "When other men lose their tempers, they shout and bluster and stomp their feet. When I lose my temper, heads roll and blood spills. Men die." He strode back toward her, holding up his hands. "Look at these hands, Willow. Look at the size of them." He flexed both of them into mighty fists. "Feel the strength in them. Suppose I should lift one of them in anger against Desmond? Or even Mary Margaret? Why, I could snap one of his bones or crush her wee skull to powder with no more than a clumsy squeeze of my fingers!"

Willow did not know how it was possible for Bannor

to look so powerful and so helpless all at the same time. She only knew that if she hadn't already discovered that she loved him, she would have done so in that moment.

She closed the remaining distance between them and gently enfolded one of his rigid fists in her hand. "I only know that these hands are capable of great tenderness as well as great strength. That they're more likely to give pleasure than pain."

His expression remained grim. "They've also dealt more death than you can imagine."

She stroked her thumb over his battle-scarred knuckles. "So you've avoided punishing your children for their wretched behavior all these long months for fear you might lose your temper? You're afraid you might lapse into one of the battle frenzies that served you so well in war, and send one of their impertinent little heads rolling across the floor of the great hall?"

He eyed her warily. "I might. How am I to know I won't?"

"You're angry at me right now, aren't you?"

"Furious," he admitted.

She continued to stroke his knuckles until his hand slowly unfolded. She inclined her head to press a kiss to his callused palm, casting him a glance from beneath her lashes. "And am I in danger at this moment?"

"More than you know," he breathed, lifting his other hand to brush a snowflake from her hair.

"I'm not the least bit afraid," she lied, hoping her tender smile would hide the true extent of her fear. "You are a kind and honorable man, Bannor of Elsinore. A man who would never hurt anyone weaker and more helpless than himself."

"Ah, but you're not helpless, my lady." He stroked

his thumb over the softness of her bottom lip, deliberately reminding them both of the tender boon she had lavished upon him the day before. "On the contrary. I've never faced an enemy who posed more of a risk to my heart."

When Bannor came marching through the list a short time later with Willow trailing casually behind him, his face was etched with an unyielding determination his men had previously seen only on the battlefield. They exchanged perplexed glances, wondering if perhaps France *had* broken the treaty, just as his son had predicted, and declared war upon them all.

Several of his more dedicated knights and men-at-arms scooped up their weapons and fell into step behind him, as much out of habit as curiosity. Their stern procession led them into the bailey, where a smirking Desmond had engaged some of the younger pages in a game of hazard they could never hope to win.

"When I'm lord of Elsinore," he was saying, shaking the weighted dice in his cupped palm, "the priest won't waste our time with reading and writing lessons. And I'll see to it that them arrogant squires polish their own boots, so you won't have to do it. If anyone refuses to do *my* bidding, I'll have them tossed in the dungeon 'til they come crawling to me, begging for mercy."

Desmond rattled on and on to his captive audience, completely oblivious to the fact that their little eyes kept growing bigger and bigger until a forbidding shadow fell over him. He swiveled around to find his father standing behind him, backed by a dozen grimfaced warriors. As the pages scattered, the weighted dice tumbled from his limp fingers. The dots carved on their faces might declare him a winner, but Desmond knew better.

His father's fist closed in the scruff of his tunic. As Bannor lifted him to his eye level, Desmond's feet dangled several inches above the ground.

Bannor's granite visage cracked into a smile so ripe with paternal affection it made Desmond's teeth begin to chatter. "I hate to spoil all of your grand plans, lad, but you're not lord of this castle yet. I am."

When Desmond started to squirm, Bannor simply heaved the boy over his shoulder and began to march back toward the list. Desmond twisted his head this way and that, frantically seeking an ally among the gathering crowd of gawkers. That was when he spotted Willow.

"Willow!" he shouted, his booted feet scissoring at the air. "Save me, Willow! Father's lost his wits. He's in some kind of berserker rage! Please don't let him tear my head off!"

Willow couldn't quite suppress her mocking smile as she called out, " 'Twasn't so very long ago that you were begging him to protect you from me. It appears you've learned naught since then."

As the scaffold came into sight, Desmond's whining soared to a full-blown wail. "Not the finger pillory again! I won't swear anymore, Father! I swear I won't!"

As Bannor carried him past the scaffold, Desmond cast the gallows a wistful look. Surely even hanging would be preferable to whatever grim fate his father had in store for him.

Bannor bore him through the bailey, through the list, and through the yawning doors of the stable. As the two of them disappeared inside, a dozen squires and grooms came running out as if they'd been evicted by the devil himself.

The doors slammed shut with a resounding thud, making everyone within hearing distance flinch.

Kell came running up, his eyes shining with excitement, and gave Willow's skirt a sharp tug. "Did you see that? He's done for now, isn't he?"

She put an arm around the boy's shoulder and hugged him close, suffering her first twinge of doubt. "Aye, lad, I'm afraid so."

Twenty-two

Bannor heaved his squirming son onto a bale of fresh hay. He feared the lad might cower and cry, but Desmond bounded to his feet to face him, the trembling of his jaw disguised by a mask of defiance.

Bannor could not have said how much this pleased him.

"Well, get on with it," Desmond snarled. "Go on and thrash me. We both know I deserve it."

"I have every intention of thrashing you. When *I* am ready."

Desmond threw himself back down on the bale of hay, a sneer twisting his lips. "And when will that be? After you've finished training your men? Or stitching the head back on one of Mary Margaret's dolls? Or slipping your hand beneath Willow's—"

Bannor cocked one eyebrow, daring him to continue.

Desmond tucked a piece of hay between his pursed lips, staring straight ahead.

"I wasn't aware you were so eager to be thrashed," Bannor said, folding his arms over his chest.

Desmond shrugged. "I figured you were the one eager to get it over with. I'm sure you've got duties of more import to attend to." He lowered his voice to a sullen mutter. "The king might need his pisspot emptied."

Bannor's temper flared. "While you're making sport of my loyalty to our king, you might wish to remember that if it weren't for him, I'd still be a penniless man-at-arms forced to sell my sword to the highest bidder. Everything I have, everything *you* have, has been a re-ward for serving him—my title, this castle, the food in your belly, the land beneath your feet. Why, your very mother was a gift from him! A bastard like myself would never have been allowed to so much as touch the hem of Mary's cloak without Edward's blessing. However much you resent it, I owe my allegiance to him. I had no choice but to take my place at his side during the war."

"There's no need to pretend it was such a great sac-rifice! We all saw the fire in your eyes when the time came for you to return to battle. Both my mother and Lady Margaret would cry for days after you departed, but I doubt you ever gave them or us a second thought."

Bannor was stricken by the truth in the lad's accusa-tion. It cut deeper than any lash wielded by an enemy's hand, making him want to strike out in self-defense. He paced the length of the stalls before whirling around to face his son. "War was all I knew. 'Twas the only thing I ever excelled at. I fought at the king's side all those years for all of you—to bring honor and glory to the name of Elsinore, to make you proud."

The boy gave him a wry look that aged his narrow face beyond its years. "Was it our pride that kept you on that battlefield, Father? Or your own?"

Bannor's gut wrenched as he realized that all of his glorious feats and triumphs meant nothing to this boy who had grown up without a father. He would have fallen on his own sword before deserting any one of the men beneath his command, yet he'd unwittingly done just that. All of his notions of honor and duty and service to his king echoed through his mind, as hollow as the look in his son's eyes.

He turned away from those eyes, understanding what it meant to be truly defeated for the first time in his life. "It appears I've done you a grave injustice. You wanted a father and I offered you naught but a hero. In the end, I was neither in your eyes."

When Desmond spoke again, his voice was strangely distant. "I ran away once when I was very small. 'Twas after Mama died. I took one of the swords you'd left behind on your last visit. 'Twas nearly twice my size, but I still managed to drag it all the way to Elsinore's border. It took me so long that I thought I must surely be in France. When one of your villeins found me, I struggled to lift the sword and told him he'd best make way, for I was the son of Lord Bannor the Bold and I was off to join my papa in battle."

Bannor slowly turned to face his son. "What did he do?"

Desmond lifted his shoulders in a sheepish shrug. "He took the sword away, threw me over his shoulder, and carried me straight back to Fiona. I kicked and screamed the whole way."

"I can't say that surprises me." Bannor's rueful chuckle died in his throat when he saw the tears shining in his son's eyes.

"You were my hero," Desmond whispered. "I wanted nothing more than to be just like you."

Bannor closed the distance between them in two strides, drawing the boy into his arms. "Someday you will be a fine warrior, and a much better father than I ever was. And you will be lord of this castle as well. But not today. Today you need only be my son." He stroked the boy's chestnut hair. "I still remember the day your mother laid you in my arms for the first time. She was so proud to have given me a son."

"She wouldn't be very proud now, would she?" Desmond mumbled, swiping at his nose.

Bannor tipped the boy's face up so he could gaze sternly into his eyes. "On the contrary. You've been both mother and father to your brothers and sisters all the years I was gone. Your mother would be every bit as proud of you as I am."

A tremulous grin curved the boy's lips. "Do you really think so?"

"Aye," Bannor said with all the conviction he could muster. "I'd wager my life upon it."

"Wager," Desmond repeated absently. He scratched his head as if trying to remember something, then snapped his fingers. Hastily disengaging himself from his father's embrace, he sprinted for the barn door.

"Where do you think you're going in such haste?" Bannor demanded, striding after him.

"I'm going to collect my hazard winnings before those cheating pages make off with them."

"Not so fast, lad." Bannor clapped a hand on his shoulder, freezing him in his tracks. When Desmond cast a timid glance over his shoulder, his father was wearing a devilish grin of his own. "We still have the small matter of your thrashing to attend to."

As the morning wore on and snow began to tumble out of the darkening sky in fat, woolly flakes, Willow paced the length of the list, wondering if she'd done a terrible thing. She nibbled at her knuckle, tortured by visions of Bannor emerging from the barn with Desmond's broken body draped over his arms, his hollow eyes burning with hatred for the woman who had coaxed him into murdering his son.

Bannor's men-at-arms and knights slunk away one by one, mumbling this excuse or that. In truth, they were no longer able to bear the sight of Willow's haunted face, or to endure a silence more ominous than screams of terror or pleas for mercy.

As both Willow's apprehension and the snow deepened, the children crept out to join the grim vigil, their somber little faces silently reproaching her. Even Edward had nothing to say. Shortly after eleven, Beatrix deigned to grace them with her presence.

"I heard what he said to his father," she whispered to Willow. "If you ask me, whatever he gets is no more than he deserves."

Willow might have reproached the girl for her spite, if she hadn't noticed that several of the fingernails Beatrix took such pride in had been chewed to the quick.

When the chapel bells tolled noon, Willow sank down on a bale of hay and buried her face in her hands. She barely felt Hammish's hand gently stroking her hair.

Her head flew up as the stable door began to creak

open. A hulking figure was silhouetted against the torchlit interior. Willow blinked the snow from her lashes, fearing the worst. But her eyes beheld not a snarling monster destroyed by the curse of his temper, but a smiling man with one brawny arm draped over his son's shoulders.

Desmond looked taller—older somehow—as if the mantle of the man he would become rested on his shoulders along with his father's arm. With his green eyes and chestnut coloring, Willow had always assumed he must be the very image of his mother, but for the first time, she saw the indelible stamp of his father in the proud tilt of his head, the stubborn jut of his jaw, the sulky-sweet cant of his grin.

The children sprang to their feet with Beatrix fast on their heels. As they ran to greet their conquering hero, yapping like a pack of eager pups, Willow gathered her skirts and followed. She had a hero of her own to salute.

"Dethmond!" squealed the twins in unison.

Meg threw her chubby little arms around her brother's leg while Mary Margaret captured his free hand, swinging it like the end of a skip-rope. At the last second, Beatrix remembered to hang back.

"We was afraid Papa had kill'ded you," Mary Margaret said.

"He thrashed me," Desmond confessed, beaming up at his father. "Within an inch of my life." Despite the boy's cheerful claim, Willow couldn't find a mark on him.

Bannor struggled to look stern. "And a long overdue thrashing it was."

"Did it hurt?" Hammish asked, his brown eyes huge.

"Dreadfully," Desmond assured him.

Beatrix eyed him down the length of her patrician nose. "I'm surprised you didn't squeal like a girl."

"I didn't let out a squeak. Not even one."

Bannor cocked an eyebrow.

Desmond ducked his head. "Well, maybe just one."

Ten-year-old Mary surveyed him with newfound respect. "How very brave of you. I'm almost certain I would have cried."

"Not me," Edward claimed, hitching his hips in a clumsy swagger. " 'Cause I'm a man, and men don't cry."

Kell gave him a shove. "But you smell bad enough to make my eyes water."

Before the fists could start to flail, Bannor stepped between the two boys and flattened a hand on each of their foreheads to hold them apart. "Your brother and I had a very long talk after his thrashing, and we've decided to negotiate some changes in the terms of our treaty."

Desmond nodded, glowing with pride to be included in his father's confidence. "That's right. We'll no longer eat honeyed pomegranates and fig pudding for every meal. We'll eat good solid meat and fresh-baked bread."

"And vegetables?" Hammish piped up hopefully. "Even the foul-tasting ones?"

"Aye," Bannor said. "Three times a day." He pointed a finger at Edward. "And you'll take a bath every sennight, son. Whether you need it or not. And since everyone is exhausted from staying up until midnight the past few nights, we shall remedy that this very afternoon. With a nap."

Edward and Kell exchanged a look of sheer horror. "A nap?"

"Now?"

"In the middle of the day?"

Bannor ruffled Kell's sunny hair. "Don't look so glum, son. Just think what a pleasure 'twill be to curl up in a soft, toasty bed while a fire crackles on the hearth and the snow falls outside your window." The sidelong glance he gave Willow promised her that a soft, toasty bed and a crackling fire were only the beginning of the pleasures he had planned for her.

"Make haste, children," she blurted out, spreading her arms wide to herd them toward the castle. "The sooner you fall asleep, the sooner you can wake up and join your father and me in a hearty supper of meat and vegetables."

They'd traveled several steps before she realized that one of her sheep had gone astray.

Mary Margaret had plopped down in the snow and folded her arms over her chest. The little girl stared straight ahead, her bottom lip protruding at a baleful angle. "Won't take no nap. Don't want to do it. Can't make me."

Desmond arched an eyebrow in Bannor's direction. All the children were watching their father to determine if this overt act of rebellion would be tolerated beneath the terms of their new treaty.

Bannor blew out a long-suffering sigh, and gave Willow a look heavy with regret. "If she refuses her nap, I suppose I shall have to forgo mine as well." Rolling his eyes heavenward, he scooped his daughter into his arms, tossed her over his shoulder, and strode back toward the barn.

Unlike her brother, Mary Margaret took no pride in suffering in silence. Long after Willow had the other children tucked snugly into their beds, the little girl's outraged shrieks rang through the castle with a fiendish glee that made all who heard them cross themselves and clap their hands over their ears. It wasn't until her shrill howls had ceased that a trembling Father Humphries dared to waddle out to the barn. He eased open the barn door, expecting the worst, only to discover the exhausted little demon napping in her father's arms.

Bannor glanced up as the priest crept into the barn. "Shhhh," he whispered, touching a finger to his lips. "I just got her to sleep." He brushed a damp ringlet from his daughter's tear-streaked cheek, the harsh planes of his face softened by tender pride. "Doesn't she put you in mind of an angel?"

Father Humphries beamed down at the child, all the while fumbling to tuck his crucifix and flask of holy water back into the sleeve of his robe before her father saw it. "Aye, my lord. An angel indeed."

Twenty-three

Anyone who saw Lord Bannor's children gathered around the high table in the great hall that evening would have sworn Father Humphries had driven demons from the lot of them. Even the knights, who were still grumbling and sulking at being banished from their seats of honor by their master's whelps, had to admit they'd never seen a more angelic band of children.

Bright-eyed from their afternoon naps, freshly scrubbed, and garbed in their finest velvets and damasks, they lacked only wings and halos to be mistaken for the most divine of celestial beings. Beneath the flickering radiance of the torchlight, their hair gleamed and their skin glowed with the dewy vigor common only to those in the first blush of youth. Fiona had even spread a quilt before the hearth, allowing a chortling Peg and a cooing Mags to join the merriment.

The children ignored the platters of sweetmeats and confections passing just beneath their noses, choosing instead to heap their plates with crispy morsels of mutton and plump onions seasoned with saffron. They murmured "please" and "thank you" and "Might I have some more?" with exquisite courtesy, so dumbfounding the squires that they kept crashing into each other and spilling sauces on the linen-draped table.

Reclining in his chair at the center of the table, Bannor took a sip of Bordeaux from his silver goblet and shook his head, marveling that the fairies had been so kind as to steal his ill-behaved brood and leave him with these sweet-tempered changelings.

In truth, 'twas not the fairies who deserved his gratitude, but a slender sprite named Willow. His gaze strayed to the stairs. Mary Margaret's tantrum had deprived him of more than just an afternoon nap. It had robbed him of the few precious hours he might have spent in his bride's arms. A wicked smile quirked his lips. If he'd have had his way, they'd have done very little napping and ended up more deliciously drowsy than before.

All thoughts of exhaustion vanished as Willow appeared on the landing. She wore a gown as soft and blue as the underbelly of a finch. A thin band of beaten gold crowned her brow, leaving her dusky curls free to frame her face.

As she approached the table, he smiled and lifted his goblet, paying her the tribute she deserved. "My compliments on a battle well fought." He nodded toward his brood. "You shall henceforth be known as The Lady of the Bath."

"I feared I was going to have to request reinforcements from the king," she said, sliding into the chair next to him. "Mary Margaret leaned too close to the brazier and singed one of her ringlets clean off. I had to dunk Edward three times for dunking Kell. And Hammish ate an entire cake of soap."

Bannor stole a sidelong glance at his son, only to discover he was still burping up bubbles. "Given his foul tongue, perhaps I should have offered Desmond similar fare a long time ago."

"Oh, that won't be necessary. Desmond got his mouth washed out with a soapy rag after Beatrix caught him peering down her dress while she scrubbed the grime from his ears."

Bannor sighed. "That doesn't surprise me. After I thrashed him this morning, we had a most enlightening conversation about how he might provoke your little maidservant into sitting on him again. 'Her tongue might be sharp, Papa,' he told me, 'but she is exceedingly soft.' "

Willow rolled her eyes. "Lord in heaven, help us. He is his father's son after all. I suppose 'twill only be a matter of time before you'll be raising his brood as well as your own."

Bannor snorted. "Don't be ridiculous. He's naught but a lad."

Willow fluttered her lashes at him, feigning innocence. "And how old were you, my lord, when a pretty maiden first caught your eye?"

Bannor paled, then drained the rest of his wine in a single gulp. "That does it. I'm locking the boy away this very night."

"Will you lock yourself away as well?"

He leaned closer, warming the curve of Willow's cheek with his breath. "Only if you possess the key."

As Willow lifted her smoky eyes to his, everyone

else in the hall seemed to disappear, leaving them all alone in a cloud of musky jasmine.

The children shattered that illusion by bursting into enthusiastic applause. A squire bearing a fully dressed peacock had just marched into the hall. The bird's iridescent plumage had been plucked before roasting, then each feather had been painstakingly restored to its original magnificence.

Watching his children bounce up and down in excitement, Bannor whispered, "The naps may have been a grave mistake. I fear they will not sleep at all tonight."

"Nor might you, my lord."

The saucy look Willow slanted him only made Bannor more determined to devise an escape for them both. He was beginning to feel like some desperate squire, seeking to lure a serving wench into some shadowy corner so he could have his way with her against the nearest wall. It galled him that he could snap his chains and battle his way out of a heavily guarded dungeon, but couldn't seem to evade a dozen bright-eyed children.

He was on the verge of throwing Willow over his shoulder, drawing his sword, and threatening to skewer anyone who dared to stand in their way, when, to the children's delight, a troupe of musicians and tumblers who had sought shelter from the snowy night decided to earn their supper. A pair of tumblers somersaulted to and fro across the hall, winning a shower of coins and hoots of appreciation from even the most jaded of Bannor's knights.

One of the musicians leapt onto a table and began to beat upon the rawhide skins of his nakers with a pair of sticks while another cranked the handle of a hurdy-gurdy. The merry notes rippling out from the instrument sent a brindle-colored terrier dancing across the hall on its hind legs. Willow laughed aloud as the trained dog plucked a morsel of peacock from her outstretched hand before prancing in a jaunty circle.

Bannor studied his bride's profile, as enchanted by her as she was by the tumbler's pup. With her hands clapping in time to the music and her eyes shining with delight, she didn't look much older than Mary Margaret.

He could not resist wrapping an arm around her shoulders and giving her a tender squeeze. "The little fellow is quite the charmer, isn't he, princess?"

She went utterly still. He glanced down to find her gazing up at him with the most peculiar expression. Her gray eyes had gone all huge and misty. "Bannor, I have something to confess." She bowed her head, wringing her hands in her lap. "I . . . I . . ."

He leaned closer, struggling to hear her stammered words over the twins' high-pitched squeals. Before he could make them out, a thunderous banging sounded on the door. Willow started violently.

" 'Tis probably naught but another weary traveler seeking shelter from the storm," Bannor assured her, covering her trembling hands with his own. "Now what is it you would like to confess? Some naughty sin you've committed?" He lowered his voice to a husky whisper. "Or perhaps one I can help you commit, if we can steal away for a few moments."

Bannor's wicked grin faded as a man-at-arms strode into the hall, his face grim. Relinquishing Willow's hands with great reluctance, Bannor rose. He expected the guard to approach him with whatever report he had to deliver, but the man seemed to be taking great care not to even look in his direction. Instead, he wended his way to the hearth and leaned down to whisper something in Fiona's ear.

The old woman frowned, then rose and followed him, leaving Mags and Peg in the care of a grimacing Bea. Bannor felt a chill of foreboding that had nothing to do with the icy draft that had billowed into the hall when the door had flown open.

His instincts were proved sound when Fiona reappeared a moment later, cradling a ragged bundle to her chest. As she shuffled toward him with her burden, a hush fell over the hall. The tumblers crept back to their benches, and even the children lapsed into an awkward silence. Bannor's spirits sank as he realized that it was no longer him everyone was struggling not to look at, but his bride.

He dared not look at her himself. But he could feel her. He knew when she drew in a shuddering breath, and painstakingly measured each second before she released it.

Fiona held out the bundle, giving him no choice but to take it. "One o' the guards found it outside the portcullis, m'lord. The poor wee thing's near blue from the cold."

Bannor drew back a fold of swaddling too threadbare to be called anything but a rag. The creature within was so tiny it hardly looked human. Its skin seemed too loose for its bones. Although it was too weak to do anything more than mewl like a half-starved kitten, its cloudy blue eyes told Bannor it had only recently been born, perhaps even this very night. 'Twas a pity, he thought savagely, that the child had to be born into such a cold, merciless world.

"There was a note," Fiona said. Since Bannor's

hands were already occupied, she handed the crumpled scrap of parchment to Sir Hollis.

The knight squinted at the crude lettering. He had to clear his throat twice before he could rasp out the words, " 'Care for him, m'lord. He is yours.' "

Bannor cast Willow a stricken look. She was staring straight ahead, her face as pale as a bolt of Egyptian linen.

He returned his gaze to the helpless creature in his arms. The child was too weak to even clutch at the finger Bannor used to stroke his tiny palm.

"Of course, he's mine," he said firmly, thrusting the babe back into Fiona's arms. "Warm him up before the fire, won't you, before his wee nose falls off. And send Bea to fetch Mags's wet nurse. The woman should have enough milk to satisfy the both of them."

He swept the same penetrating gaze that had been known to send his enemies scurrying for cover across the silent hall. "Why are you all looking so somber?" he demanded, splashing a fresh stream of wine into his goblet and lifting it high in the air. " 'Tis not every day your lord welcomes a new son to Elsinore!"

Taking their cue from him, his men-at-arms hefted their own goblets and sent up a rousing cheer. The musicians struck up a round dance while the children spilled off their benches and crowded around Fiona, eager to steal a peek at their new brother.

A fresh-faced knight slapped Bannor on the back with a familiarity he wouldn't have dared only a few minutes ago. "The war may be over, my lord, but 'tis gratifying to know your lance has lost none of its thrust."

"Pay no mind to the impudent whelp," Sir Darrin

said, an impish grin wreathing his grizzled face. "I've heard he's so eager to drive home his own lance, he misses the target more often than not."

"Better an overeager lance than a withered one," the young knight shot back, his ears flaming.

The rest of Bannor's knights roared with laughter. They crowded around him, eager to add their own ribald jests to the speculation about his legendary prowess. It took Bannor several minutes to escape their jovial clutches. By the time he did, Willow's chair was empty.

She was gone.

Willow lay rigid in her bed, watching downy feathers of snow drift past the window and listening to the chapel bells chime midnight. 'Twas all she could do not to flinch at each of their crystalline peals. They went on forever, yet seemed to cease too soon, leaving her in a silence broken only by her stepsister's less than delicate snores. She wondered if Bannor was prowling his tower, waiting for her to come to him.

She rested with her back to Beatrix, her icy hands folded beneath her cheek. She had feigned sleep when the girl had crawled into the bed, knowing she could not bear to listen to Beatrix prattle on and on about the dramatic arrival of Lord Bannor's bastard babe.

She supposed she ought to be grateful that the babe had arrived before she could humble herself beyond redemption. Before she could blurt out those three words that would have left her heart defenseless against every blow.

Willow squeezed her eyes tightly shut as Bannor's voice echoed through her mind, rich with affection and amusement. *The little fellow is quite the charmer, isn't he, princess?*

She might have been able to resist the sweet seduction of being wrapped in his embrace, of gazing at the shining faces of his children and feeling as if she belonged to a family for the very first time in her life. But his casual endearment had been her undoing, reducing her to that same pathetic little girl who had been too proud to believe that anyone could not love her. It had set her mind to spinning a tapestry of the future in shimmering threads of silver and gold. A future where Elsinore became the home she had always dreamed of having.

The minute Fiona had come marching into the hall with the babe Bannor had sired on another woman cradled in her arms, that tapestry had began to unravel. Willow had realized that the home she thought she'd found was naught but a castle of dreams built on a foundation of clouds.

Willow buried her face in her damp pillow, stricken by a wave of self-loathing. She remained that way for a long time, not even stirring when the chapel bells tolled a single melancholy note, heavy with doom.

That note was still hanging in the air when the tower door came crashing open, and she scrambled to her knees to meet the smoldering eyes of her husband.

Twenty-four

Beatrix sat bolt upright in bed and let out an ear-splitting shriek. Willow had never truly pitied Bannor's enemies until that moment. His sulky-sweet mouth was set in a grim line, and his eyes had gone as dark as a cloudless midnight. They glinted with ferocious determination, warning her that no barricade of splintered furniture or vat of boiling pitch would have kept him from her side on this night.

She was almost relieved when he shifted those eyes to Beatrix. "Out," he said, the flat command more damning than a bellow.

"B-b-but, my lord," Beatrix stammered, clutching the bedclothes to her chin without even a hint of her usual coquettishness, " 'tis my habit to sleep in naught but my skin."

Bannor took a step toward the bed, as if he had every intention of tossing her out of it himself. Snatching up one of the pelts, Beatrix lunged across Willow and off the opposite side of the bed. She all but flew past Bannor and out the door, flashing her naked backside. When the frantic slap-slap of her bare feet had faded, he shut the door with deliberate care, betraying just how badly he wanted to slam it.

For some reason, that glimpse of the raw emotion seething just beneath his icy control gave Willow courage. If he expected her to stammer and cower beneath the blankets as Beatrix had done, he was doomed to be sorely disappointed.

She tossed back the pelts and rose to stand beside the bed, wearing the chemise she had found in the cupboard her very first night at Elsinore. The night she had feared that her new husband might be naught but a rutting satyr, intent upon making her a slave to his lusts.

As Bannor's bold gaze raked up and down her, taking in every inch of her with a thoroughness that raised gooseflesh on her skin, she had to admit that he bore more than a passing resemblance to that creature. His shirt was unlaced at the throat and his hair was tousled, as if he had dragged his fingers through it more than once. Since Willow could do nothing to hide the way the sheer sendal clung to her rosy nipples or pooled between her thighs, she refused to even try.

As she had expected, Bannor did not waste time on pleasantries. "What would you have had me do, Willow? Toss the child back into the snow?"

"Of course not! Is that the kind of woman you believe me to be?"

"I almost wish I did." He paced to the window and back again, raking a hand through his hair. "All of this would be much easier then, wouldn't it? I could marvel that your flesh could be so warm and sweet, when naught but a lump of ice beats within your breast. I could justify my own sins by condemning yours." He swung around to gaze at her, the hoarse passion in his voice belying his words. "Perhaps I could even learn to hate you."

"I'm sorry to disappoint you, my lord, but 'twas not your charity toward that unfortunate child that cut me to the heart. 'Twas the pity in the eyes of Sir Hollis. Fiona. Your men." Her voice faded to a ragged whisper as she struggled to swallow around the lump in her throat. "Your children."

He shook his head. " 'Twas never my intention to make you an object of pity or ridicule to any of them. I would have spared you that if I could have."

"How? By denying the child? A child you sired on another woman, when you've made it painfully clear you have no desire to sire one on me."

Willow had not meant to blurt out the words, but there they were, lying like a carelessly tossed gauntlet on the floor between them.

Bannor trampled her invisible challenge as he closed the distance between them in two strides. "I thought we were in accord on that, my lady. If I was mistaken, then I can assure you that I am more than willing to fulfill my husbandly duties. If 'tis a child of your own that you want, 'tis a child I shall give you. The first of many, I can assure you." His hands went to his hips, preparing to unfasten the chain of braided silver that rested low upon them.

A flare of panic made Willow reach out and close her hand over his. She thought only to stop him from drawing off the belt, but as the backs of her fingers brushed the thin skein of his hose, she realized he was not only more than willing to give her a child, but more than able as well.

His eyes met hers without a hint of shame. She was the one to blush.

She jerked her hand back, wrapping it around the bedpost to hide its trembling, and tilted her chin to a defiant angle. "I'm not one of your knights, my lord, to be impressed by the size and vigor of your lance. Nor am I one of your many paramours, to be pacified with a hasty cuddle and a babe in my belly for nine months out of every year."

He barked out a helpless laugh. "Surely you must realize that the babe who was brought to the castle tonight was conceived months before I even considered taking a wife." Bannor feathered his fingers across her cheek, both his touch and his voice gentling. "Months before I ever saw your face."

Willow held herself stiffly, terrified her pride would shatter beneath his caress. "Can you promise me 'twill never happen again? Can you swear an oath here and now that there will be no more babies delivered to your doorstep after we've been wed nine months? A year? Five years?"

Bannor gazed at her, his face more haunted than she had ever seen it. After a moment, he withdrew his hand from her cheek and bowed his head. "I have yet to swear an oath that I could not keep."

Willow pressed her cheek to the bedpost, no longer able to hide the tears that were trickling down it. "Then I am afraid I shall have to claim the freedom you so generously offered me."

Bannor jerked up his head, anger sparking in his eyes. "And where will you go, my lady? Will you return to your father's household?" He took her hands, forcing her fists open. He stroked the calluses that still scarred her palms with his powerful thumbs. It would take more than a few weeks of leisure to erase a lifetime of toil. "Is being treated as less than the lowliest of servants preferable to being my wife?"

Willow tried to twist out of his grasp, but he held her fast. "I don't have to return to Bedlington. Was it not you who suggested I seek shelter in a convent?"

Bannor's harsh laugh held little humor. "And you accused me of trying to lock you away so you could die a dried-up old virgin." He cupped her face in his hands, his hungry eyes searching her face. "Is that what you want, Willow? To lie awake on a hard, narrow cot every night, dreaming of me? Dreaming of this?"

Had he seized her lips as roughly as he had seized her hands, she might have been able to resist him. But his mouth closed over hers with such unspeakable tenderness, she feared she might already be dreaming. A kiss so enchanting should have broken every curse, granted every wish, given even the saddest story a happy ending. As he explored the moist warmth of her mouth with his tongue, Willow knew she would not die a dried-up old virgin. When she lay upon her hard, narrow cot in the convent, gazing out the window at the falling snow and dreaming of this moment, her body would weep for him just as it was weeping now.

Bannor wrapped his arms around her, crushing his beard-shadowed cheek to the softness of her curls. "Stay with me, Willow," he said hoarsely. "Be my wife. You'll lack for naught, I swear it."

Even as she clung to his waist as if she would never let him go, Willow knew she had no choice but to leave him. If she stayed, she would lack the one thing she could not live without.

Her pride.

She gazed up at him through a veil of tears. "If you have no use for my heart, my lord, then I have no choice but to offer it to God. Will you grant me my freedom, or will you keep me here as your wife against my will?"

Willow had never felt as cold as she did in that moment when Bannor lowered his arms and stepped away from her. His motions were heavy, his face grave. "I told you before that I've never sworn an oath I could not keep. If 'tis your freedom I promised you, then 'tis your freedom you shall have. Hollis will escort you to Wayborne Abbey in the morning. Since our union has never been consummated, an annulment should not be difficult to obtain." Bannor started for the door, then turned back, no longer able keep the bitter note from his voice. "I'd appreciate it if you could be gone before the children awaken. I'd prefer to spare them the pain of bidding a third mother farewell."

When he was gone, Willow staggered to the window and pressed her brow to the icy glass. Fresh tears scalded her eyes. She wanted to hate him, but the only contempt she felt was for herself. She had fled Bedlington hoping to escape the ghost of the pathetic little girl she had been, yet it was her tear-streaked reflection that gazed back at Willow from the window.

She was the same little girl who had surrendered her father to Blanche without a fight. And now that she had finally found a man who just might be worth marching into battle for, she was conceding defeat without ever bothering to take up her arms.

Willow furiously swiped the tears from her cheeks,

watching the reflection of that girl disappear. A woman gazed back at her, her gray eyes burning with resolve.

Determined to seek out the one person who might be able to show her the face of the enemy, Willow jerked on her kirtle and shoes, snatched up her cloak, and strode from the chamber.

"Who is she?"

Netta's eyes flew open as the lady of Elsinore burst into her cottage, shedding feathers of snow like some molting angel of wrath. Netta peered over the brawny shoulder of the drunken knight moving between her legs, reluctantly admiring Willow's aplomb. Bannor's lady didn't blush or stammer at the sight of the young man's naked backside, which continued to plunge up and down with far more enthusiasm than rhythm.

"Who is she?" Willow repeated, as if the two of them were all alone in the firelit cottage.

Netta punched the knight in the arm. "Get off me, you oaf. We've got company."

"But I'm not done," he whined, his eyes still squeezed tightly shut. "I've paid my coin. The next fellow can wait his turn."

" 'Tis not a fellow, but a lady, you jackass," she hissed in his ear.

Groaning, he rolled off of her. Netta hastily jerked the sheet up to his waist, hoping to spare Willow from seeing anything more unsightly than she already had. She had only to draw her own skirt down over her legs, since she hadn't deemed the callow dolt worth the trouble of removing it.

The knight squinted at the intruder, his aspect

brightening as his eyes devoured her slender form. "And what have we here? A little lost lamb seeking a shepherd?"

"Get out," Willow commanded, her tone icier than the wind whistling down the chimney.

He splayed his arms behind his head, an arrogant smile quirking his lips. "Don't be so hasty, sweeting. I can assure you that my staff is vigorous enough to pleasure the both of you."

Netta snorted. " 'Tis barely vigorous enough to pleasure the one of us."

Willow recognized him as the cocky young knight who had praised the thrust of Bannor's lance. With deliberate malice, she reached up and drew back her hood.

The knight's eyes widened in horror. He jerked the blanket up to his chin, quivering so hard the entire bedstead began to rattle. "M-m-my lady, please forgive me. I had no inkling 'twas you."

She pointed toward the door. "Out."

He shot Netta a helpless look, then scrambled out of the bed, clutching the sheet to his privates. He was so busy bowing and fawning he could barely hop up and down on one foot long enough to don his hose.

"You won't tell Lord Bannor about this, will you?" he pleaded. "He'll have my head for sure."

Willow smiled sweetly. "Considering the amorous nature of your proposal, sir, I doubt 'twill be your head he seeks to sever."

Muttering beneath his breath, the knight snatched up his sword and spurs and fled into the snowy night, slamming the door behind him.

Willow whirled around to face Netta, in no mood to

mince words. "How do you bear it? I can't imagine allowing anyone but the man I love to touch me that way."

"Not all of us can afford to be so finicky, my lady." Netta shrugged as she tucked her generous breasts back into her bodice and jerked the laces tight. "Besides, once you've had a dozen men, what difference does one more make? Or a hundred more?" She lifted her eyes to Willow's. "At least that's what my mother told me, to comfort me after she sold me for the first time. She was so relieved not to have to service an entire regiment of the king's guard all by herself that she let me keep one of the shillings I had earned."

Desperate to escape the woman's uncompromising gaze, Willow jerked off her cloak and tossed it across the stool in front of the hearth. "I suppose you've already heard what happened at Elsinore tonight."

Netta waved a hand at the door. "When Sir Lacklance came bursting in, he was babbling all about it. Although I fail to see why the arrival of another bastard on Lord Bannor's doorstep should rouse such excitement. 'Tis a common enough occurrence, is it not?"

Willow stiffened. Netta seemed to be deliberately baiting her. "I want to know who the mother of that child is. I want to know who they all are."

Shaking back her tousled mane, Netta gave her a sloe-eyed glance. "And what then, my fine lady? Will you have them tarred and feathered? Driven from the village? Stoned?"

Willow lifted her chin. "I might."

"And if I refuse to tell you? Will you do the same to me?"

"No." Before Netta's mocking smile could spread, Willow added flatly, "I'll have you cast into Elsinore's dungeon until you decide to use that caustic tongue of yours for something more useful than pleasuring Bannor's men."

Netta tilted her head to the side, eyeing Willow the way a mastiff might eye a harmless-looking kitten who has just raked bloody furrows across its nose. When she rose from the bed, her smile was more bemused than mocking.

"Sit, my lady," she said, pouring a stream of ale into a chipped earthenware cup and thrusting it into Willow's hand, "and I shall tell you everything you seek to know about this woman who holds your husband's heart in thrall."

Feeling her own heart falter at Netta's words, Willow sank down on the stool. Although she rarely drank anything stronger than mulled wine, she took a hearty gulp of the ale, welcoming its fortifying warmth.

Netta perched on the edge of the bed, sipping directly from the flagon. "She first came to Elsinore on a snowy night much like this one. The wind was whistling down from the mountains, cold enough to freeze a man's spit before it hit the ground. 'Twas Twelfth Night, and even from a distance she could hear the sounds of music and merriment drifting over the castle walls. She clutched her little boy's hand, terrified, yet knowing if she couldn't find the courage to storm that mighty fortress, he would die. She'd already been forced to peddle her flesh to keep bread in his mouth, but now that flesh was wasting away because she'd been giving him her portion of their food."

Netta's eyes grew distant. "A hush fell when they led her into the great hall. The lord of the castle presided over the high table, flanked by his beautiful wife and his handsome children. She drew her son in front of her. Swallowing the last of her pride, she whispered, 'He is yours, m'lord. I pray you will welcome him into your household and your heart.'

"The lord looked the boy up and down. Although he couldn't have been more than six or seven, he planted his little legs and boldly met the gaze of the man he had been told was his father.

"The lord reached down to rumple his hair, then boomed out a hearty laugh. 'Why would I want to claim the bastard of a whore' he inquired of the hall, 'when I have all of these fine children of my own?'"

Willow set aside the cup of ale, unable to urge another sip past her chattering teeth.

"At their master's signal, his men-at-arms seized her and dragged her from the hall. They hurled her and her child into the snow outside the castle gates, laughing and taunting her all the while. Too shamed to seek shelter in one of the nearby cottages, she snatched up her child and began trudging across the meadows. She thought only to return to her own village, but the wind whipped snow into her eyes, causing her to roam in ever widening circles. She believed if she could just sit down and rest her trembling legs for a little while, she would surely find the strength to go on. Hugging her son to her breast, she sank to her knees in the snow."

Netta fixed her gaze on Willow, her eyes as bleak as that snowswept vista. "The lad was strong and sturdy. She was not. When they found them the next morning, he was still clinging to her, crying so hard they swore he'd tried to melt the ice from her stiff, frozen body with his tears. It took three men to drag him away from her."

Willow surged to her feet, tears streaming openly down her own cheeks. "You're lying! I know Bannor. I know what manner of man he is. He would never be so cruel and heartless as to cast a woman and her child out into a blizzard!"

Netta's eyes blazed. "Of course he wouldn't, you little fool. But his father would."

Willow sank back down on the stool, her knees betraying her. *What would you have had me do? Toss the child back into the snow?* Bannor had asked her, his eyes smoldering with primal fury.

Those same eyes had watched his mother die. Had wept scorching tears of anguish over her icy corpse. Had shone with compassion as he stroked his finger over the palm of the tiny, half-frozen creature given into his care this night.

A helpless wave of emotion broke over her. "The babies?" she whispered, lifting her tear-streaked face to Netta. "They're not his, are they?"

"No," Netta said flatly. "They're mine."

Twenty-five

Netta came to her feet, her eyes glinting with stubborn pride. "I can't claim the youngest two, but Meg, the twins, the babe you brought to the cottage with you that morning—all mine."

Willow was staggered by the memory of Netta cradling Peg in her arms—the tenderness in her touch, the wonder in her eyes. She had never dreamed the woman was gazing into the face of her own daughter.

As Netta's words sank into her dazed mind, she frowned. "If Mags and the baby left at the castle gates tonight aren't yours, then who do they belong to?"

"The one you call Mags belongs to a woman who already has twelve mouths to feed. The other babe was born this night to a girl of twelve, who believed the honeyed lies of a handsome young troubadour who passed through the village nine months ago."

Willow shook her head. "I don't understand how they could just abandon their babies."

"*Abandon?*" Netta all but spat the word. "Annie's father threatened to drown her baby in a bucket if she didn't rid herself of it. She was so weak from giving birth that she would have had to crawl to reach the castle gates. But crawl she would have, had I not promised to deliver the baby to Lord Bannor myself." Netta paced to the hearth, then whirled around, her skirts snapping. "What fate would you choose for your child, my lady? To have her raised as I was, as the daughter of the village whore?" She flung a finger toward the rumpled bed with its stained sheets and musky odor. "To have every man in the village expect her to take your place in that bed when you grew too old or eaten up with pox to endure their fumbling and grunting?" Her voice softened. "Or to have her raised as the cherished child of a lord, lacking for naught except a mother's love?"

Willow bowed her head, deeply shamed. "Why didn't he tell me?" she whispered. "Why did he let me believe the worst of him?"

"Because he swore to me that no one would ever know those babes were not his. I made him promise that they would never have to endure the stares, the ugly whispers, the shame of being the misbegotten bastards of a whore."

Willow didn't know whether to laugh or cry. To protect the children entrusted into his hands, Bannor had been willing to let her believe he was naught but a rutting stallion, eager to mount every mare whose scent drifted to his nostrils. He had been willing to let her leave Elsinore with Sir Hollis on this very morn, never to return.

She laughed softly, but with a trace of bitterness. "He warned me that he has never sworn an oath he could not keep."

"Aye," Netta agreed, sinking down on the edge of the hearth. "He is a man of his word. When I left the first babe outside of his gates one chill November eve, I never dreamed he would claim her as his own. I could only pray that one of the laundresses or maidservants might take her in." She shivered. "When two of his men-at-arms appeared on my doorstep the next day to escort me to him, I was terrified he was going to have me cast into the dungeon, or perhaps imprisoned in the stocks, so that everyone would know the dreadful thing I had done."

Willow almost smiled, remembering how reluctant Bannor had been to so much as spank his rebellious son.

"I was trembling like a leaf when they brought me before him." Although Willow would have sworn it was impossible, a becoming blush crept into the woman's cheeks as she bowed her head. "When he dismissed his guards and turned away to pour a goblet of mead, I began to disrobe, thinking that he meant for me to trade my favors in exchange for his mercy."

Willow arched one eyebrow. "That must have been quite a shock for him."

"Oh, it was," Netta assured her. "At first I thought he was going to bolt from the chamber. But then he realized my knees were knocking with fright. He jerked a tapestry down from the wall, wrapped it around me, and bade me to sit in a chair by the fire before I collapsed. 'Twas then that he told me about his mother, and promised me that no child would ever be turned away from the gates of Elsinore, not so long as he was lord there."

Willow recognized the fierce glow in Netta's eyes. She had seen it in the eyes of her own reflection only a short while ago.

"Why, you're half in love with him, aren't you?" Willow regretted the words almost immediately, sensing that nothing else she could have said would have so cut Netta to the quick.

Netta's lips tipped in a rueful smile. She did not bother to blink back her tears. "How could I not be, my lady?"

"Aye," Willow murmured, reaching out to clasp the woman's rawboned hand. "How could you not be?"

Willow slipped through the darkened passages of Elsinore. 'Twas not yet dawn, and the castle was silent except for the whisper of her cloak against the flagstones. 'Twas almost as if its inhabitants had fallen beneath the same enchanted hush as the snow-glazed world beyond the windows.

As she traversed the second level, a half-ajar door beckoned her forward.

A peculiar pang seized her heart when she saw that Bannor's children had reverted to their old habit of sharing the same immense bed. In truth, she could not blame them on a morning as cold as this. The fire had dwindled to glowing embers, and she could see the ghost of her sigh drifting in the air. Desmond's crow dozed on a perch near the window, his head tucked into his sleek breast. His yellow tomcat was curled up at the foot of the bed. As Willow drew nearer, the cat opened his one golden eye and blinked at her.

A tousled flaxen head rested next to Desmond's chestnut one. After being banished from her own bed,

Beatrix must have sought sanctuary in theirs. Willow wondered what Desmond would do when he awoke to find the girl nestled against his back, naked except for a fur pelt. She smiled. He'd be lucky if the shock of it didn't cause him to tumble out of the bed and crack his noggin.

When she'd first arrived at Elsinore, she'd seen the children as naught but a passel of faceless brats, but as she traced their slumbering faces with her gaze, she realized she had come to know them in a way she had never known her own brothers and sisters.

Gangly Ennis, who strove to be the voice of reason; sober little Mary with her amusing habit of always looking at the glum side of things; generous, sweet-natured Hammish; chattering Edward; Kell with his sunny hair and sarcastic quips; strong-willed Mary Margaret; Meg and the twins, looking like a litter of cherubs with their plump limbs and dimpled cheeks.

And Desmond—still a boy, yet poised on the brink of manhood, revealing more of his father than he knew in his fierce protectiveness toward his brothers and sisters and his kindness to animals that no one else wanted.

Willow might have drifted right past the nursery had it not been for Fiona's rattling snores. The old woman was curled up on a narrow bedstead at the foot of a wooden cradle. Peg and Mags slept side by side in the cradle, bundled up like a pair of fat, woolly lambs. Willow touched both of their downy cheeks with her fingertip before turning to go.

She was almost to the door when she heard a soft sound—not quite a whimper, not quite a coo. She slowly turned. A wicker basket rested on the hearth. She knelt to find the newborn baby nestled within. A baby who would soon grow into a sturdy little boy. A boy who would never lack for bread or have to sit shivering in the snow and watch his mother draw her last breath.

Seized by a strange urgency, Willow tucked the blanket around the baby and slipped from the chamber. As soon as she was out of earshot of the nursery, she broke into a run. She raced up the stairs and threw open the door of Bannor's tower without bothering to knock. The chamber was deserted, the grate cold. The feather mattress bore no imprint of his body. A goblet was overturned on the hearth, as if someone had flung it there in a fit of anger.

Willow flew down the stairs to the great hall. Although the yeasty aroma of baking bread was beginning to drift out from the kitchens, most of the stragglers who had sought shelter from the snowstorm were still sleeping off the effects of the ale that had been served after Lord Bannor had welcomed his new son into his household. When Willow tripped over one of the tumblers, he simply mumbled an oath and snuggled deeper into his cloak.

Bursting into the deserted bailey, she spun around, at an utter loss. The sun drifted over the eastern horizon at that moment, striking the snow with a force that nearly blinded her. It wasn't until Willow shaded her eyes against the dazzling glare that she spotted the lone man standing between the merlons of the battlement high above her, his dark hair whipping in the wind.

By the time Willow reached the wall walk, she had managed to steady her breathing, but not the hammering of her heart.

Bannor stood gazing across the snowswept meadows, his hands resting on the stone embrasure between the merlons. He did not turn, not even when he heard the crunch of her slippers against the crust of snow. "Did it never occur to you, my lady," he asked, his voice as hard as the glittering crystals of ice that laced the scattered trees, "that I might also seek to spare myself the pain of bidding a third wife farewell?"

Despite the chill in Bannor's voice, his words warmed her. He had never before addressed her as his wife. "Did it never occur to you, my lord, that I might seek to spare you that pain as well?"

"Quite frankly, it did not."

"I just came from the nursery." She dared to draw nearer despite his lack of welcome. "Your new son is pinking up nicely. I dare say that, thanks to your kindness, he'll be battling wee Mags for a teat before the day is over."

"I'm pleased that the babe will survive, but I'm in no mood to be lauded for my generosity. Not when the cost of it is so high."

Willow kicked at the snow with the toe of her slipper, keeping her voice deliberately light. "Oh, I haven't come to praise you for your charity, but to chastise you for your pride."

He snorted. " 'Tis the second time I've been accused of such a sin in as many days. Have you been talking to Desmond?"

"No, I've been talking to a friend." Willow was thankful he could not see the wry twist of her lips. "One who is more devoted than you realize."

"Devoted enough to brand me an arrogant fool, it seems."

"Arrogant perhaps, but not a fool." She paced behind him, expelling a mocking sigh. "If I were a mighty warrior, so feared that my name was spoken only in whispers by my enemies, I might also prefer that everyone believe my seed was as potent as my sword. 'Twould no doubt damage your ferocious reputation if word got out that you were so tender of heart, you couldn't bear to turn a child away from your gates." She stood on tiptoe to whisper in his ear. "Even one you did not sire."

Bannor relinquished his white-knuckled grip on the stone, and slowly turned to face her. "Idle gossip, my lady, coaxed from the treacherous throat of someone who is surely not a friend, but a foe."

Despite the intensity of his gaze, Willow refused to retreat. "And is it also idle gossip that a woman died in a meadow not far from here? That she froze to death after your father branded her a whore, and ordered his men to cast both her and her innocent child out into a blizzard?"

If not for the rhythmic twitching of the muscle in his jaw, Bannor might have been carved from ice himself. "That child was no innocent, my lady. He had already spent countless nights huddled in the cold outside the door of his mother's cottage, while she took a succession of grunting, stinking strangers to her bed. Even though it made him gag, he had learned to choke down every bite of moldy bread she gave him, knowing just how much it had cost her."

Bannor turned back to the battlement, his profile as harsh as the snow-capped crags of the distant mountains. "When she died, I swore that all of this would one day be mine. I only wish my father could have lived long enough to see that day come."

Willow stroked his rigid forearm. "Perhaps if he

had, you wouldn't have been waging war against him all these years. Tell me, Bannor, have you ever slain a foe who did not wear his leering face?"

Bannor's dry chuckle held no humor at all. " 'Tis not his face that haunts me, but hers. She is the one I cannot forgive."

Willow knew then that as terrible as the story had been, Netta had spared her the worst of it. "She loved him, didn't she?" she asked in a choked whisper.

"She adored him. She was only fifteen when he seduced her, and she never stopped believing that he'd come back for her someday. Never accepted that he had a girl just like her in every village within a hundred leagues of Elsinore." The bitterness in his voice ripened. "She used to tell me what a fine man my father was. How generous! How kind! How noble! When she was forced to take up whoring, she wept not because she had sold her body and soul for a crust of bread, but because she feared she would no longer be worthy of him." Bannor flashed Willow a look that was both entreaty and warning. "Her love was a sickness of the heart. And in the end, it killed her."

With a sinking sensation in the pit of her stomach, Willow realized that the deadly weapons he had collected through the years, the gleaming shields that adorned his walls, had all been painstakingly chosen to make him invulnerable to the poisoned arrow that had felled his mother. He had spent the years since she died armoring his own heart against every threat.

Including her.

It was Willow's turn to clutch the embrasure, to gaze out over the barren beauty of the snow-shrouded meadows while the wind whipped her unbound curls from her stinging eyes. "I can certainly understand why you want no more children of your own," she said softly. "If word continues to spread that the mighty lord of Elsinore will claim any babe left on his doorstep, we'll soon be overrun with the little imps."

"We?" Bannor echoed softly, as if afraid he had misheard her.

She could feel him behind her, his warmth as palpable as a caress. She had not realized how cold she was until that moment. Once Willow had been arrogant enough to pity Bannor's first two wives for contenting themselves with less than his love. Now she felt only a strange kinship with them.

She swung around to face him, her chin steady, her eyes dry. "You're a man of your word, Bannor of Elsinore. You're not given to uncontrollable rages, strong drink, or blasphemy. A woman can ask no more than that of her husband. If you have naught but crumbs of affection to offer me, then I shall make do as I always have."

"Is that all you think I have to offer you? *Crumbs?*" Bannor lifted his hand to her cheek, his eyes darkening with a fierce hunger of their own. "On the contrary, my lady. If you dine at my table, I can promise you a banquet sweeter than any you've ever imagined."

Willow held her breath as his mouth descended on hers. His warm, rough tongue dipped into her mouth, offering her not just a sip of ambrosia, but a taste of heaven itself. She curled her hand around his nape, clinging helplessly as he swept her up into his arms.

Bannor's mouth never left hers. Not when he carried her down the narrow flight of stairs that led to her tower. Not when he blindly kicked the door shut behind them. Not when he lowered her to her feet, unfastened the catch of her cloak, and shoved it from her shoulders. Only when he fisted his hands in her kirtle and began to draw it over her head was he forced to surrender her lips. He did so with the most heartfelt of groans.

Willow should have been shivering in her thin chemise, but it seemed both of them were immune to the chill in the fireless chamber. As Bannor bore her back against the bedpost, his powerful body trembled all over, burning with the same fever that threatened to consume her.

"I can't bear it when you cry," he muttered, seeking to kiss the tearstains from her cheeks.

"Not even when I'm weeping for your touch?" Willow murmured against his ear, seized by a spirit of boldness.

Not even in her boldest fantasy would Willow have dared to imagine that Bannor would drop to his knees at her feet, ease up her chemise, and seek a taste of those pearly tears. She gasped as he used his broad thumbs to part the softness of her nether curls, exposing her to the silken wonder of his tongue.

Her first instinct was to clench her thighs together, to prevent the both of them from committing a sin so deliciously shocking it must surely be mortal.

Bannor pressed his stubbled cheek to the pale cream of her thigh, his voice raw with longing. "Please, Willow ..."

Willow knew he was not a man to beg. Nor a man to kneel before anyone but his king. But he was willing to humble himself so he might exalt her. By generously granting her such sway over him, he rendered her powerless to deny him anything. Stroking her fingers through his hair, she allowed him to coax her thighs apart, then pressed her eyes shut, too shy to bear the primal beauty of his dark head between her legs.

As Bannor took his first sip from her brimming chalice, Willow was seized by a pleasure so piercing she feared she might swoon. She fisted her hands in his hair, whimpering his name with her every breath. He cupped her naked bottom in his palms, making it clear that she could beg and writhe all she wanted, but to no avail. With the rigid bedpost at her back and his hot mouth pressed against her, there was no escaping the unholy rapture of his kiss.

His tongue flickered over her, probing the delicate shell of her flesh as if to seek a priceless treasure. When he finally found the glistening pearl tucked within, he suckled it until her head rolled back and her knees crumpled. His fingers dug into the soft flesh of her buttocks as shudder after shudder of raw ecstasy wracked her.

When they subsided, Willow could only collapse over his shoulder, clinging as if to keep from drowning in a fathomless sea. Their sin had indeed proved mortal. She had died in his arms, and he had stolen her soul as surely as he had stolen her heart.

"Not enough, sweeting," Bannor whispered fiercely against her quivering belly. "Not this time. This time I promised you more."

Rising, he drew off her chemise and heaved her back on the feather mattress, then dragged his shirt over his head, his expression as relentless as if he was preparing to march into battle. Willow reached for him with both hands, unable to resist the primitive allure of his battle-scarred chest. Kicking off his boots, he fell on her like a starving man, devouring her lips, her throat, her throbbing nipples. Before she could catch her breath, his fingers were sifting through the damp curls at the juncture of her thighs, gliding through the warm honey his tongue had melted from her womanhood.

He dipped his longest finger in and out of that virgin hollow, causing exquisite shivers of anticipation to wrack her womb. Without even realizing it, Willow began to arch her hips in a rhythm as old as time itself, inviting him to go deeper, entreating him to be rougher, panting with a need she could barely comprehend.

But Bannor seemed to know exactly what she needed. Even as he was kissing her mouth with a sinuous tenderness that made her want to weep, he was joining another finger to the first. He pressed them both deep within her, then began to circle that throbbing pearl with the callused pad of his thumb. A broken sob escaped her as the pleasure crested without warning, leaving her limp with delight, yet strangely unfulfilled.

She opened her misty eyes to find Bannor resting on his back beside her, with one arm flung over his eyes. "Bannor?" she whispered.

He grunted a reply, but did not lower his arm.

Willow rolled to her side and began to stroke his chest, thinking how curious it was to be naked while he was still half-clothed, yet feel no hint of shyness. "I know how you hate these frank discussions, but if we're to stay wed and don't want any more children, perhaps you'd best share how you kept all the women who weren't your wives from breeding."

" 'Twas never a concern. I wasn't willing to risk scattering a bunch of bastards like myself about the countryside. I didn't want some son or daughter I'd never met to grow up despising me."

Willow's hand froze in its motion. "Do you mean to tell me that when you wed Mary, you were a—"

Bannor lowered his arm to glare at her. "If you laugh, I shall petition the church for that annulment. *After* I strangle you."

But Willow's smile was one of bemused wonder. "And in the years since Margaret died, you've never ... ?"

"Not even once. Although God knows I've wanted to." His glare deepened to a full-blown scowl. "Never more than the first time I laid eyes on you, my lady."

Willow's heart melted at his reluctant confession. Her hand skated down his abdomen, making his taut flesh ripple in reaction. "Netta told me of another trick we might try."

He cocked an eyebrow at her. "Do you really think 'twould be wise to heed the advice of a woman who has had four children?"

She leaned over and whispered something in his ear. He lay utterly still for a moment, then sprang to his knees and began to work at a stubborn knot in the drawstring of his hose.

Willow was somewhat unnerved by his sudden burst of enthusiasm. "Of course, I should warn you that Netta said there was only one sure way for a woman to keep from getting with child."

"And that would be?" Bannor gave the hapless drawstring a savage tug that snapped it in two.

As the hose slid from his hips, Willow blushed and turned her face away, suffering a latent pang of shyness. "Swear a vow of chastity."

Bannor hurled his hose into a far corner and seized Willow's face in the cup of his hands. "I'll leave it up to you, sweeting. Will it be chastity?" He lowered himself on top of her, settling his weight between her splayed thighs. "Or me?"

"You," Willow whispered, mesmerized by the wicked sparkle in his heavy-lidded eyes.

She was still gazing into those eyes when Bannor buried himself deep inside of her. He had promised to serve her a banquet sweeter than any she had ever known, but he'd failed to warn her it would be so filling. As her body struggled to contain him, a hoarse moan—half pleasure and half pain—spilled from her throat. The pain was sharp and fleeting, but the pleasure seemed to go on and on, pulsing in time with each shuddering beat of her heart.

Kissing away the tears that had sprung unbidden to her eyes, Bannor began to glide in and out of her, stroking her honeyed sheath with such paralyzing tenderness that his absence soon became more painful than his presence. He was so much bigger than she was, so much stronger. Yet she sensed he was holding his lust in check, much as he had held his bloodlust in check when he had feared harming his children.

She clung to his powerful shoulders and turned her head from side to side, gasping for breath. "Bannor, please . . . oh, sweet heaven, please . . ."

He mistook her whimper as a plea for freedom. When he began to roll off of her, Willow wrapped her legs around his waist and rolled with him, impaling herself on the full measure of his manhood. Bannor collapsed against the mattress, groaning as if it had been he, and not she, who had been struck the mortal blow.

Willow shook her hair out of her eyes, marveling that she could contain such power and passion within her fragile body. Her exultation swelled as she watched the flickers of rapture dance across the rugged beauty of Bannor's features with each rise and fall of her hips. He closed his hands around her waist and arched against her, urging her to take more of him when she would have sworn she'd already taken all she could hold.

Still clutching her waist, he rolled again, imprisoning her beneath him. A thrill of raw delight coursed through her veins as his hips increased their tempo. His tongue swept through her mouth, wordlessly promising that this time he would hold nothing back. He would grant her no mercy and no reprieve until she'd surrendered the last shred of her self-control to his tender mastery.

Willow had no choice but to do just that, as he angled his hips, deliberately rubbing his rigid length against that live ember buried at the crux of her curls. A scarlet haze descended over her eyes as the world burst into flames. As her womb convulsed in an agony of pleasure, Bannor's own massive body began to shudder.

Willow could not help but reach for him as he tore himself from her, spilling his seed against the softness of her belly with a mighty roar.

Twenty-six

Sir Hollis was haggling over the price of a barrel of wine with a traveling tinker when his master's roar resounded through the castle. He might not have started so violently, had Bannor not been bellowing *his* name. Muttering an excuse to escape from the bandy-legged little man, Hollis began to back out of the buttery. As soon as he rounded the corner, he forsook the dignity of his position and went flying up the stairs to the north tower, fearing the worst. The last time his lord had summoned him in such an earsplitting manner, he had found Bannor barricaded in the tower, cursing the treaty with France and bemoaning the fact that he was being held hostage by his own offspring.

This time the tower door had been flung wide open, spilling a puddle of golden sunshine onto the landing. As Hollis came stumbling into the chamber, Bannor swung away from the unshuttered window, giving him a bemused look.

"You bellowed, my lord?" Hollis inquired, still gasping for breath.

"There was no need for you to make such haste. The tower wasn't afire, and neither was my beard." Bannor stroked the fresh growth that darkened his jaw.

Feeling a trifle bit foolish, Hollis gave his doublet a tug to straighten it and joined Bannor at the window. "Old habits die hard, my lord. How was I to know I wouldn't find you with a French dagger at your throat or with Mary Margaret bouncing up and down on your chest?"

Bannor chuckled. "Once I would have preferred the former to the latter, but now I'm not so sure."

A gleeful shriek wafted up from the courtyard, making him grin instead of wince. The day was uncommonly cold, but sunny, and after nearly two months of snowfall, relieved only by fitful spells of icy rain, the children had streamed out of the castle like a horde of eager honeybees bursting from their hive.

They were currently engaged in a rousing game of hot cockles. When Ennis asked for a new volunteer, Hammish thrust his hand into the air, bouncing up and down in his eagerness to be chosen. After he had donned a coarse linen hood, the children took turns hitting him over the head and urging him to identify his assailant. Since their halfhearted blows only made the lad giggle hysterically, they soon grew winded and bored.

'Twas Desmond who suggested a round of hood-man blind. A reluctant Bea was coaxed into being the first one to wear the hood this time. Blinded by its thick folds, she groped at the air while the rest of the children danced just out of her reach.

Bannor shook his head. "I still don't understand why Willow favors that little maidservant of hers. I've yet to see the wench do an honest lick of work."

As they watched, Desmond seized one of the fat flaxen braids protruding from beneath the hood and gave it a playful yank.

Bea snatched off the hood and whirled on him, her blue eyes pools of outrage. As he sprinted out of the bailey, casting a taunt over his shoulder, she snatched up her skirts and gave chase. With her braids flying out behind her, she looked like the little girl she was, instead of the woman she pretended to be.

"As long as the lad's legs are getting, she'll never catch him," Hollis predicted.

"Oh, she'll catch him," Bannor said, a wry grin playing around his mouth. "He'll see to that, I'll wager."

While Bannor watched them pelt through the list and disappear into the barn, Hollis's gaze was drawn to an iron gate in the far corner of the bailey. A woman had just emerged from the herb garden with chubby little Peg balanced on her hip. The baby's questing fingers tangled in the tidy bun at her nape, causing her thick mane of honey brown hair to come tumbling around her shoulders. Instead of scolding the babe, she pressed a kiss to its rosy cheek, a smile transforming her own rawboned features.

Bannor followed the direction of Hollis's gaze. "She is a handsome woman, is she not?"

"And a stubborn one," Hollis said, refusing to acknowledge the speculative look Bannor slanted him.

"As well I know. In the beginning, she refused Wil-

low's invitation to come live at the castle and help
Fiona care for the children. She didn't relent until I
threatened to marry her off to the first man who would
take her."

Hollis prayed he wasn't blushing. "Fiona was a bit
jealous at first, was she not, to have another cat sniffing
around her litter?"

Bannor shrugged. "She sulked and pouted for a few
days, but it didn't take her long to realize Netta was just
another lost child for her to mother."

Netta wasn't the only lost child who had come beneath Bannor's protection in the past two months.
Thanks to Willow's prodding, young Annie, whose father had threatened to drown her newborn baby in a
bucket, had joined the hallowed ranks of the castle
maidservants. Her father had also received a personal
visit from the lord of the castle. The village gossips
swore it had taken the blacksmith over six hours to dislodge the man's fat head from his own privy bucket.

Hollis dragged his gaze away from Netta. "I doubt
you summoned me here to admire your children or
their new nursemaid, however fair."

Bannor clamped a hand on his shoulder and steered
him toward the table. "You're quite right, Hollis. 'Tis
your keen wits I have need of. I want you to help me
plot the most important campaign of my career."

Once, Hollis might have felt a thrill of excitement at
Bannor's words. Now he felt only dismay. The solitary
life of a soldier no longer held the attraction for him
that it once did. "Have you received word from the
king? Has the peace faltered? Are we to join him in
France? If he has summoned you to his side, perhaps
'twould be best if I linger here at Elsinore. After all,

someone needs to tend to the castle and all of its business. I should hate to see it fall into disarray and neglect
again."

Unfazed by his steward's feverish urgency, Bannor
propelled him into a chair. "I don't want you to help me
make war, my friend, but to make merry."

"Merry?" Hollis repeated, hardly able to comprehend the word when it was all he could do not to bang
his head upon the table in despair.

"Aye. I want you to help me plan a wedding. A wedding the likes of which Elsinore has never seen before
and will never see again." A tender smile curved Bannor's lips. "I want to marry Willow."

Hollis shook his head, baffled. "But you've already
married Willow. I should know. I was there."

"Precisely. But I wasn't. This time, I want to stand before the priest myself and make my vows. I want to en-
dow her with all my worldly goods." Bannor's voice
and his gaze softened as he glanced toward the bed that
stayed rumpled more often than not, now that Willow
was sharing it with him. "I want to promise to worship
her with my body."

"A task you've no doubt already been giving your
most pious attention."

Ignoring Hollis's smirk, Bannor shoved a crisp sheet
of parchment at him. "We shall begin by penning an invitation to her family."

Hollis's amusement quickly shifted to disbelief.
"Have you taken leave of your senses, my lord? She
was naught to them but a piece of chattel, to be bartered
away to the highest bidder."

Bannor's face darkened. "That's precisely why I
want them here to witness her triumph. Why I intend

to make them grovel at her feet, as I take her to be my bride with all of the splendor and honor she deserves. Why, I can hardly wait to see the astonishment on her face when they arrive to pay homage to her."

Hollis swallowed. "Willow does not know of this invitation?"

Bannor looked nonplussed by the very suggestion. "Of course not. I want it to be a surprise. Just as the wedding itself will be."

Hollis nearly groaned aloud. "Do you really believe 'tis wise to stage a wedding without the bride's sanction?"

"What protest could she possibly have? We've been living as man and wife for over three months."

"I doubt that Willow will have any objections to having your union blessed twice. But it has been my personal experience that women prefer to believe they have a say in such matters, whether they do or not."

Bannor waved away his counsel. "No offense, my friend, but Willow has taught me more about women than I'd previously learned in my entire thirty-two years. Oh, I knew all there was to know about pleasuring a woman, but very little about pleasing one. I knew they were tender of flesh, but not so very tender of heart." A shadow of regret passed over his face. "If I had, I might have been a far better husband to Mary and Margaret."

"From what I witnessed, my lord, those two noble ladies, God rest their souls, had few complaints."

Bannor flashed him a grateful smile. "If I have anything to say about it, Willow will have none."

Hollis chuckled. "It does my heart good to see you behaving like a love-struck swain."

Bannor's smile faded. "Don't be ridiculous," he said stiffly. "I'm no love-struck swain, simply a man who appreciates the value of a good wife."

"And a good sword. And a good saddle. And a good piece of horseflesh," Hollis could not resist adding.

Bannor glowered at him. "And a steward who knows when to hold his tongue and mind his own affairs."

Wisely heeding the warning, Hollis devoted all of his attention to dipping a freshly sharpened quill into a flask of ink.

"We must make haste," Bannor said, pacing behind him. "We have no way of knowing how long this break in the weather will last."

As Bannor began to dictate, Hollis wished it was possible to capture the excoriating edge of sarcasm in his voice. It didn't take him long to finish with the pleasantries, or the pointed lack of them.

" 'Tis my great pleasure to invite you . . .' " Bannor paused, the gleam in his eye sharpening to a wicked glint, "No, change that to *command*. 'Tis my great pleasure to *command* you to attend the wedding of your cherished daughter a sennight hence . . .' "

"Desmond?" Beatrix whispered, slipping into the deserted barn.

The vexsome boy appeared to have vanished, leaving her all alone to wend her way through the shadows. Shafts of sunlight slanted through the cracks in the walls, gilding the dust motes that drifted through the air. With its towering rafters and steeply pitched ceiling, the barn possessed the hushed and holy ambiance of a cathedral. Beatrix shivered. She'd never much cared for churches. She had too many wicked thoughts, and despaired of ever atoning for them all.

"Desmond?" This time, her plaintive call was greeted by a muffled whicker and some halfhearted shuffling of hooves. Most of the horses and all the grooms were out taking advantage of the brief spell of sunshine. The scent of hay tickled her nose.

She choked back a sneeze, then froze. She would have almost sworn she heard a rustling in the loft above her head. She cocked her head to the side, but it did not come again. 'Twas probably naught but a mouse, she told herself firmly.

"Or a bat," she whispered, beginning to edge toward the door. Which was really naught but a mouse with razor-sharp fangs, poised to swoop down and tangle itself in one of her braids.

Spooked by the image, she whirled around to flee. From the corner of her eye she saw a great shadow descending upon her. A scream tore from her throat as the frightful creature wrapped its wings around her and tumbled her into a bristling mound of hay.

Beatrix was still screaming and beating at her hair when she realized the thing that had collapsed on top of her was not some behemoth of a bat, but Desmond. His entire body was quaking with laughter.

"Get off me, you horrid boy!" she yelled, struggling to wiggle out from underneath him.

Her squirming was to no avail. Once, she might have unseated him with little effort, but in the past two months, his shoulders seemed to have doubled in breadth, keeping pace with the length of his legs. If the wretched lad didn't stop growing soon, he'd be looking down his nose at her.

His moss green eyes sparkled with mischief. "I should

have just let you keep wandering around the barn, bleating like a lost sheep."

"I may have been bleating, but you're going to be
bleeding if you don't let me go." Beatrix caught his earlobe between her thumb and forefinger and twisted.

He gritted his teeth, but refused to budge. "Stop
pinching me, wench, or I swear I'll . . . I'll . . ." As he
struggled to come up with a threat vile enough to subdue her, his gaze lit upon her trembling lips. "Why, I'll
kiss you!"

Beatrix abruptly stopped struggling. "You wouldn't
dare."

Desmond cocked one eyebrow, looking even more
devilish than his father. "Oh, wouldn't I?"

Beatrix was unprepared for the blush that scorched
her cheeks.

So was Desmond. His mouth fell open, then snapped
shut. "You've never been kissed, have you?"

Taking advantage of the shock that had weakened
his grasp, Beatrix shoved him off of her and sat up,
brushing the hay from her apron with brisk motions.
"Don't be ridiculous. I've had scores of suitors and at
least a dozen proposals."

"But you haven't been kissed," he repeated, this
time with a smug certainty that made her want to box
his ears.

"Have too," she retorted, scrambling away from him.

"Have not." As her back came up against a bale of
hay, Desmond looped an arm around one knee and
shook his head, hooting with laughter. "Fancy that!
Sweet Bea struts around flaunting her cleavage, twitching her saucy little rump, and working the squires into
a fine lather, and she's never even been kissed."

A shriek of defeat escaped her. "Oh, all right! So I've never been kissed! Mock me if you must, but if anyone else ever finds out, especially Willow, I shall perish of shame. Why, I'll fling myself into the river, I swear I will!" She choked up a pathetic sniffle. "If you were a man of honor, you'd vow to tell no one."

Desmond gazed at her for a long moment. "You've never called me a man before. I rather like the sound of it on your lips." He ducked his head, a flush working its way from his bobbing Adam's apple to his squared jaw. "It occurs to me that I couldn't tell anyone you'd never been kissed"—he eyed her through the unruly hank of hair that had tumbled over his brow—"if you had."

If there had been even a hint of mischief in Desmond's eyes, Beatrix would have flung his bargain back in his face. But their crystalline depths were curiously somber, mirroring her own breathless uncertainty. She was too dazed to protest when he captured the flaxen rope of her braid, winding it around his fist to coax her nearer.

Her eyes fluttered shut. She wouldn't have been surprised had he sought to poke his tongue into her mouth, as her older sisters had warned her men were wont to do. But his lips simply grazed hers in a whisper-soft caress. The two of them lingered that way for as long as they dared, nothing touching but their mouths. Beatrix breathed deeply through her nose, amazed that even in the depths of winter, he could smell so much like sunshine.

When he finally drew away, it took her a moment to work up the courage to open her eyes. If he laughed, she decided, she would snatch up the pitchfork propped against the wall and stab him through the heart.

She opened her eyes. Desmond was smiling. It wasn't the mocking smirk she had feared, but a lopsided grin that tugged at her heart as inexorably as his hand had tugged at her braid.

"Since you wouldn't want anyone to know you've only been kissed once," he murmured, the husky note in his voice making her quiver, "I feel 'tis my duty, as a man of honor, to kiss you again."

"How very chivalrous of you, sir." Beatrix leaned forward, her full lips puckering in the seductive pout that had always come as naturally to her as breathing. Desmond's lips were only an uneven breath away from her own when she whispered, "But you'll have to catch me first."

Bursting into laughter, she sprang to her feet and darted for the barn door, her braid slipping through his fingers like cornsilk.

"Why, you treacherous little wench!" he shouted, bounding to his own feet. But as he cleared a bale of hay in a single leap and went racing after her, he was laughing nearly as heartily as she was.

Willow stood at a narrow arched window on the second level of the castle, blinking down in disbelief at the barren garden below. For the past five minutes, Desmond had been chasing Beatrix around and around a stone bench, his breathless demands for her surrender mingling with her shrieks of laughter. That didn't surprise Willow, since the two of them spent most of their waking hours at each other's throats.

The shock had come when Desmond had vaulted *over* the bench and wrapped his arms around Beatrix. Instead of boxing his ears, as Willow had expected her to do, Beatrix had ducked her head and cast him a shy glance utterly foreign to the bold little vixen.

Willow's mouth fell open as Desmond cupped Beatrix's chin in his hand and awkwardly tilted her face to his. The warm mist of their breath mingled as their lips met in a kiss so innocent and full of promise that Willow had to look away, her eyes stinging.

Ashamed of herself for spying upon their tender interlude, she silently drew the shutter closed. Surely she wasn't so petty as to still be suffering twinges of envy over her stepsister's good fortune! How could she begrudge Beatrix the devotion of a besotted lad, when she herself was among the most fortunate of women?

She had a home. She had a family. She no longer had to labor from dawn to dusk in a vain quest to please a mistress who could never be satisfied.

And she had Bannor.

As Willow leaned against the window embrasure, a tender smile softened her lips. Her husband was indeed a man of his word. He had promised her a banquet, and delivered nightly a feast of the senses. He eagerly sought new ways to pleasure her without getting her with child, each more delicious than the last.

Only last night he had challenged her to a chess game, in which they were each forced to surrender not only their captured pieces, but an item of clothing as well. Willow had won by forfeit, since the sight of her naked breasts licked by tongues of firelight had maddened Bannor to the point of distraction. Growling beneath his breath, he had swept the chessboard to the floor and lunged across the table at her. Willow had been unable to resist murmuring "Checkmate" in his ear as he lowered her to the wolfskin rug in front of the hearth.

It wasn't until she was curled up in the warm cocoon of his arms, listening to the oddly soothing rumble of his snores, that a faint melancholy had stolen over her. Bannor might be her prince, but he would never utter those three magical words that would transform her into his princess.

Willow was not so naive as to believe most marriages were built on a foundation of love. On the contrary, most were arranged when the parties were still too young to understand the meaning of the word. Her own papa certainly hadn't married Blanche for love, but for the generous dowry provided by the king.

But Willow could still remember the look on her papa's face when he had told her that he would never love any woman as he had loved her mama.

Shaking her head at her own folly, she turned away from the window. No matter how cherished Bannor made her feel, perhaps somewhere deep inside, she would always be that awkward little girl who had groped for her papa's hand, only to have him draw it out of her reach.

Twenty-seven

Sir Rufus's hands trembled as he uncorked the silver flask and brought it to his lips. The chariot chose that moment to buck its way through yet another jagged rut. Ale dribbled down his chin. Feeling more like an old man than ever before, he swiped it away, then took a deep draught from the flask.

The spicy-sweet brew settled heavily in his belly, but not even its agreeable warmth could take the strident edge off his wife's laughter or soften the smirk curving his stepson's lips. Blanche and Stefan had been whispering and giggling together for most of the journey, behaving more like lovers than mother and son.

There was no denying that his strapping blond stepson looked even more satisfied with himself than usual. He reclined on the padded seat next to Blanche, his long, muscular legs taking up more than their share of the chariot's scant room. As the wagon jolted through another rut, the lad's knee struck Rufus's gouty one with a thump that made Rufus wince.

"Sorry." Stefan flashed his teeth in a wolfish grin, looking less than penitent, then drew a scrap of parchment from the satin purse dangling from his belt and began to study it.

The vellum was yellowed and creased, as if it had been opened, read, then lovingly refolded, countless times. A dab of crimson wax still clung to its broken seal. Rufus craned his neck, but still couldn't make out the words formed by the smudged ink.

"Would you care for a cushion, dear?" Blanche inquired, blocking his view with one of the plump pillows she had embroidered with her own pale, graceful hands.

Rufus shifted his gaze to his wife. She was always so kind. So solicitous. So mindful of his comfort. Yet he couldn't quite banish the notion that she'd rather be pressing the pillow over his face.

"No, thank you," he said, leaning away from her. "We should reach the godforsaken castle soon enough. That is, if we're not buried alive by the blizzard that's coming." He drew back the velvet curtain and glared at the clouds brooding over the hostile crags. "Don't you find it rather odd that Lord Bannor would summon us in such a high-handed manner? After all, he's already wed Willow once. In my day, that was more than sufficient."

Stefan and Blanche blinked at him, looking like a pair of cats who had just shared a particularly tasty canary.

"Perhaps Lord Bannor simply seeks to give Willow the sort of wedding she deserves," Blanche ventured.

"That's what we all desire, isn't it?" Stefan murmured, tucking the parchment back into his purse. "To see Willow get what she deserves."

Unsettled by the hungry gleam in the lad's eyes, Rufus nodded toward Blanche. "At least 'twill give you the opportunity to fetch home that rebellious daughter of yours."

Stefan exchanged another enigmatic glance with his mother. "Beatrix might very well choose to remain at Elsinore. In her last missive, she assured me that Lord Bannor had taken quite a fancy to her."

" 'Tis fortunate we left the rest of the children at home," Rufus muttered. "He might have taken a fancy to them and decided to keep them as well."

His hands were still trembling when he let the curtain fall. He had no idea why the prospect of seeing his daughter again should make him quiver with both anticipation and foreboding.

He could still remember the last time he had seen her—standing before the priest in the chapel at Bedlington, pale and steadfast. Her voice had not faltered, not even when she had made her vows to a stranger who would soon hand her off to another stranger.

I'll not sell my only daughter!

And why not, Papa? 'Twouldn't be the first time, would it?

As he recalled her accusing words, Rufus's heart twisted with a painful mixture of anger and regret. The girl had no right to reproach him! He had always striven to do what was best for her, had he not? After all, everyone knew that a little girl needed a mother. It wouldn't have done to let her keep running through the castle and meadows that surrounded Bedlington like some wild, wee sprite.

And hadn't Blanche assured him that after giving birth to six children of her own, she knew just how to handle a headstrong little girl? Hadn't she promised to temper Willow's natural exuberance with maidenly restraint? Whenever Rufus had protested that Blanche might be being a bit too harsh on the child, had she not soothed him with her gentle words, her honeyed lips? How could he protest the heaviness of her hand against his child's flesh when it was wielded with such tender skill against his own? How could he protest the sharpness of the same tongue that wreaked such delicious havoc in the privacy of their bedchamber?

The sparkle might have faded from Willow's eyes and her bubbling laughter become naught more than a memory, but Blanche had assured him 'twas only the ransom the girl must pay for leaving behind the frivolous pleasures of childhood to seek the more satisfying joys of womanhood.

Rufus took another swig of the wine, grimacing to find it more bitter than sweet.

As the carriage rocked its way up a steep hill, Rufus settled deeper into his cloak. The wine might have failed to ease his foreboding or steady his hands, but it had cast a leaden net over his eyelids. He closed his eyes, dreaming that they had already arrived at Elsinore. Dreaming that he descended from the chariot with the sprightly step of the man he had been before the war and Blanche had robbed him of his pride. Dreaming that a little girl with bouncing dark curls and sparkling gray eyes came racing across the bailey to greet him, an adoring cry on her lips. As she flung herself into his arms and smothered his beard with kisses, he had to bury his face in her curls to hide his tears.

Willow raced through the bailey in desperate pursuit of the pig Mary Margaret had just liberated from the irate butcher's ax-wielding clutches.

"Ennis!" she shrieked. "He's coming your way!"

Laughter rippled from her throat as the creature darted between Ennis's gangly legs, then doubled back, in what Willow would have sworn was a deliberate charge, to knock first Margery, and then Colm, flat on their plump little backsides. Willow's laughter deepened to pained grunts as Mary raced over and began to climb her like a tree, in a frantic attempt to escape the beast's wrath.

As Edward and Kell closed in from opposite corners, the pig squealed in outrage. The boys dove for the animal at the precise same moment. They missed it entirely, knocking heads with a crack loud enough to make Willow wince.

As Hammish appeared in the doorway to the herb garden, the pig slowed to a trot. The boy crept forward, his cupped hand extended before him. "Here, piggy-piggy," he crooned. "I've a treat for you."

Mesmerized by the lad's singsong invitation, the pig snuffled once at the air, then buried his snout in Hammish's palm, rooting blissfully among the acorns he found there.

"Nice piggy," Hammish crooned, scratching behind the animal's bristly ears. "Sweet piggy."

"Tasty piggy," Ennis muttered, snorting in disgust as he tried to brush the mudstains from his breeches.

"Little does he know that Hammish is more likely to eat him than the butcher," Mary predicted from her perch atop Willow's shoulders.

"Do you really think Hammish would eat the butcher?" Edward asked, staggering to his feet.

"He would if he was hungry enough," Kell replied, rubbing his own head.

Mary Margaret chose that moment to flounce into

the courtyard like some sort of pygmy princess. "Oh, there you are, you naughty pig. I was wondering where you got off to." Looping a lavender ribbon around the animal's neck, she began to parade him around the courtyard, utterly oblivious to the chaos she had caused.

Willow dislodged the toe of Mary's slipper from her ear, and lowered the little girl to the ground. "There you go, dear. I do believe 'tis safe now."

As the child went scampering off to admire the newly docile pig, Willow examined the damage done to her kirtle. Muddy handprints and footprints stained the once plush purple wool of her skirt. Her damask bodice had fared little better. Its jeweled buttons had all been driven into the dirt when she'd fallen flat in a vain attempt to tackle the fleet-hooved pig. She lifted her hem to discover that her stockings were torn in several places and one of her shoes was missing.

Chuckling ruefully, Willow drew off her sash and used it as a kerchief to bind back her disheveled hair. If she was going to behave like a swineherd, she might as well look like one, too. As she went in search of her shoe, the icy bite of the wind whipped roses into her cheeks. If the black-edged underbellies of the clouds massing in the north were any indication, their reprieve from the snow might very well be coming to an end.

She crawled beneath a drummer's cart, but earned naught for her trouble but a fresh smudge of mud on her nose. When she emerged, Bannor and Hollis were striding toward her.

Bannor looked every inch the prince with his neatly trimmed beard, ivory hose, and doublet cut from sapphire blue wool. He was so handsome he took her breath away.

Unable to resist teasing him, Willow hitched up her

skirts in a mocking curtsy that revealed her shredded stockings, and wiggled the grubby toes of her shoeless foot at him in a most impudent manner. "Good day, my lord. Do you fancy my new attire?"

Bannor pressed a distracted kiss to her brow and murmured, " 'Tis most enchanting, my dear," before proceeding toward the gatehouse.

Willow dropped her skirts and gazed after him, baffled. He'd been behaving in a most peculiar manner all day—pacing the length of the great hall one moment, flinging himself into a chair to restlessly drum his fingers on its arm the next. Even now, his uneasy gaze kept darting between the winding road that led to the castle and the inky clouds brewing over the mountains. He didn't even seem to notice that his daughter was dragging a full-grown pig around the courtyard by a lavender ribbon.

At least Sir Hollis's glum demeanor was no mystery. Bannor's steward was no doubt still suffering from Netta's chilly rebuffs of his every overture. Despite the knight's engaging warmth toward her, the woman's frosty pride showed no sign of thawing.

"Stop following me, you wretched little boy, or I'll box your impertinent ears." Willow whirled around as Beatrix came marching out of the herb garden, clanging the gate shut behind her.

Desmond vaulted over it, landing gracefully on the balls of his feet. "I'd rather be a wretched little boy than a great haughty girl, with my prissy nose always stuck up in the air."

The two of them had been making an almost comical effort to keep up their pretense of despising each other. Their constant bickering was at such odds with the yearning glances they cast each other when they thought no one was looking that Willow could not resist laughing out loud. When Desmond went stalking off toward the other children in a mock huff, Willow began to limp toward her stepsister, intending to recruit her in the search for her shoe.

A majestic blast from a hunting horn froze Willow in her tracks. A wave of excitement rippled through the bailey. Visitors were a rare occurrence in the heart of winter. Especially visitors consequential enough to be announced by the lookout in the gatehouse watchtower.

Willow turned, squinting toward the road.

A single chariot was wending its way up the hill, accompanied not by a retinue of knights, but by three scruffy-looking men-at-arms who slouched low in their saddles.

Even from a distance, Willow could see the slivers of gilt peeling from the chariot's cream-colored wheels. The chariot wasn't drawn by six snowy white steeds, but by a team of mismatched cart horses. Yet the bells threaded through their bridles struck a discordant note in Willow's memory.

That off-key echo seemed to go on and on, deafening her to everything but the sound of Beatrix behind her, breathing out the one word guaranteed to send a jagged splinter of dread plunging through Willow's heart.

"Mama?"

With each revolution of the chariot's wheels, time seemed to roll backward, hurtling her into the past. As the chariot grew larger and larger, Willow could feel herself growing smaller and smaller. She almost wished she would just go on shrinking until she disappeared altogether.

Her gaze still riveted on the road, she touched a

hand to the dusty kerchief that bound her curls, then absently smoothed her bodice, half expecting to find a row of clumsily stitched roses embroidered there.

She never saw Bannor emerge from the gatehouse, beaming with anticipation. She never saw him nudge Hollis and murmur, "See the look of surprise on her face," or heard Hollis hiss, "If you ask me, she looks as if she's going to be ill."

She only saw that familiar chariot rumbling up the drawbridge, passing beneath the arch of the gatehouse, and rolling to a halt not twenty feet in front of her. One of Bannor's squires hastened forward to throw open the door.

Everyone in the bailey seemed to hold their breath as one elegant hand, shrouded to the elbow in a pristine white glove, emerged from that silken cocoon to take the blushing squire's arm. Time might have tinted Blanche's blond hair with silver, but the smile that played around her lips had lost none of its enigmatic charm. The pearl-encrusted girdle that had once belonged to Willow's mother hugged her shapely hips.

Her gaze flickered across the bailey, lighting briefly on Willow. Stepping down from the carriage, she cried, "Oh, my beloved daughter, how I have missed you!"

As she started toward Willow with arms flung wide, Bannor frowned. "Is it possible I could have misjudged the woman so sorely?"

But at that precise moment, Blanche went flying past Willow as if she didn't exist, and threw her arms around an open-mouthed Bea.

Twenty-eight

Beatrix hung awkwardly in her mother's embrace, looking as confused and miserable as a fox with its paw caught in a poacher's trap. Blanche was crooning, Bannor was glowering, and Desmond was glaring at Beatrix as if she'd deliberately betrayed him. Willow watched it all through a murky veil of shock.

That veil did not lift until her papa clambered stiffly down from the carriage, cradling his weak arm to his chest.

"Papa?" she whispered, taking an involuntary step toward him.

He turned toward her, a tremulous smile hovering on his lips. Before Willow could take another step, Stefan descended from the carriage behind her father. They both froze as Stefan strode past Sir Rufus, seized Willow by the shoulders, and planted a less than brotherly kiss upon her mouth.

He held her at arm's length, his features cast in a mask of concern. "Don't grieve yourself just because the heartless knave has decided to cast you aside, my dear sister. As long as I am master of Bedlington," he said, ignoring Sir Rufus's outraged gasp, "you'll always have a home." He touched his lips to her temple, lowering his voice to a husky whisper intended only for her ears. "And a bed."

Before Willow could jerk herself out of her stepbrother's possessive grip, the heartless knave in question came striding toward Stefan with his hand on his sword hilt and murder in his eyes. Blanche stepped between the two men. Beatrix managed to squirm out of her mother's grip and duck behind her while Stefan wisely sidled away from Willow, a triumphant smirk still playing around his lips.

"Explain yourself, woman," Bannor thundered, still glaring daggers at Stefan. "What is the meaning of this?"

Blanche spread the ferret-trimmed skirts of her cloak in a graceful curtsy. "Ah, you must be Lord Bannor. Allow me to introduce myself. I am Blanche of Bedlington."

"I know damn well who you are." Bannor stabbed a finger at Beatrix, who was peeping over her mother's shoulder, her eyes huge and her face ashen. "I want to know who the hell she is."

Blanche looked briefly taken aback, but it didn't take her long to recover her aplomb and slant Bannor a flirtatious glance. "Surely you tease me with your riddles, my lord. She is my daughter and your betrothed, is she not?"

Sir Rufus began to sputter in earnest, but Bannor was too dumbfounded to even form a denial.

Blanche spared Willow a pitying glance. "I must confess that I wasn't terribly surprised to learn that our Willow simply wouldn't do. I hope you don't blame us for foisting the unfortunate girl off upon you. We would have never done so, had your steward not insisted." Digging her gloved fingers into the girl's arm, Blanche hauled Beatrix back in front of her. "You can be assured that my daughter will make you a marvelous bride."

"Have you taken leave of your senses, woman?" Sir Rufus thundered. "Lord Bannor already has a bride. *My* daughter."

Bannor finally found his own voice. "You, my lady, are the one speaking in riddles. Contrary to what you may believe, I have no intention of wedding this—this child!"

Stefan's smirk faded and Blanche's smile turned frosty. "I don't understand, my lord. You were the one who sent the missive inviting us to attend the wedding of our cherished daughter. You were the one who insisted we journey to Elsinore for the event."

"You?" The word was spoken softly, but with such crystalline clarity that they all swiveled around to stare at Willow.

Although Bannor had never backed down from a fight in his life, the bruised accusation in his wife's eyes made him itch to bolt.

"*You?*" she repeated. "You did this? You invited them here without asking my leave? Without doing me the courtesy of warning me that they were coming? You're the one who made me the butt of this terrible jest?"

Bannor shot Hollis a desperate look, wishing that he was on some battlefield in the heart of France, dodging enemy arrows. Or perhaps chained in the stygian gloom of a dungeon, with only rats and skeletons for company. Hollis just shrugged, as if to say that this was one battle he would have to fight alone.

Bannor stretched out a hand, using the same tone he had once used to disarm a French spy disguised as a camp follower, who had ended up spilling her own secrets against his lips before he gently removed her from his bed. "I summoned them here so they could pay tribute to you, sweeting, while I hosted a magnificent wedding in your honor."

"And is this how you believe I would choose to greet our guests?" She shook her mudstained skirts at him, her voice rising. "Just look at me, Bannor!"

Bannor could hardly believe that this spitting feline was the same sweet-tempered kitten who had spent last night cuddled in his arms, purring with pleasure. He raked his gaze up and down her, drinking in her glittering gray eyes, the roses in her cheeks, the row of saucy pink toes peeping out from her torn stocking.

He shook his head in genuine bewilderment. "I don't know that I've ever seen you look more beautiful." His confession only made her groan. "I never intended to do you a discourtesy. 'Twas meant to be a surprise."

"Oh, it was. A delightful surprise! Nearly as delightful as an unexpected visit from the king's tax collectors. Or an outbreak of the plague."

It was Blanche's turn to sputter. "Well, I must say, that's not very hospitable of you."

As Willow turned to Blanche, an eerie calm descended over her. She was not a child anymore, but a woman grown. She no longer had to swallow whatever bitter poison her stepmother decided to ladle down her throat. "What would you know about being hospitable, Blanche? You made me feel unwelcome in my own home for thirteen years."

Blanche stomped her slippered foot. "How dare you address me in such a disrespectful manner? I won't stand for it!"

"And what will you do to stop me?" Willow jerked off the kerchief to reveal her cropped curls, eliciting a strangled gasp from Stefan. "Threaten to cut off all my hair? Thrash me? Force Papa to send me to bed without supper?"

As if inspired by Willow's words, Blanche whirled on Rufus. "She's *your* daughter. *You* should be the one to deal with her insolence. If you're man enough, that is."

"Why, I-I . . ." Sir Rufus drew out a kerchief and mopped his florid brow, his bravado deserting him in the face of his wife's scorn. "Perhaps if the two of you made a better effort . . ."

As the man she had once idolized stood there, trapped between his daughter and his wife, Willow wished desperately that she could feel something for him besides a weary mixture of pity and contempt.

She patted his stooped shoulder. "Don't trouble yourself, Papa. We shall strive to make amends."

Willow faced her stepmother, her eyes still glittering with defiance. "Forgive me, my lady. I spoke in haste." She could tell from the acid curl of her stepmother's mouth that the words meant no more to Blanche than they did to her.

Willow's unyielding grace made Bannor's heart swell with pride. He rested his hands on her shoulders, sweeping his most formidable glower across Blanche, Beatrix, and the rest of their misbegotten clan. "I don't know what sort of scheme you and this *daughter* of yours have devised, but 'tis Willow who is, and always shall be, my wife. She is the woman I . . . the woman I . . ." As Bannor caressed the gentle curve of Willow's collarbone, the tenderness he harbored in his heart seemed to swell into his throat, choking him.

Willow cast him a look over her shoulder, her gray eyes enormous. Not even at the height of their love-making had he seen such utter vulnerability in their misty depths.

She seemed to be holding her breath, while Bannor was suddenly having difficulty catching his. He knew instinctively that he had it within his power to atone for every sin committed by man since a sniveling Adam had pointed his finger at Eve and blamed her for giving him the apple.

When the words finally came, they spilled out in a desperate rush. "She is the woman I intend to marry for a second time this very night."

Hollis groaned and buried his face in his hand. Stefan's lips curled into a scornful sneer he did not bother to mask.

Willow disengaged herself from Bannor's embrace with an icy precision that chilled him to the bone. "I think not, my lord," she said. "For had I known what a churlish lout you were, I would have never married you the first time." Tugging Beatrix from her mother's arms, Willow gave the girl a halfhearted shove toward Bannor. "I hope the two of you will be very happy together!"

As she went stalking toward the castle, her head held high, Beatrix burst into tears and fled the bailey, her noisy sobs lingering long after she'd gone.

Bannor was still gazing after Willow, his empty hands hanging helplessly at his sides, when Hollis sidled up behind him. " 'Tis fortunate that you've become such an expert on women, is it not? A less able man might have bungled that entire situation."

• • •

Desmond found Beatrix in the barn, perched on the very same mound of hay where they had shared their first kiss. As he approached, she hugged her knees and shot him a petulant look from beneath her tear-dampened lashes. "If you've come to scowl and growl at me, I'm in no mood for it."

"Can you blame me for being angry? You led me to believe you were naught but a common maidservant, when all along you were a . . . a . . ." he grimaced in distaste, ". . . a *lady*."

" 'Twas Willow's idea to disguise me as her maidservant. She was afraid that if Lord Bannor knew I'd run away from home, he'd make her send me back." Beatrix swiped at her nose with the back of her hand. "Now Willow hates me, and Lord Bannor will probably send me back anyway."

Desmond swung around to stare at her. 'Twas the first time the possibility had occurred to him. "No, he won't," he said with an arrogance that would serve him well when he was master of the castle. "I won't stand for it."

"What do you care?" she flung at him. "You're behaving as if you hate me, too."

Desmond paced away from her, stroking the sparse stubble on his chin as if it were a full beard. "As long as you were a maidservant, I was free to dally with you as I pleased. I could chase you around the garden and steal all the kisses I wanted." He swung around to glare at her. "But now that you're a lady, I can't very well just tumble you into a haystack and seduce you. Damned if I won't have to marry you first!"

Beatrix blinked up at him, tears of joy flooding her

misty blue eyes. "Why, I do believe that's the nicest proposal I've ever received," she whispered.

Desmond's eyes glowed with both tenderness and
resolve as he stretched out one freckled hand and drew
her to her feet. "If I have anything to say about it, Lady
Beatrix of Bedlington, 'twill be the last one as well."

When Bannor arrived at the top of the stairs just before
dusk, he found ten of his children huddled on the landing outside Willow's bedchamber, their hushed whispers proclaiming the gravity of their vigil. Desmond
and Beatrix shared the top step, their clasped hands
poorly hidden by the folds of her skirt. When Bannor
appeared, they gave a guilty start and edged away
from each other, twin blushes darkening their cheeks.

So *that* was to be the way of it, Bannor thought with
a wry glimmer of amusement, as he picked his way
between them. Although he didn't look forward to negotiating a betrothal contract with the girl's grasping
mother, at least he didn't have to worry about his
son and heir wooing the laziest maidservant in all of
England.

He cast the arrow loop a grim glance. If the snow
kept tumbling from the sky as it had in the past few
hours, he feared he'd have ample time to negotiate that
contract. Bannor shuddered at the thought of being
trapped in the castle with the nest of adders Willow
called a family until the spring thaw. Her father had
been drinking himself into a stupor ever since that
scene in the bailey and Bannor couldn't so much as
catch a glimpse of her stepbrother's sullen smirk without wanting to drive his fist into it.

The rising wail of the wind was the only sound on the landing. Muffled sobs, outraged shrieks, or the crash of pottery shattering would have been preferable to the piteous silence seeping out from behind the door of Willow's bedchamber. Bannor closed his eyes briefly, cursing himself and all of his male ancestors for being so damnably thickheaded. If he had just heeded Hollis's counsel, he might be sharing Willow's bed right now instead of standing outside the door of her bedchamber, as empty-handed as a beggar.

As he lifted his hand to knock, his children regarded him with a disconcerting mixture of chagrin and pity.

"She won't let you in," Mary predicted, her round little face more doleful than usual.

"How can you be sure?"

"Are you the last man on earth?" Mary Margaret demanded, tugging on the leg of his hose.

"I don't believe so," he ventured.

The little girl pondered his reply for a moment before shrugging. "Well, even if you were, Willow still wouldn't let you in."

"Or stay married to you," Ennis muttered.

"Or throw you a rope if you tumbled headfirst down a well," Edward added cheerfully.

"How do you know that?" Bannor inquired.

Hammish cringed in sympathy. "She told Fiona, then Fiona told us."

Bannor blew out a pensive breath. It seemed this was going to be much more difficult than he'd anticipated.

Swallowing his trepidation, he rapped his knuckles softly against the door. "Willow? Sweeting? Might I have a word with you?"

He would have thought it impossible, but the silence became even more pronounced. He pressed his ear to the oak, encouraged by a faint rustling within. His heart soared as the door slowly creaked open.

Then plummeted when Fiona's wizened visage appeared in the crack. The chamber behind the stooped old woman was veiled in shadows.

Fiona greeted him with a sorrowful shake of her head. "Ye'd best take yerself off, lad. She'll not see ye right now."

Still shaking her head, Fiona began to shut the door. Bannor jammed the toe of his boot into the narrowing crack. "Wait, Fiona! Tell her . . ."

Tell her what? That his arms ached with emptiness whenever she wasn't in them? That he was a stubborn fool with more pride than courage?

Gazing down into Fiona's expectant face, Bannor shook his own head before saying softly, "Just tell her that I'm sorry."

Fiona nodded before gently closing the door in his face.

Once Bannor might have called for a battering ram to pound it down, but if Willow had taught him anything in the past few months, it was that such reckless posturing might destroy the very prize he sought to win.

Willow could not seem to stop crying. It was as if all the tears she'd choked back since she was six years old had decided to come pouring out of her in one bitter torrent. She longed to wail and rage and kick her feet as Mary Margaret would have done, but she'd spent too many years crying into her pillow, her body wracked by silent sobs.

Every time the salty flood subsided, she would relive

the scene in the bailey, remembering her papa's painful confusion, Blanche's frosty contempt, and Stefan's blatant sneer at witnessing her humiliation.

Most damning of all had been the raw panic she'd glimpsed on Bannor's face, when he had been unable to choke out the one word that would have forever redeemed her pride in the eyes of her family.

Willow's shuddering hiccups deepened to sniffles, her sniffles to snuffles, and her snuffles to sobs. Before long she was weeping full force again, and Fiona was patting her back and crooning soothing words in a language she did not understand. Although the snow was still falling in a blinding veil outside the window, Willow refused to let the old woman light a candle. The gloom suited her.

"Oh, Fiona," Willow mumbled, "I think I hate him!"

"Of course, ye do, darlin'," Fiona murmured. "He's a loathsome toad. All men are."

Willow stopped crying long enough to cast the old woman a look over her shoulder, her eyes still brimming with tears. "But he's not loathsome at all. He's kind and strong and gentle." She collapsed face first into the feather pillow. "Oh, God, that only makes me hate him more! How did Mary and Margaret bear it? They're probably glad they're dead. I wish I was dead, too!" She seized upon the idea with savage satisfaction. "Perhaps I'll cry myself to death, and then he'll be sorry he never loved me."

Fiona gently stroked her hair. "There, there, lass. Don't take on so. 'Tis only natural that yer feelin's would be more tender right now." She chuckled. "Why, when I was breedin' fer the first time, I used to weep and wail until me poor Liam was fair near to burstin' into tears himself."

Twenty-nine

Willow's tears ceased abruptly. She rolled to a sitting position, eyeing Fiona as if the saintly old woman had just sprouted horns and a tail. "Breeding?"

Fiona gave Willow's taut little belly a fond pat. "Surely it couldn't have come as a surprise to ye, lass. Not when ye've been sharin' Lord Bannor's bed fer almost two months."

"D-Don't be ridiculous," Willow stammered. "I can't be breeding. Bannor doesn't want any more children. Why, we've taken great care to—" Blushing, she leaned over and whispered something in the old woman's ear.

Hooting with laughter, Fiona rocked backward so far she nearly tumbled off the bed. "Such shenanigans might work fer a less potent man. But I'd wager, if ye were on one side of the moat and he was on the other, our Bannor would still find a way to tuck his babe into yer belly."

Scrubbing the last of the tears from her cheeks, Willow rose from the bed and began to pace around the tower, no longer able to keep still with so much turmoil roiling around inside of her. "My monthly courses were a bit light last month, but I haven't felt the least bit faint or sick to my stomach. Why, I've been hungry as a horse! You saw me at supper last night. I ate three partridge pasties, an entire blancmange, a bowl of oysters, and three enormous . . ." She trailed off, silenced by Fiona's knowing smile. "Oh," she whispered, groping for the stool behind her. "I'd better sit down. I do believe I'm feeling a little faint after all."

"You'll soon adjust to the shiftin' o' yer moods—laughin' one minute, cryin' the next." Fiona chuckled. " 'Tis a wonder any man survives nine months o' such devilry."

Willow brought her trembling hand to rest against the curve of her belly, before lifting wondering eyes to Fiona. "How did you know?"

Fiona grimaced. "The last time I ate a bowl of oysters and a blancmange in one sittin', I was pregnant with me first set o' twins."

Willow gazed down at her stomach, marveling that something so fragile as an invisible life could reside within. "I never thought I wanted a babe of my own," she said softly. "But 'tis a part of me, is it not?"

Fiona nodded. "And a part of him. The very best part."

Willow knew she ought to be weeping in earnest now, but a shimmering thread of joy had began to unfurl in her heart. "How can I help but love it?" She lifted her chin, giving in to a rush of stubborn pride. "Bannor may not love me, but perhaps his child will."

Fiona cocked her head to the side, giving Willow a

pitying look. "Just what do ye think love is, child? Me Liam and I were wed for forty-seven years, and the stubborn old cuss never once spoke the words. Yet not a day went by in all those years that he didn't reach fer me hand or sneak up behind me to give me a cuddle. Love isn't a burst o' trumpets and a flock o' doves descendin' out o' the heavens to roost on yer heads. 'Tis sharin' a cup o' tea by the hearth on a cold winter's night. 'Tis the look in yer husband's eyes when ye lay yer first child in his arms." Sorrow touched the old woman's face. " 'Tis the ache in yer heart when ye watch the light in his eyes dim fer the last time, and know a part o' ye has gone out o' this world with him."

Willow did not realize she was crying again, until a tear splashed on her hand.

Fiona reached over to take that hand. "There's a reason Mary and Margaret never regretted weddin' Bannor. They knew in their hearts that the lad loved them, even if he didn't know it himself."

The old woman gave Willow's hand a firm squeeze, then rose and shuffled toward the door.

Willow stood and swiped the fresh tears from her cheeks. With what she hoped was a dignified sniff, she said, "You may inform my husband that I will see him now."

Fiona bobbed a curtsy, her wizened face crumpling into an impish smile. " 'Twill be a pleasure, m'lady."

As Willow waited for Bannor to arrive, she pawed frantically through her cupboard, tossing kirtles, gloves, stockings, and chemises over her shoulder left and right.

She was going to have a baby. A vexsome creature

who would wriggle and fret and rub its sticky little hands all over her. When she cradled it against her shoulder, it would burp in her ear and spit milk down her back. She would never in her entire life know another moment of peace, because she would always be worrying that it might fall down a privy shaft, get its chubby head caught in a window grate, or grow up to fall in love with someone who was overly fond of cabbage or chewed with their mouth open.

She'd never been happier.

She finally settled upon a gown woven from the finest camlet, with flowing sleeves trimmed in miniver. She plopped down on the stool and drew on a fresh pair of stockings and garters, then slipped her feet into one of the delicate pairs of doeskin slippers Bannor had given her for a wedding present.

Once she might have dreaded telling Bannor that she was carrying his child. Once she might have feared that his heart would grow cold toward her, as her papa's had done. The girl she had been before she came to Elsinore might even have run away without telling him so she'd never have to take that chance.

But Willow was no longer that girl. She was a woman now—a woman who would soon be mother to the child of the man she loved. And perhaps 'twas time for her to offer that man not only her love, but her trust as well.

As Willow lifted the mirror to survey her reflection, her hand was steady, her eyes clear. She doubted her own family would recognize her now. She'd scrubbed her face clean and combed her shoulder-length curls to a glossy sheen. She could not resist turning the mirror this way and that, searching for the fabled glow promised to breeding women. It wasn't until she angled the mirror toward her stomach to search for any hint of a bulge that she realized how ridiculous she was being. If she didn't stop admiring herself, she would soon be as vain as Beatrix!

A sharp knock sounded on the door. Willow sprang to her feet, tossing the mirror on the table. She smoothed her skirts, tucked a rebellious curl behind one ear, and forced herself to draw in a deep breath, determined that she would not appear too eager. She made it halfway across the tower before her ruse of dignity deserted her. She raced the rest of the way to the door and flung it open, her welcoming smile fading as she saw the man leaning against the wall.

Bannor took the stairs two at a time. Willow's summons had come while he was in the gatehouse, seeking refuge from her family. He would have gladly lingered there for the remainder of the winter to escape their company. When he had slunk through the great hall only a few minutes ago, that wretched stepbrother of hers had been nowhere in sight, but her hapless father had still been trying to drink himself insensible, while Lady Blanche berated him for not boxing Willow's ears when the chit had insulted her.

A grim smile curved Bannor's lips. If the man had dared to lift a hand to Willow in his presence, he'd have ended up with two maimed arms instead of one.

Bannor slowed as he approached the landing. He gave his doublet a tug, smoothed his hair, and drew in a deep breath, not wanting to appear too eager. His tongue might stumble when he begged Willow's forgiveness, but he hoped that its eloquence in bed could coax her into pardoning him for any offense, even being a churlish lout.

Bannor had lifted his hand to knock when he realized that the door was already ajar.

It creaked open at his touch. "Willow?"

The snow falling outside the glazed window cast an eerie half-light over the tower. The bed was thrown into sharp relief, as were the kirtles and stockings scattered about the tower like the victims of some tragic battle. Some primal instinct urged Bannor to dull his footfalls to a whisper, as if he was sneaking up on an enemy whose face he might not recognize until it was too late.

A hollow silence had settled over the deserted chamber, making a familiar knot of dread curl in Bannor's gut. It took him a moment to realize why it was so familiar. 'Twas the same silence that had plagued the chamber after Mary and Margaret had died. 'Twas not so much the absence of sound, as the lingering sigh of someone who has left and is never coming back. He had forgotten how terrible it was, because Willow had banished its haunting echo with her husky laughter, her tender smile, her loving touch.

Bannor whirled around, scanning the chamber as he would an enemy battlefield. 'Twasn't the scattered gloves and gowns that sent a shiver of dread coursing down his spine. 'Twas the doeskin slipper resting on its side next to the door. The slipper he might never have seen, if his every nerve wasn't prickling with foreboding.

An ethereal hint of jasmine taunted him as he clawed through the piles of gowns, frantically searching for its mate. He dropped to his hands and knees to look beneath the bed, then tore all the bedclothes from the mattress and hurled them to the floor. He emptied the cupboard with a single swipe of his hand, nearly overturning it in his zeal to explore every nook and cranny.

He was left standing in the middle of the ransacked chamber, his breath coming in savage pants, still holding one slipper. A single doeskin slipper, so delicate he could have crushed it to dust with one hand.

As Bannor raced from the chamber, still clutching the slipper, the wind began to rise, howling a warning he could no longer ignore.

"Fiona!"

Bannor's bellow thundered through the castle, shaking the rafters and making every page, squire, and man-at-arms within hearing distance of the great hall tremble with dread. If Fiona hadn't learned long ago that Bannor's bellows rarely preceded anything more taxing than a mild tongue-lashing, followed by a sheepish apology, she might have dropped the baby she was bouncing on her knee. She would have probably ignored him completely if she hadn't caught a glimpse of his face as he descended the stairs.

She handed the baby off to young Annie, and scrambled over to meet him at the foot of the stairs. "What is it, m'lord? Ye look as if ye've seen a haint."

Bannor's eyes smoldered like live coals against the drawn planes of his face. "If this is a jest, 'tis not very funny."

"I don't know what ye're talkin' about."

He thrust the slipper in his hand at her. "I'm talking about this. If my wife thinks to punish me by scaring me witless, I'll thank you to tell me where she's hidden herself."

"I left her in the south tower, waitin' fer ye."

"Well, she's not there now. I've combed the entire castle. The children haven't seen her, and I can't find a trace of her anywhere."

As if sensing a spill of blood in the water, Lady Blanche came cruising over, her nostrils flaring. "Don't fret yourself, my lord. Willow's probably just gone off somewhere to sulk. 'Twas always an unfortunate habit of hers, wasn't it, Rufus? To whine, pout, or throw a tantrum whenever she didn't get her way."

When Willow's father only muttered something unintelligible and went back to nursing his goblet of ale, Blanche's smile tightened. "My Beatrix, however, was always as sweet-tempered as a lamb. Never did so much as a word of complaint pass those comely lips of hers."

Bannor shot the woman a look that plainly proclaimed he thought she was a raving lunatic, before returning his attention to Fiona. "Think, Fiona. Think hard. Did Willow give you any hint, any clue, as to where she might have gone?"

Fiona shook her head, mumbling more to herself than to him. "Perhaps I shouldn't have told the lass about the babe. But I thought she knew. I never dreamed 'twould distress her so."

"Is there something amiss with one of the babes? Which one?" Bannor's desperate gaze swept the hall. "Peg? Mags? That one?" He pointed to the child in Annie's arms, forgetting its name in his alarm.

Fiona blinked up at him, her rheumy blue eyes beginning to water. "Yer babe, m'lord. The one she's carryin'."

Blanche swore a bitter and distinctly unladylike oath. "We might as well pack up and go home, Rufus. The church will never grant them an annulment now."

"Willow is carrying my child?" Bannor whispered, dizzied by a rush of shock.

Fiona nodded. "She was just as surprised to learn she was breedin' as ye are, m'lord, if not more. Why, she stopped cryin' right off when I told her. Her eyes grew round as two silvery moons, and she said . . ." The old woman trailed off, biting her lip as if she wished she'd never spoken at all.

Bannor seized her arm. "What? What did she say?"

Fiona ducked her head. "She said, 'Don't be ridiculous. Bannor doesn't want any more children.' "

Bannor groaned. "Dear God, what have I done? Was she afraid I'd be angry with her? Did she threaten to run away? Surely she wouldn't have been so foolish as to brave this blizzard just to escape me."

Almost as if his words had invoked the storm's wrath, the main doors at the far end of the hall flew open, letting in a deafening howl of wind and a blinding swirl of snow. Bannor took two long strides toward the door, hope warring with his despair. But the figure that staggered out of that icy cloud was not Willow, but Beatrix.

The girl had one arm wrapped around Desmond's waist. Her face was nearly as pale as her hair, making the crimson hue of the blood streaming from his son's brow even more shocking.

Bannor caught them both before they could fall. Clutching at his doublet, Beatrix gazed up at him, her blue eyes murky with terror. "Willow's gone," she whispered. "He's taken her."

Thirty

It took three squires to wrestle the door closed against the hammering fists of the wind. After making sure that his son was suffering from nothing more serious than being knocked senseless, Bannor handed the boy over to Fiona's care. While the old woman sat him down on a bench and used her own kerchief to dab the blood from the shallow gash on his brow, Bannor jerked a tapestry from the wall and wrapped it around Beatrix's shoulders. The girl's teeth were chattering so hard she could barely talk.

"What happened, Bea?" Bannor asked, striving to keep his tone gentle despite his growing panic. "Who took Willow?"

"S-S-S-Stefan. Desmond and I were in the barn, h-hiding in the hayloft, when he came looking for a horse. He held a d-d-dagger to Willow's throat and forced her to climb astride. When Desmond realized what was happening, he jumped down out of the loft and demanded that Stefan surrender. Stefan nearly ran him down."

Bannor shot his son a fierce look. "That was very foolish of you, lad. And very brave."

Desmond gave him a woozy salute. The lad's half-hearted attempts to duck Fiona's crooning ministrations were thwarted when she seized him by the ear and held him fast.

Blanche wagged one long, patrician finger at Beatrix. "And just what were you doing alone in a hayloft with that . . . that . . . *boy*? I'll have you know, my lord, that if your son has compromised my daughter in any way, her stepfather and I will settle for naught less than a betrothal contract." Her lips curved in a pious smile. "Or at the very least, a generous purse to compensate us for her virtue."

Forcing himself to ignore both the woman's jabbering and her daughter's painful blush, Bannor caught Bea gently by the shoulders. "Why, Bea? I don't understand. Why would Stefan believe he had any right to Willow?"

Beatrix's voice dropped to an agonized whisper. " 'Twas all my doing. Stefan sent me here to seduce you, so he could have Willow all to himself. Then when you and Willow were quarreling and she told me I was welcome to you, I sent him a letter telling him all was going according to plan and 'twas only a matter of time before I'd be sending for him. In truth, I forgot all about the letter, but when Stefan received your summons, he must have assumed our scheme had been successful. He didn't come to Elsinore to attend Willow's wedding . . ."

"He came to claim her for his own," Bannor finished

grimly. He whirled on Blanche, who took a hasty step backward. "Did you know of your son's plot to abduct my bride, my lady?"

One of Blanche's pale hands fluttered around her throat. "I should say not. Stefan has always been a headstrong lad. He doesn't take well to not getting his way."

Bannor stalked the woman, backing her up with each step. "I should warn you that I don't take well to not getting my way, either. If your son harms so much as one hair on my wife's head, I'll settle for naught less than your own head on a platter."

Blanche trotted backward the last few steps, stumbling right into her husband's lap. "Are you going to allow him to speak to me that way, Rufus?"

Willow's father lurched to his feet, dumping his wife to the floor in a spill of skirts. Although he was none too steady on his feet, he managed to get the goblet in his hand to his lips without spilling a single drop of ale. "And why not? If I'd had the courage to speak to you that way a long time ago, that wretched brat of yours might not have made off with my little girl."

Savagely thinking 'twas a pity Willow had not been there to witness *that*, Bannor strode back to Beatrix and seized her by the shoulders, no longer striving to gentle his grip. "I need to know which way they headed. If they kept to the road, I should be able to overtake them within the hour."

"North," Desmond mumbled, lurching to his feet. "They headed north. Across the meadows."

Bannor had been known to bear even the harshest blow without flinching, but his son's words staggered him. He sank down on the bottom step of the stairs, raking both hands through his hair.

Willow was out there somewhere. In the cold. In the snow. Without her shoe. Without him. In the time it had taken Beatrix and Desmond to stumble across the bailey, the ruthless hand of the wind would have already swept clean any trail Stefan might have left.

Bannor could almost see her—her pearly white teeth beginning to chatter, her warm, pink skin growing stiff and blue. She would shiver so hard she would swear her very bones were knocking together. Icy blades of pain would stab her fingers and toes.

Then the shivering would stop. The pain would fade away. The blue tinge would creep into her eyelids, her fingertips, her lips. The pearls of frost clinging to her skin would crystallize into an icy shroud so hard that all the tears in the world wouldn't melt it. Instead of dying with a child in her arms, as his mother had done, she would die with his child in her belly.

She would die without ever knowing how very much he loved both her and that child.

Bannor dropped his head into his hands. Somewhere in the darkest corner of his soul, he had believed that if he could somehow stop himself from loving Willow, he could keep her safe. If he never uttered the words, she would never leave him as his mother had done.

A gentle hand brushed his hair. For one crazy moment, Bannor thought it might be Willow's, but he lifted his head to find Beatrix kneeling before him.

Tears spilled down her cheeks in a swelling torrent. " 'Tis all my fault, my lord. I would have never wished her harm, you know. Why, she's the only real mother I've ever known."

Ignoring Blanche's outraged gasp, Bannor folded the girl into his arms, muffling her sobs against his chest. "Don't cry, child," he said fiercely. "I'll find her. As God is my witness, I swear I shall find her and bring her back."

As he pressed his eyes shut, Bannor could only pray that God wouldn't have allowed him to swear such an oath if He wasn't going to help him keep it.

"Listen!" Desmond cried, lunging to his feet.

Bannor cocked his head to the side, but all he could hear were Bea's watery hiccups. He rose, gently guiding the girl into Fiona's arms, but it still took him a bewildered moment to realize exactly what it was his son wanted him to hear.

Silence.

The wind had ceased its terrible wailing, leaving behind a hush as sweet and crystalline as the tolling of the chapel bells. Bannor rushed to the doors and flung them open. Feathers of snow no longer driven by the relentless lash of the wind brushed like angel wings against his face. A jolly pearl of a moon seemed to wink at him from amongst the scattering clouds, its luminous light drenching the snow in silver.

Bannor would have fallen to his knees right then and there, had he not been determined to make the most of the blessing God had given him.

Bannor the Bold strode through the great hall of Elsinore, girded for battle. Beneath the saffron tunic emblazoned with his coat of arms, he wore a hauberk woven of mail, and a steel breastplate. The scabbard sheathing his massive broadsword clanked against the plates armoring his calves and thighs, in a discordant counterpoint to his jingling spurs. From the other side of his belt hung a jeweled scabbard, outfitted with a short but deadly dagger.

His expression was grim, the glint in his eye lethal. He was not marching into battle to defend his country or his honor, but to seek a prize more precious than any the king could offer.

Hollis trotted along beside him, forced to take two steps for every one of his master's long strides. "I wish you'd let me accompany you. It doesn't feel right for you to go riding off without me by your side."

"No, it doesn't," Bannor agreed. "But I need you here at Elsinore. If this break in the storm doesn't last, you'll have to look after the castle—" he hesitated for a painful moment, "—until I can find my way home." His brow clouded. "And the children."

"Fiona and Netta can look after the children. But I feel so damned helpless. Surely there must be something I can do to help bring Willow back."

"There is," Bannor said, pausing just long enough to clap a firm hand on his steward's shoulder. "Go to the chapel, my friend, and pray."

Bannor threw open the main doors, trusting that his squires would have his mount ready for him. They did not disappoint. The pale stallion seemed to rise out of the moonlit snow, puffing steam from his nostrils like some mythical dragon. Bannor accepted the horse's reins from a somber-faced lad and swung himself astride. Giving Hollis one last salute, he guided the horse in a prancing half-circle, only to find his path to the drawbridge blocked.

Thirty-one

Desmond, Ennis, Mary, Hammish, Edward, Kell, and Mary Margaret awaited him, their mounts lined up as neatly as they themselves had once stood in this very courtyard to welcome their new mother to Elsinore. Bannor supposed he ought to at least be thankful that Mary Margaret was riding a pony instead of a pig. The miniature bow Willow had shot him with was slung over the child's shoulder, along with a quiver of tiny arrows.

They'd armored themselves in a motley assortment of kitchen pots, platters, fur leggings, and mangy pelts. Edward looked as if he might be wearing an entire bear, while Hammish sported an iron kettle for a helm. They were armed with a menacing array of pitchforks, scythes, awls, and clubs, much as they had been the night they'd battered down the wall of his tower. The night he'd savored his first taste of Willow's lips. They sat in absolute silence, awaiting his command.

"Stand aside," he called out, "or I'll have my men throw the lot of you in the dungeon."

Desmond urged his dappled gray mare forward. Bannor couldn't be sure if it was the stark white of the bandage against his chestnut hair, or the beautiful blonde riding side-saddle behind him, that lent his son a startling new air of maturity.

"We wish to accompany you, Father. Willow is our lady as well as yours."

"I cannot argue with that, son. But 'tis distressing enough to know that my wife's life is in the hands of a lunatic. I'll not risk the lives of my children as well."

"That lunatic is my brother," Beatrix reminded him. "I might be able to talk some sense into him."

Bannor arched one eyebrow. "And if you can't?"

The girl gave his sword a meaningful glance. "Then I'll let you do it."

Bannor leaned back in his saddle, surveying them all as if for the first time. He knew only too well what formidable adversaries they could be. They possessed equal amounts of cunning and determination, the two qualities no warrior could survive without.

"Please, Father," Desmond said, his green eyes betraying a hint of desperation. "Don't leave us behind again. We only want to help you find the loathsome churl who took Willow."

A crooked smile slowly spread across Bannor's face. "And may God help him when we do."

At his father's words, an answering grin spread across Desmond's face. Bannor guided his stallion between them to take the lead. Mary Margaret unleashed a gleeful war cry as they all went cantering through the castle gates and down the drawbridge, the snow beneath their horses' hooves exploding in a glittering cloud of stardust.

Hollis found Netta in the chapel, kneeling before the altar of burnished oak. With her eyes pressed shut and her face bathed by the glow of the candlelight, she was as beautiful to him as the marble Madonna who kept watch over the nave. He cast a wry glance heavenward, praying God wouldn't consider such a tribute blasphemy.

At the whisper of his footfalls, Netta scrambled to her feet, blushing as if she'd been caught defiling the altar instead of worshipping at it. When she recognized him, an all too familiar mask of wariness descended over her features, making him want to swear a less than pious oath.

"I was praying for our lady," she said, cocking her head at a defiant angle. "Although I don't suppose you believe God listens to the prayers of whores."

"On the contrary. 'Tis written that after His resurrection, our Lord appeared first to Mary Magdalene, a woman of some questionable virtue."

"That may be true, but I've found that his followers are more likely to cast the first stone than to confess their own failings."

"You must not believe that of Lady Willow, or you wouldn't be here praying for her safe return."

Netta shrugged, but the downward flicker of her eyes betrayed her distress. "She has been kind to me. As has Lord Bannor. I do not wish to see either of them come to any harm. Now if you'll excuse me, sir, I shall leave you to examine your own conscience."

"Don't go," Hollis said, weary of their endless game of wits.

She brushed past him. "If you want the pleasure of my company, 'twill cost you a shilling. Twice that if you want—"

She faltered when he grabbed her wrist. 'Twas the first time he had ever dared to touch her. The first time he'd ever allowed her to see the flash of his temper. "Do you honestly believe you're worth naught more than the coins a man will pay you to share his bed? Did it never occur to you that a man might simply wish to converse with you, or to sit quietly by your side?"

She tipped her head back, deliberately taunting him with the nearness of her lips. "You can pretend your interest in me is prompted by naught but the most chaste of motives, but I know that look in your eyes. I've seen it oft enough in the eyes of the countless men who came before you."

Hollis freed her arm and took a step backward, wishing he could despise her for her cruelty. "I won't deny that I want you in my bed. I won't pretend that I don't wake up in the night, shivering with desire, and reach for you." His voice softened. "But I would be content only to adore you from afar for the rest of my life. How much will that cost me, Netta? If my undying devotion isn't enough for you, then perhaps this will be." Hollis jerked a velvet purse from his belt and tossed it down. It landed with a solid jingle at her feet.

Knowing he could not bear to see her pick it up, he turned to stride from the chapel.

"Sir?"

Refusing to sell himself so cheaply, Hollis kept walking.

"Hollis?" This time Netta's plea was only a whisper, but it stopped him in his tracks.

He slowly turned. Netta's hand was outstretched, but the purse still lay on the floor at her feet.

Hollis gazed at her, as mesmerized by the tremble of her hand as he was by the tears sparkling in her eyes. "Would you care to join your prayers to mine?" she asked. "Perhaps then they'd be more likely to reach the ears of God."

Hollis closed the distance between them, and gently folded her hand in his. He kept a firm grip on that hand as they knelt side by side and inclined their heads to pray that God would shine His infinite mercy upon their lord and lady.

Willow forced herself to put one trembling leg in front of the other, all of her concentration centered on wading through the sea of snow, when all she wanted to do was sink deep into its powdery waves and drift off to sleep.

If she succumbed to that seductive temptation, she knew she would never wake up. Whenever its siren call became too loud, she would almost swear she could hear Bannor's mother whispering in her ear—urging her to keep slogging forward, to keep moving, to keep hoping. But perhaps it was only the wind, wailing a lament for her dying dreams.

She hugged her cloak tight around her, but the embrace of her own arms was too feeble to stop her shivering. She yearned for Bannor. For the warmth of his arms, the sizzling sweetness of his kiss, the fevered press of his flesh against her own.

The chill settled deep into her bones, making her

flesh quake and her teeth rattle. As her stockings froze solid, her feet went from tingling to numb.

It took her a dark eternity to realize that the wind was no longer driving stinging needles of snow into her face. She stumbled to a halt at the bottom of a hill and lifted her head, surveying the glittering tundra with childlike wonder. Brittle motes of snow sparkled like fairy dust beneath the shimmering caress of the moon, breathtakingly beautiful even in their cruelty.

Something slammed into her back, driving her to her hands and knees. If not for the scalding surge of fury that coursed through her veins, Willow might have remained there, her head hung low in defeat. But that fury gave her the strength to stagger to her feet and swing around to face her assailant.

"There's no need to glare at me like that," Stefan spat, his lips tinted the same icy blue as his eyes. "If you hadn't spooked the horse into running away, we'd be halfway to Scotland by now."

"If I hadn't spooked the horse," Willow bit off through her chattering teeth, "we'd be at the bottom of the river. You were the lackwit who nearly drove him over the edge of the cliff."

"Only because you had your hands over my eyes."

"Do forgive me. I was aiming for your mouth."

An ugly smirk twisted his lips. "You can sneer down your nose at me all you want, Willow, but scrubbing the mud off your face and donning a fine gown won't make you a lady. Nor will being swived by a lord." Stefan stroked his thumb along her cheek, his touch making Willow's stomach churn. "I wanted to be the first," he whispered, his breath a blast of brimstone against her icy skin. "I wanted to be the one to make you bleed."

Trembling with more than just the cold, Willow

knocked his hand away. "You'll be the only one bleeding when Bannor finds us."

Stefan snorted. "He'll probably be glad to be rid of you. With you out of the way, he'll be free to marry Beatrix as he should have done in the beginning."

Willow drew herself up, refusing to let that old taunt draw blood. "I doubt that he'll be so glad to be rid of the mother of his child."

As Stefan's gaze darted to the hand she'd curved possessively over her abdomen, a gratifying shadow of fear and distaste darkened his eyes. "Do you mean to tell me you've already got that wretch's brat in your belly?"

She tilted her chin to a proud angle. "Aye, I do, and I can promise you that Bannor will hunt you down to the ends of the earth if you harm his babe."

Stefan cocked his head to the side, eyeing her thoughtfully. "He probably would at that."

As her stepbrother slowly uncoiled a length of rope from his belt, Willow took a step backward, realizing too late that she might have misjudged the depths of his depravity. "What do you think you're doing?"

Stefan shrugged his broad shoulders. "It seems that if I'm to have any hope of escaping your husband's wrath, I shall have to disappear." He lunged toward her. "And so shall you."

Before Willow could coax her numb limbs into motion, Stefan had lashed out, snaking the rope around her wrists. He jerked it tight and knotted it off before casting a second rope around her ankles.

Willow tugged against him, striving to keep the panic from her voice. "You can't do this, Stefan. If I don't keep moving, I'll freeze to death."

"Don't worry, sister, dear," he said, giving the rope a

last vicious jerk before shoving her down in the snow. "I'm sure your devoted husband will find you. *After* the spring thaw."

"Stefan!" she shouted as her stepbrother went loping away, without so much as a backward glance.

Willow screamed until her throat was raw. She thrashed about in the snow like a turtle on its back, praying her fury and frustration would keep the blood pumping through her veins.

When her strength began to desert her, she glared up at the impassive face of the moon, cursing the unfairness of it all. She'd fought so hard to stay on her feet, to keep moving, to keep believing that Bannor would find her, no matter what. But it had all been for naught. He would never know how brave she had tried to be, or how hard she had fought for their child. As she struggled against the ropes, bitter tears began to course down her cheeks, freezing before they could fall.

She curled into a ball, trying to shelter the babe in her belly from the bite of the wind. As the snow began to fall harder, enveloping her in a downy white blanket, a delicious lethargy began to steal over her. She was tired, so very tired. Pearls of frost weighted her lashes, making her eyes ache with the effort it took to keep them open. Perhaps if she just closed them for a little while, she might be able to sleep. She might be able to dream once more of her prince and his magical kisses.

Willow no longer had to imagine his face. She had traced every inch of its rugged beauty with her fingertips and her lips. Those lips curved into a wistful half-smile, as she closed her eyes, snuggled her cheek into a pillow of snow, and waited for her prince to come.

Thirty-two

As Bannor and the children started up a rolling hill, he kicked his stallion into a gallop. Ever since they had discovered the rambling set of tracks in the snow, his urgency had been mounting along with his hopes. It had hardly surprised him that Willow's idiot of a step-brother had managed to lose his horse somewhere along the way. The beast had probably cantered straight back to Elsinore and was even now munching oats in the toasty warmth of the stables.

One set of tracks was too erratic to even be called footprints. But they still made Bannor's heart surge with joy. Their shambling awkwardness could mean only one thing: Willow was alive.

He drove his horse up the hill, desperate to follow the tracks across the shallow valley before the rising wind could obliterate them. The snow was coming down harder now, and as he crested the hill, a bank of clouds shrouded the moon, throwing the valley into darkness.

Bannor reined in his horse, swearing beneath his breath. The children followed suit, flanking him on both sides.

They waited, each impatient breath a silvery puff of fog, until the moon shook off its veil, flooding the valley with an almost supernatural brilliance.

Bannor's worst fears were realized. The wind gusting through the valley had swept the tracks away, leaving behind a pristine carpet of snow undefiled by human feet.

"Look, Papa!" Mary Margaret cried, pointing toward the bottom of the hill.

Bannor was forced to blink the snowflakes from his lashes before he could focus. There was something peeping out of a deep drift—a splash of color billowing against the virgin snow.

His hands tightened on the reins. Although it shivered him to the bone to imagine Willow out there without her cloak, Bannor prayed the garment had simply slipped off her shoulders, and Stefan had been either too viciously stupid or too savagely cruel to allow her to retrieve it.

"Wait here," he commanded his children, slipping off the horse.

For once, they obeyed him without questioning.

Bannor scrambled down the hill, but his steps began to slow as he reached the floor of the valley.

As the moon ducked behind another cloud, he stretched a hand toward that billowing scrap of fabric, already anticipating the moment when he could unearth it from its grave of snow, laugh, and hold it aloft to show his children that it was nothing they should be afraid of.

The moon reappeared, bringing each detail into focus with an almost deliberate cruelty.

A single dark curl, frosted with ice; a glimpse of marble flesh; a slender foot that should have been safely encased in the doeskin slipper he carried in a pouch next to his heart.

Bannor staggered to his knees and began to claw at the snow. As he gathered Willow into his arms, a cry that mirrored his own anguish wafted down from the hillside above. Through a haze of agony, he saw Beatrix start down the hill, saw Desmond snatch her back and cradle her face to his chest.

Bannor tore the rope from Willow's wrists and struggled to brush the snow from her face and hair, a low keening rising from deep within his throat. Time seemed to roll backward until he was no longer Bannor the Bold, Lord of Elsinore, but simply a frightened six-year-old boy who couldn't understand why his mama wouldn't wake up. As he gazed down upon Willow's face, frozen forever in sweet repose, he finally understood that it was not love that had killed his mother, but the lack of it.

"Oh, God in heaven, forgive me!" he cried, snatching her to his breast. He buried his face in her cold, stiff curls, rocking back and forth. "I love you, Willow," he whispered, tears beginning to course down his cheeks. "I loved you from the first moment I laid eyes on you, and I'll love you until the day I die."

Bannor pressed a fierce kiss to her icy lips, his tears pattering against her skin like a warm spring rain. He was so dazed with grief that it took him a moment to realize she was kissing him back.

A sharp cry escaped his lips as he scrambled backward, nearly dropping her. "Sweet holy Christ, I thought you were—"

"Dead?" Willow smothered a yawn in the cup of her hand, her eyelids drooping. "Don't be silly. I was only sleeping." She shivered. "I was so cold, then the snow covered me up and made me warm. I knew if I went to sleep that you'd come to me." She gave him an endearingly silly grin. "You always came to me in my dreams. Ever since I was a little girl."

Bannor smoothed the frozen curls away from her face, still unsettled by her abrupt resurrection. "And who do you think I am?"

She beamed up at him. "You're my prince. And my husband. And the man I love." Her smile softened as she captured his hand and brought it to bear against the curve of her belly. "And the father of my child."

Bannor's breath caught at the wonder of it all. Life growing beneath his hand like the most rare and precious of blooms. Life warming Willow's skin, flushing her cheeks with rose, pulsing like the sweetest of saps through her veins.

As Bannor drew her into his arms, raining kisses upon every inch of her beautiful face, his children's jubilant cries rang like music in his ears. He had been both right and wrong about Willow from the very beginning. Her name did suit her. But not because she was so fragile as to snap in the slightest breeze. On the contrary, she was strong and supple enough to bend with the wind instead of breaking. Her arms were generous enough to provide shelter and respite from every storm. Her grace and her courage had shot tender, yet unbreakable, roots deep into his heart.

He could not have said if it was his words, his tears, or his kiss that had awoken Willow from her enchanted slumber. He only knew that in the end, love hadn't been his destruction, but his salvation.

"I love you," he whispered, pressing a fierce kiss to her brow.

Willow cupped his cheek in her hand, her own eyes brimming with tenderness. "I know."

Epilogue

Bannor's trembling hand was hovering between his rook and his queen when a woman's shrill scream tore through the castle.

"God's blood!" he swore, slamming his mighty fist down on the table. Both chessboard and pieces went flying.

Hollis surveyed his fallen men with a dour expression. "I do believe I might have actually won that game."

Bannor rose from his chair, raking both hands through his already disheveled hair. "How can you expect me to concentrate on some ridiculous game, when my wife is being subjected to the most monstrous of tortures?"

Hollis shrugged. "It never seemed to bother you when Mary or Margaret was giving birth."

"I was in France, you idiot. And besides," he added, prowling the tower like some great wounded animal,

"I had no idea 'twas such an ordeal. I thought the babes just sort of shot out"—he waved his hand—"like missiles from a catapult."

Hollis rolled his eyes. "Perhaps if we spoke of something else." He fished about for a cheerier topic. "So how is that stepbrother of Willow's doing?"

It was Bannor's turn to roll his eyes. "He still refuses to leave the dungeon. He's terrified I'll throw him to the children again."

Hollis chuckled. "I'll never forget the night they dragged him back to the castle. He had all of those tiny little arrows poking out of his back."

Bannor grinned. "When he punched Hammish in the nose, he never expected the lad to laugh in his face, then butt him in the stomach. Of course, 'twouldn't have been so painful if Hammish hadn't been wearing an iron kettle on his head at the time."

"Ah, but it was seeing Edward all wrapped up in that mangy pelt that finally broke his spirit. Stefan thought he was a real bear!"

Both of the men were roaring with laughter when another scream wafted through the window, this one even more heart-wrenching than the last.

Bannor hesitated for the briefest second, then went racing for the door. Hollis beat him there. It took the steward three tries, but he finally managed to slide the bench in front of the door and throw himself in front of the bench. "Fiona threatened to have my head if I let you walk out of here. You heard what she said. The birthing chamber is no place for a man."

"From the sound of it," Bannor growled, " 'tis no place for a woman either."

"Weren't you the one born with an almost inhuman tolerance for pain?"

"*My* pain, not hers." Snatching a sword down from the wall, Bannor planted its tip against Hollis's bobbing Adam's apple. "I wouldn't let one of my men march into battle alone, would I? Especially not if I was the one who gave the order that sent him there."

Hollis sighed and lifted his hands in surrender, wise enough to know when he'd been bested. Bannor heaved the bench out of the way and dragged open the door.

"I told Fiona we should have chained you up in the dungeon," Hollis muttered as he fell into step behind him.

"Oh, no, you don't!" Netta cried, flinging her arms across the doorway of the south tower as Bannor came storming up the stairs. "You can't go in there, my lord. 'Tis not seemly."

Since Bannor couldn't very well hold a sword to the throat of a woman who was over six months pregnant, he whirled around, seeking his steward's assistance. "She's *your* wife. Appeal to her reason."

"She's also a woman," Hollis teased, winking at Netta. "She doesn't have any reason."

He expected Bannor to growl and bluster. He did not expect him to drop to one knee and tenderly enfold Netta's hand in his own.

"Hey!" Hollis tapped him on the shoulder. "As you just reminded me, she's *my* wife."

"And a kinder and more compassionate helpmeet is not to be found in all of England." Bannor gave Netta a look from beneath his sweeping dark lashes that had been known to melt even the sternest of hearts. "Which is why I know she would not be so cruel as to deny a wife her husband's comfort during this time of travail."

Hollis gritted his teeth, only too aware of his wife's lingering weakness for Bannor's charm.

"Well, I suppose 'twouldn't hurt to let you steal a peek at her," Netta whispered, a becoming blush creeping into her cheeks. "As long as you promise not to tell Fiona I was the one who let you in."

Bannor pressed a fervent kiss to the back of her hand. "You have my oath on it. I'll tell her 'twas Hollis who did the deed."

Before Hollis could protest, Bannor had swept open the door. He retreated just as quickly when an earthenware pitcher shattered against the door frame. They all ducked when the matching basin followed, its flight accompanied by Willow's outraged shriek.

Bannor exchanged a shaken look with Hollis, not sure what to make of the unexpected attack. "Do you want me to go away, sweeting?" he called, timidly poking his head around the corner of the door frame.

"No," Willow wailed, stretching out her arms to him. "I want you to stay."

"She wants me to stay," he whispered, a grateful smile curving his lips. As he tiptoed into the chamber, Netta gently closed the door behind him.

'Twas the bloodiest and most exhausting battle Bannor had ever fought. But when it was done, and Fiona laid the squirming bundle in his wife's arms, his heart surged with a triumph beyond anything he'd ever known on the battlefield.

He smoothed Willow's sweat-tangled hair away from her face as they both gazed down into the angry, red face of their baby daughter with pure adoration. "Before you came into my life," he said, "I believed that

God had abandoned me. Now I know that He has blessed me beyond measure."

As if to confirm his words, Netta threw open the door, allowing his other children to come creeping into the tower, one by one.

"Might we see her?" Desmond shyly asked, holding Beatrix's hand.

"I wants to pway wif her," Mary Margaret demanded, clutching a headless doll in her arms.

"Don't let Hammish hold her," Kell quipped. "He might be hungry."

While the children were laughing, another man slipped into the tower. Sir Rufus of Bedlington had ignored his wife's shrill protests to journey to Elsinore for the birth of his first grandchild. He ducked his head and gave Willow a sheepish look, unsure of his welcome.

Bannor eyed him warily, but Willow smiled and stretched out a hand to him. "Hello, Papa. I'm so glad you could come."

He took her hand and brought it to his lips. "I was hoping you'd give this stubborn old fool a chance to prove he can be a better grandfather than he was a father. And I know I don't deserve it, but I wished to entreat a boon from you."

He leaned down to whisper something in Willow's ear. As she nodded, a joyful smile broke over his face.

Relinquishing her papa's hand, Willow caught hold of Bannor's sleeve. "Papa has requested that we name our new daughter after my mother. Do you have any objections?"

Bannor chuckled. "Not unless her name was Mary or Margaret."

"Don't be a silly goose. My mother was French." A mischievous spark lit Willow's eyes as she crooked a finger at her husband. Bannor leaned over, then groaned aloud when her whisper reached his ears.

He straightened. Drawing in a bracing breath, he held out his hands. Ignoring their pronounced tremble, Willow gently laid the babe across his palms and gave him a heartening smile.

"Boys and girls," he said, turning around. "I would like to present to you your new sister"—he rolled his eyes—"Marie Marguerite."

As the children gathered around, oohing and aahing over their new sibling, Bannor gazed down at the child, dizzied by a rush of pride and love. He'd never held anything quite so tiny. Or fragile. Or squirmy. Or bloody.

Noticing his deepening pallor, Fiona gestured to Hollis and plucked the babe from his arms. And not a moment too soon.

For just as Sir Hollis shoved a chair beneath him, Lord Bannor the Bold, pride of the English and terror of the French, fainted dead away.

About the Author

USA TODAY bestseller Teresa Medeiros has well over three and a half million copies of her books in print. She was recently chosen one of the Top Ten Favorite Romance Authors by *Affaire de Coeur* magazine and won the *Romantic Times* Reviewer's Choice Award for Best Historical Love and Laughter. A former Army brat and registered nurse, Teresa wrote her first novel at the age of twenty-one and has since gone on to win the hearts of critics and readers alike. Teresa currently lives in Kentucky with her husband, Michael, and four lovably neurotic cats. Writing romance allows her to express her own heartfelt beliefs in faith, hope, and the enduring power of love to bring about a happy ending.